D1562656

Weird Women

Weird Women

Classic Supernatural Fiction by Groundbreaking Female Writers: 1852–1923

EDITED BY

Lisa Morton AND Leslie S. Klinger

PEGASUS BOOKS
NEW YORK LONDON

Introduction

by Lisa Morton and Leslie S. Klinger

". . . if our authoress can forget the gentleness of her sex, it is no reason why we should; and we shall therefore dismiss the novel without further comment."

—from *The British Critic*'s 1818 review of
Mary Wollstonecraft Shelley's *Frankenstein*

Any student of the literary history of the weird or horror story can hardly be faulted for expecting to find a genre bereft of female writers, at least in its first two centuries. A few of the authors included in this volume—Charlotte Perkins Gilman, Mary Wilkins Freeman, Clemence Housman—were discussed in early studies like H. P. Lovecraft's *Supernatural Horror in Literature* (1927); some would be acclaimed in later, more exhaustive works like *The Penguin Encyclopedia of Horror and the Supernatural* (1986); and others would find later fame thanks largely to filmed adaptations of their work (Herminie Templeton Kavanagh with Disney's 1959 *Darby O'Gill and the Little People,* and Edith Nesbit with the BBC adaptation of *The Railway Children* in 1968). But reprint anthologies of horror published throughout the twentieth century could routinely be counted on to include few or no stories by women. Perhaps the editors of those books were concerned about "the gentleness of her sex."

Yet there *were* women writing early terror tales—in fact, there were a *lot* of them. During the second half of the nineteenth century, when printing technologies enabled the mass production of cheap newspapers and magazines that needed a steady supply of material, many of the writers supplying that work were women. The middle classes were demanding reading material, and the plethora of magazines, newspapers, and cheap books meant a robust marketplace for authors. Women had limited career opportunities, and writing was probably more appealing than some of the other avenues open to them. Though the publishing world was male-dominated, writing anonymously or using masculine-sounding names (such as "M.E. Braddon") gave women a chance to break into the market. It was also still a time when writers were freer than today's writers to write work in a variety of both styles and what we now call *genres*. A prolific writer might pen adventure stories, romantic tales, domestic stories, mystery or detective fiction, stories of the supernatural—there were really no limits.

Spiritualism—the belief that spirit communication could be conducted by a medium at a séance, and could be scientifically proven (despite continued evidence to the contrary)—was widely popular, and so one might expect to find that many writers of this period were producing ghost stories. But ghost stories were just one type of supernatural story produced by women writers at this time. Women were also writing stories of mummies, werewolves, mad scientists, ancient curses, and banshees. They were writing tales of cosmic horror half a century before Lovecraft ever put pen to paper, and crafting weird westerns, dark metaphorical fables, and those delicious, dread-inducing gems that are simply unclassifiable.

This range of subjects is, of course, not unique to women writers, but there are nonetheless certain attributes to much of their work that are distinctly feminine. Not surprisingly, many stories from the nineteenth and early twentieth century feature women involved in traditional feminine pursuits—family, children, and even gardening all figure prominently in their fiction. Look, for example, at the terror and pathos surrounding the children at the heart of Charlotte Perkins Gilman's "The Giant Wistaria," Mary Wilkins Freeman's "The Wind in the Rose-bush," Elizabeth Stuart Phelps's "What Was the Matter?," and Olivia Howard Dunbar's "The Dream-baby." In the latter story, the author addresses head-on the self-worth of childless women, even when their lives are otherwise satisfying.

These early female authors often introduced social commentary into their works, especially issues of the role of women and class struggles. The suffragette movement and labor reform were important throughout this period of time; in fact, the vast majority of the women included in this book were involved in these movements, as well as socialism (and, of course, spiritualism). During the nineteenth century, work as a domestic was one of the few options available to women who were either not born into the middle or upper classes, or were unfortunate enough to fall from them, and several of these stories—Elizabeth Gaskell's "The Old Nurse's Story," Dora Sigerson Shorter's "Transmigration," Frances Hodgson Burnett's "In the Closed Room"—are told from the point of view of either domestics in a wealthy household or the very poor. A story like Marjorie Bowen's "Twilight" took the reverse tactic of turning one of history's most decadent, wealthy figures (Lucrezia Borgia) into a nightmarish vision that terrifies a young man, while Ellen Glasgow's "Jordan's End" traces the macabre fall of a once-great family. Olive Schreiner's "In a Far-off World" and Regina Miriam Bloch's "The Swine-Gods" use rich, dark metaphors—complete with bloody sacrifices—to illustrate societal ills like war, greed, and disparity between the genders in relationships. And then there are the ghost stories, which speak to how these authors both romanticized and feared the past.

While it seems downright shocking today to think that anyone could decide to support a family by writing and actually *do it* in a relatively short period of time, a number of the writers included here—women who abruptly found themselves without a father or a husband and with siblings, children, or elderly parents to support—entered the writing field for precisely that reason. Ann Radcliffe, one of the greatest female novelists in the years prior to Jane Austen and the Brontë sisters, was the highest-paid writer of the 1790s, and a century later Marie Corelli (whose lovely and eerie "The Lady with the Carnations" is a fine example of her work) would hold that honor in the 1890s. But even a writer of moderately successful short stories could keep a family on her earnings during this time, and without resorting to a life of drudgery in a factory or wealthy household. Writing also gave women the chance to receive the same pay as men, especially if they were satisfied with anonymity. Two of the most famous authors of the period who originally took up writing out of financial need (and both of whom appear in this book) were feminist icon Charlotte Perkins Gilman—who, by the way, was also an early user of self-publishing—and Frances Hodgson Burnett, who, like Louisa May Alcott, became known for her children's books although both enjoyed writing supernatural tales (Alcott, in fact, actually *preferred* writing them.). Charlotte Riddell—another author who took up the pen to support herself and her mother—produced ghost stories that felt drenched in the folklore of the past, with their plots often depending on the time-honored tradition of a haunting that originated from a murder (see "Nut Bush Farm"). Sarah Orne Jewett's "The Gray Man," written about fifty years after Nathaniel Hawthorne's "The Gray Champion," almost reads as a feminine answer to that earlier story; whereas Hawthorne's ghost returns to engage in battle, Jewett's specter is a participant in gentler activities like teaching and gardening (however, Jewett also captures the hint of irony underscoring Hawthorne's tale).

While many of these women certainly wrote as much from the simple, basic writer's need to tell a story, there's another key difference between them and their male counterparts: call it ego or ambition . . . or lack thereof, because many of these women wrote under pseudonyms, used their married name (Riddell and Gaskell were usually known as Mrs. J. H. Riddell and Mrs. Gaskell), or in some situations—like Harriet Spofford's astonishing weird tale "The Moonstone Mass"—under no byline whatsoever. Many of these authors were friendly with male writers who would go on to achieve greater fame, or they were tremendously admired by famous men, only to see their own names fade into semi-obscurity. Emma Frances Dawson, whose collection *An Itinerant House and Other Stories* is now a sought-after rarity in the secondhand market, was a great favorite of Ambrose Bierce, who frequently served as her editor, yet there's conjecture that Dawson died (at the age of 87) of starvation. Similarly, the mysterious Regina Miriam Bloch, once rumored to be the great Rebecca West, and who had been acclaimed by the British newspapers when her two short story collections, *The Swine-Gods and Other Visions* and *The Book of Strange Loves*, were released in 1917 and 1918 respectively, didn't merit a single mention in any paper upon her death in 1939.

Fortunately, the rise of the academic genre and feminist studies over the last few years has (deservedly) brought some of these authors back into the limelight; and fine small presses like Ash-Tree Press have provided lovely new editions of their works. We hope this volume will serve to continue introducing more of these gifted—and *very* dark—works to modern readers.

A Note on the Selection Process: we seriously considered well over fifty stories (by fifty authors) for inclusion in this book. We read critical studies, scoured old periodicals and anthologies, and in one case (that of Regina Miriam Bloch) even photographed the pages of a book from a university library's Special Collections. Unfortunately, in the end a publisher can only print so many pages, so we were forced to winnow our initial list down to less than half of those we loved. We weighed our final selections for their importance in the genre and how well they fit in with our vision for the book, but—first and foremost—we chose stories that frightened, disturbed, entranced, amused, and generally entertained us. We apologize to readers who may have a favorite story that isn't reflected here; if you'd like to hear more about our decisions—and read some of the stories we couldn't use—please check out our site www.weirdwomenbook.com.

Weird Women

Elizabeth Cleghorn Gaskell (1810–1865) was a British author who is often known simply as "Mrs. Gaskell." At the age of 22, Elizabeth married an assistant minister, William Gaskell, and bore four daughters. A son, born in 1845, died at nine months from scarlet fever. To distract her from her grief, her husband suggested she write a novel. Her first novel, *Mary Barton*, a story of impoverished workers, was published in 1848 and had a tremendous impact on British readers. Charles Dickens was a fan (although their relationship as editor and writer for his magazines was sometimes tumultuous), and Gaskell was also acclaimed for her biography of her friend Charlotte Brontë. Although she's now known primarily for social realism, she was also a gifted teller of ghostly tales. "The Old Nurse's Story" first appeared in 1852, in a special section of Dickens's periodical *Household Words* entitled "A Round of Stories by the Christmas Fire."

The Old Nurse's Story

by Elizabeth Gaskell

You know, my dears, that your mother was an orphan, and an only child; and I dare say you have heard that your grandfather was a clergyman up in Westmoreland, where I come from. I was just a girl in the village school, when, one day, your grandmother came in to ask the mistress if there was any scholar there who would do for a nurse-maid; and mighty proud I was, I can tell ye, when the mistress called me up, and spoke to my being a good girl at my needle, and a steady, honest girl, and one whose parents were very respectable, though they might be poor. I thought I should like nothing better than to serve the pretty young lady, who was blushing as deep as I was, as she spoke of the coming baby, and what I should have to do with it. However, I see you don't care so much for this part of my story, as for what you think is to come, so I'll tell you at once. I was engaged and settled at the parsonage before Miss Rosamond (that was the baby, who is now your mother) was born. To be sure, I had little enough to do with her when she came, for she was never out of her mother's arms, and slept by her all night long; and proud enough was I sometimes when missis trusted her to me. There never was such a baby before or since, though you've all of you been fine enough in your turns; but for sweet, winning ways, you've none of you come up to your mother. She took after her mother, who was a real lady born; a Miss Furnivall, a grand-daughter of Lord Furnivall's, in Northumberland. I believe she had neither brother nor sister, and had been brought up in my lord's family till she had married your grandfather, who was just a curate, son to a shop-keeper in Carlisle—but a clever, fine gentleman as ever was—and one who was a right-down hard worker in his parish, which was very wide, and scattered all abroad over the Westmoreland Fells. When your mother, little Miss Rosamond, was about four or five years old, both her parents died in a fortnight—one after the other. Ah! that was a sad time. My pretty young mistress and me was looking for another baby, when my master came home from one of his long rides, wet and tired, and took the fever he died of; and then she never held up her head again, but just lived to see her dead baby, and have it laid on her breast, before she sighed away her life. My mistress had asked me, on her death-bed, never to leave Miss Rosamond; but if she had never spoken a word, I would have gone with the little child to the end of the world.

The next thing, and before we had well stilled our sobs, the executors and guardians came to settle the affairs. They were my poor young mistress's own cousin, Lord Furnivall, and Mr. Esthwaite, my master's brother, a shopkeeper in Manchester; not so well-to-do then as he was afterwards, and with a large family rising about him. Well! I don't know if it were their settling, or because of a letter my mistress wrote on her death-bed to her cousin, my lord; but somehow it was settled that Miss Rosamond and me were to go to Furnivall Manor House, in Northumberland; and my lord spoke as if it had been her mother's wish that she should live with his family, and as if he had no objections, for that one or two more or less could make no difference in so grand a household. So, though that was not the way in which I should have wished the coming of my bright and pretty pet to have been looked at—who was like a sunbeam in any family, be it never so grand—I was well pleased that all the folks in the Dale should stare and admire, when they heard I was going to be young lady's maid at my Lord Furnivall's at Furnivall Manor.

But I made a mistake in thinking we were to go and live where my lord did. It turned out that the family had left Furnivall Manor House fifty years or more. I could not hear that my poor young mistress had ever been there, though she had been brought up in the family; and I was sorry for that, for I should have liked Miss Rosamond's youth to have passed where her mother's had been.

My lord's gentleman, from whom I asked as many questions as I durst, said that the Manor House was at the foot of the Cumberland Fells,[*] and a very grand place; that an old Miss Furnivall, a great-aunt of my lord's, lived there, with only a few servants; but that it was a very healthy place, and my lord had thought that it would suit Miss Rosamond very well for a few years, and that her being there might perhaps amuse his old aunt.

I was bidden by my lord to have Miss Rosamond's things ready by a certain day. He was a stern, proud man, as they say all the Lords Furnivall were; and he never spoke a word more than was necessary. Folk did say he had loved my young mistress; but that, because she knew that his father would object, she would never listen to him, and married Mr. Esthwaite; but I don't know. He never married, at any rate. But he never took much notice of Miss Rosamond; which I thought he might have done if he had cared for her dead mother. He sent his gentleman with us to the Manor House, telling him to join him at Newcastle[†] that same evening; so there was no great length of time for him to make us known to all the strangers before he, too, shook us off; and we were left, two lonely young things (I

---

* Cumberland County is located in the far northwest of Great Britain, bordered by Scotland on the north; the Fells are the harsh uplands of the Pennines.

† Newcastle is on the east coast of Great Britain, almost directly opposite the Cumberland area.

was not eighteen) in the great old Manor House. It seems like yesterday that we drove there. We had left our own dear parsonage very early, and we had both cried as if our hearts would break, though we were travelling in my lord's carriage, which I thought so much of once. And now it was long past noon on a September day, and we stopped to change horses for the last time at a little smoky town, all full of colliers* and miners. Miss Rosamond had fallen asleep, but Mr. Henry told me to waken her, that she might see the park and the Manor House as we drove up. I thought it rather a pity; but I did what he bade me, for fear he should complain of me to my lord. We had left all signs of a town, or even a village, and were then inside the gates of a large wild park—not like the parks here in the south, but with rocks, and the noise of running water, and gnarled thorn-trees, and old oaks, all white and peeled with age.

The road went up about two miles, and then we saw a great and stately house, with many trees close around it, so close that in some places their branches dragged against the walls when the wind blew, and some hung broken down; for no one seemed to take much charge of the place;—to lop the wood, or to keep the moss-covered carriage-way in order. Only in front of the house all was clear. The great oval drive was without a weed; and neither tree nor creeper was allowed to grow over the long, many-windowed front; at both sides of which a wing projected, which were each the ends of other side fronts; for the house, although it was so desolate, was even grander than I expected. Behind it rose the Fells, which seemed unenclosed and bare enough; and on the left hand of the house, as you stood facing it, was a little, old-fashioned flower-garden, as I found out afterwards. A door opened out upon it from the west front; it had been scooped out of the thick, dark wood for some old Lady Furnivall; but the branches of the great forest-trees had grown and overshadowed it again, and there were very few flowers that would live there at that time.

When we drove up to the great front entrance, and went into the hall, I thought we should be lost—it was so large, and vast, and grand. There was a chandelier all of bronze, hung down from the middle of the ceiling; and I had never seen one before, and looked at it all in amaze. Then, at one end

* A coal miner.

of the hall, was a great fireplace, as large as the sides of the houses in my country, with massy andirons and dogs to hold the wood; and by it were heavy, old-fashioned sofas. At the opposite end of the hall, to the left as you went in—on the western side—was an organ built into the wall, and so large that it filled up the best part of that end. Beyond it, on the same side, was a door; and opposite, on each side of the fireplace, were also doors leading to the east front; but those I never went through as long as I stayed in the house, so I can't tell you what lay beyond.

The afternoon was closing in, and the hall, which had no fire lighted in it, looked dark and gloomy; but we did not stay there a moment. The old servant, who had opened the door for us, bowed to Mr. Henry, and took us in through the door at the further side of the great organ, and led us through several smaller halls and passages into the west drawing-room, where he said that Miss Furnivall was sitting. Poor little Miss Rosamond held very tight to me, as if she were scared and lost in that great place; and as for myself, I was not much better. The west drawing-room was very cheerful-looking, with a warm fire in it, and plenty of good, comfortable furniture about. Miss Furnivall was an old lady not far from eighty, I should think, but I do not know. She was thin and tall, and had a face as full of fine wrinkles as if they had been drawn all over it with a needle's point. Her eyes were very watchful, to make up, I suppose, for her being so deaf as to be obliged to use a trumpet. Sitting with her, working at the same great piece of tapestry, was Mrs. Stark, her maid and companion, and almost as old as she was. She had lived with Miss Furnivall ever since they both were young, and now she seemed more like a friend than a servant; she looked so cold, and grey, and stony, as if she had never loved or cared for any one; and I don't suppose she did care for any one, except her mistress; and, owing to the great deafness of the latter, Mrs. Stark treated her very much as if she were a child. Mr. Henry gave some message from my lord, and then he bowed good-bye to us all—taking no notice of my sweet little Miss Rosamond's outstretched hand—and left us standing there, being looked at by the two old ladies through their spectacles.

I was right glad when they rung for the old footman who had shown us in at first, and told him to take us to our rooms. So we went out of that great drawing-room, and into another sitting-room, and out of that, and then up a great flight of stairs, and along a broad gallery—which was something like a library, having books all down one side, and windows and writing-tables all down the other—till we came to our rooms, which I was not sorry to hear were just over the kitchens; for I began to think I should be lost in that wilderness of a house. There was an old nursery, that had been used for all the little lords and ladies long ago, with a pleasant fire burning in the grate, and the kettle boiling on the hob, and tea-things spread out on the table; and out of that room was the night-nursery, with a little crib for Miss Rosamond close to my bed. And old James called up Dorothy, his wife, to bid us welcome; and both he and she were so hospitable and kind, that by-and-by Miss Rosamond and me felt quite at home; and by the time tea was over, she was sitting on Dorothy's knee, and chattering away as fast as her little tongue could go. I soon found out that Dorothy was from Westmoreland, and that bound her and me together, as it were; and I would never wish to meet with kinder people than were old James and his wife. James had lived pretty nearly all his life in my lord's family, and thought there was no one so grand as they. He even looked down a little on his wife; because, till he had married her, she had never lived in any but a farmer's household. But he was very fond of her, as well he might be. They had one servant under them, to do all the rough work. Agnes they called her; and she and me, and James and Dorothy, with Miss Furnivall and Mrs. Stark, made up the family; always remembering my sweet little Miss Rosamond! I used to wonder what they had done before she came, they thought so much of her now. Kitchen and drawing-room, it was all the same. The hard, sad Miss Furnivall, and the cold Mrs. Stark, looked pleased when she came fluttering in like a bird, playing and pranking hither and thither, with a continual murmur, and pretty prattle of gladness. I am sure, they were sorry many a time when she flitted away into the kitchen, though they were too proud to ask her to stay with them, and were a little surprised at her taste; though to be sure, as Mrs. Stark said, it was not to be wondered at, remembering what stock her father had come of. The great, old rambling house was a famous place for little Miss Rosamond. She made expeditions all over it, with me at her heels: all, except the east wing, which was never opened, and whither we never thought of going. But in the western and northern part was many a pleasant room; full of things that were curiosities to us, though they might not have been to people who had seen more. The windows were darkened by the sweeping boughs of the trees, and the ivy which had overgrown them; but, in the green gloom, we could manage to see old china jars and carved ivory boxes, and great heavy books, and, above all, the old pictures!

Once, I remember, my darling would have Dorothy go with us to tell us who they all were; for they were all portraits of some of my lord's family, though Dorothy could not tell us the names of every one. We had gone through most of the rooms, when we came to the old state drawing-room over the hall, and there was a picture of Miss Furnivall; or, as she was called in those days, Miss Grace, for she was the younger sister. Such a beauty she must have been! but with such a set, proud look, and such scorn looking out of her handsome eyes, with her eyebrows just a little raised, as if she wondered how any one could have the impertinence to look at her, and her lip curled at us, as we stood there gazing. She had a dress on, the like of which I had never seen before, but it was all the fashion when she was young: a hat of some soft white stuff like beaver, pulled a little over her brows, and a beautiful plume of feathers sweeping round it on one side; and her gown of blue satin was open in front to a quilted white stomacher.

"Well, to be sure!" said I, when I had gazed my fill. "Flesh is grass, they do say; but who would have thought that Miss Furnivall had been such an out-and-out beauty, to see her now?"

"Yes," said Dorothy. "Folks change sadly. But if what my master's father used to say was true, Miss Furnivall, the elder sister, was handsomer than Miss Grace. Her picture is here somewhere; but, if I show it you, you must never let on, even to James, that you have seen it. Can the little lady hold her tongue, think you?" asked she.

I was not so sure, for she was such a little sweet, bold, open-spoken child, so I set her to hide herself; and then I helped Dorothy to turn a great picture, that leaned with its face towards the wall, and was not hung up as the others were. To be sure, it beat Miss Grace for beauty; and I think, for scornful pride, too, though in that matter it might be hard to choose. I could have looked at it an hour but Dorothy seemed half frightened at having shown it to me, and hurried it back again, and bade me run and find Miss Rosamond, for that there were some ugly places about the house, where she should like ill for the child to go. I was a brave, high-spirited girl, and thought little of what the old woman said, for I liked hide-and-seek as well as any child in the parish; so off I ran to find my little one.

As winter drew on, and the days grew shorter, I was sometimes almost certain that I heard a noise as if some one was playing on the great organ in the hall. I did not hear it every evening; but, certainly, I did very often, usually when I was sitting with Miss Rosamond, after I had put her to bed, and keeping quite still and silent in the bedroom. Then I used to hear it booming and swelling away in the distance. The first night, when I went down to my supper, I asked Dorothy who had been playing music, and James said very shortly that I was a gowk* to take the wind soughing among the trees for music; but I saw Dorothy look at him very fearfully, and Bessy, the kitchen-maid, said something beneath her breath, and went quite white. I saw they did not like my question, so I held my peace till I was with Dorothy alone, when I knew I could get a good deal out of her. So, the next day, I watched my time, and I coaxed and asked her who it was that played the organ; for I knew that it was the organ and not the wind well enough, for all I had kept silence before James. But Dorothy had had her lesson, I'll warrant, and never a word could I get from her. So then I tried Bessy, though I had always held my head rather above her, as I was evened to James and Dorothy, and she was little better than their servant. So she said I must never, never tell; and if ever told, I was never to say she had told me; but it was a very strange noise, and she had heard it many a time, but most of all on winter nights, and before storms; and folks did say it was the old lord playing on the great organ in the hall, just as he used to do when he was alive; but who the old lord was, or why he played, and why he played on stormy winter evenings in particular, she either could not or would not tell me. Well! I told you I had a brave heart; and I thought it was rather pleasant to have that grand music rolling about the house, let who would be the player; for now it rose above the great gusts of wind, and wailed and triumphed just like a living creature, and then it fell to a softness most complete, only it was always music, and tunes, so it was nonsense

* A Northern English/Scottish term for a foolish person.

to call it the wind. I thought at first, that it might be Miss Furnivall who played, unknown to Bessy; but one day, when I was in the hall by myself, I opened the organ and peeped all about it and around it, as I had done to the organ in Crosthwaite Church once before, and I saw it was all broken and destroyed inside, though it looked so brave and fine; and then, though it was noon-day, my flesh began to creep a little, and I shut it up, and run away pretty quickly to my own bright nursery; and I did not like hearing the music for some time after that, any more than James and Dorothy did. All this time Miss Rosamond was making herself more and more beloved. The old ladies liked her to dine with them at their early dinner; James stood behind Miss Furnivall's chair, and I behind Miss Rosamond's all in state; and, after dinner, she would play about in a corner of the great drawing-room as still as any mouse, while Miss Furnivall slept, and I had my dinner in the kitchen. But she was glad enough to come to me in the nursery afterwards; for, as she said Miss Furnivall was so sad, and Mrs. Stark so dull; but she and I were merry enough; and, by-and-by, I got not to care for that weird rolling music, which did one no harm, if we did not know where it came from.

That winter was very cold. In the middle of October the frosts began, and lasted many, many weeks. I remember one day, at dinner, Miss Furnivall lifted up her sad, heavy eyes, and said to Mrs. Stark, "I am afraid we shall have a terrible winter," in a strange kind of meaning way. But Mrs. Stark pretended not to hear, and talked very loud of something else. My little lady and I did not care for the frost; not we! As long as it was dry, we climbed up the steep brows behind the house, and went up on the Fells which were bleak and bare enough, and there we ran races in the fresh, sharp air; and once we came down by a new path, that took us past the two old gnarled holly-trees, which grew about half-way down by the east side of the house. But the days grew shorter and shorter, and the old lord, if it was he, played away, more and more stormily and sadly, on the great organ. One Sunday afternoon—it must have been towards the end of November—I asked Dorothy to take charge of little missy when she came out of the drawing-room, after Miss Furnivall had had her nap; for it was too cold to take her with me to church, and yet I wanted to go, And Dorothy was glad enough to promise and was so fond of the child, that all seemed well; and Bessy and I set off very briskly, though the sky hung heavy and black over the white earth, as if the night had never fully gone away, and the air, though still, was very biting.

"We shall have a fall of snow," said Bessy to me. And sure enough, even while we were in church, it came down thick, in great large flakes—so thick, it almost darkened the windows. It had stopped snowing before we came out, but it lay soft, thick, and deep beneath our feet, as we tramped home. Before we got to the hall, the moon rose, and I think it was lighter then—what with the moon, and what with the white dazzling snow—than it had been when we went to church, between two and three o'clock. I have not told you that Miss Furnivall and Mrs. Stark never went to church; they used to read the prayers together, in their quiet, gloomy way; they seemed to feel the Sunday very long without their tapestry-work to be busy at. So when I went to Dorothy in the kitchen, to fetch Miss Rosamond and take her upstairs with me, I did not much wonder when the old woman told me that the ladies had kept the child with them, and that she had never come to the kitchen, as I had bidden her, when she was tired of behaving pretty in the drawing-room. So I took off my things and went to find her, and bring her to her supper in the nursery. But when I went into the best drawing-room, there sat the two old ladies, very still and quiet, dropping out a word now and then, but looking as if nothing so bright and merry as Miss Rosamond had ever been near them. Still I thought she might be hiding from me; it was one of her pretty ways,—and that she had persuaded them to look as if they knew nothing about her; so I went softly peeping under this sofa and behind that chair, making believe I was sadly frightened at not finding her.

"What's the matter, Hester?" said Mrs. Stark sharply. I don't know if Miss Furnivall had seen me for, as I told you, she was very deaf, and she sat quite still, idly staring into the fire, with her hopeless face. "I'm only looking for my little Rosy Posy," replied I, still thinking that the child was there, and near me, though I could not see her.

"Miss Rosamond is not here," said Mrs. Stark. "She went away, more than an hour ago, to find Dorothy." And she, too, turned and went on looking into the fire.

My heart sank at this, and I began to wish I had never left my darling. I went back to Dorothy and told her. James was gone out for the day, but she, and me, and Bessy took lights, and went up into the nursery first; and then we roamed over the great, large house, calling and entreating Miss Rosamond to come out of her hiding-place, and not frighten us to death in that way. But there was no answer; no sound.

"Oh!" said I, at last, "can she have got into the east wing and hidden there?"

But Dorothy said it was not possible, for that she herself had never been in there; that the doors were always locked, and my lord's steward had the keys, she believed; at any rate, neither she nor James had ever seen them: so I said I would go back, and see if, after all, she was not hidden in the drawing-room, unknown to the old ladies; and if I found her there, I said, I would whip her well for the fright she had given me; but I never meant to do it. Well, I went back to the west drawing-room, and I told Mrs. Stark we could not find her anywhere, and asked for leave to look all about the furniture there, for I thought now that she might have fallen asleep in some warm, hidden corner; but no! we looked—Miss Furnivall got up and looked, trembling all over—and she was nowhere there; then we set off again, every one in the house, and looked in all the places we had searched before, but we could not find her. Miss Furnivall shivered and shook so much, that Mrs. Stark took her back into the warm drawing-room; but not before they had made me promise to bring her to them when she was found. Well-a-day! I began to think she never would be found, when I bethought me to look into the great front court, all covered with snow. I was upstairs when I looked out; but, it was such clear moonlight, I could see, quite plain, two little footprints, which might be traced from the hall-door and round the corner of the east wing. I don't know how I got down, but I tugged open the great stiff hall-door, and, throwing the skirt of my gown over my head for a cloak, I ran out. I turned the east corner, and there a black shadow fell on the snow but when I came again into the moonlight, there were the little footmarks going up—up to the Fells. It was bitter cold; so cold, that the air almost took the skin off my face as I ran; but I ran on, crying to think how my poor little darling must be perished and frightened. I was within sight of the holly-trees, when I saw a shepherd coming down the hill, bearing something in his arms wrapped in his maud.* He shouted

* A gray plaid cloak worn by Scottish shepherds.

to me, and asked me if I had lost a bairn; and, when I could not speak for crying, he bore towards me, and I saw my wee bairnie, lying still, and white, and stiff in his arms, as if she had been dead. He told me he had been up the Fells to gather in his sheep, before the deep cold of night came on, and that under the holly-trees (black marks on the hill-side, where no other bush was for miles around) he had found my little lady—my lamb—my queen—my darling—stiff and cold in the terrible sleep which is frost-begotten. Oh! the joy and the tears of having her in my arms once again! for I would not let him carry her; but took her, maud and all, into my own arms, and held her near my own warm neck and heart, and felt the life stealing slowly back again into her little gentle limbs. But she was still insensible when we reached the hall, and I had no breath for speech. We went in by the kitchen-door.

"Bring the warming-pan," said I; and I carried her upstairs, and began undressing her by the nursery fire, which Bessy had kept up. I called my little lammie all the sweet and playful names I could think of,—even while my eyes were blinded by my tears; and at last, oh! at length she opened her large blue eyes. Then I put her into her warm bed, and sent Dorothy down to tell Miss Furnivall that all was well; and I made up my mind to sit by my darling's bedside the live-long night. She fell away into a soft sleep as soon as her pretty head had touched the pillow, and I watched by her till morning light; when she wakened up bright and clear—or so I thought at first—and, my dears, so I think now.

She said, that she had fancied that she should like to go to Dorothy, for that both the old ladies were asleep, and it was very dull in the drawing-room; and that, as she was going through the west lobby, she saw the snow through the high window falling—falling—soft and steady; but she wanted to see it lying pretty and white on the ground; so she made her way into the great hall: and then, going to the window, she saw it bright and soft upon the drive; but while she stood there, she saw a little girl, not so old as she was, "but so pretty," said my darling; "and this little girl beckoned to me to come out; and oh, she was so pretty and so sweet, I could not choose but go." And then this other little girl had taken her by the hand, and side by side the two had gone round the east corner.

"Now you are a naughty little girl, and telling stories," said I. "What would your good mamma, that is in heaven, and never told a story in her life, say to her little Rosamond, if she heard her—and I dare say she does—telling stories!"

"Indeed, Hester," sobbed out my child, "I'm telling you true. Indeed I am."

"Don't tell me!" said I, very stern. "I tracked you by your foot-marks through the snow; there were only yours to be seen: and if you had had a little girl to go hand-in-hand with you up the hill, don't you think the footprints would have gone along with yours?"

"I can't help it, dear, dear Hester," said she, crying, "if they did not; I never looked at her feet, but she held my hand fast and tight in her little one, and it was very, very cold. She took me up the Fell-path, up to the holly-trees; and there I saw a lady weeping and crying; but when she saw me, she hushed her weeping, and smiled very proud and grand, and took me on her knee, and began to lull me to sleep, and that's all, Hester—but that is true; and my dear mamma knows it is," said she, crying. So I thought the child was in a fever, and pretended to believe her, as she went over her story—over and over again, and always the same. At last Dorothy knocked at the door with Miss Rosamond's breakfast; and she told me the old ladies were down in the eating parlour, and that they wanted to speak to me. They had both been into the night-nursery the evening before, but it was after Miss Rosamond was asleep; so they had only looked at her—not asked me any questions.

"I shall catch it," thought I to myself, as I went along the north gallery. "And yet," I thought, taking courage, "it was in their charge I left her; and it's they that's to blame for letting her steal away unknown and unwatched."So I went in boldly, and told my story. I told it all to Miss Furnivall, shouting it close to her ear; but when I came to the mention of the other little girl out in the snow, coaxing and tempting her out, and wiling her up to the grand and beautiful lady by the holly-tree, she threw her arms up—her old and withered arms—and cried aloud, "Oh! Heaven forgive! Have mercy!"

Mrs. Stark took hold of her; roughly enough, I thought; but she was past Mrs. Stark's management, and spoke to me, in a kind of wild warning and authority.

"Hester! keep her from that child! It will lure her to her death! That evil child! Tell her it is a wicked, naughty child." Then, Mrs. Stark hurried me out of the room; where, indeed, I was glad enough to go; but Miss Furnivall kept shrieking out, "Oh, have mercy! Wilt thou never forgive! It is many a long year ago"—

I was very uneasy in my mind after that. I durst never leave Miss Rosamond, night or day, for fear lest she might slip off again, after some fancy or other; and all the more, because I thought I could make out that Miss Furnivall was crazy, from their odd ways about her; and I was afraid lest something of the same kind (which might be in the family, you know) hung over my darling. And the great frost never ceased all this time; and, whenever it was a more stormy night than usual, between the gusts, and through the wind we heard the old lord playing on the great organ. But, old lord, or not, wherever Miss Rosamond went, there I followed; for my love for her, pretty, helpless orphan, was stronger than my fear for the grand and terrible sound. Besides, it rested with me to keep her cheerful and merry, as beseemed her age. So we played together, and wandered together, here and there, and everywhere; for I never dared to lose sight of her again in that large and rambling house. And so it happened, that one afternoon, not long before Christmas-day, we were playing together on the billiard-table in the great hall (not that we knew the right way of playing, but she liked to roll the smooth ivory balls with her pretty hands, and I liked to do whatever she did); and, by-and-by, without our noticing it, it grew dusk indoors, though it was still light in the open air, and I was thinking of taking her back into the nursery, when, all of a sudden, she cried out—

"Look, Hester! look! there is my poor little girl out in the snow!"

I turned towards the long narrow windows, and there, sure enough, I saw a little girl, less than my Miss Rosamond—dressed all unfit to be out-of-doors such a bitter night—crying, and beating against the window panes, as if she wanted to be let in. She seemed to sob and wail, till Miss Rosamond could bear it no longer, and was flying to the door to open it, when, all of a sudden, and close upon us, the great organ pealed out so loud and thundering, it fairly made me tremble; and all the more, when I remembered me that, even in the stillness of that dead-cold weather, I had heard no sound of little battering hands upon the window-glass, although the phantom child had seemed to put forth all its force; and, although I had seen it wail and cry, no faintest touch of sound had fallen upon my ears. Whether I remembered all this at the very moment, I do not know; the great organ sound had so stunned me into terror; but this I know, I caught up Miss Rosamond before she got the hall-door opened, and clutched her, and carried her away, kicking and screaming, into the large, bright kitchen, where Dorothy and Agnes were busy with their mince-pies.

"What is the matter with my sweet one?" cried Dorothy, as I bore in Miss Rosamond, who was sobbing as if her heart would break.

"She won't let me open the door for my little girl to come in; and she'll die if she is out on the Fells all night. Cruel, naughty Hester," she said, slapping me; but she might have struck harder, for I had seen a look of ghastly terror on Dorothy's face, which made my very blood run cold.

"Shut the back-kitchen door fast, and bolt it well," said she to Agnes. She said no more; she gave me raisins and almonds to quiet Miss Rosamond; but she sobbed about the little girl in the snow, and would not touch any of the good things. I was thankful when she cried herself to sleep in bed. Then I stole down to the kitchen, and told Dorothy I had made up my mind. I would carry my darling back to my father's house in Applethwaite; where, if we lived humbly, we lived at peace. I said I had been frightened enough with the old lord's organ-playing; but now that I had seen for myself this little moaning child, all decked out as no child in the neighbourhood could be, beating and battering to get in, yet always without any sound or noise—with the dark wound on its right shoulder; and that Miss Rosamond had known it again for the phantom that had nearly lured her to death (which Dorothy knew was true); I would stand it no longer.

I saw Dorothy change colour once or twice. When I had done, she told me she did not think I could take Miss Rosamond with me, for that she was my lord's ward, and I had no right over her; and she asked me would I leave the child that I was so fond of just for sounds and sights that could do me no harm; and that they had all had to get used to in their turns? I was all in a hot, trembling passion; and I said it was very well for her to talk, that knew what these sights and noises betokened, and that had, perhaps, had something to do with the spectre child while it was alive. And I taunted her so, that she told me all she knew at last; and then I wished I had never been told, for it only made me more afraid than ever.

She said she had heard the tale from old neighbours that were alive when she was first married; when folks used to come to the hall sometimes, before it had got such a bad name on the country side: it might not be true, or it might, what she had been told.

The old lord was Miss Furnivall's father—Miss Grace, as Dorothy called her, for Miss Maude was the elder, and Miss Furnivall by lights. The old lord was eaten up with pride. Such a proud man was never seen or heard of; and his daughters were like him. No one was good enough to wed them, although they had choice enough; for they were the great beauties of their day, as I had seen by their portraits, where they hung in the state drawing-room. But, as the old saying is, "Pride will have a fall;" and these two haughty beauties fell in love with the same man, and he no better than a foreign musician, whom their father had down from London to play music with him at the Manor House. For, above all things, next to his pride, the old lord loved music. He could play on nearly every instrument that ever was heard of; and it was a strange thing it did not soften him; but he was a fierce, dour old man, and had broken his poor wife's heart with his cruelty, they said. He was mad after music, and would pay any money for it. So he got this foreigner to come; who made such beautiful music, that they said the very birds on the trees stopped their singing to listen. And, by degrees, this foreign gentleman got such a hold over the old lord, that nothing would serve him but that he must come every year; and it was he that had the great organ brought from Holland, and built up in the hall, where it stood now. He taught the old lord to play on it; but many and many a time, when Lord Furnivall was thinking of nothing but his fine organ, and his finer music, the dark foreigner was walking abroad in the woods, with one of the young ladies: now Miss Maude, and then Miss Grace.

Miss Maude won the day and carried off the prize, such as it was; and he and she were married, all unknown to any one; and, before he made his next yearly visit, she had been confined of a little girl at a farm-house on the Moors, while her father and Miss Grace thought she was away at Doncaster Races.* But though she was a wife and a mother, she was not a

* The Doncaster Racecourse in South Yorkshire is home to the Doncaster Cup, the world's oldest continuing regulated horse race.

bit softened, but as haughty and as passionate as ever; and perhaps more so, for she was jealous of Miss Grace, to whom her foreign husband paid a deal of court—by way of blinding her—as he told his wife. But Miss Grace triumphed over Miss Maude, and Miss Maude grew fiercer and fiercer, both with her husband and with her sister; and the former—who could easily shake off what was disagreeable, and hide himself in foreign countries—went away a month before his usual time that summer, and half-threatened that he would never come back again. Meanwhile, the little girl was left at the farm-house, and her mother used to have her horse saddled and gallop wildly over the hills to see her once every week, at the very least; for where she loved she loved, and where she hated she hated. And the old lord went on playing—playing on his organ; and the servants thought the sweet music he made had soothed down his awful temper, of which (Dorothy said) some terrible tales could be told. He grew infirm too, and had to walk with a crutch; and his son—that was the present Lord Furnivall's father—was with the army in America, and the other son at sea; so Miss Maude had it pretty much her own way, and she and Miss Grace grew colder and bitterer to each other every day; till at last they hardly ever spoke, except when the old lord was by. The foreign musician came again the next summer, but it was for the last time; for they led him such a life with their jealousy and their passions, that he grew weary, and went away, and never was heard of again. And Miss Maude, who had always meant to have her marriage acknowledged when her father should be dead, was left now a deserted wife, whom nobody knew to have been married, with a child that she dared not own, although she loved it to distraction; living with a father whom she feared, and a sister whom she hated. When the next summer passed over, and the dark foreigner never came, both Miss Maude and Miss Grace grew gloomy and sad; they had a haggard look about them, though they looked handsome as ever. But, by-and-by, Miss Maude brightened; for her father grew more and more infirm, and more than ever carried away by his music, and she and Miss Grace lived almost entirely apart, having separate rooms, the one on the west side, Miss Maude on the east—those very rooms which were now shut up. So she thought she might have her little girl with her, and no one need ever know except those who dared not speak about it, and were bound to believe that it was, as she said, a cottager's child she had taken a fancy to. All this, Dorothy said, was pretty well known; but what came afterwards no one knew, except Miss Grace and Mrs. Stark, who was even then her maid, and much more of a friend to her than ever her sister had been. But the servants supposed, from words that were dropped, that Miss Maude had triumphed over Miss Grace, and told her that all the time the dark foreigner had been mocking her with pretended love—he was her own husband. The colour left Miss Grace's cheek and lips that very day for ever, and she was heard to say many a time that sooner or later she would have her revenge; and Mrs. Stark was for ever spying about the east rooms.

One fearful night, just after the New Year had come in, when the snow was lying thick and deep; and the flakes were still falling—fast enough to blind any one who might be out and abroad—there was a great and violent noise heard, and the old lord's voice above all, cursing and swearing awfully, and the cries of a little child, and the proud defiance of a fierce woman, and the sound of a blow, and a dead stillness, and moans and wailings, dying away on the hill-side! Then the old lord summoned all his servants, and told them, with terrible oaths, and words more terrible, that his daughter had disgraced herself, and that he had turned her out of doors—her, and her child—and that if ever they gave her help, or food, or shelter, he prayed that they might never enter heaven. And, all the while, Miss Grace stood by him, white and still as any stone; and, when he had ended, she heaved a great sigh, as much as to say her work was done, and her end was accomplished. But the old lord never touched his organ again, and died within the year; and no wonder! for, on the morrow of that wild and fearful night, the shepherds, coming down the Fell side, found Miss Maude sitting, all crazy and smiling, under the holly-trees, nursing a dead child, with a terrible mark on its right shoulder. "But that was not what killed it," said Dorothy: "it was the frost and the cold. Every wild creature was in its hole, and every beast in its fold, while the child and its mother were turned out to wander on the Fells! And now you know all! and I wonder if you are less frightened now?"

I was more frightened than ever; but I said I was not. I wished Miss Rosamond and myself well out of that dreadful house for ever; but I would not leave her, and I dared not take her away. But oh, how I watched her, and guarded her! We bolted the doors, and shut the window-shutters fast, an hour or more before dark, rather than leave them open five minutes too late. But my little lady still heard the weird child crying and mourning; and not all we could do or say could keep her from wanting to go to her, and let her in from the cruel wind and snow. All this time I kept away from Miss Furnivall and Mrs. Stark, as much as ever I could; for I feared them—I knew no good could be about them, with their grey, hard faces, and their dreamy eyes, looking back into the ghastly years that were gone. But, even in my fear, I had a kind of pity for Miss Furnivall, at least. Those gone down to the pit can hardly have a more hopeless look than that which was ever on her face. At last I even got so sorry for her—who never said a word but what was quite forced from her—that I prayed for her; and I taught Miss Rosamond to pray for one who had done a deadly sin; but often, when she came to those words, she would listen, and start up from her knees, and say, "I hear my little girl plaining and crying, very sad,—oh, let her in, or she will die!"

One night—just after New Year's Day had come at last, and the long winter had taken a turn, as I hoped—I heard the west drawing-room bell ring three times, which was the signal for me. I would not leave Miss Rosamond alone, for all she was asleep—for the old lord had been playing wilder than ever—and I feared lest my darling should waken to hear the spectre child; see her I knew she could not. I had fastened the windows too well for that. So I took her out of her bed, and wrapped her up in such outer clothes as were most handy, and carried her down to the drawing-room, where the old ladies sat at their tapestry-work as usual. They looked up when I came in, and Mrs. Stark asked, quite astounded, "Why did I bring Miss Rosamond there, out of her warm bed?" I had begun to whisper, "Because I was afraid of her being tempted out while I was away, by the wild child in the snow," when she stopped me short (with a glance at Miss Furnivall), and said Miss Furnivall wanted me to undo some work she had done wrong, and which neither of them could see to unpick. So I laid my pretty dear on the sofa, and sat down on a stool by them, and hardened my heart against them, as I heard the wind rising and howling.

Miss Rosamond slept on sound, for all the wind blew so; and Miss Furnivall said never a word, nor looked round when the gusts shook the windows. All at once she started up to her full height, and put up one hand, as if to bid us listen.

"I hear voices!" said she. "I hear terrible screams—I hear my father's voice!"

Just at that moment my darling wakened with a sudden start: "My little girl is crying, oh, how she is crying!" and she tried to get up and go to her, but she got her feet entangled in the blanket, and I caught her up; for my flesh had begun to creep at these noises, which they heard while we could catch no sound. In a minute or two the noises came, and gathered fast, and filled our ears; we, too, heard voices and screams, and no longer heard the winter's wind that raged abroad. Mrs. Stark looked at me, and I at her, but we dared not speak. Suddenly Miss Furnivall went towards the door, out into the ante-room, through the west lobby, and opened the door into the great hall. Mrs. Stark followed, and I durst not be left, though my heart almost stopped beating for fear. I wrapped my darling tight in my arms, and went out with them. In the hall the screams were louder than ever; they seemed to come from the east wing—nearer and nearer—close on the other side of the locked-up doors—close behind them. Then I noticed that the great bronze chandelier seemed all alight, though the hall was dim, and that a fire was blazing in the vast hearth-place, though it gave no heat; and I shuddered up with terror, and folded my darling closer to me. But as I did so the east door shook, and she, suddenly struggling to get free from me, cried, "Hester! I must go. My little girl is there; I hear her; she is coming! Hester, I must go!"

I held her tight with all my strength; with a set will, I held her. If I had died, my hands would have grasped her still, I was so resolved in my mind. Miss Furnivall stood listening, and paid no regard to my darling, who had got down to the ground, and whom I, upon my knees now, was holding with both my arms clasped round her neck; she still striving and crying to get free.

All at once, the east door gave way with a thundering crash, as if torn open in a violent passion, and there came into that broad and mysterious light, the figure of a tall old man, with grey hair and gleaming eyes. He drove before him, with many a relentless gesture of abhorrence, a stern and beautiful woman, with a little child clinging to her dress.

"O Hester! Hester!" cried Miss Rosamond; "it's the lady! the lady below the holly-trees; and my little girl is with her. Hester! Hester! let me go to her; they are drawing me to them. I feel them—I feel them. I must go!"

Again she was almost convulsed by her efforts to get away; but I held her tighter and tighter, till I feared I should do her a hurt; but rather that than let her go towards those terrible phantoms. They passed along towards the great hall-door, where the winds howled and ravened for their prey; but before they reached that, the lady turned; and I could see that she defied the old man with a fierce and proud defiance; but then she quailed—and then she threw up her arms wildly and piteously to save her child—her little child—from a blow from his uplifted crutch.

And Miss Rosamond was torn as by a power stronger than mine, and writhed in my arms, and sobbed (for by this time the poor darling was growing faint).

"They want me to go with them on to the Fells—they are drawing me to them. Oh, my little girl! I would come, but cruel, wicked Hester holds me very tight." But when she saw the uplifted crutch, she swooned away, and I thanked God for it. Just at this moment—when the tall old man, his hair streaming as in the blast of a furnace, was going to strike the little shrinking child—Miss Furnivall, the old woman by my side, cried out, "O father! father! spare the little innocent child!" But just then I saw—we all saw—another phantom shape itself, and grow clear out of the blue and misty light that filled the hall; we had not seen her till now, for it was another lady who stood by the old man, with a look of relentless hate and triumphant scorn. That figure was very beautiful to look upon, with a soft, white hat drawn down over the proud brows, and a red and curling lip. It was dressed in an open robe of blue satin. I had seen that figure before. It was the likeness of Miss Furnivall in her youth; and the terrible phantoms moved on, regardless of old Miss Furnivall's wild entreaty,—and the uplifted crutch fell on the right shoulder of the little child, and the younger sister looked on, stony, and deadly serene. But at that moment, the dim lights, and the fire that gave no heat, went out of themselves, and Miss Furnivall lay at our feet stricken down by the palsy—death-stricken.

Yes! she was carried to her bed that night never to rise again. She lay with her face to the wall, muttering low, but muttering always: "Alas! alas! what is done in youth can never be undone in age! What is done in youth can never be undone in age!"

The American writer **Harriet Prescott Spofford** (1835–1921) lived in New England her entire life. In a career spanning more than 60 years, she wrote a large quantity of novels, short stories, and poetry, making her one of the most widely-published authors in America. She married in 1865, taking her husband's name Spofford, and continued to write extensively in various genres. Her first crime story "In a Cellar," published in 1859, was submitted under an assumed name, causing editors to believe that it was a translation of Dumas or Balzac. In her 1865 "Mr. Furbush," she created the first "series" detective character, the eponymous policeman, who appeared in a second story in 1868. Her 1860 tale "Circumstance" was said by Emily Dickinson to have shocked her badly. The following, which first appeared in *Harper's New Monthly Magazine* for October 1868 without her byline, is a Lovecraftian tale of a man's uncanny experience with a phenomenon from beyond, in an Arctic setting that both Mary Shelley and Lovecraft used to explore the weird.

The Moonstone Mass

by Harriet Prescott Spofford

There was a certain weakness possessed by my ancestors, though in nowise peculiar to them, and of which, in common with other more or less undesirable traits, I have come into the inheritance.

It was the fear of dying in poverty. That, too, in the face of a goodly share of pelf* stored in stocks, and lands, and copper-bottomed clippers, or what stood for copper-bottomed clippers, or rather sailed for them, in the clumsy commerce of their times.

* Money or wealth, usually applied to that acquired via theft or fraud.

There was one old fellow in particular—his portrait is hanging over the hall stove today, leaning forward, somewhat blistered by the profuse heat and wasted fuel there, and as if as long as such an outrageous expenditure of caloric was going on he meant to have the full benefit of it—who is said to have frequently shed tears over the probable price of his dinner, and on the next day to have sent home a silver dish to eat it from at a hundred times the cost. I find the inconsistencies of this individual constantly cropping out in myself; and although I could by no possibility be called a niggard, yet I confess that even now my prodigalities make me shiver.

Some years ago I was the proprietor of the old family estate, unencumbered by any thing except timber, that is worth its weight in gold yet, as you might say; alone in the world, save for an unloved relative; and with a sufficiently comfortable income, as I have since discovered, to meet all reasonable wants. I had, moreover, promised me in marriage the hand of a woman without a peer, and which, I believe now, might have been mine on any day when I saw fit to claim it.

That I loved Eleanor tenderly and truly you can not doubt; that I desired to bring her home, to see her flitting here and there in my dark old house, illuminating it with her youth and beauty, sitting at the head of my table that sparkled with its gold and silver heir-looms, making my days and nights like one delightful dream, was just as true.

And yet I hesitated. I looked over my bankbook—I cast up my accounts. I have enough for one, I said; I am not sure that it is enough for two. Eleanor, daintily nurtured, requires as dainty care for all time to come; moreover, it is not two alone to be considered, for should children come, there is their education, their maintenance, their future provision and portion to be found. All this would impoverish us, and unless we ended by becoming mere dependents, we had, to my excited vision, only the cold charity of the world and the work-house to which to look forward. I do not believe that Eleanor thought me right in so much of the matter as I saw fit to explain, but in maiden pride her lips perforce were sealed. She laughed though, when I confessed my work-house fear, and said that for her part she was thankful there was such a refuge at all, standing as it did on its knoll in the midst of green fields, and shaded by broad-limbed oaks—she had always envied the old women sitting there by their evening fireside, and mumbling over their small affairs to one another. But all her words seemed merely idle badinage—so I delayed. I said—when this ship sails in, when that dividend is declared, when I see how this speculation turns out—the days were long that added up the count of years, the nights were dreary; but I believed that I was actuated by principle, and took pride to myself for my strength and self-denial.

Moreover, old Paul, my great-uncle on my mother's side, and the millionaire of the family, was a bitter misogynist, and regarded women and marriage and household cares as the three remediless mistakes of an overruling Providence. He knew of my engagement to Eleanor, but so long as it remained in that stage he had nothing to say. Let me once marry, and my share of his million would be best represented by a cipher. However, he was not a man to adore, and he could not live forever.

Still, with all my own effort, I amassed wealth but slowly, according to my standard; various ventures had various luck; and one day my old Uncle Paul, always intensely interested in the subject, both scientifically and from a commercial point of view, too old and feeble to go himself, but fain to send a proxy, and desirous of money in the family, made me an offer of that portion of his wealth on my return which would be mine on his demise, funded safely subject to my order, provided I made one of those who sought the discovery of the Northwest Passage.*

I went to town, canvassed the matter with the experts—I had always an adventurous streak, as old Paul well knew—and having given many hours to the pursuit of the smaller sciences, had a turn for danger and discovery as well. And when the *Albatross* sailed—in spite of Eleanor's shivering remonstrance and prayers and tears, in spite of the grave looks of my friends—I was one of those that clustered on her deck, prepared for either fate. They—my companions—it is true, were led by nobler lights; but as for me, it was much as I told Eleanor—my affairs were so regulated that they would go on uninterruptedly in my absence; I should be no worse off for going, and if I returned, letting alone the renown of the thing, my

* Nineteenth-century explorers and merchants sought the Northwest Passage, a sea route from the Atlantic to Pacific Ocean navigating through the ice to the north of Canada. It wasn't achieved until nearly forty years after this story was written.

Uncle Paul's donation was to be appropriated; every thing then was assured, and we stood possessed of lucky lives. If I had any keen or eager desire of search, any purpose to aid the growth of the world or to penetrate the secrets of its formation; as indeed I think I must have had, I did not at that time know any thing about it. But I was to learn that death and stillness have no kingdom on this globe, and that even in the extremest bitterness of cold and ice perpetual interchange and motion is taking place. So we went, all sails set on favorable winds, bounding over blue sea, skirting frowning coasts, and ever pushing our way up into the dark mystery of the North.

I shall not delay here to tell of Danish posts and the hospitality of summer settlements in their long afternoon of arctic daylight; nor will I weary you with any description of the succulence of the radishes that grew under the panes of glass in the Governor's scrap of moss and soil, scarcely of more size than a lady's parlor fernery, and which seemed to our dry mouths full of all the earth's cool juices—but advance, as we ourselves hastened to do, while that chill and crystalline sun shone, up into the ice-cased dens and caverns of the Pole. By the time that the long, blue twilight fell, when the rough and rasping cold sheathed all the atmosphere, and the great stars pricked themselves out on the heavens like spears' points, the *Albatross* was hauled up for winter-quarters, banked and boarded, heaved high on fields of ice; and all her inmates, during the wintry dark, led the life that prepared them for further exploits in higher latitudes the coming year, learning the dialects of the Esquimaux, the tricks of the seal and walrus, making long explorations with the dogs and Glipnu, their master, breaking ourselves in for business that had no play about it.

Then, at last, the August suns set us free again; inlets of tumultuous water traversed the great ice-floes; the *Albatross*, refitted, ruffled all her plumage and spread her wings once more for the North—for the secret that sat there domineering all its substance.

It was a year since we had heard from home; but who staid to think of that while our keel spurned into foam the sheets of steely seas, and day by day brought us nearer to the hidden things we sought? For myself I confess that, now so close to the end as it seemed, curiosity and research absorbed every other faculty; Eleanor might be mouldering back to the parent earth—I could not stay to meditate on such a possibility; my Uncle Paul's donation might enrich itself with gold-dust instead of the gathered dust of idle days—it was nothing to me. I had but one thought, one ambition, one desire in those days—the discovery of the clear seas and open passage. I endured all our hardships as if they had been luxuries: I made light of scurvy, banqueted off train-oil,* and met that cold for which there is no language framed, and which might be a new element; or which, rather, had seemed in that long night like the vast void of ether beyond the uttermost star, where was neither air nor light nor heat, but only bitter negation and emptiness. I was hardly conscious of my body; I was only a concentrated search in myself.

The recent explorers had announced here, in the neighborhood of where our third summer at last found us, the existence of an immense space of clear water. One even declared that he had seen it.

My Uncle Paul had pronounced the declaration false, and the sight an impossibility. The North he believed to be the breeder of icebergs, an ever-welling fountain of cold; the great glaciers there forever form, forever fall; the ice-packs line the gorges from year to year unchanging; peaks of volcanic rock drop their frozen mantles like a scale only to display the fresher one beneath. The whole region, said he, is Plutonic,† blasted by a primordial convulsion of the great forces of creation; and though it may be a few miles nearer to the central fires of the earth, allowing that there are such things, yet that would not in itself detract from the frigid power of its sunless solitudes, the more especially when it is remembered that the spinning of the earth, while in its first plastic material, which gave it greater circumference and thinness of shell at its equator, must have thickened the shell correspondingly at the poles; and the character of all the waste and wilderness there only signifies the impenetrable wall between its surface and centre, through which wall no heat could enter or escape. The great rivers, like the White and the Mackenzie, emptying to the north of the continents, so far from being enough in themselves to form any body of ever fresh and flowing water, can only pierce the opposing ice-fields in narrow streams and bays and inlets as they seek the Atlantic and the Pacific seas. And as for the

* Whale-oil, that is—made from blubber.

† Igneous rock formed deep beneath the earth's surface.

theory of the currents of water heated in the tropics and carried by the rotary motion of the planet to the Pole, where they rise and melt the ice-floes into this great supposititious sea,* it is simply an absurdity on the face of it, he argued, when you remember that warm water being in its nature specifically lighter than cold it would have risen to the surface long before it reached there. No, thought my Uncle Paul, who took nothing for granted; it is as I said, an absurdity on the face of it; my nephew shall prove it, and I stake half the earnings of my life upon it.

To tell the truth, I thought much the same as he did; and now that such a mere trifle of distance intervened between me and the proof, I was full of a feverish impatience that almost amounted to insanity.

We had proceeded but a few days, coasting the crushing capes of rock that every where seemed to run out in a diablerie of tusks and horns to drive us from the legion that they warded, now cruising through a runlet of blue water just wide enough for our keel, with silver reaches of frost stretching away into a ghastly horizon—now plunging upon tossing seas, the sun wheeling round and round, and never sinking from the strange, weird sky above us, when again to our look-out a glimmer in the low horizon told its awful tale—a sort of smoky lustre like that which might ascend from an army of spirits—the fierce and fatal spirits tented on the terrible field of the ice-floe.

We were alone, our single little ship speeding ever upward in the midst of that untraveled desolation. We spoke seldom to one another, oppressed with the sense of our situation. It was a loneliness that seemed more than a death in life, a solitude that was supernatural. Here and now it was clear water; ten hours later and we were caught in the teeth of the cold, wedged in the ice that had advanced upon us and surrounded us, fettered by another winter in latitudes where human life had never before been supported.

We found, before the hands of the dial had taught us the lapse of a week, that this would be something not to be endured. The sun sank lower every day behind the crags and silvery horns; the heavens grew to wear a hue

* The idea of a warmer climate at the North Pole held sway for many years prior to its exploration. This myth is mentioned in the opening letters of the Arctic explorer Robert Walton in Mary Shelley's *Frankenstein*.

of violet, almost black, and yet unbearably dazzling; as the notes of our voices fell upon the atmosphere they assumed a metallic tone, as if the air itself had become frozen from the beginning of the world and they tinkled against it; our sufferings had mounted in their intensity till they were too great to be resisted.

It was decided at length—when the one long day had given place to its answering night, and in the jet-black heavens the stars, like knobs of silver, sparkled so large and close upon us that we might have grasped them in our hands—that I should take a sledge with Glipnu and his dogs, and see if there were any path to the westward by which, if the *Albatross* were forsaken, those of her crew that remained might follow it, and find an escape to safety. Our path was on a frozen sea; if we discovered land we did not know that the foot of man had ever trodden it; we could hope to find no cache of snow-buried food—neither fish nor game lived in this desert of ice that was so devoid of life in any shape as to seem dead itself. But, well provisioned, furred to the eyes, and essaying to nurse some hopefulness of heart, we set out on our way through this Valley of Death, relieving one another, and traveling day and night.

Still night and day to the west rose the black coast, one interminable height; to the east extended the sheets of unbroken ice; sometimes a huge glacier hung pendulous from the precipice; once we saw, by the starlight, a white, foaming, rushing river arrested and transformed to ice in its flight down that steep. A south wind began to blow behind us; we traveled on the ice; three days, perhaps, as days are measured among men, had passed, when we found that we made double progress, for the ice traveled too; the whole field, carried by some northward-bearing current, was afloat; it began to be crossed and cut by a thousand crevasses; the cakes, an acre each, tilted up and down, and made wide waves with their ponderous plashing in the black body of the sea: we could hear them grinding distantly in the clear dark against the coast, against each other. There was no retreat—there was no advance; we were on the ice, and the ice was breaking up. Suddenly we rounded a tongue of the primeval rock, and recoiled before a narrow gulf—one sharp shadow, as deep as despair, as full of aguish* fears. It was

* Shivering, as in an ague or fever.

just wide enough for the sledge to span. Glipnu made the dogs leap; we could be no worse off if they drowned. They touched the opposite block; it careened; it went under; the sledge went with it; I was left alone where I had stood. Two dogs broke loose, and scrambled up beside me; Glipnu and the others I never saw again. I sank upon the ice; the dogs crouched beside me; sometimes I think they saved my brain from total ruin, for without them I could not have withstood the enormity of that loneliness, a loneliness that it was impossible should be broken—floating on and on with that vast journeying company of spectral ice. I had food enough to support life for several days to come, in the pouch at my belt; the dogs and I shared it—for, last as long as it would, when it should be gone there was only death before us—no reprieve—sooner or later that; as well sooner as later—the living terrors of this icy hell were all about us, and death could be no worse.

Still the south wind blew, the rapid current carried us, the dark skies grew deep and darker, the lanes and avenues between the stars were crowded with forebodings—for the air seemed full of a new power, a strange and invisible influence, as if a king of unknown terrors here held his awful state. Sometimes the dogs stood up and growled and bristled their shaggy hides; I, prostrate on the ice, in all my frame was stung with a universal tingle. I was no longer myself. At this moment my blood seemed to sing and bubble in my veins; I grew giddy with a sort of delirious and inexplicable ecstasy; with another moment unutterable horror seized me; I was plunged and weighed down with a black and suffocating load, while evil things seemed to flap their wings in my face, to breathe in my mouth, to draw my soul out of my body and carry it careering through the frozen realm of that murky heaven, to restore it with a shock of agony. Once as I lay there, still floating, floating northward, out of the dim dark rim of the water-world, a lance of piercing light shot up the zenith; it divided the heavens like a knife; they opened out in one blaze, and the fire fell sheetingly down before my face—cold fire, curdlingly cold—light robbed of heat, and set free in a preternatural anarchy of the elements; its fringes swung to and fro before my face, pricked it with flaming spiculæ,* dissolving in a thousand colors that spread every where over the low field, flashing,

* A spike-shaped or needle-like structure.

flickering, creeping, reflecting, gathering again in one long serpentine line of glory that wavered in slow convolutions across the cuts and crevasses of the ice, wreathed ever nearer, and, lifting its head at last, became nothing in the darkness but two great eyes like glowing coals, with which it stared me to a stound,* till I threw myself face down to hide me in the ice; and the whining, bristling dogs cowered backward, and were dead.

I should have supposed myself to be in the region of the magnetic pole of the sphere, if I did not know that I had long since left it behind me. My pocket-compass had become entirely useless, and every scrap of metal that I had about me had become a loadstone.† The very ice, as if it were congealed from water that held large quantities of iron in solution; iron escaping from whatever solid land there was beneath or around, the Plutonic rock that such a region could have alone veined and seamed with metal. The very ice appeared to have a magnetic quality; it held me so that I changed my position upon it with difficulty, and, as if it established a battery by the aid of the singular atmosphere above it, frequently sent thrills quivering through and through me till my flesh seemed about to resolve into all the jarring atoms of its original constitution; and again soothed me, with a velvet touch, into a state which, if it were not sleep, was at least haunted by visions that I dare not believe to have been realities, and from which I always awoke with a start to find myself still floating, floating. My watch had long since ceased to beat. I felt an odd persuasion that I had died when that stood still, and only this slavery of the magnet, of the cold, this power that locked every thing in invisible fetters and let nothing loose again, held my soul still in the bonds of my body. Another idea, also, took possession of me, for my mind was open to whatever visitant chose to enter, since utter despair of safety or release had left it vacant of a hope or fear. These enormous days and nights, swinging in their arc six months long, were the pendulum that dealt time in another measure than that dealt by the sunlight of lower zones; they told the time of what interminable years, the years of what vast generations far beyond the span that covered the age of the primeval men of Scripture—they measured time on this gigantic and enduring scale for what

* Amazement or astonishment.

† Variant spelling of "lodestone," a piece of naturally magnetic rock.

wonderful and mighty beings, old as the everlasting hills, as destitute as they of mortal sympathy, cold and inscrutable, handling the two-edged javelins of frost and magnetism, and served by all the unknown polar agencies. I fancied that I saw their far-reaching cohorts, marshaling and manœuvring at times in the field of an horizon that was boundless, the glitter of their spears and casques, the sheen of their white banners; and again, sitting in fearful circle with their phantasmagoria they shut and hemmed me in and watched me writhe like a worm before them.

I had a fancy that the perpetual play of magnetic impulses here gradually disintegrated the expanse of ice, as sunbeams might have done. If it succeeded in unseating me from my cold station I should drown, and there would be an end of me; it would be all one; for though I clung to life I did not cling to suffering. Something of the wild beast seemed to spring up in my nature; that ignorance of any moment but the present. I felt a certain kinship to the bear in her comfortable snowiness whom I had left in the parallels far below this unreal tract of horrors. I remembered traditions of such metempsychoses;* the thought gave me a pang that none of these fierce and subtle elements had known how to give before. But all the time my groaning, cracking ice was moving with me, splitting now through all its leagues of length along the darkness, with an explosion like a cannon's shot, that echoed again and again in every gap and chasm of its depth, and seemed to be caught up and repeated by a thousand airy sprites, and snatched on from one to another till it fell dead through the frozen thickness of the air.

It was at about this time that I noticed another species of motion than that which had hitherto governed it seizing this journeying ice. It bent and bent, as a glacier does in its viscous flow between mountains; it crowded, and loosened, and rent apart, and at last it broke in every direction, and every fragment was crushed and jammed together again; and the whole mass was following, as I divined, the curve of some enormous whirlpool that swept it from beneath. It might have been a day and night, it might have been an hour, that we traveled on this vast curve—I had no more means of knowing than if I had veritably done with time. We were one

* Transmigrations of the soul.

expanse of shadow; not a star above us, only a sky of impenetrable gloom received the shimmering that now and again the circling ice cast off. It was a strange slow motion, yet with such a steadiness and strength about it that it had the effect of swiftness. It was long since any water, or the suspicion of any, had been visible; we might have been grinding through some gigantic hollow for all I could have told; snow had never fallen here; the mass moved you knew as if you felt the prodigious hand that grasped and impelled it from beneath. Whither was it tending, in the eddy of what huge stream that went, with the smoke of its fall hovering on the brink, to plunge a tremendous cataract over the limits of the earth into the unknown abyss of space? Far in advance there was a faint glimmering, a sort of powdery light glancing here and there. As we approached it—the ice and I—it grew fainter, and was, by-and-by, lost in a vast twilight that surrounded us on all sides; at the same time it became evident that we had passed under a roof, an immense and vaulted roof. As crowding, stretching, rending, we passed on, uncanny gleams were playing distantly above us and around us, now and then overlaying all things with a sheeted illumination as deathly as a grave-light, now and then shooting up in spires of blood-red radiance that disclosed the terrible aurora. I was in a cavern of ice, as wide and as high as the heavens; these flashes of glory, alternated with equal flashes of darkness, as you might say, taught me to perceive. Perhaps tremendous tide after tide had hollowed it with all its fantastic recesses; or had that Titantic race of the interminable years built it as a palace for their monarch, a temple for their deity, with its domes that sprung far up immeasurable heights and hung palely shining like mock heavens of hazy stars; its aisles that stretched away down colonnades of crystal columns into unguessed darkness; its high-heaved arches, its pierced and open sides? Now an aurora burned up like a blue-light, and went skimming under all the vaults far off into far and farther hollows, revealing, as it went, still loftier heights and colder answering radiances. Then these great arches glowed like blocks of beryl. Wondrous tracery of delicate vines and leaves, greener than the greenest moss, wandered over them, wreathed the great pillars, and spread round them in capitals of flowers; roses crimson as a carbuncle; hyacinths like bedded cubes of amethyst; violets bluer than sapphires—all as if the flowers had been turned to flame, yet all so cruelly cold, as if the power that wrought such wonders could simulate a sparkle beyond even the lustre of light, but could not give it heat, that principle of life, that fountain of first being. Yonder a stalactite of clustered ruby—that kept the aurora and glinted faintly, and more faintly, till the thing came again, when it grasped a whole body-full of splendor—hung downward and dropped a thread-like stem and a blossom of palest pink, like a transfigured Linnæa,* to meet the snow-drop in its sheath of green that shot up from a spire of aqua marine below. Here living rainbows hew from buttress to buttress and frolicked in the domes—the only things that dared to live and sport where beauty was frozen into horror. It seemed as if that shifting death-light of the aurora photographed all these things upon my memory, for I noted none of them at the time. I only wondered idly whither we were tending as we drove in deeper and deeper under that ice-roof, and curved more and more circlingly upon our course while the silent flashes sped on overhead. Now we were in the dark again crashing onward; now a cold blue radiance burst from every icicle, from every crevice, and I saw that the whole enormous mass of our motion bent and swept around a single point—a dark yet glittering form that sat as if upon the apex of the world. Was it one of those mightier than the Anakim,† more than the sons of God, to whom all the currents of this frozen world converged? Sooth I know not—for presently I imagined that my vision made only an exaggeration of some brown Esquimaux sealed up and left in his snow-house to die. A thin sheathing of ice appeared to clothe him and give the glister to his duskiness. Insensible as I had thought myself to any further fear, I cowered beneath the stare of those dead and icy eyes. Slowly we rounded, and ever rounded; the inside, on which my place was, moving less slowly than the outer circle of the sheeted mass in its viscid flow; and as we moved, by some fate my eye was caught by the substance on which this figure sat. It was no figure at all now, but a bare jag of rock rising in the centre of this solid whirlpool, and carrying on its summit something which held a light that not one of these icy freaks, pranking

* A subarctic woodland shrub, *Linnaea borealis*, until 2013 the only known member of the genus *Linnaea*.

† A race of giants, mentioned in Genesis.

in the dress of gems and flowers, had found it possible to assume. It was a thing so real, so genuine, my breath became suspended; my heart ceased to beat; my brain, that had been a lump of ice, seemed to move in its skull; hope, that had deserted me, suddenly sprung up like a second life within me; the old passion was not dead, if I was. It rose stronger than life or death or than myself. If I could but snatch that mass of moonstone, that inestimable wealth! It was nothing deceptive, I declared to myself. What more natural home could it have than this region, thrown up here by the old Plutonic powers of the planet, as the same substance in smaller shape was thrown up on the peaks of the Mount St. Gothard,* when the Alpine aiguilles† first sprang into the day? There it rested, limpid with its milky pearl, casting out flakes of flame and azure, of red and leaf-green light, and holding yet a sparkle of silver in the reflections and refractions of its inner axis—the splendid Turk's-eye of the lapidaries, the cousin of the water-opal and the girasole, the precious essence of feldspar. Could I break it, I would find clusters of great hemitrope crystals. Could I obtain it, I should have a jewel in that mass of moonstone such as the world never saw! The throne of Jemschid‡ could not cast a shadow beside it.

Then the bitterness of my fate overwhelmed me. Here, with this treasure of a kingdom, this jewel that could not be priced, this wealth beyond an Emperor's—and here only to die! My stolid apathy vanished, old thoughts dominated once more, old habits, old desires. I thought of Eleanor then in her warm, sunny home, the blossoms that bloomed around her, the birds that sang, the cheerful evening fires, the longing thoughts for one who never came, who never was to come. But I would! I cried, where human voice had never cried before. I would return! I would take this treasure with me! I would not be defrauded! Should not I, a man, conquer this inanimate blind matter? I reached out my hands to seize it. Slowly it receded—slowly, and less slowly; or was the motion of the ice still carrying me onward? Had we encircled this apex? and were we driving out into the open and

* An Alpine mountain pass.

† Sharp peaks.

‡ A Persian king, builder of the city of Istakhar.

uncovered North, and so down the seas and out to the open main of black water again? If so—if I could live through it—I must have this thing!

I rose, and as well as I could, with my cramped and stiffened limbs, I moved to go back for it. It was useless; the current that carried us was growing invincible, the gaping gulfs of the outer seas were sucking us toward them. I fell; I scrambled to my feet; I would still have gone back, but, as I attempted it, the ice whereon I was inclined ever so slightly, tipped more boldly, gave way, and rose in a billow, broke, and piled over on another mass beneath. Then the cavern was behind us, and I comprehended that this ice-stream, having doubled its central point, now in its outward movement encountered the still incoming body, and was to pile above and pass over it, the whole expanse bending, cracking, breaking, crowding, and compressing, till its rearing tumult made bergs more mountainous than the offshot glaciers of the Greenland continent, that should ride safely down to crumble in the surging seas below. As block after block of the rent ice rose in the air, lighted by the blue and bristling aurora-points, toppled and mounted higher, it seemed to me that now indeed I was battling with those elemental agencies in the dreadful fight I had desired—one man against the might of matter. I sprang from that block to another; I gained my balance on a third, climbing, shouldering, leaping, struggling, holding with my hands, catching with my feet, crawling, stumbling, tottering, rising high and higher with the mountain ever making underneath; a power unknown to my foes coming to my aid, a blessed rushing warmth that glowed on all the surface of my skin, that set the blood to racing in my veins, that made my heart beat with newer hope, sink with newer despair, rise buoyant with new determination. Except when the shaft of light pierced the shivering sky I could not see or guess the height that I had gained. I was vaguely aware of chasms that were bottomless, of precipices that opened on them, of pinnacles rising round me in aerial spires, when suddenly the shelf, on which I must have stood, yielded, as if it were pushed by great hands, swept down a steep incline like an avalanche, stopped half-way, but sent me flying on, sliding, glancing, like a shooting-star, down, down the slippery side, breathless, dizzy, smitten with blistering pain by awful winds that whistled by me, far out upon the level ice below that tilted up and down again with the great resonant plash of open water, and conscious for a moment that

I lay at last upon a fragment that the mass behind urged on, I knew and I remembered nothing more.

Faces were bending over me when I opened my eyes again, rough, uncouth, and bearded faces, but no monsters of the pole. Whalemen rather, smelling richly of train-oil, but I could recall nothing in all my life one fraction so beautiful as they; the angels on whom I hope to open my eyes when Death has really taken me will scarcely seem sights more blest than did those rude whalers of the North Pacific Sea. The North Pacific Sea—for it was there that I was found, explain it how you may—whether the *Albatross* had pierced farther to the west than her sailing-master knew, and had lost her reckoning with a disordered compass-needle under new stars—or whether I had really been the sport of the demoniac beings of the ice, tossed by them from zone to zone in a dozen hours. The whalers, real creatures enough, had discovered me on a block of ice, they said; nor could I, in their opinion, have been many days undergoing my dreadful experience, for there was still food in my wallet when they opened it. They would never believe a word of my story, and so far from regarding me as one who had proved the Northwest Passage in my own person, they considered me a mere idle maniac, as uncomfortable a thing to have on ship-board as a ghost or a dead body, wrecked and unable to account for myself, and gladly transferred me to a homeward-bound Russian man-of-war, whose officers afforded me more polite but quite as decided skepticism. I have never to this day found any one who believed my story when I told it—so you can take it for what it is worth. Even my Uncle Paul flouted it, and absolutely refused to surrender the sum on whose expectation I had taken ship; while my old ancestor, who hung peeling over the hall fire, dropped from his frame in disgust at the idea of one of his hard-cash descendants turning romancer. But all I know is that the *Albatross* never sailed into port again, and that if I open my knife today and lay it on the table it will wheel about till the tip of its blade points full at the NorthStar.

I have never found any one to believe me, did I say? Yes, there is one—Eleanor never doubted a word of my narration, never asked me if cold and suffering had not shaken my reason. But then, after the first recital, she has never been willing to hear another word about it, and if I ever allude to my lost treasure or the possibility of instituting search for it, she asks me if I need more lessons to be content with the treasure that I have, and gathers up her work and gently leaves the room. So that, now I speak of it so seldom, if I had not told the thing to you it might come to pass that I should forget altogether the existence of my mass of moonstone. My mass of moonshine, old Paul calls it. I let him have his say; he can not have that nor any thing else much longer; but when all is done I recall Galileo and I mutter to myself, "*Per si muove**—it *was* a mass of moonstone! With these eyes I saw it, with these hands I touched it, with this heart I longed for it, with this will I mean to have it yet!"

* It is said that after Galileo was forced to recant his embrace of the teachings of Copernicus, he muttered this phrase: "And still it moves . . ."

Louisa May Alcott (1832–1888) is beloved by readers as the author of the classic *Little Women* (1868), but she also enjoyed writing horror, or what she referred to as her "blood and thunder" tales. In fact, Alcott once said, "I think my natural ambition is for the lurid style." Her thriller *A Long Fatal Love Chase* was deemed "too sensational" by Victorian publishers (Random House published the novel when it was rediscovered in 1994). "Lost in a Pyramid" was first published in Frank Leslie's 1869 *A New World*, using only the initials "L. M. A." Although it's technically not the first horror story to use a mummy, it's often considered to be the first major work to incorporate one.

Lost in a Pyramid, or the Mummy's Curse

by Louisa May Alcott

I

"And what are these, Paul?" asked Evelyn, opening a tarnished gold box and examining its contents curiously.

"Seeds of some unknown Egyptian plant," replied Forsyth, with a sudden shadow on his dark face, as he looked down at the three scarlet grains lying in the white hand lifted to him.

"Where did you get them?" asked the girl.

"That is a weird story, which will only haunt you if I tell it," said Forsyth, with an absent expression that strongly excited the girl's curiosity.

"Please tell it, I like weird tales, and they never trouble me. Ah, do tell it; your stories are always so interesting," she cried, looking up with such a pretty blending of entreaty and command in her charming face, that refusal was impossible.

"You'll be sorry for it, and so shall I, perhaps; I warn you beforehand, that harm is foretold to the possessor of those mysterious seeds," said Forsyth, smiling, even while he knit his black brows, and regarded the blooming creature before him with a fond yet foreboding glance.

"Tell on, I'm not afraid of these pretty atoms," she answered, with an imperious nod.

"To hear is to obey. Let me read the facts, and then I will begin," returned Forsyth, pacing to and fro with the far-off look of one who turns the pages of the past.

Evelyn watched him a moment, and then returned to her work, or play, rather, for the task seemed well suited to the vivacious little creature, half-child, half-woman.

"While in Egypt," commenced Forsyth, slowly, "I went one day with my guide and Professor Niles, to explore the Cheops.[*] Niles had a mania for antiquities of all sorts, and forgot time, danger and fatigue in the ardor of his pursuit. We rummaged up and down the narrow passages, half choked with dust and close air; reading inscriptions on the walls, stumbling over shattered mummy-cases, or coming face to face with some shriveled specimen perched like a hobgoblin on the little shelves where the dead used to be stowed away for ages.[†] I was desperately tired after a few hours of it, and begged the professor to return. But he was bent on exploring certain places, and would not desist. We had but one guide, so I was forced to stay; but Jumal,[‡] my

---

* This refers to the Great Pyramid, sometimes known as the Pyramid of Cheops or the Pyramid of Khufu. King Khufu (whose Greek name was Cheops) built the Great Pyramid to stand over his tomb; it was completed in 2560 B.C., and is one of the Seven Wonders of the Ancient World. When this story was written, European exploration of the Great Pyramid had been going on for over two centuries. Khufu also appears in Jane C. Loudon's 1827 novel *The Mummy! A Tale of the 22nd Century*.

† Alcott is taking fanciful liberties with her description of the pyramid's interior, which by 1869 had become such a tourist destination that the entrance was covered with graffiti left by hundreds of earlier European visitors. By the beginning of the eighteenth century, the pyramid's interior had already been thoroughly plundered.

‡ Jumal is an Arabic boys' name meaning "handsome"

man, seeing how weary I was, proposed to us to rest in one of the larger passages, while he went to procure another guide for Niles. We consented, and assuring us that we were perfectly safe, if we did not quit the spot, Jumal left us, promising to return speedily. The professor sat down to take notes of his researches, and stretching my self on the soft sand, I fell asleep.

"I was roused by that indescribable thrill which instinctively warns us of danger, and springing up, I found myself alone. One torch burned faintly where Jumal had struck it, but Niles and the other light were gone. A dreadful sense of loneliness oppressed me for a moment; then I collected myself and looked well about me. A bit of paper was pinned to my hat, which lay near me, and on it, in the professor's writing were these words:

"'I've gone back a little to refresh my memory on certain points. Don't follow me till Jumal comes. I can find my way back to you, for I have a clue. Sleep well, and dream gloriously of the Pharaohs. N N.'

"I laughed at first over the old enthusiast, then felt anxious then restless, and finally resolved to follow him, for I discovered a strong cord fastened to a fallen stone, and knew that this was the clue he spoke of. Leaving a line for Jumal, I took my torch and retraced my steps, following the cord along the winding ways. I often shouted, but received no reply, and pressed on, hoping at each turn to see the old man poring over some musty relic of antiquity. Suddenly the cord ended, and lowering my torch, I saw that the footsteps had gone on.

"'Rash fellow, he'll lose himself, to a certainty,' I thought, really alarmed now.

"As I paused, a faint call reached me, and I answered it, waited, shouted again, and a still fainter echo replied.

"Niles was evidently going on, misled by the reverberations of the low passages. No time was to be lost, and, forgetting myself, I stuck my torch in the deep sand to guide me back to the clue, and ran down the straight path before me, whooping like a madman as I went. I did not mean to lose sight of the light, but in my eagerness to find Niles I turned from the main passage, and, guided by his voice, hastened on. His torch soon gladdened my eyes, and the clutch of his trembling hands told me what agony he had suffered.

"'Let us get out of this horrible place at once,' he said, wiping the great drops off his forehead.

"'Come, we're not far from the clue. I can soon reach it, and then we are safe'; but as I spoke, a chill passed over me, for a perfect labyrinth of narrow paths lay before us.

"Trying to guide myself by such land-marks as I had observed in my hasty passage, I followed the tracks in the sand till I fancied we must be near my light. No glimmer appeared, however, and kneeling down to examine the footprints nearer, I discovered, to my dismay, that I had been following the wrong ones, for among those marked by a deep boot-heel, were prints of bare feet; we had had no guide there, and Jumal wore sandals.

"Rising, I confronted Niles, with the one despairing word, 'Lost!' as I pointed from the treacherous sand to the fast-waning light.

"I thought the old man would be overwhelmed but, to my surprise, he grew quite calm and steady, thought a moment, and then went on, saying, quietly:

"'Other men have passed here before us; let us follow their steps, for, if I do not greatly err, they lead toward great passages, where one's way is easily found.'

"On we went, bravely, till a misstep threw the professor violently to the ground with a broken leg, and nearly extinguished the torch. It was a horrible predicament, and I gave up all hope as I sat beside the poor fellow, who lay exhausted with fatigue, remorse and pain, for I would not leave him.

"'Paul,' he said suddenly, 'if you will not go on, there is one more effort we can make. I remember hearing that a party lost as we are, saved themselves by building a fire. The smoke penetrated further than sound or light, and the guide's quick wit understood the unusual mist; he followed it, and rescued the party. Make a fire and trust to Jumal.'

"'A fire without wood?' I began; but he pointed to a shelf behind me, which had escaped me in the gloom; and on it I saw a slender mummy-case. I understood him, for these dry cases, which lie about in hundreds, are freely used as firewood.* Reaching up, I pulled it down, believing it to

* Alcott is probably describing here a "mummy-pit," which were mass burials that are found in early travelers' accounts of Egypt. They seem to have disappeared by the early 20th century due to European collectors seeking mummies as souvenirs and relics.

be empty, but as it fell, it burst open, and out rolled a mummy. Accustomed as I was to such sights, it startled me a little, for danger had unstrung my nerves. Laying the little brown chrysalis aside, I smashed the case, lit the pile with my torch, and soon a light cloud of smoke drifted down the three passages which diverged from the cell-like place where we had paused.

"While busied with the fire, Niles, forgetful of pain and peril, had dragged the mummy nearer, and was examining it with the interest of a man whose ruling passion was strong even in death.

"'Come and help me unroll this. I have always longed to be the first to see and secure the curious treasures put away among the folds of these uncanny winding-sheets. This is a woman, and we may find something rare and precious here,' he said, beginning to unfold the outer coverings, from which a strange aromatic odor came.

"Reluctantly I obeyed, for to me there was something sacred in the bones of this unknown woman. But to beguile the time and amuse the poor fellow, I lent a hand, wondering as I worked, if this dark, ugly thing had ever been a lovely, soft-eyed Egyptian girl.

"From the fibrous folds of the wrappings dropped precious gums and spices, which half intoxicated us with their potent breath, antique coins, and a curious jewel or two, which Niles eagerly examined.

"All the bandages but one were cut off at last, and a small head laid bare, round which still hung great plaits of what had once been luxuriant hair. The shriveled hands were folded on the breast, and clasped in them lay that gold box."

"Ah!" cried Evelyn, dropping it from her rosy palm with a shudder.

"Nay; don't reject the poor little mummy's treasure. I never have quite forgiven myself for stealing it, or for burning her," said Forsyth, painting rapidly, as if the recollection of that experience lent energy to his hand.

"Burning her! Oh, Paul, what do you mean?" asked the girl, sitting up with a face full of excitement.

"I'll tell you. While busied with Madame la Momie, our fire had burned low, for the dry case went like tinder. A faint, far-off sound made our hearts leap, and Niles cried out: 'Pile on the wood; Jumal is tracking us; don't let the smoke fail now or we are lost!'

"'There is no more wood; the case was very small, and is all gone,' I answered, tearing off such of my garments as would burn readily, and piling them upon the embers.

"Niles did the same, but the light fabrics were quickly consumed, and made no smoke.

"'Burn that!' commanded the professor, pointing to the mummy.

"I hesitated a moment. Again came the faint echo of a horn. Life was dear to me. A few dry bones might save us, and I obeyed him in silence.

"A dull blaze sprung up, and a heavy smoke rose from the burning mummy, rolling in volumes through the low passages, and threatening to suffocate us with its fragrant mist. My brain grew dizzy, the light danced before my eyes, strange phantoms seemed to people the air, and, in the act of asking Niles why he gasped and looked so pale, I lost consciousness."

Evelyn drew a long breath, and put away the scented toys from her lap as if their odor oppressed her.

Forsyth's swarthy face was all aglow with the excitement of his story, and his black eyes glittered as he added, with a quick laugh:

"That's all; Jumal found and got us out, and we both forswore pyramids for the rest of our days."

"But the box: how came you to keep it?" asked Evelyn, eyeing it askance as it lay gleaming in a streak of sunshine.

"Oh, I brought it away as a souvenir, and Niles kept the other trinkets."

"But you said harm was foretold to the possessor of those scarlet seeds," persisted the girl, whose fancy was excited by the tale, and who fancied all was not told.

"Among his spoils, Niles found a bit of parchment, which he deciphered, and this inscription said that the mummy we had so ungallantly burned was that of a famous sorceress who bequeathed her curse to whoever should disturb her rest. Of course I don't believe that curse has anything to do with it, but it's a fact that Niles never prospered from that day. He says it's because he has never recovered from the fall and fright and I dare say it is so; but I sometimes wonder if I am to share the curse, for I've a vein of superstition in me, and that poor little mummy haunts my dreams still."

A long silence followed these words. Paul painted mechanically and Evelyn lay regarding him with a thoughtful face. But gloomy fancies were as foreign to her nature as shadows are to noonday, and presently she laughed a cheery laugh, saying as she took up the box again:

"Why don't you plant them, and see what wondrous flower they will bear?"*

"I doubt if they would bear anything after lying in a mummy's hand for centuries," replied Forsyth, gravely.

"Let me plant them and try. You know wheat has sprouted and grown that was taken from a mummy's coffin;† why should not these pretty seeds? I should so like to watch them grow; may I, Paul?"

"No, I'd rather leave that experiment untried. I have a queer feeling about the matter, and don't want to meddle myself or let anyone I love meddle with these seeds. They may be some horrible poison, or possess some evil power, for the sorceress evidently valued them, since she clutched them fast even in her tomb."

"Now, you are foolishly superstitious, and I laugh at you. Be generous; give me one seed, just to learn if it will grow. See I'll pay for it," and Evelyn, who now stood beside him, dropped a kiss on his forehead as she made her request, with the most engaging air.

But Forsyth would not yield. He smiled and returned the embrace with lover-like warmth, then flung the seeds into the fire, and gave her back the golden box, saying, tenderly:

"My darling, I'll fill it with diamonds or bonbons, if you please, but I will not let you play with that witch's spells. You've enough of your own, so forget the 'pretty seeds' and see what a Light of the Harem‡ I've made of you."

Evelyn frowned, and smiled, and presently the lovers were out in the spring sunshine reveling in their own happy hopes, untroubled by one foreboding fear.

---

* In the 1830s, as "Egyptomania" swept through England, a surgeon named Thomas Pettigrew gave public performances of unwrapping mummies (he personally conducted around 40). Pettigrew claimed that seeds found during the unwrappings ("mummy wheat" or "mummy peas") could be planted and would grow, although many suspected fraud on the part of Pettigrew.

† There were actual attempts made to grow "mummy wheat," but the seeds never germinated and in fact dissolved several months after being placed in soil.

‡ This is a reference to Thomas Moore's 1817 poem "The Light of the Harem," which is a description of a garden with a "harem of night-flowers."

II

"I have a little surprise for you, love," said Forsyth, as he greeted his cousin three months later on the morning of his wedding day.

"And I have one for you," she answered, smiling faintly.

"How pale you are, and how thin you grow! All this bridal bustle is too much for you, Evelyn." he said, with fond anxiety, as he watched the strange pallor of her face, and pressed the wasted little hand in his.

"I am so tired," she said, and leaned her head wearily on her lover's breast. "Neither sleep, food, nor air gives me strength, and a curious mist seems to cloud my mind at times. Mamma says it is the heat, but I shiver even in the sun, while at night I burn with fever. Paul, dear, I'm glad you are going to take me away to lead a quiet, happy life with you, but I'm afraid it will be a very short one."

"My fanciful little wife! You are tired and nervous with all this worry, but a few weeks of rest in the country will give us back our blooming Eve* again. Have you no curiosity to learn my surprise?" he asked, to change her thoughts.

The vacant look stealing over the girl's face gave place to one of interest, but as she listened it seemed to require an effort to fix her mind on her lover's words.

"You remember the day we rummaged in the old cabinet?"

"Yes," and a smile touched her lips for a moment.

"And how you wanted to plant those queer red seeds I stole from the mummy?"

"I remember," and her eyes kindled with sudden fire.

"Well, I tossed them into the fire, as I thought, and gave you the box. But when I went back to cover up my picture, and found one of those seeds on the rug, a sudden fancy to gratify your whim led me to send it to Niles and ask him to plant and report on its progress. Today I hear from him for the first time, and he reports that the seed has grown marvelously, has

* The phrase "blooming Eve" likely originated in Horatio Walpole's 1791 play *The Mysterious Mother*, in which it's used to describe a young woman at the peak of health and beauty.

budded, and that he intends to take the first flower, if it blooms in time, to a meeting of famous scientific men, after which he will send me its true name and the plant itself. From his description, it must be very curious, and I'm impatient to see it."

"You need not wait; I can show you the flower in its bloom," and Evelyn beckoned with the mechante* smile so long a stranger to her lips.

Much amazed, Forsyth followed her to her own little boudoir, and there, standing in the sunshine, was the unknown plant. Almost rank in their luxuriance were the vivid green leaves on the slender purple stems, and rising from the midst, one ghostly-white flower, shaped like the head of a hooded snake, with scarlet stamens like forked tongues, and on the petals glittered spots like dew.

"A strange, uncanny flower! Has it any odor?" asked Forsyth, bending to examine it, and forgetting, in his interest, to ask how it came there.

"None, and that disappoints me, I am so fond of perfumes," answered the girl, caressing the green leaves which trembled at her touch, while the purple stems deepened their tint.

"Now tell me about it," said Forsyth, after standing silent for several minutes.

"I had been before you, and secured one of the seeds, for two fell on the rug. I planted it under a glass in the richest soil I could find, watered it faithfully, and was amazed at the rapidity with which it grew when once it appeared above the earth. I told no-one, for I meant to surprise you with it; but this bud has been so long in blooming, I have had to wait. It is a good omen that it blossoms today, and as it is nearly white, I mean to wear it, for I've learned to love it, having been my pet for so long."

"I would not wear it, for, in spite of its innocent color, it is an evil-looking plant, with its adder's tongue and unnatural dew. Wait till Niles tells us what it is, then pet it if it is harmless. Perhaps my sorceress cherished it for some symbolic beauty—those old Egyptians were full of fancies. It was very sly of you to turn the tables on me in this way. But I forgive you, since in a few hours, I shall chain this mysterious hand

* "Mechante" is a French word referring to a bad character trait.

forever. How cold it is! Come out into the garden and get some warmth and color for tonight, my love."

But when night came, no-one could reproach the girl with her pallor, for she glowed like a pomegranate-flower, her eyes were full of fire, her lips scarlet, and all her old vivacity seemed to have returned. A more brilliant bride never blushed under a misty veil, and when her lover saw her, he was absolutely startled by the almost unearthly beauty which transformed the pale, languid creature of the morning into this radiant woman.

They were married, and if love, many blessings, and all good gifts lavishly showered upon them could make them happy, then this young pair were truly blest. But even in the rapture of the moment that made her his, Forsyth observed how icy cold was the little hand he held, how feverish the deep color on the soft cheek he kissed, and what a strange fire burned in the tender eyes that looked so wistfully at him.

Blithe and beautiful as a spirit, the smiling bride played her part in all the festivities of that long evening, and when at last light, life and color began to fade, the loving eyes that watched her thought it but the natural weariness of the hour. As the last guest departed, Forsyth was met by a servant, who gave him a letter marked "Haste." Tearing it open, he read these lines, from a friend of the professor's:

"DEAR SIR—Poor Niles died suddenly two days ago, while at the Scientific Club,* and his last words were: 'Tell Paul Forsyth to beware of the Mummy's Curse, for this fatal flower has killed me.' The circumstances of his death were so peculiar, that I add them as a sequel to this message. For several months, as he told us, he had been watching an unknown plant, and that evening he brought us the flower to examine. Other matters of interest absorbed us till a late hour, and the plant was forgotten. The professor wore it in his buttonhole—a strange white, serpent-headed blossom, with pale glittering spots, which slowly changed to a glittering scarlet, till the leaves looked as if sprinkled with blood. It was observed that instead of the pallor and feebleness which had recently come over him, that the professor was unusually animated, and seemed in an almost

* There is a longstanding Scientific Club at Oxford University, but Alcott is probably not referring to that specific organization here.

unnatural state of high spirits. Near the close of the meeting, in the midst of a lively discussion, he suddenly dropped, as if smitten with apoplexy.* He was conveyed home insensible, and after one lucid interval, in which he gave me the message I have recorded above, he died in great agony, raving of mummies, pyramids, serpents, and some fatal curse which had fallen upon him.

"After his death, livid scarlet spots, like those on the flower, appeared upon his skin, and he shriveled like a withered leaf. At my desire, the mysterious plant was examined, and pronounced by the best authority one of the most deadly poisons known to the Egyptian sorceresses. The plant slowly absorbs the vitality of whoever cultivates it, and the blossom, worn for two or three hours, produces either madness or death."

Down dropped the paper from Forsyth's hand; he read no further, but hurried back into the room where he had left his young wife. As if worn out with fatigue, she had thrown herself upon a couch, and lay there motionless, her face half-hidden by the light folds of the veil, which had blown over it.

"Evelyn, my dearest! Wake up and answer me. Did you wear that strange flower today?" whispered Forsyth, putting the misty screen away.

There was no need for her to answer, for there, gleaming spectrally on her bosom, was the evil blossom, its white petals spotted now with flecks of scarlet, vivid as drops of newly spilt blood.

But the unhappy bridegroom scarcely saw it, for the face above it appalled him by its utter vacancy. Drawn and pallid, as if with some wasting malady, the young face, so lovely an hour ago, lay before him aged and blighted by the baleful influence of the plant which had drunk up her life. No recognition in the eyes, no word upon the lips, no motion of the hand—only the faint breath, the fluttering pulse, and wide-opened eyes, betrayed that she was alive.

Alas for the young wife! The superstitious fear at which she had smiled had proved true: the curse that had bided its time for ages was fulfilled at last, and her own hand wrecked her happiness for ever. Death in life was her doom, and for years Forsyth secluded himself to tend with pathetic devotion the pale ghost, who never, by word or look, could thank him for the love that outlived even such a fate as this.

* Apoplexy is the word formerly used for strokes.

Elizabeth Stuart Phelps (1844–1911) was an American feminist writer whose work challenged traditional Christian views of the afterlife and the role of women in marriages. An active anti-vivisectionist and an advocate for women's clothing reform ("Burn those corsets!"), Phelps was the first woman to present a lecture series at Boston University, in 1876, in which she focused on the fiction of George Eliot. The following tale, about a woman with a very specific psychic power and its consequences to her and those around her, first appeared in Phelps's collection *Men, Women, and Ghosts* (1869).

What Was the Matter?

by Elizabeth Stuart Phelps

I could not have been more than seven or eight years old, when it happened; but it might have been yesterday. Among all other childish memories, it stands alone. To this very day it brings with it the old, utter sinking of the heart, and the old, dull sense of mystery.

To read what I have to say, you should have known my mother. To understand it, you should understand her. But that is quite impossible now, for there is a quiet spot over the hill, and past the church, and beside the little brook where the crimsoned mosses grow thick and wet and cool, from which I cannot call her. It is all I have left of her now. But after all, it is not of her that you will chiefly care to hear. My object is simply to acquaint you with a few facts, which, though interwoven with the events of her life, are quite independent of it as objects of interest. It is, I know, only my own heart that makes these pages a memorial,—but, you see, I cannot help it.

Yet, I confess, no glamour of any earthly love has ever entirely dazzled me,—not even hers. Of imperfections, of mistakes, of sins, I knew she was guilty. I know it now; even with the sanctity of those crimsoned mosses, and the hush of the rest beneath, so close to my heart, I cannot forget them. Yet somehow—I do not know how—the imperfections, the mistakes, the very sins, bring her nearer to me as the years slip by, and make her dearer.

My mother was what we call an aristocrat. I do not like the term, as the term is used. I am sure she does not now; but I have no other word. She was a royal-looking woman, and she had the blood of princes in her veins. Generations back,—how we children used to reckon the thing over!—she was cradled in a throne. A miserable race, to be sure, they were,—the Stuarts; and the most devout genealogist might deem it dubious honor to own them for great-grand-fathers by innumerable degrees removed. So she used to tell us, over and over, as a damper on our childish vanity, looking such a very queen as she spoke, in every play of feature, and every motion of her hand, that it was the old story of preachers who did not practise. The very baby was proud of her. The beauty of a face, and the elegant repose of a manner, are influences by no means more unfelt at three years than at thirty.

As insanity will hide itself away, and lie sleeping, and die out,—while old men are gathered to their fathers scathless,* and young men follow in their footsteps safe and free,—and start into life, and claim its own when children's children have forgotten it; as a single trait of a single scholar in a race of clods will bury itself in day-laborers and criminals, unto the third and fourth generation, and spring then, like a creation from a chaos, into statesmen and poets and sculptors;—so, I have sometimes fancied, the better and truer nature of voluptuaries and tyrants was sifted down through the years, and purified in our little New England home, and the essential autocracy of monarchical blood refined and ennobled, in my mother, into royalty.

A broad and liberal culture had moulded her; she knew its worth, in every fiber of her heart; scholarly parents had blessed her with their legacies of scholarly mind and name. With the soul of an artist, she quivered under every grace and every defect; and the blessing of a beauty as rare as rich had been given to her. With every instinct of her nature recoiling from the very shadow of crimes the world winks at, the family record had

* Archaic form of "unscathed"

been stainless for a generation. God had indeed blessed her; but the very blessing was a temptation.

I knew, before she left me, what she might have been, but for the merciful and tender watch of Him who was despised and rejected of men. I know, for she told me, one still night when we were alone together, how she sometimes shuddered at herself, and what those daily and hourly struggles between her nature and her Christianity *meant*.

I think we were as near to one another as mother and daughter can be, but yet as different. Since I have been talking in such lordly style of those miserable Jameses and Charleses, I will take the opportunity to confess that I have inherited my father's thorough-going democracy,—double measure, pressed down and running over. She not only pardoned it, but I think she loved it in me, for his sake.

It was about a year and a half, I think, after he died, that she sent for Aunt Alice to come to Creston. "Your aunt loves me," she said, when she told us in her quiet way, "and I am so lonely now."

They had been the only children, and they loved each other,—how much, I afterwards knew. And how much they love each other *now*, I like to think,—quite freely and fully, and without shadow or doubt between them, I dare to hope.

A picture of Aunt Alice always hung in mother's room. It was taken down years ago. I never asked her where she put it. I remember it, though, quite well; for mother's sake I am glad I do. For it was a pleasant face to look upon, and a young, pure, happy face,—beautiful too, though with none of the regal beauty crowned by my mother's massive hair, and pencilled brows. It was a timid, girlish face, with reverent eyes, and ripe, tremulous lips,—weak lips, as I remember them. From babyhood, I felt a want in the face. I had, of course, no capacity to define it; it was represented to me only by the fact that it differed from my mother's.

She was teaching school out West when mother sent for her. I saw the letter. It was just like my mother: "Alice, I need you. You and I ought to have but one home now. Will you come?"

I saw, too, a bit of postscript to the answer: "I'm not fit that you should love me so, Marie."

And how mother laughed at it!

When it was all settled, and the waiting weeks became at last a single day, I hardly knew my mother. She was so full of fitful moods, and little fantastic jokes! such a flush on her cheeks too, as she ran to the window every five minutes, like a child! I remember how we went all over the house together, she and I, to see that everything looked neat, and bright, and welcome. And how we lingered in the guest-room, to put the little finishing touches to its stillness, and coolness, and coseyness. The best spread was on the bed, and the white folds smoothed as only mother's fingers could smooth them; the curtain freshly washed, and looped with its crimson cord; the blinds drawn, cool and green; the late afternoon sunlight slanting through, in flecks upon the floor. There were flowers, too, upon the table. I remember they were all white,—lilies of the valley, I think; and the vase of Parian marble, itself a solitary lily, unfolding stainless leaves. Over the mantle she had hung the finest picture in the house,—an "Ecce Homo,"* and an exquisite engraving. It used to hang in grandmother's room in the old house. We children wondered a little that she took it upstairs.

"I want your aunt to feel at home, and see some things," she said. "I wish I could think of something more to make it pleasant in here."

Just as we left the room she turned and looked into it. "Pleasant, isn't it? I am so glad, Sarah," her eyes dimming a little. "She's a very dear sister to me."

She stepped in again to raise a stem of the lilies that had fallen from the vase and lay like wax upon the table, then she shut the door and came away.

That door was shut just so for years; the lonely bars of sunlight flecked the solitude of the room, and the lilies faded on the table. We children passed it with hushed footfall, and shrank from it at twilight, as from a room that held the dead. But into it we never went.

Mother was tired out that afternoon; for she had been on her feet all day, busied in her loving cares to make our simple home as pleasant and as welcome as home could be. But yet she stopped to dress us in our Sunday clothes,—and it was no sinecure to dress three persistently undressable children; Winthrop was a host in himself. "Auntie must see us look our prettiest," she said.

* A depiction of Jesus.

She was a sight for an artist when she came down. She had taken off her widow's cap and coiled her heavy hair low in her neck, and she always looked like a queen in that lustreless black silk. I do not know why these little things should have made such an impression on me then. They are priceless to me now. I remember how she looked, framed there in the doorway, while we were watching for the coach,—the late light ebbing in golden tides over the grass at her feet, and touching her face now and then through the branches of trees, her head bent a little, with eager, parted lips, and the girlish color on her cheeks, her hand shading her eyes as they strained for a sight of the lumbering coach. She must have been a magnificent woman when she was young,—not unlike, I have heard it said, to that far-off ancestress whose name she bore, and whose sorrowful story has made her sorrowful beauty immortal. Somewhere abroad there is a reclining statue of Queen Mary, to which, when my mother stood beside it, her resemblance was so strong that the by-standers clustered about her, whispering curiously. "Ah, mon Dieu!" said a little Frenchman aloud, "c'est une résurrection."

We must have tried her that afternoon, Clara and Winthrop and I; for the spirit of her own excitement had made us completely wild. Winthrop's scream of delight, when, stationed on the gate-post, he caught the first sight of the old yellow coach, might have been heard a quarter of a mile.

"Coming?" said mother, nervously, and stepped out to the gate, full in the sunlight that crowned her like royal gold.

The coach lumbered on, and rattled up, and passed.

"Why, she hasn't come!" All the eager color died out of her face. "I am so disappointed!"—speaking like a troubled child, and turning slowly into the house.

Then, after a while, she drew me aside from the others,—I was the oldest, and she was used to make a sort of confidence between us, instinctively, as it seemed, and often quite forgetting how very few my years were. "Sarah, I don't understand. You think she might have lost the train? But Alice is so punctual. Alice never lost a train. And she said she would come." And then, a while after, "I *don't* understand."

It was not like my mother to worry. The next day the coach lumbered up and rattled past, and did not stop,—and the next, and the next.

"We shall have a letter," mother said, her eyes saddening every afternoon. But we had no letter. And another day went by, and another.

"She is sick," we said; and mother wrote to her, and watched for the lumbering coach, and grew silent day by day. But to the letter there was no answer.

Ten days passed. Mother came to me one afternoon to ask for her pen, which I had borrowed. Something in her face troubled me vaguely.

"What are you going to do, mother?"

"Write to your aunt's boarding-place. I can't bear this any longer." She spoke sharply. She had already grown unlike herself.

She wrote, and asked for an answer by return of mail.

It was on a Wednesday, I remember, that we looked for it. I came home early from school. Mother was sewing at the parlor window, her eyes wandering from her work, up the road. It was an ugly day. It had rained drearily from eight o'clock till two, and closed in suffocating mist, creeping and dense and chill. It gave me a childish fancy of long-closed tombs and low-land graveyards, as I walked home in it.

I tried to keep the younger children quiet when we went in, mother was so nervous. As the early, uncanny twilight fell, we grouped around her timidly. A dull sense of awe and mystery clung to the night, and clung to her watching face, and clung even then to that closed room upstairs where the lilies were fading.

Mother sat leaning her head upon her hand, the outline of her face dim in the dusk against the falling curtain. She was sitting so when we heard the first rumble of the distant coach-wheels. At the sound, she folded her hands in her lap and stirred a little, rose slowly from her chair, and sat down again.

"Sarah."

I crept up to her. At the near sight of her face, I was so frightened I could have cried.

"Sarah, you may go out and get the letter. I—I can't."

I went slowly out at the door and down the walk. At the gate I looked back. The outline of her face was there against the window-pane, white in the gathering gloom.

It seems to me that my older and less sensitive years have never known such a night. The world was stifling in a deluge of gray, cold mists, unstirred by a breath of air. A robin with feathers all ruffled, and head hidden, sat on the gate-post, and chirped a little mournful chirp, like a creature dying in a vacuum. The very daisy that nodded and drooped in the grass at my feet seemed to be gasping for breath. The neighbor's house, not forty paces across the street, was invisible. I remember the sensation it gave me, as I struggled to find its outlines, of a world washed out, like the figures I washed out on my slate. As I trudged, half frightened, into the road, and the fog closed about me, it seemed to my childish superstition like a horde of long-imprisoned ghosts let loose, and angry. The distant sound of the coach, which I could not see, added to the fancy.

The coach turned the corner presently. On a clear day I could see the brass buttons on the driver's coat at that distance. There was nothing visible now of the whole dark structure but the two lamps in front, like the eyes of some evil thing, glaring and defiant, borne with swift motion down upon me by a power utterly unseen,—it had a curious effect. Even at this time, I confess I do not like to see a lighted carriage driven through a fog.

I summoned all my little courage, and piped out the driver's name, standing there in the road.

He reined up his horses with a shout,—he had nearly driven over me. After some searching, he discovered the small object cowering down in the mist, handed me a letter, with a muttered oath at being intercepted on such a night, and lumbered on and out of sight in three rods.*

I went slowly into the house. Mother had lighted a lamp, and stood at the parlor door. She did not come into the hall to meet me.

She took the letter and went to the light, holding it with the seal unbroken. She might have stood so two minutes.

"Why don't you read, mamma?" spoke up Winthrop. I hushed him.

She opened it then, read it, laid it down upon the table, and went out of the room without a word. I had not seen her face. We heard her go upstairs and shut the door.

She had left the letter open there before us. After a little awed silence, Clara broke out into sobs. I went up and read the few and simple lines.

Aunt Alice had left for Creston on the appointed day.

* About 50 feet.

Mother spent that night in the closed room where the lilies had drooped and died. Clara and I heard her pacing the floor till we cried ourselves to sleep. When we woke in the morning, she was pacing it still.

Weeks wore into months, and the months became many years. More than that we never knew. Some inquiry revealed the fact, after a while, that a slight accident had occurred, upon the Erie Railroad, to the train which she should have taken. There was some disabling, but no deaths, the conductor had supposed. The car had fallen into the water. She might not have been missed when the half-drowned passengers were all drawn out.

So mother added a little crape to her widow's weeds,* the key of the closed room lay henceforth in her drawer, and all things went on as before. To her children my mother was never gloomy,—it was not her way. No shadow of household affliction was placed like a skeleton confronting our uncomprehending joy. Of what those weeks and months and years were to her—a widow, and quite uncomforted in their dark places by any human love—she gave no sign. We thought her a shade paler, perhaps. We found her often alone with her little Bible. Sometimes, on the Sabbath, we missed her, and knew that she had gone into that closed room. But she was just as tender with us in our little faults and sorrows, as merry with us in our plays, as eager in our gayest plans, as she had always been. As she had always been,—our mother.

And so the years slipped from her and from us. Winthrop went into business in Boston; he never took to his books, and mother was too wise to *push* him through college; but I think she was disappointed. He was her only boy, and she would have chosen for him the profession of his father and grandfather. Clara and I graduated in our white dresses and blue ribbons, like other girls, and came home to mother, crochet-work, and Tennyson. Just about here is the proper place to begin my story.

I mean that about here our old and long-tried cook, Bathsheba, who had been an heirloom in the family, suddenly fell in love with the older sexton, who had rung the passing-bell for every soul who died in the village for forty years, and took it into her head to marry him, and desert our kitchen for his little brown house under the hill.

* Mourning clothes (usually black) worn by a widow.

So it came about that we hunted the township for a handmaiden; and it also came about that our inquiring steps led us to the poor-house. A stout, not over-brilliant-looking girl, about twelve years of age, was to be had for her board and clothes, and such schooling as we could give her,—in country fashion to be "bound out" till she should be eighteen. The economy of the arrangement decided in her favor; for, in spite of our grand descent and grander notions, we were poor enough, after father died, and the education of three children had made no small gap in our little principal, and she came.

Her name was a singular one,—Selphar. It always savored too nearly of brimstone to please me. I used to call her Sel, "for short." She was a good, sensible, uninteresting-looking girl, with broad face, large features, and limp, tow-colored curls. They used to hang straight down about her eyes, and were never otherwise than perfectly smooth. She proved to be of good temper, which is worth quite as much as brains in a servant, as honest as the daylight, dull enough at her books, but a good, plodding worker, if you marked out every step of the way for her beforehand. I do not think she would ever have discovered the laws of gravitation; but she might have jumped off a precipice to prove them, if she had been bidden.

Until she was seventeen, she was precisely like any other rather stupid girl; never given to novel-reading or fancies; never frightened by the dark or ghost-stories; proving herself warmly attached to us, after a while, and rousing in us, in return, the kindly interest naturally felt for a faithful servant; but she was not in any respect *un*common,—quite far from it,—except in the circumstance that she never told a false-hood.

At seventeen she had a violent attack of diphtheria, and her life hung by a thread. Mother was as tender and unwearying in her care of her as the girl's own mother might have been.

From that time, I believe, Sel was immovable in her faith in her mistress's divinity. Under such nursing as she had, she slowly recovered, but her old, stolid strength never came back to her. Severe headaches became of frequent occurrence. Her stout, muscular arms grew weak. As weeks went on, it became evident in many ways that, though the diphtheria itself was quite out of her system, it had left her thoroughly diseased. Strange fits of silence came over her; her volubility had been the greatest objection we had to her hitherto. Her face began to wear a troubled look. She was often found in places where she had stolen away to be alone.

One morning she slept late in her little garret-chamber, and we did not call her. The girl had gone upstairs the night before crying with the pain in her temples, and mother, who was always thoughtful of her servants, said it was a pity to wake her, and, as there were only three of us, we might get our own breakfast for once. While we were at work together in the kitchen, Clara heard her kitten mewing out in the snow, and went to the door to let her in. The creature, possessed by some sudden frolic, darted away behind the well-curb. Clara was always a bit of a romp, and, with never a thought of her daintily slippered feet, she flung her trailing dress over one arm and was off over the three-inch snow. The cat led her a brisk chase, and she came in flushed and panting, and pretty, her little feet drenched, and the tip of a Maltese tail just visible above a great bundle she had made of her apron.

"Why!" said mother, "you have lost your ear-ring."

Clara dropped the kitten with unceremonious haste on the floor, felt of her little pink ear, shook her apron, and the corners of her mouth went down into her dimpled chin.

"They're the ones Winthrop sent, of all things in the world!"

"You'd better put on your rubbers, and have a hunt out-doors," said mother.

We hunted out-doors,—on the steps, on the well-boards, in the woodshed, in the snow; Clara looked down the well till her nose and fingers were blue, but the ear-ring was not to be found. We hunted in-doors, under the stove and the chairs and the table, in every possible and impossible nook, cranny, and crevice, but gave up the search in despair. It was a pretty trinket,—a leaf of delicately wrought gold, with a pearl dew-drop on it,—very becoming to Clara, and the first present Winthrop had sent her from his earnings. If she had been a little younger she would have cried. She came very near it as it was, I suspect, for when she went after the plates she stayed in the cupboard long enough to set two tables.

When we were half through breakfast, Selphar came down, blushing, and frightened half out of her wits, her apologies tumbling over each other with such skill as to render each one unintelligible, and evidently undecided in her own mind whether she was to be hung or burnt at the stake.

"It's no matter at all," said mother, kindly; "I knew you felt sick last night. I should have called you if I had needed you."

Having set the girl at her ease, as only she could do, she went on with her breakfast, and we forgot all about her. She stayed, however, in the room to wait on the table. It was afterwards remembered that she had not been out of our sight since she came down the garret-stairs. Also, that her room looked out upon the opposite side of the house from that on which the well-curb stood.

"Why, look at Sel!" said Clara, suddenly, "she has her eyes shut."

The girl was just passing the toast. Mother spoke to her. "Selphar, what is the matter?"

"I don't know."

"Why don't you open your eyes?"

"I can't."

"Hand the salt to Miss Sarah."

She took it up and brought it round the table to me, with perfect precision.

"Sel, how you act!" said Clara, petulantly. "Of course you saw."

"Yes'm, I saw," said the girl in a puzzled way, "but my eyes are shut, Miss Clara."

"Tight?"

"Tight."

Whatever this freak meant, we thought best to take no notice of it. My mother told her, somewhat gravely, that she might sit down until she was wanted, and we returned to our conversation about the ear-ring.

"Why!" said Sel, with a little jump, "I see your ear-ring. Miss Clara,—the one with a white drop on the leaf. It's out by the well."

The girl was sitting with her back to the window, her eyes, to all appearance, tightly closed.

"It's on the right-hand side, under the snow, between the well and the wood-pile. Why, don't you see?"

Clara began to look frightened, mother displeased.

"Selphar," she said, "this is nonsense. It is impossible for you to see through the walls of two rooms and a wood-shed."

"May I go and get it?" said the girl, quietly.

"Sel," said Clara, "on your word and honor, are your eyes shut *perfectly* tight?"

"If they ain't, Miss Clara, then they never was."

Sel never told a lie. We looked at each other, and let her go. I followed her out and kept my eyes on her closed lids. She did not once raise them; nor did they tremble, as lids will tremble, if only partially closed.

She walked without the slightest hesitation directly to the well-curb, to the spot which she had mentioned, stooped down, and brushed away the three-inch fall of snow. The ear-ring lay there, where it had sunk in falling. She picked it up, carried it in, and gave it to Clara.

That Clara had the thing on when she started after her kitten, there could be no doubt. She and I both remembered it. That Sel, asleep on the opposite side of the house, could not have seen it drop, was also settled. That she, with her eyes closed and her back to the window, had seen through three walls and through three inches of snow, at a distance of fifty feet, was an inference.

"I don't believe it!" said my mother, "it's some nonsensical mistake." Clara looked a little pale, and I laughed.

We watched her carefully through the day. Her eyes remained tightly closed. She understood all that was said to her, answered correctly, but did, not seem inclined to talk. She went about her work as usual, and performed it without a mistake. It could not be seen that she groped at all with her hands to feel her way, as is the case with the blind. On the contrary, she touched everything with her usual decision. It was impossible to believe, without seeing them, that her eyes were closed.

We tied a handkerchief tightly over them; see through it or below it she could not, if she had tried. We then sent her into the parlor, with orders to bring from the book-case two Bibles which had been given as prizes to Clara and me at school, when we were children. The books were of precisely the same size, color, and texture. Our names in gilt letters were printed upon the binding. We followed her in, and watched her narrowly. She went directly to the book-case, laid her hands upon the books at once, and brought them to my mother. Mother changed them from hand to hand several times, and turned them with the gilt lettering downwards upon her lap.

"Now, Selphar, which is Miss Sarah's?"

The girl quietly took mine up. The experiment was repeated and varied again and again. In every case the result was the same. She made no mistake. It was no guess-work. All this was done with the bandage tightly drawn about her eyes. *She did not see those letters with them.*

That evening we were sitting quietly in the dining-room. Selphar sat a little apart with her sewing, her eyes still closed. We kept her with us, and kept her in sight. The parlor, which was a long room, was between us and the front of the house. The distance was so great that we had often thought, if prowlers were to come around at night, how impossible it would be to hear them. The curtains and shutters were closely drawn. Sel was sitting by the fire. Suddenly she turned pale, dropped her sewing, and sprang from her chair.

"Robbers, robbers!" she cried. "Don't you see? they're getting in the east parlor window! There's three of 'em, and a lantern. They've just opened the window,—hurry, hurry!"

"I believe the girl is insane," said mother, decidedly. Nevertheless, she put out the light, opened the parlor door noiselessly, and went in.

The east window was open. There was a quick vision of three men and a dark lantern. Then Clara screamed, and it disappeared. We went to the window, and saw the men running down the street. The snow the next morning was found trodden down under the window, and their footprints were traced out to the road.

When we went back to the other room, Selphar was standing in the middle of it, a puzzled, frightened look on her face, her eyes wide open.

"Selphar," said my mother, a little suspiciously, "how did you know the robbers were there?"

"Robbers!" said the girl, aghast.

She knew nothing of the robbers. She knew nothing of the ear-ring. She remembered nothing that had happened since she went up the garret-stairs to bed, the night before. And, as I said, the girl was as honest as the sun-light. When we told her what had happened, she burst into terrified tears.

For some time after this there was no return of the "tantrums," as Selphar had called the condition, whatever it was. I began to get up vague theories of a trance state. But mother said, "Nonsense!" and Clara was too much frightened to reason at all about the matter.

One Sunday morning Sel complained of a headache. There was service that evening, and we all went to church. Mother let Sel take the empty seat in the carryall beside her.

It was very dark when we started to come home. But Creston was a safe old Orthodox town, the roads were filled with returning church-goers like ourselves, and mother drove like a man. A darker night I think I have never seen. Literally, we could not see a hand before our eyes. We met a carriage on a narrow road and the horses' heads touched, before either driver had seen the other.

Selphar had been quite silent during the drive. I leaned forward, looked closely into her face, and could dimly see through the darkness that her eyes were closed.

"Why!" she said at last, "see those gloves!"

"Where?"

"Down in the ditch; we passed them before I spoke. I see them on a blackberry-bush; they've got little brass buttons on the wrist."

Three rods past now, and we could not see our horse's head.

"Selphar," said my mother, quickly, "what *is* the matter with you?"

"If you please, ma'am, I don't know," replied the girl, hanging her head. "May I get out and bring 'em to you?"

Prince was reined up, and Sel got out. She went so far back, that, though we strained our eyes to do it, we could not see her. In about two minutes she came up, a pair of gentleman's gloves in her hand. They were rolled together, were of cloth so black that on a bright night it would never have been seen, and had small brass buttons at the wrist.

Mother took them without a word.

The story leaked out somehow, and spread all over town. It raised a great hue and cry. Four or five antediluvian ladies declared at once that we were nothing more nor less than a family of "them spirituous mediums,"* and seriously proposed to expel mother from the prayer-meeting. Masculine Creston did worse. It smiled a pitying smile, and pronounced the whole thing the fancy of "scared women-folks." I could endure with calmness any slander upon earth but that. I bore it a number of weeks, till at last, driven by despair, I sent for Winthrop, and stated the case to him in a condition of suppressed fury. He very politely bit back an incredulous smile, and said he should be *very* happy to see her perform. The answer was somewhat dubious. I accepted it in silent suspicion.

* This story was written at the peak of the spiritualist movement in America.

He came on a Saturday noon. That afternoon we attended *en masse* one of those refined inquisitions commonly known as picnics, and Winthrop lost his pocket-knife. Selphar, of course, kept house at home.

When we returned, Winthrop made some careless reference to his loss in her presence, and thought no more of it. About half an hour after, we observed that she was washing the dishes with her eyes shut. The condition had not been upon her five minutes before she dropped the spoon suddenly into the water, and asked permission to go out to walk. She "saw Mr. Winthrop's knife somewhere under a stone, and wanted to get it." It was fully two miles to the picnic grounds, and nearly dark. Winthrop followed the girl, unknown to her, and kept her in sight. She went rapidly, and without the slightest hesitation or search, to an out-of-the-way gully down by the pond, where Winthrop afterwards remembered having gone to cut some willow-twigs for the girls, parted a thick cluster of bushes, lifted a large, loose stone under which the knife had rolled, and picked it up. She returned it to Winthrop, quietly, and hurried away about her work to avoid being thanked.

I observed that, after this incident, masculine Creston became more respectful.

Of several peculiarities in this development of the girl I made at the time careful memoranda, and the exactness of these can be relied upon.

1. She herself, so far from attempting to bring on these trance states, or taking any pride therein, was intensely troubled and mortified by them,—would run out of the room, if she felt them coming on in the presence of visitors.
2. They were apt to be preceded by severe headaches, but came often without any warning.
3. She never, in any instance, recalled anything that happened during the trance, after it was passed.
4. She was powerfully and unpleasantly affected by electricity from a battery, or acting in milder forms. She was also unable at any time to put her hands and arms into hot water; the effect was to paralyze them at once.
5. Space proved to be no impediment to her vision. She has been known to follow the acts, words, and expressions of

countenance of members of the family hundreds of miles away, with accuracy as was afterwards proved by comparing notes as to time.

6. The girl's eyes, after her trances became habitual, assumed, and always retained, the most singular expression I ever saw on any face. They were oblong and narrow, and set back in her head like the eyes of a snake. They were not—smile if you will, O practical and incredulous reader! but they were not—eyes. The eyes of Elsie Venner* are the only eyes I can think of as at all like them. The most horrible circumstance about them—a circumstance that always made me shudder, familiar as I was with it—was, that, though turned fully on you, *they never looked at you*. Something behind them or out of them did the seeing, not they.
7. She not only saw substance, but soul. She has repeatedly told me my thoughts when they were upon subjects to which she could not by any possibility have had the slightest clew.
8. We were never able to detect a shadow of deceit about her.
9. The clairvoyance never failed in any instance to be correct, so far as we were able to trace it.

As will be readily imagined, the girl became a useful member of the family. The lost valuables restored and the warnings against mischances given by her quite balanced her incapacity for peculiar kinds of work. This incapacity, however, rather increased than diminished; and, together with her fickle health, which also grew more unsettled, caused us a great deal of care. The Creston physician—who was a keen man in his way, for a country doctor—pronounced the case altogether undreamt of before in Horatio's philosophy, and kept constant notes of it. Some of these have, I believe, found their way into the medical journals.

* *Elsie Venner: A Romance of Destiny* is an 1861 novel written by Oliver Wendell Holmes. The titular character is a young woman born to a mother who was bitten by a poisonous snake and consequently develops various serpentine traits (including snake-like eyes).

After a while there came, like a thief in the night, that which I suppose was poor Selphar's one unconscious, golden mission in this world. It came on a quiet summer night, that ended a long trance of a week's continuance. Mother had gone out into the kitchen to give an order for breakfast. I heard a few eager words in Selphar's voice, and then the door shut quickly, and it was an hour before it was opened.

Then my mother came to me without a particle of color in lips or cheek, and drew me away alone, and told the secret to me.

Selphar had seen Aunt Alice.

We sat down and looked at one another. There was a singular, pinched look about my mother's mouth.

"Sarah."

"Yes."

"She says"—and then she told me what she said. She had seen Alice Stuart in a Western town, seven hundred miles away. Among the living, she desired to be counted of the dead. And that was all.

My mother paced the room three times back and forth, her hands locked.

"Sarah." There was a chill in her voice—it had been such a gentle voice!—that froze me. "Sarah, the girl is an impostor."

"Mother!"

She paced the room once more, three times, back and forth. "At any rate, she is a poor, self-deluded creature. How *can* she see, seven hundred miles away, a dead woman who has been an angel all these years? Think! an *angel*, Sarah! So much better than I, and I—I loved—"

Before or since, I never heard my mother speak like that. She broke off sharply, and froze back into her chilling voice.

"We will say nothing about this, if you please. I do not believe a word of it."

We said nothing about it but Selphar did. The delusion, if delusion it were, clung to her, haunted her, pursued her, week after week. To rid her of it, or to silence her, was impossible. She added no new facts to her first statement, but insisted that the long-lost dead was yet alive, with a quiet pertinacity that it was simply impossible to ridicule, frighten, threaten, or cross-question out of her. Clara was so thoroughly alarmed that she would not have slept alone for any mortal—perhaps not for any immortal—considerations. Winthrop and I talked the matter over often and gravely when we were alone and in quiet places. Mother's lips were sealed. From the day when Sel made the first disclosure, she was never heard once to refer to the matter. A perceptible haughtiness crept into her manner towards the girl. She even talked of dismissing her, but repented it, and melted into momentary gentleness. I could have cried over her that night. I was beginning to understand what a pitiful struggle her life had become, and how alone she must be in it. She *would* not believe—she knew not what. She could not doubt the girl. And with the conflict even her children could not intermeddle.

To understand the crisis into which she was brought, the reader must bear in mind our long habit of belief, not only in Selphar's personal honesty, but in the infallibility of her mysterious power. Indeed, it had almost ceased to be mysterious to us, from daily familiarity. We had come to regard it as the curious working of physical disease, had taken its results as a matter of course, and had ceased, in common with converted Creston, to doubt the girl's capacity for seeing anything that she chose to, at any place.

Thus a year worried on. My mother grew sleepless and pallid. She laughed often, in a nervous, shallow way, as unlike her as a butterfly is unlike a sunset; and her face settled into an habitual sharpness and hardness unutterably painful to me.

Once only I ventured to break into the silence of the haunting thought that, she knew and we knew, was never escaped by either. "Mother, it would do no harm for Winthrop to go out West, and—"

She interrupted me sternly: "Sarah, I had not thought you capable of such childish superstition, I wish that girl and her nonsense had never come into this house!"—turning sharply away, and out of the room.

But year and struggle ended. They ended at last, as I had prayed every night and morning of it that they should end. Mother came into my room one night, locked the door behind her, and walking over to the window, stood with her face turned from me, and softly spoke my name.

But that was all, for a little while. Then,—"Sick and in suffering, Sarah! The girl,—she may be right; God Almighty knows! *Sick and in suffering*, you see! I am going—I think." Then her voice broke.

Creston put on its spectacles and looked wise on learning, the next day, that Mrs. Dugald had taken the earliest morning train for the West, on sudden and important business. It was precisely what Creston expected, and just like the Dugalds for all the world—gone to hunt up material for that genealogical book, or map, or tree, or something, that they thought nobody knew they were going to publish. O yes, Creston understood it perfectly.

Space forbids me to relate in detail the clews which Selphar had given as to the whereabouts of the wanderer. Her trances, just at this time, were somewhat scarce and fragmentary, and the information she had professed to give had come in snatches and very imperfectly,—the trance being apt to end suddenly at the moment when some important question was pending, and then, of course, all memory of what she had said, or was about to say, was gone. The names and appearance of persons and places necessary to the search had, however, been given with sufficient distinctness to serve as a guide in my mother's rather chimerical undertaking. I suppose ninety-nine persons out of a hundred would have thought her a candidate for the State Lunatic Asylum. Exactly what she herself expected, hoped, or feared, I think it doubtful if she knew. I confess to a condition of simple bewilderment, when she was fairly gone, and Clara and I were left alone with Selphar's ghostly eyes forever on us. One night I had to lock the poor thing into her garret-room before I could sleep.

Just three weeks from the day on which mother started for the West, the coach rattled up to the door, and two women, arm in arm, came slowly up the walk. The one, erect, royal, with her great steadfast eyes alight; the other, bent and worn, gray-haired and shallow and dumb, crawling feebly through the golden afternoon sunshine, as the ghost of a glorious life might crawl back to its grave.

Mother threw open the door, and stood there like a queen. "Children, your aunt has come home. She is too tired to talk just now. By and by she will be glad to see you."

We took her gently upstairs, into the room where the lilies were mouldering to dust, and laid her down upon the bed. She closed her eyes wearily, turned her face over to the wall, and said no word.

What was the story of those tired eyes I never asked and I never knew. Once, as I passed the room, I saw,—and have always been glad that I saw,—through the open door, the two women lying with their arms about each other's neck, as they used to do when they were children together, and above them, still and watchful, the wounded Face that had waited there so many years for this.

She lingered weakly there, within the restful room, for seven days, and then one morning we found her with her eyes upon the thorn-crowned Face, her own quite still and smiling.

A little funeral train wound away one night behind the church, and left her down among those red-cup mosses that opened in so few months again to cradle the sister who had loved her. Her name only, by mother's orders, marked the headstone.

I have given you facts. Explain them as you will. I do not attempt it, for the simple reason that I cannot.

A word must be said as to the fate of poor Sel, which was mournful enough. Her trances grew gradually more frequent and erratic, till she became so thoroughly diseased in mind and body as to be entirely unfitted for household work, and, in short, nothing but an encumbrance. We kept her, however, for the sake of charity, and should have done so till her poor, tormented life wore itself out; but after the advent of a new servant, and my mother's death, she conceived the idea that she was a burden, cried over it a few weeks, and at last, one bitter winter's night, she disappeared. We did not give up all search for her for years, but nothing was ever heard from her. He, I hope, who permitted life to be such a terrible mystery to her, has cared for her somehow, and kindly and well.

Emma Frances Dawson (1839–1926) was born in Bangor, Maine, but didn't start writing until she moved to San Francisco in the 1870s. Dawson's mother Lola was divorced and very ill by the time they relocated, and Emma supported them both by writing and teaching music. Although she never wrote a novel, she produced just over a dozen short stories (plus some poetry). Dawson—who was described as "an old maid" and "an eccentric recluse"—wrote work that was admired by Ambrose Bierce and that continues to be anthologized and studied. This tale first appeared in *The Argonaut* magazine in 1878 and gave the title to Dawson's 1897 collection *An Itinerant House and Other Stories,* which has become scarce in the first edition because most copies were destroyed in the 1906 San Francisco earthquake.

An Itinerant House

by Emma Frances Dawson

"Eternal longing with eternal pain,
Want without hope, and memory saddening all.
All congregated failure and despair
Shall wander there through some old maze of wrong." *

His *wife*?" cried Felipa.

"Yes," I answered, unwillingly; for until the steamer brought Mrs. Anson I believed in this Mexican woman's right to that name. I felt sorry for the bright eyes and kind heart that had cheered Anson's lodgers through weary months of early days in San Francisco.

* From the 1859 poem "The Wanderer" by Owen Meredith.

She burst into tears. None of us knew how to comfort her. Dering spoke first: "Beauty always wins friends."

Between her sobs she repeated one of the pithy sayings of her language: "It is as easy to find a lover as to keep a friend, but as hard to find a friend as to keep a lover."

"Yes," said Volz, "a new friendship is like a new string to your guitar—you are not sure what its tone may prove, nor how soon it may break."

"But at least its falsity is learned at once," she sobbed.

"Is it possible," I asked, "that you had no suspicion?"

"None. He told me—" She ended in a fresh gust of tears.

"The old story," muttered Dering. "Marryatt's skipper was right in thinking everything that once happened would come again somewhere."*

Anson came. He had left the new-comer at the Niantic,† on pretense of putting his house in order. Felipa turned on him before we could go.

"Is this true?" she cried.

Without reply he went to the window and stood looking out. She sprang toward him, with rage distorting her face.

"Coward!" she screamed, in fierce scorn.

Then she fell senseless. Two doctors were called. One said she was dead. The other, at first doubtful, vainly tried hot sealing-wax‡ and other tests. After thirty-six hours her funeral was planned. Yet Dering, once medical student, had seen an electric current used in such a case§ in Vienna, and wanted to try it. That night, he, Volz, and I offered to watch. When all was still, Dering, who had smuggled in the simple things needed, began his weird work.

"Is it not too late?" I asked.

---

* This may be a reference to the novel *Jacob Faithful* by Captain F. Marryatt, in which a character named Stapleton laments his wife's continuous cheating.

† The *Niantic* was a whaling vessel that ran aground in San Francisco in 1849 and served as a hotel until it was demolished in 1872.

‡ Dropping hot wax or scalding water on skin was a common way in the 19th century of testing for the presence of life.

§ Galvanism, or applying electricity to test muscular response, was first used in 1805.

"Every corpse," said he, "can be thus excited soon after death, for a brief time only, and but once. If the body is not lifeless, the electric current has power at any time."

Volz, too nervous to stay near, stood in the door open to the dark hall. It was a dreadful sight. The dead woman's breast rose and fell; smiles and frowns flitted across her face.

"The body begins to react finely," cried Dering, making Volz open the windows, while I wrapped hot blankets round Felipa, and he instilled clear coffee and brandy.

"It seems like sacrilege! Let her alone!" I exclaimed. "Better dead than alive!"

"My God! say not that!" cried Volz; "the nerve which hears is last to die. She may know all we say."

"Musical bosh!" I muttered.

"Perhaps not," said Dering; "in magnetic sleep* that nerve can be roused."

The night seemed endless. The room gained an uncanny look, the macaws on the gaudy, old-fashioned wall-paper seemed fluttering and changing places. Volz crouched in a heap near the door. Dering stood by Felipa, watching closely. I paced the shadowy room, looked at the gleam of the moon on the bay, listened to the soughing wind in the gum-trees mocking the sea, and tried to recall more cheerful scenes, but always bent under the weight of that fearful test going on beside me. Where was her soul? Beyond the stars, in the room with us, or "like trodden snowdrift melting in the dark?"† Volz came behind, startling me by grasping my elbow.

"Shall I not play?" he whispered. "Familiar music is remembrance changed to sound—it brings the past as perfume does. Gypsy music in her ear would be like holding wild flowers to her nostrils."

"Ask Dering," I said; "he will know best."

I heard him urging Dering.

"She has gypsy blood," he said; "their music will rouse her."

---

* Magnetic sleep is a 19th-century term for the hypnotic trance.

† This is the final line from the poem "Liz" by Robert Williams Buchanan.

Dering unwillingly agreed. "But nothing abrupt—begin low," said he.

Vaguely uneasy, I turned to object; but Volz had gone for his violin. Far off arose a soft, wavering, sleepy strain, like a wind blowing over a field of poppies. He passed, in slow, dramatic style, through the hall, playing on the way. As he came in, oddly sustained notes trembled like sighs and sobs; these were by degrees subdued, though with spasmodic outbursts, amid a grand movement as of phantom shapes through cloud-land. One heart-rending phrase recurring as of one of the shadowy host striving to break loose, but beaten back by impalpable throngs, numberless grace-notes trailing their sparks like fireworks. No music of our intervals and our rhythms, but perplexing in its charm like a draught that maddens. Time, space, our very identities, were consumed in this white heat of sound. I held my breath. I caught his arm.

"It is too bold and distracting," I cried. "It is enough to kill us! Do you expect to torment her back? How can it affect us so?"

"Because," he answered, laying down his violin and wiping his brow, "in the gypsy minor scale the fourth and seventh are augmented. The sixth is diminished. The frequent augmentation of the fourth makes that sense of unrest."

"Bah! Technical terms make it no plainer," I said, returning to the window.

He played a whispered, merry discordance, resolving into click of castanets, laugh, and dance of a gypsy camp. Out of the whirl of flying steps and tremolo of tambourines rose a tender voice, asking, denying, sighing, imploring, passing into an over-ruling, long-drawn call that vibrated in widening rings to reach the farthest horizon—nay, beyond land or sea, "east of the sun, west of the moon." With a rush returned the wild jollity of men's bass laughter, women's shrill reply, the stir of the gypsy camp. This dropped behind vague, rolling measures of clouds and chaos, where to and fro floated grotesque goblins of grace-notes like the fancies of a madman; struggling, rising, falling, vain-reaching strains; fierce cries like commands. The music seemed another vital essence thrilling us with its own emotion.

"No more, no more!" I cried, half gasping, and grasping Volz's arm. "What is it, Dering?"

He had staggered from the bed and was trying to see his watch. "It is just forty-four hours!" he said, pointing to Felipa.

Her eyes were open! We were alarmed as if doing wrong and silently watched her. Fifteen minutes later her lips formed one word:

"Idiots!"

Half an hour after she flung the violin from bed to floor, but would not speak. People began to stir about the house. The prosaic sounds jarred on our strained nerves. We felt brought from another sphere. Volz and I were going, but Felipa's upraised hand kept us. She sat up, looking a ghastly vision. Turning first toward me she quoted my words:

"'Better dead than alive!' True. You knew I would be glad to die. What right had you to bring me back? God's curses on you! I was dead. Then came agony. I heard your voices. I thought we were all in hell. Then I found how by your evil cunning I was to be forced to live. It was like an awful nightmare. I shall not forget you, nor you me. These very walls shall remember—here, where I have been so tortured no one shall have peace! Fools! Leave me! Never come in this room again!"

We went, all talking at once, Dering angry at her mood; Volz, sorry he had not reached a soothing *pianissimo* passage; I, owning we had no right to make the test. We saw her but once more, when with a threatening nod toward us she left the house.

From that time a gloom settled over the place. Mrs. Anson proved a hard-faced, cold-hearted, Cape Cod woman, a scold and drudge, who hated us as much as we disliked her. Home-sick and unhappy, she soon went East and died. Within a year, Anson was found dead where he had gone hunting in the Saucelitowoods,* supposed a suicide; Dering was hung by the Vigilantes,† and the rest were scattered on the four winds. Volz and I were last to go. The night before we sailed, he for Australia, I for New York, he said:

* Rancho Saucelito, where the popular city of Sausalito is now located, although located just two miles from San Francisco, was mainly accessible only by boat at the time this story was written, so it was still wild enough to hold bear and elk.

† San Francisco saw two major uprisings of vigilantes, the last in 1856. The vigilantes hanged, kidnapped, and banished corrupt politicians, criminals, and immigrants.

"I am sorry for those who come after us in this house."

"Not knowing of any tragedy here," I said, "they will not feel its influence."

"They must feel it," he insisted; "it is written in the Proverbs, 'Evil shall not depart from his house.'"*

Some years later, I was among passengers embarking at New York for California, when there was a cry of "Man overboard!" In the confusion of his rescue, among heartless and pitiful talk, I overheard one man declare that the drowned might be revived.

"Oh, yes!" cried a well-known voice behind me. "But they might not thank you."

I turned—to find Volz! He was coming out with Wynne, the actor. Enjoying our comradeship on the voyage, on reaching San Francisco we took rooms together, on Bush Street,† in an old house with a large garden. Volz became leader of the orchestra, and Wynne, leading man at the same theatre. Lest my folks, a Maine deacon's family, should think I was on the road to ruin, I told in letters home only of the city missionary in the house.

Volz was hard worked. Wynne was not much liked. My business went wrong. It rained for many weeks; to this we laid the discomfort that grew to weigh on us. Volz wreaked his sense of it on his violin, adding to the torment of Wynne and myself, for to lonesome anxious souls "the demon in music" shows horns and cloven foot in the trying sounds of practice. One Sunday Volz played the "Witches Dance,"‡ the "Dream,"§ and "The long, long weary day."¶

---

* Proverbs 17:13 reads in full, "Whoso rewardeth evil for good, evil shall not depart from his house."

† A real street that runs through the heart of San Francisco between Nob Hill and the Tenderloin.

‡ "Witches Dance" is found in the first movement of Paganini's Violin Concerto No. 5 in A Minor (1830).

§ This may refer to "The Devil's Dream," a popular 19th-century jig and favorite of fiddlers.

¶ "The Long, Long Weary Day" is a Civil War song from 1861.

"I can bear it no longer!" said Wynne. "I feel like the haunted Matthias in 'The Bells.'* If I could feel so when acting such parts, it would make my fortune. But I feel it only here."

"I think," said Volz, "it is the *gloriafonda*† bush near the window; the scent is too strong." He dashed off Strauss' fretful, conflicting "Hurry and Delay."‡

"There, there! It is too much," said I. "You express my feelings."

He looked doubtful. "Put it in words," said he.

"How can I?" I said. "When our firm sent me abroad, I went sight-seeing among old palaces, whose Gobelin tapestries§ framed in their walls were faded to gray phantoms of pictures, but out of some the thrilling eyes followed me till I could not stay in their range. My feeling here is the uneasy one of being watched."

"Ha!" said Volz. "You remind me of Heine, when he wrote from Livorno.¶ He knew no Italian, but the old palaces whispered secrets unheard by day. The moon was interpreter, knew the lapidary style, translated to dialect of his heart."

"'Strange effects after the moon,'" mused Wynne. "That gives new meaning to Kent's threat: 'I'll make a sop o' the moonshine of you!'"**

Volz went on: "Heine wrote: 'The stones here speak to me, and I know their mute language. Also, they seem deeply to feel what I think. So a broken column of the old Roman times, an old tower of Lombardy, a weather-beaten Gothic piece of a pillar understands me well. But I am a ruin myself, wandering among ruins.'"††

---

* "The Bells" was a hit play from 1871.

† This may be a reference to the sweet-smelling *Jasminum grandiflorum*

‡ There's no obvious reference for this; it may be an alternate title.

§ The Gobelin tapestry factory is located in Paris, and has been in continuous operation since 1602.

¶ Heinrich Heine (1797–1856) was a German poet and writer who also produced several profitable travel memoirs.

** Kent uses this line to threaten Oswald in Act 2, Scene 2 of Shakespeare's *King Lear.*

†† A quote from Edgar Allan Poe's story "Manuscript Found in a Bottle."

"Perhaps, like Poe's hero," said I, "'I have imbibed shadows of fallen columns at Balbec, and Tadmor, and Persepolis, until my very soul has become a ruin.'"

"But I, too," said Wynne, "feel the unrest of Tannhauser:

'Alas! what seek I here, or anywhere,
Whose way of life is like the crumbled stair
That winds and winds about a ruined tower,
And leads no whither.'"*

"I am oppressed," Volz owned, "as if some one in my presence was suffering deeply."

"I feel," said Wynne, "as if the scene was not set right for the performance now going on. There is a hitch and drag somewhere—scene-shifters on a strike. Happy are you poets and musicians, who can express what is vague."

Volz laughed. "As in Liszt's oratorio of 'Christus,'" said he, "where a sharp, ear-piercing *sostenuto* on the piccolo-flute shows the shining of the star of Bethlehem." He turned to me. "Schubert's 'Wanderer' always recalls to me a house you and I know to be under a ban."

"Haunted?" asked Wynne. "Of all speculative theories, St. Martin's sends the most cold thrills up one's back. He said none of the dead come back, but some stay."†

"What we Germans call *gebannt*—tied to one spot," said Volz. "But this is no ghost, only a proof of what a German psychologist holds, that the magnetic man is a spirit."‡

"Go on, 'and tell quaint lies'—I like them," said Wynne.

---

* From Owen Meredith's "Tannhauser; or, the Battle of the Bards."

† A few sources actually credit this quote to St. John the Divine, but the attribution is uncertain.

‡ The "German psychologist" is Franz Mesmer (1734–1815), who created the theory of "animal magnetism," which held that miraculous healings could be effected by aligning a body's magnetic energy.

I told in brief outline, with no names, the tale Volz and I knew, while we strolled to Telegraph Hill, passing five streets blocked by the roving houses common to San Francisco.*

Wynne said: "They seem to have minds of their own, with their entrances and exits in a *moving* drama."

"Sort of 'Poor Jo's,'"† said I.

"Castles in chess," said Volz.

"Io-like,"‡ said Wynne, "with a gad§ in their hearts that forever drives them on."

A few foreign sailors lounged on the hill top, looking at the view. The wind blew such a gale we did not stay. The steps we had known, cut in the side, were gone. Where the old house used to be, goats were browsing.

"Perchance we do inhabit it but now," mockingly cried Wynne; "methinks it must be so."

"Then," said Volz, thoughtfully, "it might be what Germans call 'far-working'—acted in distance—that affects us."

"What do you mean?" I asked. "Do you know anything of her now?"

"I know she went to Mexico," said he; "that is all."

"What is 'far-working?'" asked Wynne. "If I could act in the distance, and here too—'what larks!'"¶

"Yes—'if,'" said I. "Think how all our lives turn on that pivot. Suppose Hawthorne's offer to join Wilkes' exploring expedition had been taken!"**

---

* This is probably a reference to the architectural practice of moving entire houses rather than tearing them down and rebuilding.

† "Poor Jo" is the crossing sweeper in Dickens's *Bleak House* (1853). The character was so popular that when the novel was first dramatized, the title of the play was "Bleak House, or Poor Jo."

‡ In Greek mythology, Io was a mortal lover of Zeus who was turned into a heifer.

§ As a noun, a gad is a chisel or long stick; as a verb, it means to roam about aimlessly.

¶ This phrase is most commonly associated with Dickens' 1861 *Great Expectations.*

** The Wilkes Expedition (1838–1842) was an exploratory mission to map the Pacific Ocean and surrounding areas. Nathaniel Hawthorne had lobbied to be included as official historian of the expedition, but in the end the commanding officer Charles Wilkes took on that job himself.

"Only to wills that know no 'if' is 'far-working' possible," said Volz. "Substance or space can no more hinder this force than the one of mineral magnetism. Passavent* joins it with pictures falling, or watches stopping at the time of a death. In sleep-walking, some kinds of illness, or nearness of death, the nervous ether is not so closely allied to its material conductors, the nerves, and may be loosened to act from afar, the surest where blood or feeling makes attraction or repulsion."

Wynne in the two voices of the play repeated:

"VICTOR.—Where is the gentleman?
CHISPE. As the old song says:
'His body is in Segovia,
His soul is in Madrid.'"†

We could learn about the house we were in only that five families had moved in and out during the last year. Wynne resolved to shake off the gloom that wrapped us. In struggles to defy it, he on the strength of a thousand-dollar benefit, made one payment on the house and began repairs.

On an off-night he was vainly trying to study a new part. Volz advised the relief to his nerves of reciting the dream scene from "The Bells," reminding him he had compared it with his restlessness there. Wynne denied it.

"Yes," said Volz, "where the mesmerizer forces Matthias to confess."

But Wynne refused, as if vexed, till Volz offered to show in music his own mood, and I agreed to read some rhymes about mine. Volz was long tuning his violin.

"I feel," he said, "as if the passers-by would hear a secret. Music is such a subtle expression of emotion—like flower-odor rolls far and affects the stranger. Hearken! In Heine's 'Reisebilder,'‡ as the cross was thrown ringing on the banquet table of the gods, they grew dumb and pale, and even paler

---

* Dr. Johann Karl Passavant was a German physician and writer who was frequently quoted in spiritualist writings.

† From Henry Wadsworth Longfellow's 1893 play *The Spanish Student.*

‡ *Reisebilder* translates to "travel pictures," and is the title of Heine's series of travel books.

till they melted in mist. So shall you at the long-drawn wail of my violin grow breathless, and fade from each other's sight."

The music closed round us, and we waited in its deep solitude. One brief, sad phrase fell from airy heights to lowest depths into a sea of sound, whose harmonious eddies as they widened breathed of passion and pain, now swooning, now reviving, with odd pauses and sighs that rose to cries of despair, but the tormenting first strain recurring fainter and fainter, as if drowning, drowning, drowned—yet floating back for repeated last plaint, as if not to be quelled, and closing, as it began, the whole.

As I read the name of my verses, Volz murmured: "*Les Nuits Blanches.* No. 4. Stephen Heller."*

SLEEPLESS NIGHTS

Against the garden's mossy paling
I lean, and wish the night away,
Whose faint, unequal shadows trailing
Seem but a dream of those of day.

Sleep burdens blossom, bud, and leaf,
My soul alone aspires, dilates,
Yearns to forget its care and grief—
No bath of sleep its pain abates.

How dread these dreams of wide-eyed nights!
What is, and is not, both I rue,
My wild thoughts fly like wand'ring kites,
No peace falls with this balmy dew.

Through slumb'rous stillness, scarcely stirred
By sudden trembles, as when shifts
O'er placid pool some skimming bird,
Its Letheanbowl a poppy lifts.

* Stephen Heller (1815–1888) was an accomplished pianist and composer.

If one deep draught my doubts could solve,
The world might bubble down its brim,
Like Cleopatra's pearl dissolve,
With all my dreams within its rim.

What should I know but calm repose?
How feel, recalling this lost sphere?
Alas! the fabled poppy shows
Upon its bleeding heart—a tear!

Wynne unwillingly began to recite: "'I fear nothing, but dreams are dreams—'"

He stammered, could not go on, and fell to the floor. We got him to bed. He never spoke sanely after. His wild fancies appalled us watching him all night.

"Avaunt Sathanas! That's not my cue," he muttered. "A full house to-night. How could Talma forget how the crowd looked, and fancy it a pack of skeletons? Tell Volz to keep the violins playing through this scene, it works me up as well as thrills the audience. Oh, what tiresome nights I have lately, always dreaming of scenes where rival women move, as in 'Court and Stage,' where, all masked, the king makes love to Frances Stewart before the queen's face![*] How do I try to cure it? 'And being, thus frighted, swear a prayer or two and sleep again.'[†] Madame, you're late; you've too little rouge; you'll look ghastly. We're not called yet; let's rehearse our scene. Now, then, I enter left, pass to the window. You cry 'is this true?' and faint. All crowd about. Quick curtain."

Volz and I looked at each other.

"Can our magnetism make his senses so sharp that he knows what is in our minds?" he asked me.

"Nonsense!" I said. "Memory, laudanum, and whisky."

---

* *The King's Rival; or, The Court and the Stage* is a five-act play by Tom Taylor and Charles Reade, published in 1850 and set in the court of Charles II; Frances Stewart, a real-life beauty who refused to become Charles's mistress, is a main character.

† Mercutio speaks this line in Shakespeare's 1595 *Romeo and Juliet.*

"There," Wynne went on, "the orchestra is stopping. They've rung up the curtain. Don't hold me. The stage waits, yet how can I go outside my door to step on dead bodies? Street and sidewalk are knee-deep with them. They rise and curse me for disturbing them. I lift my cane to strike. It turns to a snake, whose slimy body writhes in my hand. Trying to hold it from biting me, my nails cut my palm till blood streams to drown the snake."

He awed us not alone from having no control of his thoughts, but because there came now and then a strange influx of emotion as if other souls passed in and out of his body.

"Is this hell?" he groaned. "What blank darkness! Where am I? What is that infernal music haunting me through all space? If I could only escape it I need not go back to earth—to that room where I feel choked, where the very wall-paper frets me with its flaunting birds flying to and fro, mocking my fettered state. 'Here, here in the very den of the wolf!'[*] Hallo, Benvolio,[†] call-boy's hunting you. Romeo's gone on.

'See where he steals—
Locked in some gloomy covert under key
Of cautionary silence, with his arms
Threaded, like these cross-boughs, in sorrow's knot.'[‡]

"What is this dread that weighs like a nightmare? 'I do not fear; like Macbeth, I only inhabit trembling.'[§] For one of them—she is in hell already, and burns, poor soul! For the other'—Ah! must I die here, alone in the woods, felled by a coward, Indian-like, from behind a tree? None of the boys will know. 'I just now come from a whole world of mad women that had almost—what, is she dead?'[¶] Poor Felipa!"

---

* This is a line from Tom Taylor's 1853 play *Plot and Passion.*

† Romeo's cousin in *Romeo and Juliet.*

‡ Spoken by Mercutio in *Romeo and Juliet.*

§ A reference to this line from Shakespeare's 1623 *Macbeth*: "If trembling I inhabit then, protest me/The baby of a girl."

¶ A line from George Farquhar's 1700 play *The Constant Couple.*

"Did you tell him her name?" I asked Volz.

"No," said he. "Can one man's madness be another's real life?"

"Blood was spilt—the avenger's wing hovered above my house,"* raved Wynne. "What are these lights, hundreds of them—serpent's eyes? Is it the audience—coiled, many-headed monster, following me round the world? Why do they hiss? I've played this part a hundred times. 'Taught by Rage, and Hunger, and Despair?' Do they, full-fed, well-clothed, light-hearted, know how to judge me? 'A plague on both your houses!'† What is that flame? Fire that consumes my vitals—spon-ta-neous combustion! It is then possible. Water! water!"

The doctor said there had been some great strain on Wynne's mind. He sank fast, though we did all we could. Toward morning I turned to Volz with the words:

"He is dead."

The city missionary was passing the open door. He grimly muttered:

"Better dead than alive!"

"My God! say not that!" cried Volz. "The nerve which hears is last to die. He may know—"

He faltered. We stood aghast. The room grew suddenly familiar. I tore off a strip of the gray tint on the walls. Under it we found the old paper with its bright macaws.

"Ah, ha!" Volz said; "will you now deny my theory of 'far-working?'"

Dazed, I could barely murmur: "Then people *can* be affected by it!"

"Certainly," said he, "as rubbed glasses gain electric power."

Within a week we sailed—he for Brazil, I for New York.

Several years after, at Sacramento, Arne, an artist I had known abroad, found me on the overland train, and on reaching San Francisco urged me to go where he lodged.

"I am low-spirited here," he said; "I don't know why."

I stopped short on the crowded wharf. "Where do you live?" I asked.

"Far up Market Street," said he.

---

* From George Lovell's 1633 play *Love's Sacrifice.*

† Mercutio's famous line from *Romeo and Juliet.*

"What sort of a house?" I insisted.

"Oh—nothing modern—over a store," he answered.

Reassured, I went with him. He lived in a jumble of easels, portfolios, paint, canvas, bits of statuary, casts, carvings, foils, red curtains, Chinese goatskins, woodcuts, photographs, sketches, and unfinished pictures. On the wall hung a scene from "The Wandering Jew,"* as we saw it at the Adelphi, in London, where in the Arctic regions he sees visions foreshadowing the future of his race. Under it was quoted:

—All in my mind is confused, nor can I dissever

The mould of the visible world from the shape of my
thought in me—

The Inward and Outward are fused, and through them
murmur forever

The sorrow whose sound is the wind and the roar of the
limitless sea."†

"Do you remember," Arne asked, "when we saw that play? Both younger and more hopeful. How has the world used you? As for me, I have done nothing since I came here but that sketch, finished months ago. I have not lost ambition, but I feel fettered."

"Absinthe?—opium?—tobacco?" I hinted.

"Neither," he answered. "I try to work, but visions, widely different from what I will, crowd on me, as on the Jew in the play. Not the unconscious brain action all thinkers know, but a dictation from without. No rush of creative impulses, but a dragging sense of something else I ought to paint."

"Briefly," I said, "you are a 'Haunted Man.'"

---

* The play *The Wandering Jew*, adopted from Eugene Sue's novel by Leopold Lewis (author of *The Bells*), opened at London's Adelphi Theatre in 1873.

† From the 1859 poem "The Shore" by Owen Meredith.

"Haunted by a willful design," said he. "I feel as if something had happened somewhere which I *must* show."

"What is it like?" I asked.

"I wish I could tell you," he replied. "But only odd bits change places, like looking in a kaleidoscope; yet all cluster around one centre."

One day, looking over his portfolios, I found an old *Temple Bar*,* which he said he kept for this passage—which he read to me—from T. A. Trollope's "Artist's Tragedy:"†

"The old walls and ceilings and floors must be saturated with the exhalations of human emotions! These lintels, doorways, and stairs have become, by long use and homeliness, dear to human hearts, and have become so intimately blended a portion of the mental furniture of human lives, that they have contributed their part to the formation of human characters. Such facts and considerations have gone to the fashioning of the mental habitudes of all of us. If all could have been recorded! If emotion had the property of photographing itself on the surfaces of the walls which had witnessed it! Even if only passion, when translated into acts, could have done so! Ah, what palimpsests! What deciphering of tangled records! What skillful separation of successive layers of 'passionography!'"

"I know a room," said Arne, "thronged with acts that elbow me from my work and fill me with unrest."

I looked at him in mute surprise.

"I suppose," he went on, "such things do not interest you."

"No—yes," I stammered. "I have marked in traveling how lonely houses change their expression as you come near, pass, and leave them. Some frown, others smile. The Bible buildings had life of their own and human diseases; the priests cursed or blessed them as men."

"Houses seem to remember," said he. "Some rooms oppress us with a sense of lives that have been lived in them."

---

* *Temple Bar* was a British literary periodical that ran from 1860 to 1906.

† Thomas Adolphus Trollope's article "An Artist's Tragedy", about the painter Andrea del Sarto, appeared in the July 1870 issue of *Temple Bar.*

"That," I said, "is like Draper's theory of shadows on walls always staying.[*] He shows how after a breath passes over a coinor key, its spectral outline remains for months after the substance is removed. But can the mist of circumstance sweeping over us make our vacant places hold any trace of us?"

"Why not? Who can deny it? Why do you look at me so?" he asked.

I could not tell him the sad tale. I hesitated; then said: "I was thinking of Volz, a friend I had, who not only believed in what Bulwer calls 'a power akin to mesmerism and superior to it, once called Magic, and that it might reach over the dead, so far as their experience on earth,'[†] but also in animal magnetism from any distance."

Arne grew queerly excited. "If Time and Space exist but in our thoughts, why should it not be true?" said he. "Macdonald's lover cries, 'That which has been is, and the Past can never cease. She is mine, and I shall find her—what matters it when, or where, or how?'"[‡] He sighed, "In Acapulco, a year ago, I saw a woman who has been before me ever since—the centre of the circling, changing, crude fancies that trouble me."

"Did you know her?" I asked.

"No, nor anything about her, not even her name. It is like a spell. I must paint her before anything else, but I cannot yet decide how. I feel sure she has played a—tragic part in some life-drama."

"Swinburne's queen of panthers,"[§] I hinted.

"Yes. But I was not in love. Love I must forego. I am not a man with an income."

"I know you are not a nincompoop!" I said, always trying to change such themes by a jest. I could not tell him I knew a place which had the influence he talked of. I could not re-visit that house.

---

* Dr. John W. Draper put forth these theories in his 1856 *Human Physiology, Statical and Dynamical.*

† From Sir Edward Bulwer Lytton's "The Haunted and the Haunters," a short work published in 1861.

‡ From George MacDonald's 1860 story "The Portent."

§ From Swinburne's poem "At a Month's End"; at the end of the poem, the narrator bears "the wild-beast mark of panther fangs" from his lover.

Soon after he told me he had begun his picture, but would not show it. He complained that one figure kept its back toward him. He worked on it till he fell ill. Even then he hid it. "Only a layer of passionography," he said.

I grew restless. I thought his mood affected mine. It was a torment as well as a puzzle to me that his whole talk should be of the influence of houses, rooms, even personal property that had known other owners. Once I asked him if he had anything like the brown coat Sheridan swore drew ill-luck to him.*

"Sometimes I think," he answered, "it is this special brown paint artists prize which affects me. It is made from the best asphaltum, and that can be got only from Egyptian mummy-cloths.† Very likely dust of the mummies is ground in it. I ought to feel their ill-will."

One day I went to Saucelito. In the still woods I forgot my unrest till coming to the stream where, as I suddenly remembered, Anson was found dead, a dread took me which I tried to lose by putting into rhyme. Turning out my pockets at night, I crumpled the page I had written on, and threw it on the floor.

In uneasy sleep I dreamed I was again in Paris, not where I liked to recall being, but at "Bullier's,"‡ and in war-time. The bald, spectacled leader of the orchestra, leaning back, shamming sleep, while a dancing, stamping, screaming crowd wave tri-colored flags, and call for the "Chant du Depart."§ Three thousand voices in a rushing roar that makes the twenty thousand lights waver, in spasmodic but steady chorus:

"Les departs—parts—parts!
Les departs—parts—parts!
Les departs—parts—parts!"

---

* Unknown reference.

† Asphaltum is a bituminous mineral substance that was indeed used in the preparation of mummies, although they were hardly a primary source of it.

‡ Bullier's was a popular Parisian dance hall.

§ Although this patriotic French song was originally written during the French Revolution, it became more popular in the nineteenth century.

Roused, I supposed by passing rioters, I did not try to sleep again, but rose to write a letter for the early mail. As I struck a light I saw, smoothed out on the table, the wrinkled page I had cast aside. The ink was yet wet on two lines added to each verse. A chill crept over me as I read:

FOREST MURMURS

Across the woodland bridge I pass,
And sway its three long, narrow planks,
To mark how gliding waters glass
Bright blossoms doubled ranks on ranks;
And how through tangle of the ferns
Floats incense from veiled flower-urns,
What would the babbling brook reveal?
What may these trembling depths conceal?
Dread secret of the dense woods, held
With restless shudders horror-spelled!

How shift the shadows of the wood,
As if it tossed in troubled sleep!
Strange whispers, vaguely understood,
Above, below, around me creep;
While in the sombre-shadowed stream
Great scarlet splashes far down gleam,
The odd-reflected, stately shapes
Of cardinals in crimson capes;
Not those—but spectral pools of blood
That stain these sands through strongest flood!

Like blare of trumpets through black nights—
Or sunset clouds before a storm—
Are these red phantom water-sprites

That mock me with fantastic form;
With flitting of the last year's bird

Fled ripples that its low flight stirred—
How should these rushing waters learn
Aught but the bend of this year's fern?
The lonesome wood, with bated breath,
Hints of a hidden blow—and death!

I could not stay alone. I ran to Arne's room. As I knocked, the falling of some light thing within made me think he was stirring. I went in. He sat in the moonlight, back to me before his easel. The picture on it might be the one he kept secret. I would not look. I went to his side and touched him. He had been dead for hours! I turned the unseen canvas to the wall.

Next day I packed and planned to go East. I paid the landlady not to send Arne's body to the morgue, and watched it that night, when a sudden memory swept over me like a tidal wave. There was a likeness in the room to one where I had before watched the dead. Yes—there were the windows, there the doors—just here stood the bed, in the same spot I sat. What wildness was in the air of San Francisco!

To put such crazy thoughts to flight I would look at Arne's last work. Yet I wavered, and more than once turned away after laying my hand on it. At last I snatched it, placed it on the easel and lighted the nearest gas-burner before looking at it. Then—great heavens! How had this vision come to Arne? It was the scene where Felipa cursed us. Every detail of the room reproduced, even the gay birds on the wall-paper, and her flower-pots. The figures and faces of Dering and Volz were true as hers, and in the figure with averted face which Arne had said kept its back to him, I knew—myself! What strange insight had he gained by looking at Felipa? It was like the man who trembled before the unknown portrait of the Marquise de Brinvilliers.*

How long I gazed at the picture I do not know. I heard, without heeding, the door-bell ring and steps along the hall. Voices. Some one looking at rooms. The landlady, saying this room was to let, but unwilling to show

* The Marquise de Brinvilliers (1630–1676) was a French aristocrat convicted of the murders (by poison) of three; she was tortured, beheaded, and her body burned. She was a popular subject for writers and artists after her death, although the story of the man trembling before her portrait is unknown.

it, forced to own its last tenant lay there dead. This seemed no shock to the stranger.

"Well," said her shrill tones, "poor as he was he's better dead than alive!"

The door opened as a well-known voice cried: "My God! say not that! The nerve which hears is last to die—"

Volz stood before me! Awe-struck, we looked at each other in silence. Then he waved his hand to and fro before his eyes.

"Is this a dream?" he said. "There," pointing to the bed; "you"—to me; "the same words—the very room! Is it our fate?"

I pointed to the picture and to Arne. "The last work of this man, who thought it a fancy sketch?"

While Volz stood dumb and motionless before it, the landlady spoke:

"Then you know the place. Can you tell what ails it? There have been suicides in this room. No one prospers in the house. My cousin, who is a house-mover, warned me against taking it. He says before the store was put under it here it stood on Bush Street, and before that on Telegraph Hill."

Volz clutched my arm. "It is 'The Flying Dutchman'* of a house!" he cried, and drew me fast down stairs and out into a dense fog which made the world seem a tale that was told, blotting out all but our two slanting forms, bent as by what poor Wynne would have called "a blast from hell," hurrying blindly away. I heard the voice of Volz as if from afar: "The magnetic man *is* a spirit!"

* The Flying Dutchman is a famous ghost ship destined to sail the seas forever, unable to make port.

Mrs. J. H. (Charlotte) Riddell (1832–1906) was an influential Irish-born writer who was widely popular during her lifetime. Born of an Irish father and English mother, she lived most of her life in England. She penned 56 works, including short stories and novels, and was part-owner and editor of *St. James's Magazine* in London in the 1860s. Riddell wrote many ghost stories, including five novels. The following, noteworthy also for its description of a thoroughly independent woman, first appeared in 1882 in her collection *Weird Stories*. It shares many of the finer characteristics of the picturesque, mysterious atmosphere of tales by a contemporary of hers, Sheridan LeFanu, whose principal work appeared in the two decades preceding this story.

Nut Bush Farm

by Mrs. J. H. (Charlotte) Riddell

I

When I entered upon the tenancy of Nut Bush Farm almost the first piece of news which met me, in the shape of a whispered rumour, was that "something" had been seen in the "long field."

Pressed closely as to what he meant, my informant reluctantly stated that the "some thing" took the "form of a man," and that the wood and the path leading thereto from Whittleby were supposed to be haunted.

Now, all this annoyed me exceedingly. I do not know when I was more put out than by the intelligence. It is unnecessary to say I did not believe in ghosts or anything of that kind, but my wife being a very nervous, impressionable woman, and our only child, a delicate weakling, in the habit of crying himself into fits if left alone at night without a candle, I really felt at my wit's end to imagine what I should do if a story of this sort reached their ears.

And reach them I knew it must if they came to Nut Bush Farm, so the first thing I did when I heard people did not care to venture down the Beech Walk or through the copse, or across the long field after dark, or indeed by day, was to write to say I thought they had both better remain on at my father-in-law's till I could get the house thoroughly to rights.

After that I lit my pipe and went out for a stroll; when I knocked the ashes out of my pipe and re-entered the sitting room I had made up my mind. I could not afford to be frightened away from my tenancy. For weal or for woe* I must stick to Nut Bush Farm.

It was quite by chance I happened to know anything of the place at first. When I met with that accident in my employers' service, which they rated far too highly and recompensed with a liberality I never can feel sufficiently grateful for, the doctors told me plainly if I could not give up office work and leave London altogether, they would not give a year's purchase for my life.

Life seemed very sweet to me then—it always has done—but just at that period I felt the pleasant hopes of convalescence, and with that thousand pounds safely banked, I *could* not let it slip away from me.

"Take a farm," advised my father-in-law, "though people say a farmer's is a bad trade, I know many a man who is making money out of it. Take a farm, and if you want a helping hand to enable you to stand the racket for a year or two, why you know I am always ready."

I had been bred and born on a farm. My father held something like fifteen hundred acres under the principal landowner in his county, and though it so happened, I could not content myself at home, but must needs come up to London to see the lions and seek my fortune, still I had never forgotten the meadows and the cornfields, and the cattle, and the orchards, and the woods and the streams, amongst which my happy boyhood had been spent. Yes, I thought I should like a farm—one not too far from London; and "not too big," advised my wife's father.

* Old idiom meaning "for better or worse."

"The error people make now-a-days," he went on, "is spreading their butter over too large a surface. It is the same in business as in land—they stretch their arms out too far—they will try to wade in deep waters—and the consequence is they never know a day's peace, and end mostly in the bankruptcy court."

He spoke as one having authority, and I knew what he said was quite right. He had made his money by a very different course of procedure, and I felt I could not follow a better example.

I knew something about farming, though not very much. Still, agriculture is like arithmetic, when once one knows the multiplication table the rest is not so difficult. I had learned unconsciously the alphabet of soils and crops and stock when I was an idle young dog, and liked nothing better than talking to the labourers, and accompanying the woodman when he went out felling trees; and so I did not feel much afraid of what the result would be, more especially as I had a good business head on my shoulders, and enough money to "stand the racket," as my father-in-law put it, till the land began to bring in her increase.

When I got strong and well again after my long illness—I mean strong and well enough to go about—I went down to look at a farm which was advertised as to let in Kent.

According to the statement in the newspaper, there was no charm that farm lacked; when I saw it I discovered the place did not possess one virtue, unless, indeed, an old Tudor house fast falling to ruins, which would have proved invaluable to an artist, could be so considered. Far from a railway, having no advantages of water carriage, remote from a market, apparently destitute of society. Nor could these drawbacks be accounted the worst against it. The land, poor originally, seemed to have been totally exhausted. There were fields on which I do not think a goose could have found subsistence—nothing grew luxuriantly save weeds; it would have taken all my capital to get the ground clean. Then I saw the fences were dilapidated, the hedges in a deplorable condition, and the farm buildings in such a state of decay I would not have stabled a donkey in one of them.

Clearly, the King's Manor, which was the modest name of the place, would not do at any price, and yet I felt sorry, for the country around was beautiful, and already the sweet pure air seemed to have braced up my nerves and given me fresh energy. Talking to mine host at the "Bunch of Hops," in Whittleby, he advised me to look over the local paper before returning to London.

"There be a many farms vacant," he said, "mayhap you'll light on one to suit."

To cut a long story short, I did look in the local paper and found many farms to let, but not one to suit. There was a drawback to each—a drawback at least so far as I was concerned. I felt determined I would not take a large farm. My conviction was then what my conviction still remains, that it is better to cultivate fifty acres thoroughly, than to crop, stock, clean, and manure a hundred insufficiently. Besides, I did not want to spend my strength on wages, or take a place so large I could not oversee the workmen on foot. For all these reasons and many more I came reluctantly to the conclusion that there was nothing in that part of the country to suit a poor unspeculative plodder like myself.

It was a lovely afternoon in May when I turned my face towards Whittleby, as I thought, for the last time. In the morning I had taken train for a farm some ten miles distant and worked my way back on foot to a "small cottage with land" a local agent thought might suit me. But neither the big place nor the little answered my requirements, much to the disgust of the auctioneer, who had himself accompanied us to the cottage under the impression I would immediately purchase it and so secure his commission.

Somewhat sulkily he told me a short cut back to Whittleby, and added as a sort of rider to all previous statements, the remark:

"You had best look out for what you want in Middlesex. You'll find nothing of that sort hereabouts."

As to the last part of the foregoing sentence I was quite of his opinion, but I felt so oppressed with the result of all my wanderings that I thought upon the whole I had better abandon my search altogether, or else pursue it in some county very far away indeed—perhaps in the land of dreams for that matter!

As has been said, it was a lovely afternoon in May—the hedges were snowy with hawthorn blossom, the chestnuts were bursting into flower, the birds were singing fit to split their little throats, the lambs were dotting the hillsides, and I—ah! well, I was a boy again, able to relish all the rich banquet God spreads out day by day for the delight and nourishment of His too often thankless children.

When I came to a point half way up some rising ground where four lanes met and then wound off each on some picturesque diverse way, I paused to look around regretfully.

As I did so—some distance below me—along a long and never-before-traversed lane, I saw the gleam of white letters on a black board.

"Come," I thought, "I'll see what this is at all events," and bent my steps towards the place, which might, for all I knew about it, have been a ducal mansion or a cockney's country villa.

The board appeared modestly conspicuous in the foreground of a young fir plantation, and simply bore this legend-

"TO BE LET, HOUSE AND LAND,"

Apply at the "White Dragon."

"It is a mansion," I thought, and I walked on slowly, disappointed.

All of a sudden the road turned a sharp corner and I came in an instant upon the prettiest place I had ever seen or ever desire to see.

I looked at it over a low laurel hedge growing inside an open paling about four feet high. Beyond the hedge there was a strip of turf, green as emeralds, smooth as a bowling green—then came a sunk fence,* the most picturesque sort of protection the ingenuity of man ever devised; beyond that, a close-cut lawn which sloped down to the sunk fence from a house with projecting gables in the front, the recessed portion of the building having three windows on the first floor. Both gables were covered with creepers, the lawn was girt in by a semi-circular sweep of forest trees, the afternoon sun streamed over the grass and tinted the swaying foliage with a thousand tender lights. Hawthorn bushes, pink and white, mingled with their taller and grander brothers. The chestnuts here were in flower, the copper beech made a delightful contrast of colour, and a birch rose delicate and graceful close beside.

It was like a fairy scene. I passed my hand across my eyes to assure myself it was all real. Then I thought "if this place be even nearly within my means

* A retaining wall sunk into a ditch, used to divide lands without marring the landscape.

I will settle here. My wife will grow stronger in this paradise—my boy get more like other lads. Such things as nerves must be unknown where there is not a sight or sound to excite them. Nothing but health, purity, and peace."

Thus thinking, I tore myself away in search of the "White Dragon," the landlord of which small public sent a lad to show me over the farm.

"As for the rent," he said, "you will have to speak to Miss Gostock herself—she lives at Chalmont, on the road between here and Whittleby."

In every respect the place suited me; it was large enough, but not too large; had been well farmed, and was amply supplied with water—a stream indeed flowing through it; a station was shortly to be opened, at about half-a-mile's distance; and most of the produce could be disposed of to dealers and tradesmen at Crayshill, a town to which the communication by rail was direct.

I felt so anxious about the matter, it was quite a disappointment to find Miss Gostock from home. Judging from the look of her house, I did not suppose she could afford to stick out for a long rent, or to let a farm lie idle for any considerable period. The servant who appeared in answer to my summons was a singularly red armed and rough handed Phyllis. There was only a strip of carpeting laid down in the hall, the windows were bare of draperies, and the avenue gate, set a little back from the main road, was such as I should have felt ashamed to put in a farm yard.

Next morning I betook myself to Chalmont, anxiously wondering as I walked along what the result of my interview would prove.

When I neared the gate, to which uncomplimentary reference has already been made, I saw standing on the other side a figure, wearing a man's broad-brimmed straw hat, a man's coat, and a woman's skirt.

I raised my hat in deference to the supposed sex of this stranger. She put up one finger to the brim of hers, and said "Servant, Sir."

Not knowing exactly what to do I laid my hand upon the latch of the gate and raised it, but she did not alter her position in the least.

She only asked—"What do you want?"

"I want to see Miss Gostock," was my answer.

"I am Miss Gostock," she said; "what is your business with me?"

I replied meekly that I had come to ask the rent of Nut Bush Farm.

"Have you viewed it?" she enquired "Yes." I told her I had been over the place on the previous afternoon.

"And have you a mind to take it?" she persisted—"for I am not going to trouble myself answering a lot of idle enquiries."

So far from my being an idle enquirer, I assured the lady that if we could come to terms about the rent, I should be very glad indeed to take the farm. I said I had been searching the neighbourhood within a circuit of ten miles for some time unsuccessfully, and added, somewhat unguardedly, I suppose, Nut Bush Farm was the only place I had met with which at all met my views.

Standing in an easy attitude, with one arm resting on the top bar of the gate and one foot crossed over the other, Miss Gostock surveyed me, who had unconsciously taken up a similar position, with an amused smile.

"You must think me a very honest person, young man," she remarked.

I answered that I hoped she was, but I had not thought at all about the matter.

"Or else," proceeded this extraordinary lady, "you fancy I am a much greater flat* than I am."

"On the contrary," was my reply. "If there be one impression stronger than another which our short interview has made upon me it is that you are a wonderfully direct and capable woman of business."

She looked at me steadily, and then closed one eye, which performance, done under the canopy of that broad-brimmed straw hat, had the most ludicrous effect imaginable.

"You won't catch me napping," she observed, "but, however, as you seem to mean dealing, come in; I can tell you my terms in two minutes," and opening the gate—a trouble she would not allow me to take off her hands—she gave me admission.

Then Miss Gostock took off her hat, and swinging it to and fro began slowly walking up the ascent leading to Chalmont, I beside her.

"I have quite made up my mind," she said, "not to let the farm again without a premium; my last tenant treated me abominably—"

I intimated I was sorry to hear that, and waited for further information.

---

* A greenhorn, a rube or gull, an easy mark.

"He had the place at a low rent—a very low rent. He should not have got it so cheap but for his covenanting to put so much money in the soil; and well—I'm bound to say he acted fair so far as that—he fulfilled that part of his contract. Nearly two years ago we had a bit of a quarrel about—well it's no matter what we fell out over—only the upshot of the affair was he gave me due notice to leave at last winter quarter. At that time he owed about a year and a-half's rent—for he was a man who never could bear parting with money—and like a fool I did not push him for it. What trick do you suppose he served me for my pains?"

It was simply impossible for me to guess, so I did not try.

"On the twentieth of December," went on Miss Gostock, turning her broad face and curly grey head—she wore her hair short like a man—towards me, "he went over to Whittleby, drew five thousand pounds out of the bank, was afterwards met going towards home by a gentleman named Waite, a friend of his. Since then he has never been seen nor heard of."

"Bless my soul," I exclaimed involuntarily.

"You may be very sure I did not bless his soul," she snarled out angrily. "The man bolted with the five thousand pounds, having previously sold off all his stock and the bulk of his produce, and when I distrained for my rent, which I did pretty smart, I can tell you, there was scarce enough on the premises to pay the levy."

"But what in the world made him bolt?" I asked, quite unconsciously adopting Miss Gostock's expressive phrase; "as he had so much money, why did he not pay you your rent?'

"Ah! why, indeed," mocked Miss Gostock. "Young sir, I am afraid you are a bit of a hum-bug, or you would have suggested at once there was a pretty girl at the bottom of the affair. He left his wife and children, and me—all in the lurch—and went off with a slip of a girl, whom I once took, thinking to train up as a better sort of servant, but was forced to discharge. Oh, the little hussey!"

"Hussey" is not exactly an elegant word to hear used by a lady, but that employed by Miss Gostock was in one syllable and less refined still. Her Saxon was very nervous, and she was not a bit above helping her meaning out occasionally by an oath that would have delighted Queen Bess, and a vigorous expression which might have won her virgin Majesty's approval by its coarseness.

Somehow I did not fancy I wanted to hear anything more about her late tenant and the pretty girl, and consequently ventured to inquire how that gentleman's defalcations bore upon the question of the rent I should have to pay.

"I'll tell you directly," she said, and as we had by this time arrived at the house, she invited me to enter, and led the way into an old-fashioned parlour that must have been furnished about the time chairs and tables were first invented and which did not contain a single feminine belonging—not even a thimble.

"Sit down," she commanded, and I sat. "I have quite made up my mind," she began, "not to let the farm again, unless I get a premium sufficient to insure me against the chances of possible loss. I mean to ask a very low rent and—a premium."

"And what amount of premium do you expect?" I inquired, doubtfully.

"I want—," and here Miss Gostock named a sum which fairly took my breath away.

"In that case," I said as soon as I got it again, "it is useless to prolong this interview; I can only express my regret for having intruded, and wish you good morning," and rising I was bowing myself out when she stopped me.

"Don't be so fast," she cried, "I only said what I wanted. Now what are you prepared to give?"

"I can't be buyer and seller too," I answered, repeating a phrase the precise meaning of which, it may here be confessed, I have never been able exactly to understand.

"Nonsense," exclaimed Miss Gostock—I am really afraid the lady used a stronger term—"if you are anything of a man of business, fit at all to commence farming, you must have an idea on the subject. You shall have the land at a pound an acre, and you will give me for premium—come, how much?"

By what mental process I instantly jumped to an amount it would be impossible to say, but I did mention one which elicited from Miss Gostock the remark—

"That won't do at any price."

"Very well then," I said, "we need not talk any more about the matter."

"But what *will* you give?" asked the lady.

"I have told you," was my answer, "and I am not given either to haggling or beating down."

"You won't make a good farmer," she observed.

"If a farmer's time were of any value, which it generally seems as if it were not," I answered, "he would not waste it in splitting a sixpence."

She laughed, and her laugh was not musical.

"Come now," she said, "make another bid."

"No," I replied, "I have made one and that is enough. I won't offer another penny."

"Done then," cried Miss Gostock, "I accept your offer—we'll just sign a little memorandum of agreement, and the formal deeds can be prepared afterwards. You'll pay a deposit, I suppose?"

I was so totally taken aback by her acceptance of my offer I could only stammer out I was willing to do anything that might be usual.

"It does not matter much whether it is usual or not," she said, "either pay it or I won't keep the place for you. I am not going to have my land lying idle and my time taken up for your pleasure."

"I have no objection to pay you a deposit," I answered.

"That's right," she exclaimed, "now if you will just hand me over the writing-desk we can settle the matter, so far as those thieves of lawyers will let us, in five minutes."

Like one in a dream I sat and watched Miss Gostock while she wrote. Nothing about the transaction seemed to me real. The farm itself resembled nothing I had ever before seen with my waking eyes, and Miss Gostock appeared to me but as some monstrous figure in a story of giants and hobgoblins. The man's coat, the woman's skirt, the hob-nailed shoes, the grisly hair, the old straw hat, the bare, unfurnished room, the bright sunshine outside, all struck me as mere accessories in a play—as nothing which had any hold on the outside every-day world.

It was drawn—we signed our names. I handed Miss Gostock over a cheque. She locked one document in an iron box let into the wall, and handed me the other, adding, as a rider, a word of caution about "keeping it safe and taking care it was not lost."

Then she went to a corner cupboard, and producing a square decanter half full of spirits, set that and two tumblers on the table.

"You don't like much water, I suppose," she said, pouring out a measure which frightened me.

"I could not touch it, thank you, Miss Gostock," I exclaimed; "I dare not do so; I should never get back to Whittleby."

For answer she only looked at me contemptuously and said, "D—d nonsense."

"No nonsense, indeed," I persisted; "I am not accustomed to anything of that sort."

Miss Gostock laughed again, then crossing to the sideboard she returned with a jug of water, a very small portion of the contents of which she mixed with the stronger liquor and raised to her lips.

"To your good health and prosperity," she said, and in one instant the fiery potion was swallowed.

"You'll mend of all that," she remarked, as she laid down her glass, and wiped her lips in the simplest manner by passing the back of her hand over them.

"I hope not, Miss Gostock," I ventured to observe.

"Why you look quite shocked," she said; "did you never see a lady take a mouthful of brandy before?"

I ventured to hint that I had not, more particularly so early in the morning.

"Pooh!" she said. "Early in the morning or late at night, where's the difference? However, there was a time when I—but that was before I had come through so much trouble. Good-bye for the present, and I hope we shall get on well together."

I answered I trusted we should, and was half-way to the hall-door, when she called me back.

"I forgot to ask you if you were married," she said.

"Yes, I have been married some years," I answered.

"That's a pity," she remarked, and dismissed me with a wave of her hand.

"What on earth would have happened had I not been married," I considered, as I hurried down the drive. "Surely she never contemplated proposing for me herself? But nothing she could do would surprise me."

II

There were some repairs I had mentioned it would be necessary to have executed before I came to live at Nut Bush Farm, but when I found Miss Gostock intended to do them herself—nay, was doing them all herself—I felt thunderstruck.

On one memorable occasion I came upon her with a red handkerchief tied round her head, standing at a carpenter's bench in a stable yard, planing away, under a sun which would have killed anybody but a negro or my landlady.

She painted the gates, and put sash lines in some of the windows; she took off the locks, oiled, and replaced them; she mowed the lawn, and offered to teach me how to mow; and lastly, she showed me a book where she charged herself and paid herself for every hour's work done.

"I've made at least twenty pounds out of your place," she said, triumphantly. "Higgs at Whittleby would not have charged me a half-penny less for the repairs. The trades-men here won't give me a contract—they say it is just time thrown away, but I know that would have been about his figure. Well, the place is ready for you now, and if you take my advice, you'll get your grass up as soon as possible. It's a splendid crop, and if you hire hands enough, not a drop of rain need spoil it. If this weather stands you might cut one day and carry the next."

I took her advice, and stacked my hay in magnificent condition. Miss Gostock was good enough to come over and superintend the building of the stack, and threatened to split one man's head open with the pitchfork, and proposed burying another—she called a "lazy blackguard"—under a pile of hay.

"I will say this much for Hascot," she remarked, as we stood together beside the stream; "he was a good farmer; where will you see better or cleaner land?—a pattern I call it—and to lose his whole future for the sake of a girl like Sally Powner; leaving his wife and children on the parish, too!"

"You don't mean that?" I said.

"Indeed I do. They are all at Crayshill. The authorities did talk of shifting them, but I know nothing about what they have done."

I stood appalled. I thought of my own poor wife and the little lad, and wondered if any Sally on the face of the earth could make me desert them.

"It has given the place a bad sort of name," remarked Miss Gostock, looking at me sideways: "but of course that does not signify to you."

"Oh! of course not," I agreed.

"And don't you be minding any stories; there are always a lot of stories going about places."

I said I did not mind stories. I had lived too long in London to pay much attention to them.

"That's right," remarked Miss Gostock, and negativing my offer to see her home she started off to Chalmont.

It was not half-an-hour after her departure when I happened to be walking slowly round the meadows, from which the newly mown hay had been carted, that I heard the rumour which vexed me—"Nut Bush Farm haunted." I thought, "I said the whole thing was too good to last."

"What, Jack, lost in reverie," cried my sister, who had come up from Devonshire to keep me company, and help to get the furniture a little to rights, entering at the moment, carrying lights; "supper will be ready in a minute, and you can dream as much as you like after you have had something to eat." I did not say anything to her about my trouble, which was then indeed no bigger than a man's hand, but which grew and grew till it attained terrible proportions.

What was I to do with my wife and child? I never could bring them to a place reputed to be haunted. All in vain I sauntered up and down the Beech Walk night after night; walked through the wood—as a rule selected that route when I went to Whittleby. It did not produce the slightest effect. Not a farm servant but eschewed that path townward; not a girl but preferred spending her Sunday at home rather than venture under the interlacing branches of the beech trees, or through the dark recesses of the wood.

It was becoming serious—I did not know what to do.

One wet afternoon Lolly came in draggled, but beaming.

"I've made a new acquaintance, Jack," she said; "a Mrs. Waite—such a nice creature, but in dreadfully bad health. It came on to rain when I was coming home, and so I took refuge under a great tree at the gate of a most picturesque old house. I had not stood there long before a servant with an umbrella appeared at the porch to ask if I would not please to walk in until the storm abated. I waited there ever so long, and we had such a pleasant talk. She is a most delightful woman, with a melancholy, pathetic sort of expression that has been haunting me ever since. She apologised for not having called—said she was not strong and could not walk so far. They keep no conveyance she can drive. Mr. Waite, who is not at home at present, rides into Whittleby when anything is wanted.

"I hoped she would not think of standing on ceremony with me. I was only a farmer's daughter, and accustomed to plain, homely ways, and I asked her if I might walk round and bid her good-bye before I went home."

"You must not go home yet, Lolly," I cried, alarmed; "what in the world should I do with-out you?"

"Well, you would be a lonely boy," she answered, complacently, "with no one to sew on a button or darn your socks, or make you eat or go to bed, or do anything you ought to do."

I had not spoken a word to her about the report which was troubling me, and I knew there must be times when she wondered why I did not go up to London and fetch my wife and child to enjoy the bright summer-time; but Lolly was as good as gold, and never asked me a question, or even indirectly enquired if Lucy and I had quarrelled, as many another sister might.

She was as pleasant and fresh to look upon as a Spring morning, with her pretty brown hair smoothly braided, her cotton or muslin dresses never soiled or crumpled, but as nice as though the laundress had that moment sent them home—a rose in her belt and her hands never idle—for ever busy with curtain or blind, or something her housewifely eyes thought had need of making or mending.

About ten days after that showery afternoon when she found shelter under Mrs. Waite's hospitable roof, I felt surprised when entering the parlour a few minutes before our early dinner, I found Lolly standing beside one of the windows hopelessly lost in the depths of a brown study.

"Why, Lolly," I exclaimed, finding she took no notice of me, "where have you gone to now? A penny for your thoughts, young lady."

"They are not worth a penny," she said, and turning from the window took some work and sat down at a little distance from the spot where I was standing.

I was so accustomed to women, even the best and gayest of them, having occasional fits of temper or depression—times when silence on my part seemed the truest wisdom, that taking no notice of my sister's manner I occupied myself with the newspaper till dinner was announced.

During the progress of that meal she talked little and ate still less, but when I was leaving the room, in order to go out to a field of barley where the reapers were at work, she asked me to stop a moment.

"I want to speak to you, Jack," she said.

"Speak, then," I answered, with that lack of ceremony which obtains amongst brothers and sisters.

She hesitated for a moment, but did not speak.

"What on earth is the matter with you? Lolly," I exclaimed, "are you sick, or cross, or sorry, or what?"

"If it must be one of the four," she answered, with a dash of her usual manner, "it is "or what, Jack," and she came close up to where I stood and took me sorrowfully by the button hole.

"Well?" I said, amused, for this had always been a favourite habit of Lolly's when she wanted anything from one of the males of her family.

"Jack, you won't laugh at me."

"I feel much more inclined to be cross with you," I answered. "What are you beating about the bush for, Lolly?"

She lifted her fair face a moment and I saw she was crying.

"Lolly, Lolly!" I cried, clasping her to my heart, "what is it, dear? Have you bad news from home, or have you heard anything about Lucy or the boy? Don't keep me in suspense, there's a darling. No matter what has happened, let me know the worst."

She smiled through her tears, and Lolly has the rarest smile! It quieted my anxious heart in a moment, even before she said—

"No, Jack—it is nothing about home, or Lucy, or Teddy, but—but—but—" and then she relinquished her hold of the button-hole, and fingered each button on the front of my coat carefully and lingeringly. "Did you ever hear–Jack—anybody say anything about this place?"

I knew in a moment what she meant; I knew the cursed tattle had reached her ears, but I only asked—

"What sort of thing, Lolly?"

She did not answer me; instead she put another question.

"Is that the reason you have not brought Lucy down?" I felt vexed—but I had so much confidence in her good sense, I could not avoid answering without a moment's delay.

"Well, yes; I do not want her to come till this foolish report has completely died away."

"Are you quite sure it is a foolish report?" she enquired.

"Why, of course; it could not be anything else." She did not speak immediately, then all at once—

"Jack," she said, "I must tell you something. Lock the door that we may not be interrupted."

"No," I answered; "come into the barley field. Don't you remember Mr. Fenimore Cooper advised, if you want to talk secrets, choose the middle of a plain."

I tried to put a good face on the matter, but the sight of Lolly's tears, the sound of Lolly's doleful voice, darkened my very heart. What had she to tell me which required locked doors or the greater privacy of a half-reaped barley field. I could trust my sister—she was no fool—and I felt perfectly satisfied that no old woman's story had wrought the effect produced on her.

"Now, Lolly," I said, as we paced side by side along the top of the barley field in a solitude all the more complete because life and plenty of it was close at hand.

"You know what they say about the place, Jack?"

This was interrogative, and so I answered. "Well, no, Lolly, I can't say that I do, for the very good reason that I have always refused to listen to the gossip. What do they say?"

"That a man haunts the Beech Walk, the long meadow, and the wood."

"Yes, I have heard that," I replied.

"And they say further, the man is Mr. Hascot, the late tenant."

"But he is not dead," I exclaimed, "how then can they see his ghost?"

"I cannot tell. I know nothing but what I saw this morning. After breakfast I went to Whittleby, and as I came back I observed a man before me on the road. Following him, I noticed a curious thing, that none of the people he met made way for him or he for them. He walked straight on, without any regard to the persons on the side path, and yet no one seemed to come into collision with him. When I reached the field path I saw him going on still at the same pace. He did not look to right or left, and did not seem to walk—the motion was gliding—"

"Yes, dear."

"He went on, and so did I, till we reached the hollow where the nut-bushes grow, then he disappeared from sight. I looked down among the trees, thinking I should be able to catch a glimpse of his figure through the underwood, but no, I could see no signs of him, neither could I hear any. Everything was as still as death; it seemed to me that my ear had a spell of silence laid upon it."

"And then," I asked hoarsely, as she paused.

"Why, Jack, I walked on and crossed the little foot bridge and was just turning into the Beech Walk when the same man bustled suddenly across my path, so close to me if I had put out my hands I could have touched him. I drew back, frightened for a minute, then, as he had not seemed to see me, I turned and looked at him as he sped along down the little winding path to the wood. I thought he must be some silly creature, some harmless sort of idiot, to be running here and there without any apparent object. All at once, as he neared the wood, he stopped, and, half wheeling round, beckoned to me to follow him."

"You did not, Lolly?"

"No, I was afraid. I walked a few steps quietly till I got among the beech trees and so screened from sight, and then I began to run. I could not run fast, for my knees trembled under me; but still I did run as far nearly as that seat round the 'Priest's Tree.' I had not got quite up to the seat when I saw a man rise from it and stand upright as if waiting for me. *It was the same person, Jack!* I recognised him, instantly, though I had not seen his face clearly before. He stood quiet for a moment, and then with the same gliding motion, silently disappeared."

"Some one must be playing a very nice game about Nut Bush Farm," I exclaimed.

"Perhaps so, dear," she said, doubtfully.

"Why, Lolly, you don't believe it was a ghost you met in the broad daylight?" I cried, incredulously.

"I don't think it was a living man, Jack," she answered.

"Living or dead he dare not bring himself into close quarters with me," was my somewhat braggart remark. "Why, Lolly, I have walked the ground day after day, and night after night in the hope of seeing your friend, and not a sign of an intruder, in the flesh or out of it, could I find. Put the matter away, child, and don't ramble in that direction again. If I can ascertain the name of the person who is trying to frighten the household and disgust me with Nut Bush Farm he shall go to jail if the magistrates are of my way of thinking. Now, as you have told me this terrible story, and we have reduced your great mountain to a molehill, I will walk back with you to the house."

She did not make any reply: we talked over indifferent matters as we paced along. I went with her into the pleasant sunshiny drawing-room and looked her out a book and made her promise to read something amusing; then I was going, when she put up her lips for me to kiss her, and said—

"Jack, you won't run any risks?"

"Risks! pooh, you silly little woman," I answered; and so left my sister and repaired to the barley field once more.

When it was time for the men to leave off work I noticed that one after another began to take a path leading immediately to the main road, which was a very circuitous route to the hamlet, where most of them had either cottages or lodgings.

I noticed this for some time, and then asked a brawny young fellow,

"Why don't you go home through the Beech Walk? It is not above half the distance."

He smiled and made some almost unintelligible answer.

"Why are you all afraid of taking the shortest way," I remarked, "seeing there are enough of you to put half-a-dozen ghosts to the rout?"

"Likely, sir," was the answer; "but the old master was a hard man living, and there is not many would care to meet him dead."

"What old master?" I enquired.

"Mr. Hascot: it's him as walks. I saw him as plain as I see you now, sir, one moonlight night, just this side of the wood, and so did Nat Tyler and James Monsey, and James Monsey's father—wise Ben."

"But Mr. Hascot is not dead; how can he 'walk,' as you call it?" was my natural exclamation.

"If he is living then, sir, where is he?" asked the man. "There is nobody can tell that, and there is a many, especially just lately, think he must have been made away with. He had a cruel lot of money about him—where is all that money gone to?"

The fellow had waxed quite earnest in his interrogations, and really for the first time the singularity of Mr. Hascot's disappearance seemed to strike me.

I said, after an instant's pause, "The money is wherever he is. He went off with some girl, did he not?"

"It suited the old people to say so," he answered; "but there is many a one thinks they know more about the matter than is good for them. I can't help hearing, and one of the neighbours did say Mrs. Ockfield was seen in church last Sunday with a new dress on and a shawl any lady might have worn."

"And who is Mrs. Ockfield?" I enquired.

"Why, Sally Powner's grandmother. The old people treated the girl shameful while she was with them, and now they want to make her out no better than she should be."

And with a wrathful look the young man, who I subsequently discovered had long been fond of Sally, took up his coat and his tin bottle and his sickle, and with a brief "I think I'll be going, sir; good night," departed.

It was easy to return to the house, but I found it impossible to shake the effect produced by this dialogue off my mind.

For the first time I began seriously to consider the manner of Mr. Hascot's disappearance, and more seriously still commenced trying to piece together the various hints I had received as to his character.

A hard man—a hard master, all I ever heard speak considered him, but just, and in the main not unkind. He had sent coals to one widow, and kept a poor old labourer off the parish, and then in a minute, for the sake of a girl's face, left his own wife and children to the mercy of the nearest Union.

As I paced along it seemed to me monstrous, and yet how did it happen that till a few minutes previously I had never heard even a suspicion of foul play?

Was it not more natural to conclude the man must have been made away with, than that, in one brief day, he should have changed his nature and the whole current of his former life?

Upon the other hand, people must have had some strong reason for imagining he was gone off with Miss Powner. The notion of a man disappearing in this way—vanishing as if the earth had opened to receive him and closed again—for the sake of any girl, however attractive, was too unnatural an idea for any one to have evolved out of his internal consciousness. There must have been some substratum of fact, and then upon the other hand, there seemed to me more than a substratum of possibility in the theory started of his having been murdered.

Supposing he had been murdered, I went on to argue, what then? Did I imagine he "walked?" Did I believe he could not rest wherever he was laid?

Pooh! nonsense. It might be that the murderer haunted the place of his crime—that he hovered about to see if his guilt were still undetected, but as to anything in the shape of a ghost tenanting the Beech Walk, long meadow, and wood, I did not believe it—I could not, and I added, "if I saw it with my own eyes, I would not."

Having arrived at which decided and sensible conclusion, I went in to supper.

Usually a sound sleeper, I found it impossible that night when I lay down to close my eyes. I tossed and turned, threw off the bedclothes under the impression I was too hot and drew them tight up round me the next instant, feeling cold. I tried to think of my crops, of my land, of my wife, of my boy, of my future—all in vain. A dark shadow, a wall-like night stood between me and all the ordinary interests of my life—I could not get the notion of Mr. Hascot's strange disappearance out of my mind. I wondered if there was anything about the place which made it in the slightest degree probable I should ever learn to forget the wife who loved, the boy who was dependent on me. Should I ever begin to think I might have done better as regards my choice of a wife, that it would be nicer to have healthy merry children than my affectionate delicate lad?

When I got to this point, I could stand it no longer. I felt as though some mocking spirit were taking possession of me, which eventually would destroy all my peace of mind, if I did not cast it out promptly and effectually.

I would not lie there supine to let any demon torment me; and, accordingly, springing to the floor, I dressed in hot haste, and flinging wide the window, looked out over a landscape bathed in the clear light of a most lovely moon.

"How beautiful!" I thought. "I have never yet seen the farm by night, I'll just go and take a stroll round it and then turn in again—after a short walk I shall likely be able to sleep."

So saying, I slipped downstairs, closed the hall door softly after me, and went out into the moonlight.

III

As I stood upon the lawn, looking around with a keen and subtle pleasure, I felt, almost for the first time in my life, the full charm and beauty of night. Every object was as clearly revealed as though the time had been noon instead of an hour past midnight, but there lay a mystic spell on tree and field and stream the garish day could never equal. It was a fairy light and a fairy scene, and it would scarcely have astonished me to see fantastic elves issue from the fox-glove's flowers or dart from the shelter of concealing leaves and dance a measure on the emerald sward.

For a minute I felt—as I fancy many and many a common-place man must have done when first wedded to some miracle of grace and beauty—a sense of amazement and unreality.

All this loveliness was mine—the moonlit lawn—the stream murmuring through the fir plantation, singing soft melodies as it pursued its glittering way—the trees with a silvery gleam tinting their foliage—the roses giving out their sweetest, tenderest, perfumes—the wonderful silence around—the fresh, pure air—the soft night wind—the prosperity with which God had blessed me. My heart grew full, as I turned and gazed first on this side and then on that, and I felt vexed and angry to remember I had ever suffered myself to listen to idle stories and to be made uncomfortable by reason of village gossip.

On such a night it really seemed a shame to go to bed, and, accordingly, though the restlessness which first induced me to rise had vanished, and in doing so left the most soothing calm behind, I wandered on away from the house, now beside the stream, and again across a meadow, where faint odours from the lately-carried hay still lingered.

Still the same unreal light over field and copse—still the same witching glamour—still the same secret feeling. I was seeing something and experiencing some sensation I might never again recall on this side of the grave!

A most lovely night—one most certainly not for drawn curtains and closed eyelids—one rather for lovers tête-a-tête or a dreamy reverie—for two young hearts to reveal their secrets to each other or one soul to commune alone with God.

Still rambling, I found myself at last beside a stile, opening upon a path, which, winding upwards, led past the hollow where the nut trees grew, and then joined the footway leading through the Long field to Whittleby. The Long field was the last in that direction belonging to Nut Bush Farm. It joined upon a portion of the land surrounding Chalmont, and the field path continued consequently to pass through Miss Gostock's property till the main road was reached. It cut off a long distance, and had been used generally by the inhabitants of the villages and hamlets dotted about my place until the rumour being circulated that something might be "seen" or "met" deterred people from venturing by a route concerning which such evil things were whispered. I had walked it constantly, both on account of the time it saved and also in order to set a good example to my labourers and my neighbours, but I might as well have saved my pains.

I was regarded merely as foolhardy, and I knew people generally supposed I should one day have cause to repent my temerity.

As I cleared the stile and began winding my upward way to the higher ground beyond, the thought did strike me what a likely place for a murder Nut Bush Hollow looked. It was a deep excavation, out of which, as no one supposed it to be natural, hundreds and thousands of loads of earth must at some time or other have been carted. From top to bottom it was clothed with nut trees—they grew on every side, and in thick almost impenetrable masses. For years and years they seemed to have had no care bestowed on them, the Hollow forming in this respect a remarkable contrast to the rest of Mr. Hascot's careful farming, and, as a fir plantation ran along the base of the Hollow, while the moon's light fell clear and full on some of the bushes, the others lay in densest shadow.

The road that once led down into the pit was now completely overgrown with nut bushes which grew luxuriantly to the very edge of the Beech Walk, and threatened ere long to push their way between the trunks of the great trees, which were the beauty and the pride of my lovely farm.

At one time, so far as I could understand, the nut bushes had the whole place almost to themselves, and old inhabitants told me that formerly, in the days when their parents were boys and girls, the nuts used to pay the whole of the rent. As years passed, however, whether from want of care or some natural cause, they gradually ceased to bear, and had to be cut down and cleared off the ground—those, in the dell, however, being suffered to remain, the hollow being useless for husbandry, and the bushes which flourished there producing a crop of nuts sufficient for the farmer's family.

All this recurred to my mind as I stood for a moment and looked down into the depths of rustling green below me. I thought of the boys who must have gone nutting there, of all the nests birds had built in the branches so closely interlaced, of the summers' suns which had shone full and strong upon that mass of foliage, of the winters' snows which had lain heavy on twig and stem and happed the strong roots in a warm covering of purest white.

And then the former idea again asserted itself—what a splendid place for a tragedy; a sudden blow—a swift stab—even a treacherous push—and the deed could be done—a man might be alive and well one minute, and dead the next!

False friend, or secret enemy; rival or thief, it was competent for either in such a place at any lonely hour to send a man upon his last long journey. Had Mr. Hascot been so served? Down, far down, was he lying in a quiet, dreamless sleep? At that very moment was there any one starting from fitful slumber to grapple with his remorse for crime committed, or shrink with horror from the dread of detection?

"Where was my fancy leading me?" I suddenly asked myself. This was worse than in my own chamber preventing the night watches. Since I had been standing there my heart felt heavier than when tossing from side to side in bed, and wooing unsuccessfully the slumber which refused to come for my asking.

What folly! what nonsense! and into what an insane course of speculation had I not embarked. I would leave the eerie place and get once again into the full light of the moon's bright beams.

Hush! hark! what was that? deep down amongst the underwood—a rustle, a rush, and a scurry—then silence—then a stealthy movement amongst the bushes—then whilst I was peering down into the abyss lined with waving green below, SOMETHING passed by me swiftly, something which brought with it a cold chill as though the hand of one dead had been laid suddenly on my heart.

Instantly I turned and looked around. There was not a living thing in sight—neither on the path, nor on the sward, nor on the hill side, nor skirting the horizon as I turned my eyes upward.

For a moment I stood still in order to steady my nerves, then re-assuring myself with the thought it must have been an animal of some kind, I completed the remainder of the ascent without further delay.

"The ghost, I suspect," I said to myself as I reached the Long Field and the path leading back to the farm, "will resolve itself into a hare or pheasant—is not the whirr of a cock pheasant rising, for instance, enough, when coming unexpectedly, to frighten any nervous person out of his wits? and might not a hare, or a cat, or, better still, a stoat—yes, a stoat, with its gliding, almost noiseless, movements—mimic the footfall of a suppositious ghost?"

By this time I had gained the summit of the incline, and slightly out of breath with breasting the ascent, stood for a moment contemplating the exquisite panorama stretched out beneath me. I linger on that moment because it was the last time I ever saw beauty in the moonlight. Now I cannot endure the silvery gleam of the queen of night—weird, mournful, fantastic if you like, but to be desired—no.

Whenever possible I draw the blinds and close the shutters, yet withal on moonlight nights I cannot sleep, the horror of darkness is to my mind nothing in comparison to the terror of a full moon. But I drivel; let me hasten on.

From the crest of the hill I could see lying below a valley of dream-like beauty—woods in the foreground—a champagne country spreading away into the indefinite distance—a stream winding in and out, dancing and glittering under the moon's beams—a line of hills dimly seen against the horizon, and already a streak of light appearing above them the first faint harbinger of dawn.

"It is morning, then, already," I said, and with the words turned my face homewards. As I did so I saw before me on the path—*clearly*—the figure of a man.

He was walking rapidly and I hurried my pace in order to overtake him. Now to this part of my story I desire to draw particular attention. *Let me hurry as I might I never seemed able to get a foot nearer to him.*

At intervals he paused as if on purpose to assist my desire, but the moment I seemed gaining upon him the distance between us suddenly increased. I could not tell how he did it, the fact only remained—it was like pursuing some phantom in a dream.

All at once when he reached the bridge he stood quite still. He did not move hand or limb as I drew near—the way was so narrow I knew I should have to touch him in passing, nevertheless I pressed forward. My foot was on the bridge—I was close to him—I felt my breath coming thick and fast—I clasped a stick I had picked up in the plantation firmly in my hand—I stopped intending to speak—I opened my mouth intending to do so—and then—then—without any movement on his part—I was alone!

Yes, as totally alone as though he had never stood on the bridge—never preceded me along the field-path—never loitered upon my footsteps—never paused for my coming.

I was appalled.

"Lord, what is this?" I thought; "am I going mad?" I felt as if I were. On my honour, I know I was as nearly insane at that moment as a man ever can be who is still in the possession of his senses.

Beyond lay the farm of which in my folly I had felt so proud to be the owner, where I once meant to be so happy and win health for my wife and strength for my boy. I saw the Beech Walk I had gloried in—the ricks of hay it seemed so good to get thatched geometrically as only one man in the neighbourhood was said to be able to lay the straw.

What was farm, or riches, or beech trees, or anything, to me now? over the place there seemed a curse—better the meanest cottage than a palace with such accessories.

If I had been incredulous before, I was not so now—I could not distrust the evidence of my own eyes—and yet as I walked along, I tried after a minute or two, to persuade myself imagination had been playing some juggler's trick with me. The moon, I argued, always lent herself readily to a game of hide-and-seek. She is always open to join in fantastic gambols with shadows—with thorn bushes—with a waving branch—aye even with a clump of gorse. I must have been mistaken—I had been thinking weird thoughts as I stood by that dismal dell—I had seen no man walking—beheld no figure disappear!

Just as I arrived at this conclusion I beheld some one coming towards me down the Beech Walk. It was a man walking leisurely with a firm, free step. The sight did me good. Here was something tangible—something to question. I stood still, in the middle of the path—the Beech Walk being rather a grassy glade with a narrow footway dividing it, than anything usually understood by the term walk—so that I might speak to the intruder when he drew near, and ask him what he meant by trespassing on my property, more especially at such an hour. There were no public rights on my land except as regarded the path across the Long Field and through the wood. No one had any right or business to be in the Beech Walk, by day or night, save those employed about the Farm, and this person was a gentleman; even in the distance I could distinguish that. As he came closer I saw he was dressed in a loose Palmerston suit, that he wore a low-crowned hat, and that he carried a light cane. The moonbeams dancing down amongst the branches and between the leaves fell full upon his face, and catching sight of a ring he had on his right hand, made it glitter with as many different colours as a prism.

A middle-aged man, so far as I could judge, with a set, determined expression of countenance, dark hair, no beard or whiskers, only a small moustache. A total stranger to me. I had never seen him nor any one like him in the neighbourhood. Who could he be, and what in the wide world was he doing on my premises at that unearthly hour of the morning?

He came straight on, never moving to right or left—taking no more notice of me than if he had been blind. His easy indifference, his contemptuous coolness, angered me, and planting myself a little more in his way, I began—

"Are you aware, sir—"

I got no further. Without swerving in the slightest degree from the path, he passed me! I felt something like a cold mist touch me for an instant, and the next, I saw him pursuing his steady walk down the centre of the glade. I was sick with fear, but for all that I ran after him faster than I had ever done since boyhood.

All to no purpose! I might as well have tried to catch the wind. Just where three ways joined I stood still and looked around. I was quite alone! Neither sign nor token of the intruder could I discover. On my left lay the dell where the nut trees grew, and above it the field path to Whittleby showing white and clear in the moonlight; close at hand was the bridge; straight in front the wood looked dark and solemn. Between me and it, lay a little hollow, down which a narrow path wound tortuously. As I gazed I saw that, where a moment before no one had been, a man was walking now. But I could not follow. My limbs refused their office. He turned his head, and lifting his hand on which the ring glittered, beckoned me to come. He might as well have asked one seized with paralysis. On the confines of the wood he stood motionless as if awaiting my approach; then, when I made no sign of movement, he wrung his hands with a despairing gesture, and disappeared.

At the same moment, moon, dell, bridge, and stream faded from my sight—and I fainted.

IV

It was not much past eight o'clock when I knocked at Miss Gostock's hall door, and asked if I could see that lady.

After that terrible night vision I had made up my mind. Behind Mr. Hascot's disappearance I felt sure there lurked some terrible tragedy—living, no man should have implored my help with such passionate earnestness without avail, and if indeed one had appeared to me from the dead I would right him if I could.

But never for a moment did I then think of giving up the farm. The resolve I had come to seemed to have braced up my courage—let what might come or go, let crops remain unreaped and men neglect their labour, let monetary loss and weary anxious days be in store if they would, I meant to go on to the end.

The first step on my road clearly led in the direction of Miss Gostock's house. She alone could give me all the information I required—to her alone could I speak freely and fully about what I had seen.

I was instantly admitted and found the lady, as I had expected, at breakfast. It was her habit, I knew, to partake of that meal while the labourers she employed were similarly engaged. She was attired in an easy *négligé* of a white skirt and a linen coat which had formerly belonged to her brother. She was not taking tea or coffee like any other woman—but was engaged upon about a pound of smoking steak which she ate covered with mustard and washed down with copious draughts of home-brewed beer.

She received me cordially and invited me to join in the banquet—a request I ungallantly declined, eliciting in return the remark I should never be good for much till I ceased living on "slops" and took to "good old English" fare.

After these preliminaries I drew my chair near the table and said,

"I want you to give me some information, Miss Gostock, about my predecessor."

"What sort of information," she asked, with a species of frost at once coming over her manner.

"Can you tell me anything of his personal appearance?"

"Why do you ask?"

I did not immediately answer, and seeing my hesitation she went on.

"Because if you mean to tell me you or any one else have seen him about your place I would not believe it if you swore it—there!"

"I do not ask you to believe it, Miss Gostock," I said.

"And I give you fair warning, it is of no use coming here and asking me to relieve you of your bargain, because I won't do it. I like you well enough—better than I ever liked a tenant; but I don't intend to be a shilling out of pocket by you."

"I hope you never may be," I answered meekly.

"I'll take very good care I never am," she retorted; "and so don't come here talking about Mr. Hascot. He served me a dirty turn, and I would not put it one bit past him to try and get the place a bad name."

"Will you tell me what sort of looking man he was?" I asked determinedly.

"No, I won't," she snapped, and while she spoke she rose, drained the last drop out of a pewter measure, and after tossing on the straw hat with a defiant gesture, thumped its crown well down on her head. I took the hint, and rising, said I must endeavour to ascertain the particulars I wanted elsewhere.

"You won't ascertain them from me," retorted Miss Gostock, and so we parted as we had never done before—on bad terms.

Considerably perplexed I walked out of the house. A rebuff of this sort was certainly the last thing I could have expected, and as I paced along I puzzled myself by trying to account for Miss Gostock's extraordinary conduct, and anxiously considering what I was to do under present circumstances. All at once the recollection of mine host of the "Bunch of Hops" flashed across my mind. He must have seen Mr. Hascot often, and I could address a few casual questions to him without exciting his curiosity.

No sooner thought than done. Turning my face towards Whittleby, I stepped briskly on.

"Did I ever see Mr. Hascot," repeated the landlord—when after some general conversation about politics, the weather, the crops, and many other subjects, I adroitly turned it upon the late tenant of Nut Bush Farm—"often, sir. I never had much communication with him, for he was one of your stand-aloof, keep-your-distance, sort of gentlemen—fair dealing and honourable—but neither free nor generous. He has often sat where you are sitting now, sir, and not so much as said—'it is a fine day,' or, 'I am afraid we shall have rain.'

"You had but to see him walking down the street to know what he was. As erect as a grenadier, with a firm easy sort of marching step, he looked every inch a gentleman—just in his every-day clothes, a *Palmerston suit* and a *round hat*, he was, as many a one said, fit to go to court. His hands were not a bit like a farmer's, but white and delicate as any lady's, and the *diamond ring* he wore flashed like a star when he stroked the *slight bit of a moustache*, that *was all the hair he had upon his face.* No—not a handsome gentleman, but fine looking, with a presence—bless and save us all to think of his giving up everything for the sake of that slip of a girl."

"She was very pretty, wasn't she?" I enquired.

"Beautiful—we all said she was too pretty to come to any good. The old grandmother you see had serious cause for keeping so tight a hand over her, but it was in her, and 'what's bred in the bone,' you know, sir."

"And you really think they did go off together?"

"Oh! yes, sir; nobody had ever any doubt about that."

On this subject his tone was so decided I felt it was useless to continue the conversation, and having paid him for the modest refreshment of which I had partaken I sauntered down the High Street and turned into the Bank, where I thought of opening an account.

When I had settled all preliminaries with the manager he saved me the trouble of beating about the bush by breaking cover himself and asking if anything had been heard of Mr. Hascot.

"Not that I know of," I answered.

"Curious affair, wasn't it," he said.

"It appears so, but I have not heard the whole story."

"Well, the whole story is in a nut-shell," returned the manager. "He comes over here one day and without assigning any reason withdraws the whole of his balance, which was very heavy—is met on the road homeward but never returns home—the same day the girl Powner is also missing—what do you think of all that?"

"It is singular," I said, "very."

"Yes, and to leave his wife and family totally unprovided for."

"I cannot understand that at all."

"Nor I—it was always known he had an extreme partiality for the young person—he and Miss Gostock quarrelled desperately on the subject—but no one could have imagined an attachment of that sort would have led a man so far astray—Hascot more especially. If I had been asked to name the last person in the world likely to make a fool of himself for the sake of a pretty face I should have named the late tenant of Nut Bush Farm."

"There never was a suspicion of foul play," I suggested.

"Oh, dear, no! It was broad daylight when he was last seen on the Whittleby road. The same morning it is known he and the girl were talking earnestly together beside the little wood on your property, and two persons answering their description were traced to London, that is to say, a gentleman came forward to say he believed he had travelled up with them as far as New Cross on the afternoon in question."

"He was an affectionate father I have heard," I said.

"A *most* affectionate parent—a most devoted husband. Dear, dear! it is dreadfully sad to think how a bad woman may drag the best of men down to destruction. It is terrible to think of his wife and family being inmates of the Union."

"Yes, and it is terrible to consider not a soul has tried to get them out of it," I answered, a little tartly.

"H—m, perhaps so; but we all know we are contributing to their support," he returned with an effort at jocularity, which, in my then frame of mind, seemed singularly *mal-apropos*.

"There is something in that," I replied with an effort, and leaving the Bank next turned my attention to the Poorhouse at Crayshill.

At that time many persons thought what I did Quixotic. It is so much the way of the world to let the innocent suffer for the guilty, that I believe Mr. Hascot's wife might have ended her days in Crayshill Union but for the action I took in the matter.

Another night I felt I could not rest till I had arranged for an humble lodging she and her family could occupy till I was able to form some plan for their permanent relief. I found her a quiet, ladylike woman, totally unable to give me the slightest clue as to where her husband might be found. "He was just at the stile on the Chalmont fields," she said, "when Mr. Waite met him; no one saw him afterwards, unless it might be the Ockfields, but, of course, there is no information to be got from them. The guardians have tried every possible means to discover his whereabouts without success. My own impression is he and Sally Powner have gone to America, and that some day we may hear from him. He cannot harden his heart for ever and forget—" Here Mrs. Hascot's sentence trailed off into passionate weeping.

"It is too monstrous!" I considered; "the man never did such a thing as desert his wife and children. Some one knows all about the matter," and then in a moment I paused in the course of my meditations.

Was that person Miss Gostock?

It was an ugly idea, and yet it haunted me. When I remembered the woman's masculine strength, when I recalled her furious impetuosity when I asked her a not very exasperating question, as I recalled the way she tossed off that brandy, when I considered her love of money, her eagerness to speak ill of her late tenant, her semi-references to some great trouble prior to which she was more like other women, or, perhaps, to speak more correctly, less unlike them—doubts came crowding upon my mind.

It was when entering her ground Mr. Hascot was last seen. He had a large sum of money in his possession. She was notoriously fond of rambling about Nut Bush Farm, and what my labouring men called "spying around," which had been the cause of more than one pitched battle between herself and Mr. Hascot.

"The old master could not a-bear her," said one young fellow.

I hated myself for the suspicion; and yet, do what I would, I could not shake it off. Not for a moment did I imagine Miss Gostock had killed her former tenant in cold blood; but it certainly occurred to me that the dell was deep, and the verge treacherous, that it would be easy to push a man over, either by accident or design, that the nut-bushes grew thick, that a body might lie amongst them till it rotted, ere even the boys who went nutting there, season after season, happened to find it.

Should I let the matter drop? No, I decided. With that mute appeal haunting my memory, I should know no rest or peace till I had solved the mystery of Mr. Hascot's disappearance, and cleared his memory from the shameful stain circumstances had cast upon it.

What should I do next? I thought the matter over for a few days, and then decided to call on Mr. Waite, who never yet had called on me. As usual, he was not at home; but I saw his wife, whom I found just the sort of woman Lolly described—a fair, delicate creature, who seemed fading into the grave.

She had not much to tell me. It was her husband who saw Mr. Hascot at the Chalmont stile; it was he also who had seen Mr. Hascot and the girl Powner talking together on the morning of their disappearance. It so happened he had often chanced to notice them together before. "She was a very, very pretty girl," Mrs. Waite added, "and I always thought a modest. She had a very sweet way of speaking—quite above her station—inherited, no doubt, for her father was a gentleman. Poor little Sally!"

The words were not much but the manner touched me sensibly. I felt drawn to Mrs. Waite from that moment, and told her more of what I had beheld and what I suspected than I had mentioned to anyone else.

As to my doubts concerning Miss Gostock, I was of course silent, but I said quite plainly I did not believe Mr. Hascot had gone off with any girl or woman either, that I thought he had come to an unfair end, and that I was of opinion the stories circulated, concerning a portion of Nut Bush Farm being haunted, had some foundation in fact.

"Do you believe in ghosts then?" she asked, with a curious smile.

"I believe in the evidence of my senses," I answered, "and I declare to you, Mrs. Waite, that one night not long since, I saw as plainly as I see you, what I can only conclude to have been the semblance of Mr. Hascot."

She did not make any reply, she only turned very pale, and blaming myself for having alarmed one in her feeble state of health, I hastened to apologise and take my leave.

As we shook hands, she retained mine for a moment, and said, "When you hear anything more, if you should that is, you will tell us will you not. Naturally we feel interested in the matter, he was such a near neighbour, and—we knew him."

I assured her I would not fail to do so, and left the room.

Before I reached the front door I found I had forgotten one of my gloves, and immediately retraced my steps.

The drawing-room door was ajar, and somewhat unceremoniously, perhaps, I pushed it open and entered.

To my horror and surprise, Mrs. Waite, whom I had left apparently in her ordinary state of languid health, lay full length on the sofa, sobbing as if her heart would break. What I said so indiscreetly had brought on an attack of violent hysterics—a malady, with the signs and tokens of which I was not altogether unacquainted.

Silently I stole out of the room without my glove, and left the house, closing the front door noiselessly behind me.

A couple of days elapsed, and then I decided to pay a visit to Mrs. Ockfield. If she liked to throw any light on the matter, I felt satisfied she could. It was, to say the least of it, most improbable her grand-daughter, whether she had been murdered or gone away with Mr. Hascot, should disappear and not leave a clue by which her relatives could trace her.

The Ockfields were not liked, I found, and I flattered myself if they had any hand in Mr. Hascot's sudden disappearance, I should soon hit on some weak spot in her story.

I found the old woman, who was sixty-seven, and who looked two hundred, standing over her washing tub.

"Can I tell you where my grand-daughter is," she repeated, drawing her hands out of the suds and wiping them on her apron. "Surely, sir, and very glad I am to be able to tell everybody, gentle and simple, where to find our Sally. She is in a good service down in Cheshire. Mr. Hascot got her the place, but we knew nothing about it till yesterday; she left us in a bit of a pet, and said she wouldn't have written me only some things seemed to tell her she must. Ah! she'll have a sore heart when she gets my letter and hears how it has been said that the master and she went off together. She thought a deal of the master, did Sally; he was always kind and stood between her and her grandfather."

"Then do you mean to say," I asked, "that she knows nothing of Mr. Hascot's disappearance?"

"Nothing, sir, thank God for all His mercies; the whole of the time since the day she left here she has been in service with a friend of his. You can read her letter if you like."

Though I confess old Mrs. Ockfield neither charmed nor inspired me with confidence, I answered that I should like to see the letter very much indeed.

When I took it in my hand I am bound to say I thought it had been written with a purpose, and intended less for a private than for the public eye, but as I read I fancied there was a ring of truth about the epistle, more especially as the writer made passing reference to a very bitter quarrel which had preceded her departure from the grand-paternal roof.

"It is very strange," I said, as I returned the letter, "it is a most singular coincidence that your grand-daughter and Mr. Hascot should have left Whittleby on the same day, and yet that she should know nothing of his whereabouts, as judging from her letter seems to be the case."

"Are you quite sure Mr. Hascot ever did leave Whittleby, sir?" asked the old woman with a vindictive look in her still bright old eyes. "There are those as think he never went very far from home, and that the whole truth will come out some day."

"What do you mean?" I exclaimed, surprised.

"Least said soonest mended," she answered, shortly; "only I hopes if ever we do know the rights of it, people as do hold their heads high enough, and have had plenty to say about our girl and us too for that matter, will find things not so pleasant as they find them at present. The master had a heap of money about him, and we know that often those as has, are those as wants more!"

"I cannot imagine what you are driving at," I said, for I feared every moment she would mention Miss Gostock, and bring her name into the discussion. "If you think Mr. Hascot met with any foul play you ought to go to the police about the matter."

"Maybe I will some time," she answered, "but just now I have my washing to do."

"This will buy you some tea to have afterwards," I said, laying down half-a-crown, and feeling angry with myself for this momentary irritation. After all the woman had as much right to her suspicions as I to mine.

Thinking over Miss Powner's letter I came to the conclusion it might be well to see the young lady for myself. If I went to the address she dated from I could ascertain at all events whether her statement regarding her employment was correct. Yes, I would take train and travel into Cheshire; I had commenced the investigation and I would follow it to the end.

I travelled so much faster than Mrs. Ockfield's letter—which indeed that worthy woman had not then posted—that when I arrived at my journey's end I found the fair Sarah in total ignorance of Mr. Hascot's disappearance and the surmises to which her own absence had given rise.

Appearances might be against the girl's truth and honesty, yet I felt she was dealing fairly with me.

"A better gentleman, sir," she said, "than Mr. Hascot never drew breath. And so they set it about he had gone off with me—they little know—they little know! Why, sir, he thought of me and was careful for me as he might for a daughter. The first time I ever saw him grandfather was beating me, and he interfered to save me. He knew they treated me badly, and it was after a dreadful quarrel I had at home he advised me to go away. He gave me a letter to the lady I am now with, and a ten-pound note to pay my travelling and keep something in my pocket. 'You'll be better away from the farm, little girl,' he said the morning I left; 'people are beginning to talk, and we can't shut their mouths if you come running to me every time your grandmother speaks sharply to you.'"

"But why did you not write sooner to your relatives?" I asked.

"Because I was angry with my grandmother, sir, and I thought I would give her a fright. I did not bring any clothes or anything and I hoped—it was a wicked thing I know, sir—but I hoped she would believe I had made away with myself. Just lately, however, I began to consider that if she and grandfather had not treated me well I was treating them worse, so I made up a parcel of some things my mistress gave me and sent it to them with a letter. I am glad it reached them safely."

"What time was it when you saw Mr. Hascot last?" I enquired.

"About two o'clock, sir. I know that, because he was in a hurry. He had got some news about the bank at Whittleby not being quite safe, and he said he had too much money there to run any risk of loss. "Be a good girl," were the last words he said, and he walked off sharp and quick by the field path to Whittleby. I stood near the bridge crying for a while. Oh, sir! do you think anything ill can have happened to him?"

For answer, I only said the whole thing seemed most mysterious.

"He'd never have left his wife and children, sir," she went on; "never. He must have been made away with."

"Had he any enemies, do you think?" I asked.

"No, sir; not to say enemies. He was called hard because he would have a day's work for a day's wage, but no one that ever I heard of had a grudge against him. Except Miss Gostock and Mr. Waite, he agreed well with all the people about. He did not like Miss Gostock, and Mr. Waite was always borrowing money from him. Now Mr. Hascot did not mind giving, but he could not bear lending."

I returned to Nut Bush Farm perfectly satisfied that Mr. Hascot had been as the girl expressed the matter—"made away with." On the threshold of my house I was met with a catalogue of disasters. The female servants had gone in a body; the male professed a dislike to be in the stable-yard in the twilight. Rumour had decided that Nut Bush Farm was an unlucky place even to pass. The cattle were out of condition because the men would not go down the Beech Walk, or turn a single sheep into the Long Field. Reapers wanted higher wages. The labourers were looking out for other service.

"Poor fellow! this is a nice state of things for you to come home to," said Lolly, compassionately. "Even the poachers won't venture into the wood, and the boys don't go nutting."

"I will clear away the nut trees, and cut down the wood," I declared, savagely.

"I don't know who you are going to get to cut them," answered Lolly, "unless you bring men down from London."

As for Miss Gostock, she only laughed at my dilemma, and said, "You're a pretty fellow to be frightened by a ghost. If he was seen at Chalmont I'd ghost him."

While I was in a state of the most cruel perplexity, I bethought me of my promise to Mrs. Waite, and walked over one day to tell her the result of my enquiries.

I found her at home, and Mr. Waite, for a wonder, in the drawing-room. He was not a bad-looking fellow, and welcomed my visit with a heartiness which ill accorded with the dis-courtesy he had shown in never calling upon me.

Very succinctly I told what I had done, and where I had been. I mentioned the terms in which Sally Powner spoke of her benefactor. We discussed the whole matter fully—the *pros* and *cons* of any one knowing Mr. Hascot had such a sum of money on his person, and the possibility of his having been murdered. I mentioned what I had done about Mrs. Hascot, and begged Mr. Waite to afford me his help and co-operation in raising such a sum of money as might start the poor lady in some business.

"I'll do all that lies in my power," he said. heartily, shaking hands at the same time, for I had risen to go.

"And for my part," I remarked, "it seems to me there are only two things more I can do to elucidate the mystery, and those are—root every nut-tree out of the dell and set the axe to work in the wood."

There was a second's silence. Then Mrs. Waite dropped to the floor as if she had been shot.

As he stooped over her, he and I exchanged glances, and then *I knew*. Mr. Hascot *had* been murdered, and Mr. Waite was the murderer!

That night I was smoking and Lolly at needlework. The parlour windows were wide open, for it was warm, and not a breath of air seemed stirring.

There was a stillness on everything which betokened a coming thunderstorm; and we both were silent, for my mind was busy and Lolly's heart anxious. She did not see, as she said, how I was to get on at all, and for my part I could not tell what I ought to do.

All at once something whizzed through the window furthest from where we sat, and fell noisily to the floor.

"What is that?" Lolly cried, springing to her feet. "Oh, Jack what is it?"

Surprised and shaken, myself, I closed the windows and drew down the blinds before I examined the cause of our alarm. It proved to be an oblong package weighted with a stone. Unfastening it cautiously, for I did not know whether it might not contain some explosive, I came at length to a pocket book—opening the pocket book I found it stuffed full of bank notes.

"What are they? Where can they have come from?" exclaimed Lolly.

"They are the notes Mr. Hascot drew from Whittleby bank the day he disappeared," I answered with a sort of inspiration, but I took no notice of Lolly's last question.

For good or for evil that was a secret which lay between myself and the Waites, and which I have never revealed till now.

If the vessel in which they sailed for New Zealand had not gone to the bottom I should have kept the secret still.

When they were out of the country and the autumn well advanced, I had the wood thoroughly examined, and there in a gully, covered with a mass of leaves and twigs and dead branches, we found Mr. Hascot's body. His watch was in his waistcoat pocket—his ring on his finger; save for these possessions no one could have identified him.

His wife married again about a year afterwards and my brother took Nut Bush Farm off my hands. He says the place never was haunted—that I never saw Mr. Hascot except in my own imagination—that the whole thing originated in a poor state of health and a too credulous disposition!

I leave the reader to judge between us.

Sarah Orne Jewett (1849–1909) is too often remembered as merely an American writer of literary regionalism, whose stories center almost exclusively on the coast of Maine. She visited Boston frequently, where she met many literary figures of the day. Despite her Episcopalian practices, she took up the study of the philosophy of Emanuel Swedenborg, and much of her work stressed individual responsibility. Supernatural themes pervade many of her tales, often more implicit than explicit. The following story first appeared in her 1886 collection *A White Heron and Other Stories*. It is a prime example of that controlled ambiguity, in which the reader can only wonder about the true identity of the eponymous figure. Jewett regarded this as one of her "Tolstoyan" tales—perhaps because of its consideration of death—but it also shares many traits with the fine supernatural tales of Nathaniel Hawthorne.

The Gray Man

by Sarah Orne Jewett

High on the southern slope of Agamenticus* there may still be seen the remnant of an old farm. Frost-shaken stone walls surround a fast-narrowing expanse of smooth turf which the forest is overgrowing on every side. The cellar is nearly filled up, never having been either wide or deep, and the fruit of a few mossy apple-trees drops ungathered to the ground. Along one side of the forsaken garden is a thicket of seedling cherry-trees to which the shouting robins come year after year in busy flights; the caterpillars' nests are unassailed and populous in this untended hedge. At night, perhaps, when summer twilights are late in drawing their

* Mount Agamenticus is a 692-feet-tall isolated hill in the town of York, Maine.

brown curtain of dusk over the great rural scene,—at night an owl may sit in the hemlocks near by and hoot and shriek until the far echoes answer back again. As for the few men and women who pass this deserted spot, most will be repulsed by such loneliness, will even grow impatient with those mistaken fellow-beings who choose to live in solitude, away from neighbors and from schools,—yes, even from gossip and petty care of self or knowledge of the trivial fashions of a narrow life.

Now and then one looks out from this eyrie, across the wide-spread country, who turns to look at the sea or toward the shining foreheads of the mountains that guard the inland horizon, who will remember the place long afterward. A peaceful vision will come, full of rest and benediction into busy and troubled hours, to those who understand why some one came to live in this place so near the sky, so silent, so full of sweet air and woodland fragrance; so beaten and buffeted by winter storms and garlanded with summer greenery; where the birds are nearest neighbors and a clear spring the only wine-cellar, and trees of the forest a choir of singers who rejoice and sing aloud by day and night as the winds sweep over. Under the cherry thicket or at the edge of the woods you may find a strayaway blossom, some half-savage, slender grandchild of the old flower-plots, that you gather gladly to take away, and every year in June a red rose blooms toward which the wild pink roses and the pale sweet briars turn wondering faces as if a queen had shown her noble face suddenly at a peasant's festival.

There is everywhere a token of remembrance, of silence and secrecy. Some stronger nature once ruled these neglected trees and this fallow ground. They will wait the return of their master as long as roots can creep through mould, and the mould make way for them. The stories of strange lives have been whispered to the earth, their thoughts have burned themselves into the cold rocks. As one looks from the lower country toward the long slope of the great hillside, this old abiding-place marks the dark covering of trees like a scar. There is nothing to hide either the sunrise or the sunset. The low lands reach out of sight into the west and the sea fills all the east.

The first owner of the farm was a seafaring man who had through freak or fancy come ashore and cast himself upon the bounty of nature for support in his later years, though tradition keeps a suspicion of buried treasure and of a dark history. He cleared his land and built his house, but save the fact that he was a Scotsman no one knew to whom he belonged, and when he died the state inherited the unclaimed property. The only piece of woodland that was worth anything was sold and added to another farm, and the dwelling-place was left to the sunshine and the rain, to the birds that built their nests in the chimney or under the eaves. Sometimes a strolling company of country boys would find themselves near the house on a holiday afternoon, but the more dilapidated the small structure became, the more they believed that some uncanny existence possessed the lonely place, and the path that led toward the clearing at last became almost impassable.

Once a number of officers and men in the employ of the Coast Survey were encamped at the top of the mountain, and they smoothed the rough track that led down to the spring that bubbled from under a sheltering edge. One day a laughing fellow, not content with peering in at the small windows of the house, put his shoulder against the rain-blackened door and broke the simple fastening. He hardly knew that he was afraid as he first stood within the single spacious room, so complete a curiosity took possession of him. The place was clean and bare, the empty cupboard doors stood open, and yet the sound of his companions' voices outside seemed far away, and an awful sense that some unseen inhabitant followed his footsteps made him hurry out again pale and breathless to the fresh air and sunshine. Was this really a dwelling-place of spirits, as had been already hinted? The story grew more fearful, and spread quickly like a mist of terror among the lowland farms. For years the tale of the coast-surveyor's adventure in the haunted house was slowly magnified and told to strangers or to wide-eyed children by the dim firelight. The former owner was supposed to linger still about his old home, and was held accountable for deep offense in choosing for the scene of his unsuccessful husbandry a place that escaped the properties and restraints of life upon lower levels. His grave was concealed by the new growth of oaks and beeches, and many a lad and full-grown man beside has taken to his heels at the flicker of light from across a swamp or under a decaying tree in that neighborhood. As the world in some respects grew wiser, the good people near the mountain understood less and less the causes of these simple effects, and as they became familiar with the visible world, grew more shy of the unseen and more sensitive to unexplained foreboding.

One day a stranger was noticed in the town, as a stranger is sure to be who goes his way with quick, furtive steps straight through a small village or along a country road. This man was tall and had just passed middle age. He was well made and vigorous, but there was an unusual pallor in his face, a grayish look, as if he had been startled by bad news. His clothes were somewhat peculiar, as if they had been made in another country, yet they suited the chilly weather, being homespun of undyed wools, just the color of his hair, and only a little darker than his face or hands. Some one observed in one brief glance as he and this gray man met and passed each other, that his eyes had a strange faded look; they might, however, flash and be coal-black in a moment of rage. Two or three persons stepped forward to watch the wayfarer as he went along the road with long, even strides, like one taking a journey on foot, but he quickly reached a turn of the way and was out of sight. They wondered who he was; one recalled some recent advertisement of an escaped criminal, and another the appearance of a native of the town who was supposed to be long ago lost at sea, but one surmiser knew as little as the next. If they had followed fast enough they might have tracked the mysterious man straight across the country, threading the by-ways, the shorter paths that led across the fields where the road was roundabout and hindering. At last he disappeared in the leafless, trackless woods that skirted the mountain.

That night there was for the first time in many years a twinkling light in the window of the haunted house, high on the hill's great shoulder; one farmer's wife and another looked up curiously, while they wondered what daring human being had chosen that awesome spot of all others for his home or for even a transient shelter. The sky was already heavy with snow; he might be a fugitive from justice, and the startled people looked to the fastening of their doors unwontedly that night, and waked often from a troubled sleep.

An instinctive curiosity and alarm possessed the country men and women for a while, but soon faded out and disappeared. The newcomer was by no means a hermit; he tried to be friendly, and inclined toward a certain kindliness and familiarity. He bought a comfortable store of winter provisions from his new acquaintances, giving every one his price, and spoke more at length, as time went on, of current events, of politics and the weather, and the town's own news and concerns. There was a sober cheerfulness about the man, as if he had known trouble and perplexity, and was fulfilling some mission that gave him pain; yet he saw some gain and reward beyond; therefore he could be contented with his life and such strange surroundings. He was more and more eager to form brotherly relations with the farmers near his home. There was almost a pleading look in his kind face at times, as if he feared the later prejudice of his associates. Surely this was no common or uneducated person, for in every way he left the stamp of his character and influence upon men and things. His reasonable words of advice and warning are current as sterling coins in that region yet; to one man he taught a new rotation of crops, to another he gave some priceless cures for devastating diseases of cattle. The lonely women of those remote country homes learned of him how to achieve their household toil with less labor and drudgery, and here and there he singled out promising children and kept watch of their growth, giving freely a most affectionate companionship, and a fair start in the journey of life. He taught those who were guardians of such children to recognize and further the true directions and purposes of existence; and the easily warped natures grew strong and well-established under his thoughtful care. No wonder that some people were filled with amazement, and thought his wisdom supernatural, from so many proofs that his horizon was wider than their own.

Perhaps some envious soul, or one aggrieved by being caught in treachery or deception, was the first to find fault with the stranger. The prejudice against his dwelling-place, and the superstition which had become linked to him in consequence, may have led back to the first suspicious attitude of the community. The whisper of distrust soon started on an evil way. If he were not a criminal, his past was surely a hidden one, and shocking to his remembrance, but the true foundation of all dislike was the fact that the gray man who went to and fro, living his simple, harmless life among them, never was seen to smile. Persons who remember him speak of this with a shudder, for nothing is more evident than that his peculiarity became at length intolerable to those whose minds lent themselves readily to suspicion. At first, blinded by the gentle good fellowship of the stranger, the changeless expression of his face was scarcely observed, but as the winter wore away he was watched with renewed disbelief and dismay.

After the first few attempts at gayety nobody tried to tell a merry story in his presence. The most conspicuous of a joker's audience does a deep-rankling injustice if he sits with unconscious, unamused face at the receipt of raillery. What a chilling moment when the gray man softly opened the door of a farmhouse kitchen, and seated himself like a skeleton at the feast of walnuts and roasted apples beside the glowing fire! The children whom he treated so lovingly, to whom he ever gave his best, though they were won at first by his gentleness, when they began to prattle and play with him would raise their innocent eyes to his face and hush their voices and creep away out of his sight. Once only he was bidden to a wedding, but never afterward, for a gloom was quickly spread through the boisterous company; the man who never smiled had no place at such a festival. The wedding guests looked over their shoulders again and again in strange foreboding, while he was in the house, and were burdened with a sense of coming woe for the newly-married pair. As one caught sight of his, among the faces of the rural folk, the gray man was like a sombre mask, and at last the bridegroom flung open the door with a meaning gesture, and the stranger went out like a hunted creature, into the bitter coldness and silence of the winter night.

Through the long days of the next summer the outcast of the wedding, forbidden, at length, all the once-proffered hospitality, was hardly seen from one week's end to another's. He cultivated his poor estate with patient care, and the successive crops of his small garden, the fruits and berries of the wilderness, were food enough. He seemed unchangeable, and was always ready when he even guessed at a chance to be of use. If he were repulsed, he only turned away and went back to his solitary home. Those persons who by chance visited him there tell wonderful tales of the wild birds which had been tamed to come at his call and cluster about him, of the orderliness and delicacy of his simple life. The once-neglected house was covered with vines that he had brought from the woods, and planted about the splintering, decaying walls. There were three or four books in worn bindings on a shelf above the fire-place; one longs to know what volumes this mysterious exile had chosen to keep him company!

There may have been a deeper reason for the withdrawal of friendliness; there are vague rumors of the gray man's possession of strange powers.

Some say that he was gifted with amazing strength, and once when some belated hunters found shelter at his fireside, they told eager listeners afterward that he did not sleep but sat by the fire reading gravely while they slumbered uneasily on his own bed of boughs. And in the dead of night an empty chair glided silently toward him across the floor as he softly turned his pages in the flickering light.

But such stories are too vague, and in that neighborhood too common to weigh against the true dignity and bravery of the man. At the beginning of the war of the rebellion he seemed strangely troubled and disturbed, and presently disappeared, leaving his house key with a neighbor as if for a few days' absence. He was last seen striding rapidly through the village a few miles away, going back along the road by which he had come a year or two before. No, not last seen either; for in one of the first battles of the war, as the smoke suddenly lifted, a farmer's boy, reared in the shadow of the mountain, opened his languid pain-dulled eyes as he lay among the wounded, and saw the gray man riding by on a tall horse. At that moment the poor lad thought in his faintness and fear that Death himself rode by in the gray man's likeness; unsmiling Death who tries to teach and serve mankind so that he may at the last win welcome as a faithful friend!

Olive Schreiner (1855–1920) was a South African writer, best remembered for her novel *The Story of An African Farm* (1883). Though she stayed seven years in England, most of her life was spent in South Africa, where she became involved in the politics and issues of the day. She was friends with Cecil Rhodes but became disillusioned by his positions and satirized his actions in a novel *Trooper Peter Halket of Mashonaland.* Most of her writings were about her social concerns, including racism and labor, especially the treatment of women. The following is a dream-like tale about true love that first appeared in her 1890 collection appropriately entitled *Dreams.*

In a Far-Off World

by Olive Schreiner

There is a world in one of the far-off stars, and things do not happen here as they happen there.

In that world were a man and woman; they had one work, and they walked together side by side on many days, and were friends—and that is a thing that happens now and then in this world also.

But there was something in that star-world that there is not here. There was a thick wood: where the trees grew closest, and the stems were interlocked, and the summer sun never shone, there stood a shrine. In the day all was quiet, but at night, when the stars shone or the moon glinted on the tree-tops, and all was quiet below, if one crept here quite alone and knelt on the steps of the stone altar, and uncovering one's breast, so wounded it that the blood fell down on the altar steps, then whatever he who knelt there wished for was granted him. And all this happens, as I said, because it is a far-off world, and things often happen there as they do not happen here.

Now, the man and woman walked together; and the woman wished well to the man. One night when the moon was shining so that the leaves of all the trees glinted, and the waves of the sea were silvery, the woman walked alone to the forest. It was dark there; the moonlight fell only in little flecks on the dead leaves under her feet, and the branches were knotted tight overhead. Farther in it got darker, not even a fleck of moonlight shone. Then she came to the shrine; she knelt down before it and prayed; there came no answer. Then she uncovered her breast; with a sharp two-edged stone that lay there she wounded it. The drops dripped slowly down on to the stone, and a voice cried, "What do you seek?"

She answered, "There is a man; I hold him nearer than anything. I would give him the best of all blessings."

The voice said, "What is it?"

The girl said, "I know not, but that which is most good for him I wish him to have."

The voice said, "Your prayer is answered; he shall have it."

Then she stood up. She covered her breast and held the garment tight upon it with her hand, and ran out of the forest, and the dead leaves fluttered under her feet. Out in the moonlight the soft air was blowing, and the sand glittered on the beach. She ran along the smooth shore, then suddenly she stood still. Out across the water there was something moving. She shaded her eyes and looked. It was a boat; it was sliding swiftly over the moonlit water out to sea. One stood upright in it; the face the moonlight did not show, but the figure she knew. It was passing swiftly; it seemed as if no one propelled it; the moonlight's shimmer did not let her see clearly, and the boat was far from shore, but it seemed almost as if there was another figure sitting in the stern. Faster and faster it glided over the water away, away. She ran along the shore; she came no nearer it. The garment she had held closed fluttered open; she stretched out her arms, and the moonlight shone on her long loose hair.

Then a voice beside her whispered, "What is it?"

She cried, "With my blood I bought the best of all gifts for him. I have come to bring it him! He is going from me!"

The voice whispered softly, "Your prayer was answered. It has been given him."

She cried, “What is it?”
The voice answered, “It is that he might leave you.”
The girl stood still.
Far out at sea the boat was lost to sight beyond the moonlight sheen.
The voice spoke softly, “Art thou contented?”
She said, “I am contented.”
At her feet the waves broke in long ripples softly on the shore.

Charlotte Perkins Gilman (1860–1935) was born in Hartford, Connecticut, but grew up mainly in Providence, Rhode Island. Her father abandoned her mother and brother when she was young, and they grew up in poverty. Charlotte's aunts, who helped the family, included the novelist Harriet Beecher Stowe. As an adult, she held a variety of jobs and had relationships with both men and women. She was also devoted to a number of social causes, especially women's rights. In fact, her 1892 short story "The Yellow Wall-paper" and the 1915 novel *Herland* are often cited as early classics of feminist fiction. This story first appeared in *New England Magazine*, one year before they published "The Yellow Wall-paper."

The Giant Wistaria*

by Charlotte Perkins Gilman

"Meddle not with my new vine, child! See! Thou hast already broken the tender shoot! Never needle or distaff for thee, and yet thou wilt not be quiet!"

The nervous fingers wavered, clutched at a small carnelian cross that hung from her neck, then fell despairingly.

"Give me my child, mother, and then I will be quiet!"

"Hush! hush! thou fool—some one might be near! See—there is thy father coming, even now! Get in quickly!"

She raised her eyes to her mother's face, weary eyes that yet had a flickering, uncertain blaze in their shaded depths.

* "Wistaria" is an alternate spelling of "wisteria," a flowering vine common to the eastern United States.

"Art though a mother and hast no pity on me, a mother? Give me my child!"

Her voice rose in a strange, low cry, broken by her father's hand upon her mouth.

"Shameless!" said he, with set teeth. "Get to thy chamber, and be not seen again to-night, or I will have thee bound!"

She went at that, and a hard-faced serving woman followed, and presently returned, bringing a key to her mistress.

"Is all well with her,—and the child also?"

"She is quiet, Mistress Dwining, well for the night, be sure. The child fretteth endlessly, but save for that it thriveth with me."

The parents were left alone together on the high square porch with its great pillars, and the rising moon began to make faint shadows of the young vine leaves that shot up luxuriantly around them; moving shadows, like little stretching fingers, on the broad and heavy planks of the oaken floor.

"It groweth well, this vine thou broughtest me in the ship, my husband."

"Aye," he broke in bitterly, "and so doth the shame I brought thee! Had I known of it I would sooner have had the ship founder beneath us, and have seen our child cleanly drowned, than live to this end!"

"Thou art very hard, Samuel, art thou not afeard for her life? She grieveth sore for the child, aye, and for the green fields to walk in!"

"Nay," said he grimly, "I fear not. She hath lost already what is more than life; and she shall have air enough soon. To-morrow the ship is ready, and we return to England. None knoweth of our stain here, not one, and if the town hath a child unaccounted for to rear in decent ways—why, it is not the first, even here. It will be well enough cared for! And truly we have matter for thankfulness, that her cousin is yet willing to marry her."

"Hast thou told him?"

"Aye!Thinkest thou I would cast shame into another man's house, unknowing it? He hath always desired her, but she would none of him, the stubborn! She hath small choice now!"

"Will he be kind, Samuel? can he—"

"Kind? What call'st thou it to take such as she to wife? Kind! How many men would take her, an' she had double the fortune? and being of the family already, he is glad to hide the blot forever."

"An' if she would not? He is but a coarse fellow, and she ever shunned him."

"Art thou mad, woman? She weddeth him ere we sail to-morrow, or she stayeth ever in that chamber. The girl is not so sheer a fool! He maketh an honest woman of her, and saveth our house from open shame. What other hope for her than a new life to cover the old? Let her have an honest child, an' she so longeth for one!"

He strode heavily across the porch, till the loose planks creaked again, strode back and forth, with his arms folded and his brows fiercely knit above his iron mouth.

Overhead the shadows flickered mockingly across a white face among the leaves, with eyes of wasted fire.

"O, George, what a house! what a lovely house! I am sure it's haunted! Let us get that house to live in this summer! We will have Kate and Jack and Susy and Jim of course, and a splendid time of it!"

Young husbands are indulgent, but still they have to recognize facts.

"My dear, the house may not be to rent; and it may also not be habitable."

"There is surely somebody in it. I am going to inquire!"

The great central gate was rusted off its hinges, and the long drive had trees in it, but a little footpath showed signs of steady usage, and up that Mrs. Jenny went, followed by her obedient George. The front windows of the old mansion were blank, but in a wing at the back they found white curtains and open doors. Outside, in the clear May sunshine, a woman was washing. She was polite and friendly, and evidently glad of visitors in that lonely place. She "guessed it could be rented—didn't know." The heirs were in Europe, but "there was a lawyer in New York had the lettin' of it." There had been folks there years ago, but not in her time. She and her husband had the rent of their part for taking care of the place. "Not that they took much care on't either, but keepin' robbers out." It was furnished throughout, old-fashioned enough, but good; and if they took it she could do the work for 'em herself, she guessed—"if *he* was willin'!"

Never was a crazy scheme more easily arranged. George knew that lawyer in New York; the rent was not alarming; and the nearness to a rising sea-shore resort made it a still pleasanter place to spend the summer.

Kate and Jack and Susy and Jim cheerfully accepted, and the June moon found them all sitting on the high front porch.

They had explored the house from top to bottom, from the great room in the garret, with nothing in it but a rickety cradle, to the well in the cellar without a curb and with a rusty chain going down to unknown blackness below. They had explored the grounds, once beautiful with rare trees and shrubs, but now a gloomy wilderness of tangled shade.

The old lilacs and laburnums, the spirea and syringe,* nodded against the second-story windows. What garden plants survived were great ragged bushes or great shapeless beds. A huge wistaria vine covered the whole front of the house. The trunk, it was too large to call a stem, rose at the corner of the porch by the high steps, and had once climbed its pillars; but now the pillars were wrenched from their places and held rigid and helpless by the tightly wound and knotted arms.

It fenced in all the upper story of the porch with a knitted wall of stem and leaf; it ran along the eaves, holding up the gutter that had once supported it; it shaded every window with heavy green; and the drooping, fragrant blossoms made a waving sheet of purple from roof to ground.

"Did you ever see such a wistaria!" cried ecstatic Mrs. Jenny. "It is worth the rent just to sit under such a vine,—a fig tree beside it would be sheer superfluity and wicked extravagance!"

"Jenny makes much of her wistaria," said George, "because she's so disappointed about the ghosts. She made up her mind at first sight to have ghosts in the house, and she can't find even a ghost story!"

"No," Jenny assented mournfully; "I pumped poor Mrs. Pepperill for three days, but could get nothing out of her. But I'm convinced there is a story, if we could only find it. You need not tell me that a house like this, with a garden like this, and a cellar like this, isn't haunted!"

"I agree with you," said Jack. Jack was a reporter on a New York daily, and engaged to Mrs. Jenny's pretty sister. "And if we don't find a real ghost, you may be very sure I shall make one. It's too good an opportunity to lose!"

The pretty sister, who sat next him, resented. "You shan't do anything of the sort, Jack! This is a *real* ghostly place, and I won't have you make

* Spirea is a climbing, flowering bush; *Syringa vulgaris*, or common lilac, is a small tree.

fun of it! Look at that group of trees out there in the long grass—it looks for all the world like a crouching, hunted figure!"

"It looks to me like a woman picking huckleberries," said Jim, who was married to George's pretty sister.

"Be still, Jim!" said that fair young woman. "I believe in Jenny's ghost as much as she does. Such a place! Just look at this great wistaria trunk crawling up by the steps here! It looks for all the world like a writhing body—cringing—beseeching!"

"Yes," answered the subdued Jim, "it does, Susy. See its waist,—about two yards of it, and twisted at that! A waste of good material!"

"Don't be so horrid, boys! Go off and smoke somewhere if you can't be congenial!"

"We can! We will! We'll be as ghostly as you please." And forthwith they began to see bloodstains and crouching figures so plentifully that the most delightful shivers multiplied, and the fair enthusiasts started for bed, declaring they should never sleep a wink.

"We shall all surely dream," cried Mrs. Jenny, "and we must all tell our dreams in the morning!"

"There's another thing certain," said George, catching Susy as she tripped over a loose plank; "and that is that you frisky creatures must use the side door till I get this Eiffel tower of a portico fixed, or we shall have some fresh ghosts on our hands! We found a plank here that yawns like a trap-door—big enough to swallow you,—and I believe the bottom of the thing is in China!"

The next morning found them all alive, and eating a substantial New England breakfast, to the accompaniment of saws and hammers on the porch, where carpenters of quite miraculous promptness were tearing things to pieces generally.

"It's got to come down mostly," they had said. "These timbers are clean rotted through, what ain't pulled out o' line by this great creeper. That's about all that holds the thing up."

There was clear reason in what they said, and with a caution from anxious Mrs. Jenny not to hurt the wistaria, they were left to demolish and repair at leisure.

"How about ghosts?" asked Jack after a fourth griddle cake. "I had one, and it's taken away my appetite!"

Mrs. Jenny gave a little shriek and dropped her knife and fork.

"Oh, so had I! I had the most awful—well, not dream exactly, but feeling. I had forgotten all about it!"

"Must have been awful," said Jack, taking another cake. "Do tell us about the feeling. My ghost will wait."

"It makes me creep to think of it even now," she said. "I woke up, all at once, with that dreadful feeling as if something were going to happen, you know! I was wide awake, and hearing every little sound for miles around, it seemed to me. There are so many strange little noises in the country for all it is so still. Millions of crickets and things outside, and all kinds of rustles in the trees! There wasn't much wind, and the moonlight came through in my three great windows in three white squares on the black old floor, and those fingery wistaria leaves we were talking of last night just seemed to crawl all over them. And—O, girls, you know that dreadful well in the cellar?"

A most gratifying impression was made by this, and Jenny proceeded cheerfully:

"Well, while it was so horridly still, and I lay there trying not to wake George, I heard as plainly as if it were right in the room, that old chain down there rattle and creak over the stones!"

"Bravo!" cried Jack. "That's fine! I'll put it in the Sunday edition!"

"Be still!" said Kate. "What was it, Jenny? Did you really see anything?"

"No, I didn't, I'm sorry to say. But just then I didn't want to. I woke George, and made such a fuss that he gave me bromide,* and said he'd go and look, and that's the last I thought of it till Jack reminded me,—the bromide worked so well."

"Now, Jack, give us yours," said Jim. "Maybe, it will dovetail in somehow. Thirsty ghost, I imagine; maybe they had prohibition here even then!"

Jack folded his napkin, and leaned back in his most impressive manner.

"It was striking twelve by the great hall clock—" he began.

---

* A sedative. Bromide compounds were later withdrawn from the market because of high toxicity.

"There isn't any hall clock!"

"O hush, Jim, you spoil the current! It was one o'clock then, by my old-fashioned repeater."*

"Waterbury![†] Never mind what time it was!"

"Well, honestly, I woke up sharp, like our beloved hostess, and tried to go to sleep again, but couldn't. I experienced all those moonlight and grasshopper sensations, just like Jenny, and was wondering what could have been the matter with the supper, when in came my ghost, and I knew it was all a dream! It was a female ghost, and I imagine she was young and handsome, but all those crouching, hunted figures of last evening ran riot in my brain, and this poor creature looked just like them. She was all wrapped up in a shawl, and had a big bundle under her arm,—dear me, I am spoiling the story! With the air and gait of one in frantic haste and terror, the muffled figure glided to a dark old bureau, and seemed taking things from the drawers. As she turned, the moonlight shone full on a little red cross that hung from her neck by a thin gold chain—I saw it glitter as she crept noiselessly from the room! That's all."

"O Jack, don't be so horrid! Did you really? Is that all? What do you think it was?"

"I am not horrid by nature, only professionally. I really did. That was all. And I am fully convinced it was the genuine, legitimate ghost of an eloping chambermaid with kleptomania!"

"You are too bad, Jack!" cried Jenny. "You take all the horror out of it. There isn't a 'creep' left among us."

"It's no time for creeps at nine-thirty A.M., with sunlight and carpenters outside! However, if you can't wait till twilight for your creeps, I think I can furnish one or two," said George. "I went down cellar after Jenny's ghost!"

There was a delighted chorus of female voices, and Jenny cast upon her lord a glance of genuine gratitude.

"It's all very well to lie in bed and see ghosts, or hear them," he went on. "But the young householder suspecteth burglars, even though as a medical

---

* A watch or clock that chimes at specific intervals.

† A company that produced cheap watches and eventually became the Timex Group.

man he knoweth nerves, and after Jenny dropped off I started on a voyage of discovery. I never will again, I promise you!"

"Why, what *was* it?"

"Oh, George!"

"I got a candle—"

"Good mark for the burglars," murmured Jack.

"And went all over the house, gradually working down to the cellar and the well."

"Well?" said Jack.

"Now you can laugh; but that cellar is no joke by daylight, and a candle there at night is about as inspiring as a lightning-bug in the Mammoth Cave. I went along with the light, trying not to fall into the well prematurely; got to it all at once; held the light down and *then* I saw, right under my feet—(I nearly fell over her, or walked through her, perhaps),—a woman, hunched up under a shawl! She had hold of the chain, and the candle shone on her hands—white, thin hands,—on a little red cross that hung from her neck—*vide* Jack! I'm no believer in ghosts, and I firmly object to unknown parties in the house at night; so I spoke to her rather fiercely. She didn't seem to notice that, and I reached down to take hold of her,—then I came upstairs!"

"What for?"

"What happened?"

"What was the matter?"

"Well, nothing happened. Only she wasn't there! May have been indigestion, of course, but as a physician I don't advise any one to court indigestion alone at midnight in a cellar!"

"This is the most interesting and peripatetic and evasive ghost I ever heard of!" said Jack. "It's my belief she has no end of silver tankards, and jewels galore, at the bottom of that well, and I move we go and see!"

"To the bottom of the well, Jack?"

"To the bottom of the mystery. Come on!"

There was unanimous assent, and the fresh cambrics* and pretty boots were gallantly escorted below by gentlemen whose jokes were so frequent that many of them were a little forced.

---

* A lightweight linen garment.

The deep old cellar was so dark that they had to bring lights, and the well so gloomy in its blackness that the ladies recoiled.

"That well is enough to scare even a ghost. It's my opinion you'd better let well enough alone?" quoth Jim.

"Truth lies hid in a well, and we must get her out," said George. "Bear a hand with the chain?"

Jim pulled away on the chain, George turned the creaking windlass, and Jack was chorus.

"A wet sheet for this ghost, if not a flowing sea," said he. "Seems to be hard work raising spirits! I suppose he kicked the bucket when he went down!"

As the chain lightened and shortened there grew a strained silence along them; and when at length the bucket appeared, rising slowly through the dark water, there was an eager, half reluctant peering, and a natural drawing back. They poked the gloomy contents. "Only water."

"Nothing but mud."

"Something—"

They emptied the bucket up on the dark earth, and then the girls all went out into the air, into the bright warm sunshine in front of the house, where was the sound of saw and hammer, and the smell of new wood. There was nothing said until the men joined them, and then Jenny timidly asked:

"How old should you think it was, George?"

"All of a century," he answered. "That water is a preservative,—lime in it. Oh!—you mean?—Not more than a month; a very little baby!"

There was another silence at this, broken by a cry from the workmen. They had removed the floor and the side walls of the old porch, so that the sunshine poured down to the dark stones of the cellar bottom. And there, in the strangling grasp of the roots of the great wistaria, lay the bones of a woman, from whose neck still hung a tiny scarlet cross on a thin chain of gold.

British writer **Marie Corelli** (1855–1924) was the most popular author of her day, outselling contemporaries like Rudyard Kipling and Arthur Conan Doyle. Although she was never a critical darling, her admirers included Oscar Wilde; her books were so popular with readers that she even appeared on postcards. Her first novel, *A Romance of Two Worlds* (1886) was an instant success, establishing her as a writer who was interested in occult themes. Corelli lived for 40 years with a female companion, Bertha Vyver, to whom she dedicated several books. This romantic and eerie tale first appeared in her collection *Cameos* (1896).

The Lady with the Carnations

by Marie Corelli

It was in the Louvre that I first saw her—or rather her picture. Greuze* painted her—so I was told; but the name of the artist scarcely affected me—I was absorbed in the woman herself, who looked at me from the dumb canvas with that still smile on her face, and that burning cluster of carnations clasped to her breast. I felt that I knew her. Moreover, there was a strange attraction in her eyes that held mine fascinated. It was as though she said "Stay till I have told thee all!" A faint blush tinged her cheek—one loose tress of fair hair fell caressingly on her half-uncovered bosom. And, surely, was I dreaming?—or did I smell the odour of carnations on the air? I started from my reverie—a slight tremor shook my nerves. I turned to go. An artist carrying a large easel and painting materials just then approached,

* Jean-Baptiste Greuze was an 18th-century French painter who specialized in vivid portraits and domestic scenes. His work is on display in the Louvre.

and placing himself opposite the picture, began to copy it. I watched him at work for a few moments—his strokes were firm, and his eye accurate; but I knew, without waiting to observe his further progress, that there was an indefinable something in that pictured face that he with all his skill would never be able to delineate as Greuze had done—if Greuze indeed were the painter, of which I did not then, and do not now, feel sure. I walked slowly away. On the threshold of the room I looked back. Yes! there it was—that fleeting, strange, appealing expression that seemed mutely to call to *me*; that half-wild yet sweet smile that had a world of unuttered pathos in it. A kind of misgiving troubled me—a presentiment of evil that I could not understand—and, vexed with myself for my own foolish imaginings, I hastened down the broad staircase that led from the picture-galleries, and began to make my way out through that noble hall of ancient sculpture in which stands the defiantly beautiful *Apollo Belvedere*[*] and the world-famous *Artemis*.[†] The sun shone brilliantly; numbers of people were passing and repassing. Suddenly my heart gave a violent throb, and I stopped short in my walk, amazed and incredulous. Who was that seated on the bench close to the *Artemis*, reading? Who, if not "the Lady with the Carnations," clad in white, her head slightly bent, and her hand clasping a bunch of her own symbolic flowers! Nervously I approached her. As my steps echoed on the marble pavement she looked up; her grey-green eyes met mine in that slow wistful smile that was so indescribably sad. Confused as my thoughts were, I observed her pallor, and the ethereal delicacy of her face and form—she had no hat on, and her neck and shoulders were uncovered. Struck by this peculiarity, I wondered if the other people who were passing through the hall noticed her *dèshabille*. I looked around me enquiringly—not one passer-by turned a glance in our direction! Yet surely the lady's costume was strange enough to attract attention? A chill of horror quivered through me—was *I* the only one who saw her sitting there? This idea was so alarming that I uttered an involuntary exclamation; the next moment the seat before me

* The Apollo Belvedere is one of the great sculptures of classical antiquity, dating back to about the first century A.D. It has, however, never been displayed in the Louvre, so Corelli may have confused it with several other classical Apollo pieces at the museum.

† This probably refers to the famous statue of Artemis popularly called "Diana of Versailles," which was first displayed in the Louvre in 1602.

was empty, the strange lady had gone, and nothing remained of her but—the strong sweet odour of the carnations she had carried! With a sort of sickness at my heart I hurried out of the Louvre, and was glad when I found myself in the bright Paris streets filled with eager, pressing people, all bent on their different errands of business or pleasure. I entered a carriage and was driven rapidly to the Grand Hotel,* where I was staying with a party of friends. I refrained from speaking of the curious sensations that had overcome me—I did not even mention the picture that had exercised so weird an influence upon me. The brilliancy of the life we led, the constant change and activity of our movements, soon dispersed the nervous emotion I had undergone; and though sometimes the remembrance of it returned to me, I avoided dwelling on the subject. Ten or twelve days passed, and one night we all went to the Théâtre Français†—it was the first evening of my life that I ever was in the strange position of being witness to a play without either knowing its name or understanding its meaning. I could only realise one thing—namely, that "the Lady with the Carnations" sat in the box opposite to me, regarding me fixedly. She was alone; her costume was unchanged. I addressed one of our party in a low voice—

"Do you see that girl opposite, in white, with the shaded crimson carnations in her dress?"

My friend looked, shook her head, and rejoined—

"No; where is she sitting?"

"Right opposite!" I repeated in a more excited tone. "Surely you can see her! She is alone in that large box *en face*."

My friend turned to me in wonder. "You must be dreaming, my dear! That large box is perfectly empty!"

Empty—I knew better! But I endeavoured to smile; I said I had made a mistake—that the lady I spoke of had moved—and so changed the subject. But throughout the evening, though I feigned to watch the stage, my eyes were continually turning to the place where SHE sat so quietly, with her steadfast, mournful gaze fixed upon me. One addition to her costume she

* Le Grand Hotel was built in 1862 and is a short distance from the Louvre.

† Founded in 1680, the Théâtre Français is in Paris, situated between the Arc de Triomphe and the Louvre.

had—a fan—which from the distance at which I beheld it seemed to be made of very old yellow lace, mounted on sticks of filigree silver. She used this occasionally, waving it slowly to and fro in a sort of dreamy, meditative fashion; and ever and again she smiled that pained, patient smile which, though it hinted much, betrayed nothing. When we rose to leave the theatre "the Lady with the Carnations" rose also, and drawing a lace wrap about her head, she disappeared. Afterwards I saw her gliding through one of the outer lobbies; she looked so slight and frail and childlike, alone in the pushing, brilliant crowd, that my heart went out to her in a sort of fantastic tenderness. "Whether she be a disembodied spirit," I mused, "or an illusion called up by some disorder of my own imagination, I do not know; but she seems so sad, that even were she a dream, I pity her!"

This thought passed through my brain as in company with my friends I reached the outer door of the theatre. A touch on my arm startled me—a little white hand clasping a cluster of carnations rested there for a second—then vanished. I was somewhat overcome by this new experience; but my sensations this time were not those of fear. I became certain that this haunting image followed me for some reason; and I determined not to give way to any foolish terror concerning it, but to calmly await the course of events, that would in time, I felt convinced, explain everything. I stayed a fortnight longer in Paris without seeing anything more of "the Lady with the Carnations," except photographs of her picture in the Louvre, one of which I bought—though it gave but a feeble idea of the original masterpiece—and then I left for Brittany. Some English friends of mine, Mr. and Mrs. Fairleigh, had taken up their abode in a quaint old rambling chateau near Quimperlé* on the coast of Finisterre, and they had pressed me cordially to stay with them for a fortnight—an invitation which I gladly accepted. The house was built on a lofty rock overlooking the sea; the surrounding coast was eminently wild and picturesque; and on the day I arrived, there was a boisterous wind which lifted high the crests of the billows and dashed them against the jutting crags with grand and terrific uproar. Mrs. Fairleigh, a bright, practical woman, whose life was entirely

* Quimperlé is an ancient town built at the confluence of two rivers near the coast of the Brittany region in the northwestern part of France.

absorbed in household management, welcomed me with effusion—she and her two handsome boys, Rupert and Frank, were full of enthusiasm for the glories and advantages of their holiday resort.

"Such a beach!" cried Rupert, executing a sort of Indian war-dance beside me on the path.

"And such jolly walks and drives!" chorussed his brother.

"Yes, really!" warbled my hostess in her clear gay voice, "I'm delighted we came here. And the chateau is such a funny old place, full of odd nooks and corners. The country people, you know, are dreadfully superstitious, and they say it is haunted; but of course that's all nonsense! Though if there *were* a ghost, we should send you to interrogate it, my dear!"

This with a smile of good-natured irony at me. I laughed. Mrs. Fairleigh was one of those eminently sensible persons who had seriously lectured me on a book known as "A Romance of Two Worlds,"* as inculcating spiritualistic theories, and therefore deserving condemnation.

I turned the subject.

"How long have you been here?" I asked.

"Three weeks—and we haven't explored half the neighbourhood yet. There are parts of the house itself we don't know. Once upon a time—so the villagers say—a great painter lived here. Well, his studio runs the whole length of the chateau, and that and some other rooms are locked up. It seems they are never let to strangers. Not that we want them—the place is too big for us as it is,"

"What was the painter's name?" I enquired, pausing as I ascended the terrace to admire the grand sweep of the sea.

"Oh, I forget! His pictures were so like those of Greuze that few can tell the difference between them—and—"

I interrupted her. "Tell me," I said, with a faint smile, "have you any carnations growing here?"

"Carnations! I should think so! The place is full of them. Isn't the odour delicious?" And as we reached the highest terrace in front of the chateau I saw that the garden was ablaze with these brilliant scented blossoms, of

* An in-joke on the part of the author, since *A Romance of Two Worlds* was the title of her first novel.

every shade, varying from the palest salmon pink to the deepest, darkest scarlet. This time that subtle fragrance was not my fancy, and I gathered a few of the flowers to wear in my dress at dinner. Mr. Fairleigh now came out to receive us, and the conversation became general.

I was delighted with the interior of the house; it was so quaint, and old, and suggestive. There was a dark oaken staircase, with a most curiously carved and twisted balustrade—some ancient tapestry still hung on the walls—and there were faded portraits of stiff ladies in ruffs, and maliciously smiling knights in armour, that depressed rather than decorated the dining-room. The chamber assigned to me upstairs was rather bright than otherwise—it fronted the sea, and was cheerfully and prettily furnished. I noticed, however, that it was next door to the shut-up and long-deserted studio. The garden was, as Mrs. Fairleigh had declared, full of carnations. I never saw so many of these flowers growing in one spot. They seemed to spring up everywhere, like weeds, even in the most deserted and shady corners. I had been at the chateau some three or four days, when one morning I happened to be walking alone in a sort of shrubbery at the back of the house, when I perceived in the long dank grass at my feet a large grey stone, that had evidently once stood upright, but had now fallen flat, burying itself partly in the earth. There was something carved upon it. I stooped down, and clearing away the grass and weeds, made out the words

"MANON
Cœur perfide!"*

Surely this was a strange inscription! I told my discovery to the Fairleighs, and we all examined and re-examined the mysterious slab, without being able to arrive at any satisfactory explanation of its pictures. Even enquiries made among the villagers failed to elicit anything save shakes of the head, and such remarks as "Ah, Madame! si on savait!. . ." or "Je crois bien qu'il y a une histoire là!"†

* "Treacherous heart"

† In English: "Ah, Madame! If we knew!" followed by, "I believe that there is a story there!"

One evening we all returned to the chateau at rather a later hour than usual, after a long and delightful walk on the beach in the mellow radiance of a glorious moon. When I went to my room I had no inclination to go to bed—I was wide awake, and moreover in a sort of expectant frame of mind; expectant, though I knew not what I expected.

I threw my window open, leaning out and looking at the moon-enchanted sea, and inhaling the exquisite fragrance of the carnations wafted to me on every breath of the night wind. I thought of many things—the glory of life; the large benevolence of Nature; the mystery of death; the beauty and certainty of immortality, and then, though my back was turned to the interior of my room, I knew—I felt, I was no longer alone. I forced myself to move round from the window; slowly but determinedly I brought myself to confront whoever it was that had thus entered through my locked door; and I was scarcely surprised when I saw "the Lady with the Carnations" standing at a little distance from me, with a most woebegone, appealing expression on her shadowy lovely face. I looked at her, resolved not to fear her; and then brought all my will to bear on unravelling the mystery of my strange visitant. As I met her gaze unflinchingly she made a sort of timid gesture with her hands, as though she besought something.

"Why are you here?" I asked, in a low, clear tone. "Why do you follow me?"

Again she made that little appealing movement. Her answer, soft as a child's whisper, floated through the room—

"You pitied me!"

"Are you unhappy?"

"Very!" And here she clasped her wan white fingers together in a sort of agony. I was growing nervous, but I continued—

"Tell me, then, what you wish me to do?"

She raised her eyes in passionate supplication.

"Pray for me! No one has prayed for me ever since I died—no one has pitied me for a hundred years!"

"How did you die?" I asked, trying to control the rapid beating of my heart. The "Lady with the Carnations" smiled most mournfully, and slowly unfastened the cluster of flowers from her breast—there her white robe was darkly stained with blood. She pointed to the stain, and then replaced the flowers. I understood.

"Murdered!" I whispered, more to myself than to my pale visitor—"murdered!"

"No one knows, and no one prays for me!" wailed the faint sweet spirit voice—"and though I am dead I cannot rest. Pray for me—I am tired!"

And her slender head drooped wearily—she seemed about to vanish. I conquered my rising terrors by a strong effort, and said—

"Tell me—you *must* tell me"—here she raised her head, and her large pensive eyes met mine obediently—"who was your murderer?"

"He did not mean it," she answered. "He loved me. It was here"—and she raised one hand and motioned towards the adjacent studio—"here he drew my picture. He thought me false—but I was true. 'Manon, cœur perfide!' Oh, no, no, no! It should be 'Manon, cœur fidèle!'"*

She paused and looked at me appealingly. Again she pointed to the studio.

"Go and see!" she sighed. "Then you will pray—and I will never come again. Promise you will pray for me—it was here he killed me—and I died without a prayer."

"Where were you buried?" I asked, in a hushed voice.

"In the waves," she murmured; "thrown in the wild cold waves; and no one knew—no one ever found poor Manon; alone and sad for a hundred years, with no word said to God for her!"

Her face was so full of plaintive pathos, that I could have wept. Watching her as she stood, I knelt at the quaint old *prie-Dieu*† just within my reach, and prayed as she desired. Slowly, slowly, slowly a rapturous light came into her eyes; she smiled and waved her hands towards me in farewell. She glided backwards towards the door—and her figure grew dim and indistinct. For the last time she turned her now radiant countenance upon me, and said in thrilling accents—

"Write, 'Manon, cœur fidèle!'"

---

* "Faithful heart."

† A small piece of furniture used for prayer.

I cannot remember how the rest of the night passed; but I know that with the early morning, rousing myself from the stupor of sleep into which I had fallen, I hurried to the door of the closed studio. It was ajar! I pushed it boldly open and entered. The room was long and lofty, but destitute of all furniture save a battered-looking, worm-eaten easel that leaned up against the damp stained wall. I approached this relic of the painter's art, and examining it closely, perceived the name "Manon" cut roughly yet deeply upon it. Looking curiously about, I saw what had nearly escaped my notice—a sort of hanging cupboard, on the left-hand side of the large central bay window. I tried its handle—it was unlocked, and opened easily. Within it lay three things—a palette, on which the blurring marks of long obliterated pigments were still faintly visible; a dagger, unsheathed, with its blade almost black with rust; and—the silver filigree sticks of a fan, to which clung some mouldy shreds of yellow lace. I remembered the fan the "Lady with the Carnations" had carried at the Théâtre Français; and I pieced together her broken story. She had been slain by her artist lover—slain in a sudden fit of jealousy ere the soft colours on his picture of her were yet dry—murdered in this very studio; and no doubt that hidden dagger was the weapon used. Poor Manon! Her frail body had been cast from the high rock on which the château stood "into the wild cold waves," as she or her spirit had said; and her cruel lover had carried his wrath against her so far as to perpetuate a slander against her by writing "Cœur perfide" on that imperishable block of stone! Full of pitying thoughts I shut the cupboard, and slowly left the studio, closing the door noiselessly after me.

That morning as soon as I could get Mrs. Fairleigh alone I told her my adventure, beginning with the very first experience I had had of the picture in the Louvre. Needless to say, she heard me with the utmost incredulity.

"I know you, my dear!" she said, shaking her head at me wisely;"you are full of fancies, and always dreaming about the next world, as if this one wasn't good enough for you. The whole thing is a delusion."

"But," I persisted, "you know the studio was shut and locked; how is it that it is open now?"

"It isn't open!" declared Mrs. Fairleigh—"though I am quite willing to believe you dreamt it *was*."

"Come and see!" I exclaimed eagerly; and I took her upstairs, though she was somewhat reluctant to follow me. As I had said, the studio was open. I led her in, and showed her the name cut on the easel, and the hanging cupboard with its contents. As these convincing proofs of my story met her eyes, she shivered a little, and grew rather pale.

"Come away," she said nervously—"you are really *too* horrid! I can't bear this sort of thing! For goodness' sake, keep your ghosts to yourself!" I saw she was vexed and pettish, and I readily followed her out of the barren, forlorn-looking room. Scarcely were we well outside the door when it shut to with a sharp click. I tried it—it was fast locked! This was too much for Mrs. Fairleigh. She rushed downstairs in a perfect paroxysm of terror; and when I found her in the breakfast-room she declared she would not stop another day in the house. I managed to calm her fears, however; but she insisted on my remaining with her to brave out whatever else might happen at what she persisted now in calling the "haunted" chateâu, in spite of her practical theories. And so I stayed on. And when we left Brittany, we left all together, without having had our peace disturbed by any more manifestations of an unearthly nature. One thing alone troubled me a little—I should have liked to obliterate the word "*perfide*" from that stone, and to have had "*fidèle*" carved on it instead; but it was too deeply engraved for this. However, I have seen no more of "the Lady with the Carnations." But I know the dead need praying for—and that they often suffer for lack of such prayers—though I cannot pretend to explain the reason why. And I know that the picture in the Louvre is not a Greuze, though it is called one—it is the portrait of a faithful woman deeply wronged; and her name is here written as she told me to write it—

"MANON
Cœur fidèle!"

Clemence Housman (1861–1955) was the younger sister of the English poet A. E. Housman, and her younger brother Laurence was a well-known fantasy writer. Clemence was not only a fine writer, she also illustrated many of Laurence's books, and she lived much of her life with him. Clemence was very active in the suffrage movement, even imprisoned briefly, and used her artistic abilities to create posters and print pamphlets and signs for the movement. Despite its length, far shorter than the average novel, *The Were-Wolf* was published separately in 1896 by J. Lane at the Bodley Head, in an edition illustrated by Laurence. H. P. Lovecraft admired her work (though he did not know she was a woman, mistakenly believing "Clarence" to be her first name) and wrote that *The Were-Wolf* "attains a high degree of gruesome tension and achieves to some extent the atmosphere of authentic folklore." However, the quasi-erotic aspects of the story may have gone over Lovecraft's head, who rarely wrote of women in his fiction. Montague Summers's *The Werewolf in Lore and Legend* also expresses high praise for this story, calling it an "exquisite prose-poem," "beautiful," and "harrowing."

The Were-Wolf

by Clemence Housman

The great farm hall was ablaze with the fire-light, and noisy with laughter and talk and many-sounding work. None could be idle but the very young and the very old: little Rol, who was hugging a puppy, and old Trella, whose palsied hand fumbled over her knitting. The early evening had closed in, and the farm-servants, come from their outdoor work, had assembled in the ample hall, which gave space for a score or more of workers. Several of the men were engaged in carving, and to these were yielded the best place and light; others made or repaired fishing-tackle and harness, and a great seine net occupied three pairs of hands. Of the women most were sorting and mixing eider feather* and chopping straw to add to it. Looms were there, though not in present use, but three wheels whirred emulously, and the finest and swiftest thread of the three ran between the fingers of the house-mistress. Near her were some children, busy too, plaiting wicks for candles and lamps. Each group of workers had a lamp in its centre, and those farthest from the fire had live heat from two braziers filled with glowing wood embers, replenished now and again from the generous hearth. But the flicker of the great fire was manifest to remotest corners, and prevailed beyond the limits of the weaker lights.

Little Rol grew tired of his puppy, dropped it incontinently, and made an onslaught on Tyr, the old wolf-hound, who basked dozing, whimpering and twitching in his hunting dreams. Prone went Rol beside Tyr, his young arms round the shaggy neck, his curls against the black jowl. Tyr gave a perfunctory lick, and stretched with a sleepy sigh. Rol growled and rolled and shoved invitingly, but could only gain from the old dog placid toleration and a half-observant blink. "Take that then!" said Rol, indignant at this ignoring of his advances, and sent the puppy sprawling against the dignity that disdained him as playmate. The dog took no notice, and the child wandered off to find amusement elsewhere.

The baskets of white eider feathers caught his eye far off in a distant corner. He slipped under the table, and crept along on all-fours, the ordinary common-place custom of walking down a room upright not being to his fancy. When close to the women he lay still for a moment watching, with his elbows on the floor and his chin in his palms. One of the women seeing him nodded and smiled, and presently he crept out behind her skirts and passed, hardly noticed, from one to another, till he found opportunity to possess himself of a large handful of feathers. With these he traversed the length of the room, under the table again, and emerged near the spinners. At the feet of the youngest he curled himself round, sheltered by her knees from the observation of the others, and disarmed her of interference by secretly displaying his handful with a confiding smile. A dubious nod

* That is, feathers from the common eider duck, *Somateriamollissima.*

satisfied him, and presently he started on the play he had devised. He took a tuft of the white down, and gently shook it free of his fingers close to the whirl of the wheel. The wind of the swift motion took it, spun it round and round in widening circles, till it floated above like a slow white moth. Little Rol's eyes danced, and the row of his small teeth shone in a silent laugh of delight. Another and another of the white tufts was sent whirling round like a winged thing in a spider's web, and floating clear at last. Presently the handful failed.

Rol sprawled forward to survey the room, and contemplate another journey under the table. His shoulder, thrusting forward, checked the wheel for an instant; he shifted hastily. The wheel flew on with a jerk, and the thread snapped. "Naughty Rol!" said the girl. The swiftest wheel stopped also, and the house-mistress, Rol's aunt, leaned forward, and sighting the low curly head, gave a warning against mischief, and sent him off to old Trella's corner.

Rol obeyed, and after a discreet period of obedience, sidled out again down the length of the room farthest from his aunt's eye. As he slipped in among the men, they looked up to see that their tools might be, as far as possible, out of reach of Rol's hands, and close to their own. Nevertheless, before long he managed to secure a fine chisel and take off its point on the leg of the table. The carver's strong objections to this disconcerted Rol, who for five minutes thereafter effaced himself under the table.

During this seclusion he contemplated the many pairs of legs that surrounded him, and almost shut out the light of the fire. How very odd some of the legs were: some were curved where they should be straight, some were straight where they should be curved, and, as Rol said to himself, "they all seemed screwed on differently." Some were tucked away modestly under the benches, others were thrust far out under the table, encroaching on Rol's own particular domain. He stretched out his own short legs and regarded them critically, and, after comparison, favourably. Why were not all legs made like his, or like his?

These legs approved by Rol were a little apart from the rest. He crawled opposite and again made comparison. His face grew quite solemn as he thought of the innumerable days to come before his legs could be as long and strong. He hoped they would be just like those, his models, as straight as to bone, as curved as to muscle.

A few moments later Sweyn of the long legs felt a small hand caressing his foot, and looking down, met the upturned eyes of his little cousin Rol. Lying on his back, still softly patting and stroking the young man's foot, the child was quiet and happy for a good while. He watched the movement of the strong deft hands, and the shifting of the bright tools. Now and then, minute chips of wood, puffed off by Sweyn, fell down upon his face. At last he raised himself, very gently, lest a jog should wake impatience in the carver, and crossing his own legs round Sweyn's ankle, clasping with his arms too, laid his head against the knee. Such act is evidence of a child's most wonderful hero-worship. Quite content was Rol, and more than content when Sweyn paused a minute to joke, and pat his head and pull his curls. Quiet he remained, as long as quiescence is possible to limbs young as his. Sweyn forgot he was near, hardly noticed when his leg was gently released, and never saw the stealthy abstraction of one of his tools.

Ten minutes thereafter was a lamentable wail from low on the floor, rising to the full pitch of Rol's healthy lungs; for his hand was gashed across, and the copious bleeding terrified him. Then was there soothing and comforting, washing and binding, and a modicum of scolding, till the loud outcry sank into occasional sobs, and the child, tear-stained and subdued, was returned to the chimney-corner settle, where Trella nodded.

In the reaction after pain and fright, Rol found that the quiet of that fire-lit corner was to his mind. Tyr, too, disdained him no longer, but, roused by his sobs, showed all the concern and sympathy that a dog can by licking and wistful watching. A little shame weighed also upon his spirits. He wished he had not cried quite so much. He remembered how once Sweyn had come home with his arm torn down from the shoulder, and a dead bear; and how he had never winced nor said a word, though his lips turned white with pain. Poor little Rol gave another sighing sob over his own faint-hearted shortcomings.

The light and motion of the great fire began to tell strange stories to the child, and the wind in the chimney roared a corroborative note now and then. The great black mouth of the chimney, impending high over the hearth, received as into a mysterious gulf murky coils of smoke and brightness of aspiring sparks; and beyond, in the high darkness, were muttering and wailing and strange doings, so that sometimes the smoke rushed back in panic, and curled out and up to the roof, and condensed itself to invisibility among the rafters. And then the wind would rage after its lost prey, and rush round the house, rattling and shrieking at window and door.

In a lull, after one such loud gust, Rol lifted his head in surprise and listened. A lull had also come on the babel of talk, and thus could be heard with strange distinctness a sound outside the door—the sound of a child's voice, a child's hands. "Open, open; let me in!" piped the little voice from low down, lower than the handle, and the latch rattled as though a tiptoe child reached up to it, and soft small knocks were struck. One near the door sprang up and opened it. "No one is here," he said. Tyr lifted his head and gave utterance to a howl, loud, prolonged, most dismal.

Sweyn, not able to believe that his ears had deceived him, got up and went to the door. It was a dark night; the clouds were heavy with snow, that had fallen fitfully when the wind lulled. Untrodden snow lay up to the porch; there was no sight nor sound of any human being. Sweyn strained his eyes far and near, only to see dark sky, pure snow, and a line of black fir trees on a hill brow, bowing down before the wind. "It must have been the wind," he said, and closed the door.

Many faces looked scared. The sound of a child's voice had been so distinct—and the words "Open, open; let me in!" The wind might creak the wood, or rattle the latch, but could not speak with a child's voice, nor knock with the soft plain blows that a plump fist gives. And the strange unusual howl of the wolf-hound was an omen to be feared, be the rest what it might. Strange things were said by one and another, till the rebuke of the house-mistress quelled them into far-off whispers. For a time after there was uneasiness, constraint, and silence; then the chill fear thawed by degrees, and the babble of talk flowed on again.

Yet half-an-hour later a very slight noise outside the door sufficed to arrest every hand, every tongue. Every head was raised, every eye fixed in one direction. "It is Christian; he is late," said Sweyn.

No, no; this is a feeble shuffle, not a young man's tread. With the sound of uncertain feet came the hard tap-tap of a stick against the door, and the high-pitched voice of eld, "Open, open; let me in!" Again Tyr flung up his head in a long doleful howl.

Before the echo of the tapping stick and the high voice had fairly died away, Sweyn had sprung across to the door and flung it wide. "No one again," he said in a steady voice, though his eyes looked startled as he stared out. He saw the lonely expanse of snow, the clouds swagging low, and between the two the line of dark fir-trees bowing in the wind. He closed the door without a word of comment, and re-crossed the room.

A score of blanched faces were turned to him as though he must be solver of the enigma. He could not be unconscious of this mute eye-questioning, and it disturbed his resolute air of composure. He hesitated, glanced towards his mother, the house-mistress, then back at the frightened folk, and gravely, before them all, made the sign of the cross. There was a flutter of hands as the sign was repeated by all, and the dead silence was stirred as by a huge sigh, for the held breath of many was freed as though the sign gave magic relief.

Even the house-mistress was perturbed. She left her wheel and crossed the room to her son, and spoke with him for a moment in a low tone that none could overhear. But a moment later her voice was high-pitched and loud, so that all might benefit by her rebuke of the "heathen chatter" of one of the girls. Perhaps she essayed to silence thus her own misgivings and forebodings.

No other voice dared speak now with its natural fulness. Low tones made intermittent murmurs, and now and then silence drifted over the whole room. The handling of tools was as noiseless as might be, and suspended on the instant if the door rattled in a gust of wind. After a time Sweyn left his work, joined the group nearest the door, and loitered there on the pretence of giving advice and help to the unskilful.

A man's tread was heard outside in the porch. "Christian!" said Sweyn and his mother simultaneously, he confidently, she authoritatively, to set the checked wheels going again. But Tyr flung up his head with an appalling howl.

"Open, open; let me in!"

It was a man's voice, and the door shook and rattled as a man's strength beat against it. Sweyn could feel the planks quivering, as on the instant his hand was upon the door, flinging it open, to face the blank porch, and beyond only snow and sky, and firs aslant in the wind.

He stood for a long minute with the open door in his hand. The bitter wind swept in with its icy chill, but a deadlier chill of fear came swifter, and seemed to freeze the beating of hearts. Sweyn stepped back to snatch up a great bearskin cloak.

"Sweyn, where are you going?"

"No farther than the porch, mother," and he stepped out and closed the door.

He wrapped himself in the heavy fur, and leaning against the most sheltered wall of the porch, steeled his nerves to face the devil and all his works. No sound of voices came from within; the most distinct sound was the crackle and roar of the fire.

It was bitterly cold. His feet grew numb, but he forbore stamping them into warmth lest the sound should strike panic within; nor would he leave the porch, nor print a foot-mark on the untrodden white that declared so absolutely how no human voices and hands could have approached the door since snow fell two hours or more ago. "When the wind drops there will be more snow," thought Sweyn.

For the best part of an hour he kept his watch, and saw no living thing—heard no unwonted sound. "I will freeze here no longer," he muttered, and re-entered.

One woman gave a half-suppressed scream as his hand was laid on the latch, and then a gasp of relief as he came in. No one questioned him, only his mother said, in a tone of forced unconcern, "Could you not see Christian coming?" as though she were made anxious only by the absence of her younger son. Hardly had Sweyn stamped near to the fire than clear knocking was heard at the door. Tyr leapt from the hearth, his eyes red as the fire, his fangs showing white in the black jowl, his neck ridged and bristling; and overleaping Rol, ramped at the door, barking furiously.

Outside the door a clear mellow voice was calling. Tyr's bark made the words undistinguishable. No one offered to stir towards the door before Sweyn.

He stalked down the room resolutely, lifted the latch, and swung back the door.

A white-robed woman glided in.

No wraith! Living—beautiful—young.

Tyr leapt upon her.

Lithely she baulked the sharp fangs with folds of her long fur robe, and snatching from her girdle a small two-edged axe, whirled it up for a blow of defence.

Sweyn caught the dog by the collar, and dragged him off yelling and struggling.

The stranger stood in the doorway motionless, one foot set forward, one arm flung up, till the house-mistress hurried down the room; and Sweyn, relinquishing to others the furious Tyr, turned again to close the door, and offer excuse for so fierce a greeting. Then she lowered her arm, slung the axe in its place at her waist, loosened the furs about her face, and shook over her shoulders the long white robe—all as it were with the sway of one movement.

She was a maiden, tall and very fair. The fashion of her dress was strange, half masculine, yet not unwomanly. A fine fur tunic, reaching but little below the knee, was all the skirt she wore; below were the cross-bound shoes and leggings that a hunter wears. A white fur cap was set low upon the brows, and from its edge strips of fur fell lappet-wise about her shoulders; two of these at her entrance had been drawn forward and crossed about her throat, but now, loosened and thrust back, left unhidden long plaits of fair hair that lay forward on shoulder and breast, down to the ivory-studded girdle where the axe gleamed.

Sweyn and his mother led the stranger to the hearth without question or sign of curiosity, till she voluntarily told her tale of a long journey to distant kindred, a promised guide unmet, and signals and landmarks mistaken.

"Alone!" exclaimed Sweyn in astonishment. "Have you journeyed thus far, a hundred leagues, alone?"

She answered "Yes" with a little smile.

"Over the hills and the wastes! Why, the folk there are savage and wild as beasts."

She dropped her hand upon her axe with a laugh of some scorn.

"I fear neither man nor beast; some few fear me." And then she told strange tales of fierce attack and defence, and of the bold free huntress life she had led.

Her words came a little slowly and deliberately, as though she spoke in a scarce familiar tongue; now and then she hesitated, and stopped in a phrase, as though for lack of some word.

She became the centre of a group of listeners. The interest she excited dissipated, in some degree, the dread inspired by the mysterious voices. There was nothing ominous about this young, bright, fair reality, though her aspect was strange.

Little Rol crept near, staring at the stranger with all his might. Unnoticed, he softly stroked and patted a corner of her soft white robe that reached to the floor in ample folds. He laid his cheek against it caressingly, and then edged up close to her knees.

"What is your name?" he asked.

The stranger's smile and ready answer, as she looked down, saved Rol from the rebuke merited by his unmannerly question.

"My real name," she said, "would be uncouth to your ears and tongue. The folk of this country have given me another name, and from this" (she laid her hand on the fur robe) "they call me 'White Fell.'"

Little Rol repeated it to himself, stroking and patting as before. "White Fell, White Fell."

The fair face, and soft, beautiful dress pleased Rol. He knelt up, with his eyes on her face and an air of uncertain determination, like a robin's on a doorstep, and plumped his elbows into her lap with a little gasp at his own audacity.

"Rol!" exclaimed his aunt; but, "Oh, let him!" said White Fell, smiling and stroking his head; and Rol stayed.

He advanced farther, and panting at his own adventurousness in the face of his aunt's authority, climbed up on to her knees. Her welcoming arms hindered any protest. He nestled happily, fingering the axe head, the ivory studs in her girdle, the ivory clasp at her throat, the plaits of fair hair; rubbing his head against the softness of her fur-clad shoulder, with a child's full confidence in the kindness of beauty.

White Fell had not uncovered her head, only knotted the pendant fur loosely behind her neck. Rol reached up his hand towards it, whispering her name to himself, "White Fell, White Fell," then slid his arms round her neck, and kissed her—once—twice. She laughed delightedly, and kissed him again.

"The child plagues you?" said Sweyn.

"No, indeed," she answered, with an earnestness so intense as to seem disproportionate to the occasion.

Rol settled himself again on her lap, and began to unwind the bandage bound round his hand. He paused a little when he saw where the blood had soaked through; then went on till his hand was bare and the cut displayed, gaping and long, though only skin deep. He held it up towards White Fell, desirous of her pity and sympathy.

At sight of it, and the blood-stained linen, she drew in her breath suddenly, clasped Rol to her—hard, hard—till he began to struggle. Her face was hidden behind the boy, so that none could see its expression. It had lighted up with a most awful glee.

Afar, beyond the fir-grove, beyond the low hill behind, the absent Christian was hastening his return. From daybreak he had been afoot, carrying notice of a bear hunt to all the best hunters of the farms and hamlets that lay within a radius of twelve miles. Nevertheless, having been detained till a late hour, he now broke into a run, going with a long smooth stride of apparent ease that fast made the miles diminish.

He entered the midnight blackness of the fir-grove with scarcely slackened pace, though the path was invisible; and passing through into the open again, sighted the farm lying a furlong off down the slope. Then he sprang out freely, and almost on the instant gave one great sideways leap, and stood still. There in the snow was the track of a great wolf.

His hand went to his knife, his only weapon. He stooped, knelt down, to bring his eyes to the level of a beast, and peered about; his teeth set, his heart beat a little harder than the pace of his running insisted on. A solitary wolf, nearly always savage and of large size, is a formidable beast that will not hesitate to attack a single man. This wolf-track was the largest Christian had ever seen, and, so far as he could judge, recently made. It led from under the fir-trees down the slope. Well for him, he thought, was the delay that had so vexed him before: well for him that he had not passed through the dark fir-grove when that danger of jaws lurked there. Going warily, he followed the track.

It led down the slope, across a broad ice-bound stream, along the level beyond, making towards the farm. A less precise knowledge had doubted, and guessed that here might have come straying big Tyr or his like; but Christian was sure, knowing better than to mistake between footmark of dog and wolf.

Straight on—straight on towards the farm.

Surprised and anxious grew Christian, that a prowling wolf should dare so near. He drew his knife and pressed on, more hastily, more keen-eyed. Oh that Tyr were with him!

Straight on, straight on, even to the very door, where the snow failed. His heart seemed to give a great leap and then stop. There the track ended.

Nothing lurked in the porch, and there was no sign of return. The firs stood straight against the sky, the clouds lay low; for the wind had fallen and a few snowflakes came drifting down. In a horror of surprise, Christian stood dazed a moment: then he lifted the latch and went in. His glance took in all the old familiar forms and faces, and with them that of the stranger, fur-clad and beautiful. The awful truth flashed upon him: he knew what she was.

Only a few were startled by the rattle of the latch as he entered. The room was filled with bustle and movement, for it was the supper hour, when all tools were laid aside, and trestles and tables shifted. Christian had no knowledge of what he said and did; he moved and spoke mechanically, half thinking that soon he must wake from this horrible dream. Sweyn and his mother supposed him to be cold and dead-tired, and spared all unnecessary questions. And he found himself seated beside the hearth, opposite that dreadful Thing that looked like a beautiful girl; watching her every movement, curdling with horror to see her fondle the child Rol.

Sweyn stood near them both, intent upon White Fell also; but how differently! She seemed unconscious of the gaze of both—neither aware of the chill dread in the eyes of Christian, nor of Sweyn's warm admiration.

These two brothers, who were twins, contrasted greatly, despite their striking likeness. They were alike in regular profile, fair brown hair, and deep blue eyes; but Sweyn's features were perfect as a young god's, while Christian's showed faulty details. Thus, the line of his mouth was set too straight, the eyes shelved too deeply back, and the contour of the face flowed in less generous curves than Sweyn's. Their height was the same, but Christian was too slender for perfect proportion, while Sweyn's well-knit frame, broad shoulders, and muscular arms, made him pre-eminent for manly beauty as well as for strength. As a hunter Sweyn was without rival; as a fisher without rival. All the countryside acknowledged him to be the best wrestler, rider, dancer, singer. Only in speed could he be surpassed, and in that only by his younger brother. All others Sweyn could distance fairly; but Christian could outrun him easily. Ay, he could keep pace with Sweyn's most breathless burst, and laugh and talk the while. Christian took little pride in his fleetness of foot, counting a man's legs to be the least worthy of his members. He had no envy of his brother's athletic superiority, though to several feats he had made a moderate second. He loved as only a twin can love—proud of all that Sweyn did, content with all that Sweyn was; humbly content also that his own great love should not be so exceedingly returned, since he knew himself to be so far less love-worthy.

Christian dared not, in the midst of women and children, launch the horror that he knew into words. He waited to consult his brother; but Sweyn did not, or would not, notice the signal he made, and kept his face always turned towards White Fell. Christian drew away from the hearth, unable to remain passive with that dread upon him.

"Where is Tyr?" he said suddenly. Then, catching sight of the dog in a distant corner, "Why is he chained there?"

"He flew at the stranger," one answered.

Christian's eyes glowed. "Yes?" he said, interrogatively.

"He was within an ace of having his brain knocked out."

"Tyr?"

"Yes; she was nimbly up with that little axe she has at her waist. It was well for old Tyr that his master throttled him off."

Christian went without a word to the corner where Tyr was chained. The dog rose up to meet him, as piteous and indignant as a dumb beast can be. He stroked the black head. "Good Tyr! brave dog!"

They knew, they only; and the man and the dumb dog had comfort of each other.

Christian's eyes turned again towards White Fell: Tyr's also, and he strained against the length of the chain. Christian's hand lay on the dog's neck, and he felt it ridge and bristle with the quivering of impotent fury. Then he began to quiver in like manner, with a fury born of reason, not instinct; as impotent morally as was Tyr physically. Oh! the woman's form that he dare not touch! Anything but that, and he with Tyr would be free to kill or be killed.

Then he returned to ask fresh questions.

"How long has the stranger been here?"

"She came about half-an-hour before you."

"Who opened the door to her?"

"Sweyn: no one else dared."

The tone of the answer was mysterious.

"Why?" queried Christian. "Has anything strange happened? Tell me."

For answer he was told in a low undertone of the summons at the door thrice repeated without human agency; and of Tyr's ominous howls; and of Sweyn's fruitless watch outside.

Christian turned towards his brother in a torment of impatience for a word apart. The board was spread, and Sweyn was leading White Fell to the guest's place. This was more awful: she would break bread with them under the roof-tree!

He started forward, and touching Sweyn's arm, whispered an urgent entreaty. Sweyn stared, and shook his head in angry impatience.

Thereupon Christian would take no morsel of food.

His opportunity came at last. White Fell questioned of the landmarks of the country, and of one Cairn Hill, which was an appointed meeting-place at which she was due that night. The house-mistress and Sweyn both exclaimed.

"It is three long miles away," said Sweyn; "with no place for shelter but a wretched hut. Stay with us this night, and I will show you the way to-morrow."

White Fell seemed to hesitate. "Three miles," she said; "then I should be able to see or hear a signal."

"I will look out," said Sweyn; "then, if there be no signal, you must not leave us."

He went to the door. Christian rose silently, and followed him out.

"Sweyn, do you know what she is?"

Sweyn, surprised at the vehement grasp, and low hoarse voice, made answer:

"She? Who? White Fell?"

"Yes."

"She is the most beautiful girl I have ever seen."

"She is a Were-Wolf."

Sweyn burst out laughing. "Are you mad?" he asked.

"No; here, see for yourself."

Christian drew him out of the porch, pointing to the snow where the footmarks had been. Had been, for now they were not. Snow was falling fast, and every dint was blotted out.

"Well?" asked Sweyn.

"Had you come when I signed to you, you would have seen for yourself."

"Seen what?"

"The footprints of a wolf leading up to the door; none leading away."

It was impossible not to be startled by the tone alone, though it was hardly above a whisper. Sweyn eyed his brother anxiously, but in the darkness could make nothing of his face. Then he laid his hands kindly and re-assuringly on Christian's shoulders and felt how he was quivering with excitement and horror.

"One sees strange things," he said, "when the cold has got into the brain behind the eyes; you came in cold and worn out."

"No," interrupted Christian. "I saw the track first on the brow of the slope, and followed it down right here to the door. This is no delusion."

Sweyn in his heart felt positive that it was. Christian was given to day-dreams and strange fancies, though never had he been possessed with so mad a notion before.

"Don't you believe me?" said Christian desperately. "You must. I swear it is sane truth. Are you blind? Why, even Tyr knows."

"You will be clearer headed to-morrow after a night's rest. Then come too, if you will, with White Fell, to the Hill Cairn; and if you have doubts still, watch and follow, and see what footprints she leaves."

Galled by Sweyn's evident contempt Christian turned abruptly to the door. Sweyn caught him back.

"What now, Christian? What are you going to do?"

"You do not believe me; my mother shall."

Sweyn's grasp tightened. "You shall not tell her," he said authoritatively.

Customarily Christian was so docile to his brother's mastery that it was now a surprising thing when he wrenched himself free vigorously, and said as determinedly as Sweyn, "She shall know!" but Sweyn was nearer the door and would not let him pass.

"There has been scare enough for one night already. If this notion of yours will keep, broach it to-morrow." Christian would not yield.

"Women are so easily scared," pursued Sweyn, "and are ready to believe any folly without shadow of proof. Be a man, Christian, and fight this notion of a Were-Wolf by yourself."

"If you would believe me," began Christian.

"I believe you to be a fool," said Sweyn, losing patience. "Another, who was not your brother, might believe you to be a knave, and guess that you had transformed White Fell into a Were-Wolf because she smiled more readily on me than on you."

The jest was not without foundation, for the grace of White Fell's bright looks had been bestowed on him, on Christian never a whit. Sweyn's coxcombery* was always frank, and most forgiveable, and not without fair colour.

"If you want an ally," continued Sweyn, "confide in old Trella. Out of her stores of wisdom, if her memory holds good, she can instruct you in the orthodox manner of tackling a Were-Wolf. If I remember aright, you should watch the suspected person till midnight, when the beast's form must be resumed, and retained ever after if a human eye sees the change; or, better still, sprinkle hands and feet with holy water, which is certain death.† Oh! never fear, but old Trella will be equal to the occasion."

* A coxcomb is a vain and conceited person.

† Norse mythology and the Icelandic Sagas contain many instances of shapeshifting and transformation into a wolf, usually after donning the skin of the animal. The Völsunga Saga contains a story of "an old she-wolf" that emerges from the forest at midnight to feast on men, but otherwise Housman's werewolf lore seems to have been created by her rather than based on any existing folk beliefs.

Sweyn's contempt was no longer good-humoured; some touch of irritation or resentment rose at this monstrous doubt of White Fell. But Christian was too deeply distressed to take offence.

"You speak of them as old wives' tales; but if you had seen the proof I have seen, you would be ready at least to wish them true, if not also to put them to the test."

"Well," said Sweyn, with a laugh that had a little sneer in it, "put them to the test! I will not object to that, if you will only keep your notions to yourself. Now, Christian, give me your word for silence, and we will freeze here no longer."

Christian remained silent.

Sweyn put his hands on his shoulders again and vainly tried to see his face in the darkness.

"We have never quarrelled yet, Christian?"

"I have never quarrelled," returned the other, aware for the first time that his dictatorial brother had sometimes offered occasion for quarrel, had he been ready to take it.

"Well," said Sweyn emphatically, "if you speak against White Fell to any other, as to-night you have spoken to me—we shall."

He delivered the words like an ultimatum, turned sharp round, and re-entered the house. Christian, more fearful and wretched than before, followed.

"Snow is falling fast: not a single light is to be seen."

White Fell's eyes passed over Christian without apparent notice, and turned bright and shining upon Sweyn.

"Nor any signal to be heard?" she queried. "Did you not hear the sound of a sea-horn?"

"I saw nothing, and heard nothing; and signal or no signal, the heavy snow would keep you here perforce."

She smiled her thanks beautifully. And Christian's heart sank like lead with a deadly foreboding, as he noted what a light was kindled in Sweyn's eyes by her smile.

That night, when all others slept, Christian, the weariest of all, watched outside the guest-chamber till midnight was past. No sound, not the faintest, could be heard. Could the old tale be true of the midnight change?

What was on the other side of the door, a woman or a beast? he would have given his right hand to know. Instinctively he laid his hand on the latch, and drew it softly, though believing that bolts fastened the inner side. The door yielded to his hand; he stood on the threshold; a keen gust of air cut at him; the window stood open; the room was empty.

So Christian could sleep with a somewhat lightened heart.

In the morning there was surprise and conjecture when White Fell's absence was discovered. Christian held his peace. Not even to his brother did he say how he knew that she had fled before midnight; and Sweyn, though evidently greatly chagrined, seemed to disdain reference to the subject of Christian's fears.

The elder brother alone joined the bear hunt; Christian found pretext to stay behind. Sweyn, being out of humour, manifested his contempt by uttering not a single expostulation.

All that day, and for many a day after, Christian would never go out of sight of his home. Sweyn alone noticed how he manœuvred for this, and was clearly annoyed by it. White Fell's name was never mentioned between them, though not seldom was it heard in general talk. Hardly a day passed but little Rol asked when White Fell would come again: pretty White Fell, who kissed like a snowflake. And if Sweyn answered, Christian would be quite sure that the light in his eyes, kindled by White Fell's smile, had not yet died out.

Little Rol! Naughty, merry, fairhaired little Rol. A day came when his feet raced over the threshold never to return; when his chatter and laugh were heard no more; when tears of anguish were wept by eyes that never would see his bright head again: never again, living or dead.

He was seen at dusk for the last time, escaping from the house with his puppy, in freakish rebellion against old Trella. Later, when his absence had begun to cause anxiety, his puppy crept back to the farm, cowed, whimpering and yelping, a pitiful, dumb lump of terror, without intelligence or courage to guide the frightened search.

Rol was never found, nor any trace of him. Where he had perished was never known; how he had perished was known only by an awful guess—a wild beast had devoured him.

Christian heard the conjecture "a wolf"; and a horrible certainty flashed upon him that he knew what wolf it was. He tried to declare what he knew, but Sweyn saw him start at the words with white face and struggling lips; and, guessing his purpose, pulled him back, and kept him silent, hardly, by his imperious grip and wrathful eyes, and one low whisper.

That Christian should retain his most irrational suspicion against beautiful White Fell was, to Sweyn, evidence of a weak obstinacy of mind that would but thrive upon expostulation and argument. But this evident intention to direct the passions of grief and anguish to a hatred and fear of the fair stranger, such as his own, was intolerable, and Sweyn set his will against it. Again Christian yielded to his brother's stronger words and will, and against his own judgment consented to silence.

Repentance came before the new moon, the first of the year, was old. White Fell came again, smiling as she entered, as though assured of a glad and kindly welcome; and, in truth, there was only one who saw again her fair face and strange white garb without pleasure. Sweyn's face glowed with delight, while Christian's grew pale and rigid as death. He had given his word to keep silence; but he had not thought that she would dare to come again. Silence was impossible, face to face with that Thing, impossible. Irrepressibly he cried out:

"Where is Rol?"

Not a quiver disturbed White Fell's face. She heard, yet remained bright and tranquil. Sweyn's eyes flashed round at his brother dangerously. Among the women some tears fell at the poor child's name; but none caught alarm from its sudden utterance, for the thought of Rol rose naturally. Where was little Rol, who had nestled in the stranger's arms, kissing her; and watched for her since; and prattled of her daily?

Christian went out silently. One only thing there was that he could do, and he must not delay. His horror overmastered any curiosity to hear White Fell's smooth excuses and smiling apologies for her strange and uncourteous departure; or her easy tale of the circumstances of her return; or to watch her bearing as she heard the sad tale of little Rol.

The swiftest runner of the country-side had started on his hardest race: little less than three leagues and back, which he reckoned to accomplish in two hours, though the night was moonless and the way rugged. He rushed against the still cold air till it felt like a wind upon his face. The dim homestead sank below the ridges at his back, and fresh ridges of snowlands rose out of the obscure horizon-level to drive past him as the stirless air drove, and sink away behind into obscure level again. He took no conscious heed of landmarks, not even when all sign of a path was gone under depths of snow. His will was set to reach his goal with unexampled speed; and thither by instinct his physical forces bore him, without one definite thought to guide.

And the idle brain lay passive, inert, receiving into its vacancy restless siftings of past sights and sounds: Rol, weeping, laughing, playing, coiled in the arms of that dreadful Thing: Tyr—O Tyr!—white fangs in the black jowl: the women who wept on: the foolish puppy, precious for the child's last touch: footprints from pine wood to door: the smiling face among furs, of such womanly beauty—smiling—smiling: and Sweyn's face.

"Sweyn, Sweyn, O Sweyn, my brother!"

Sweyn's angry laugh possessed his ear within the sound of the wind of his speed; Sweyn's scorn assailed more quick and keen than the biting cold at his throat. And yet he was unimpressed by any thought of how Sweyn's anger and scorn would rise, if this errand were known.

Sweyn was a sceptic. His utter disbelief in Christian's testimony regarding the footprints was based upon positive scepticism. His reason refused to bend in accepting the possibility of the supernatural materialised. That a living beast could ever be other than palpably bestial—pawed, toothed, shagged, and eared as such, was to him incredible; far more that a human presence could be transformed from its god-like aspect, upright, free-handed, with brows, and speech, and laughter. The wild and fearful legends that he had known from childhood and then believed, he regarded now as built upon facts distorted, overlaid by imagination, and quickened by superstition. Even the strange summons at the threshold, that he himself had vainly answered, was, after the first shock of surprise, rationally explained by him as malicious foolery on the part of some clever trickster, who withheld the key to the enigma.

To the younger brother all life was a spiritual mystery, veiled from his clear knowledge by the density of flesh. Since he knew his own body to be linked to the complex and antagonistic forces that constitute one soul, it seemed to him not impossibly strange that one spiritual force should possess divers forms for widely various manifestation. Nor, to him, was it great effort to believe that as pure water washes away all natural foulness, so water, holy by consecration, must needs cleanse God's world from that supernatural evil Thing. Therefore, faster than ever man's foot had covered those leagues, he sped under the dark, still night, over the waste, trackless snow-ridges to the far-away church, where salvation lay in the holy-water stoup at the door. His faith was as firm as any that wrought miracles in days past, simple as a child's wish, strong as a man's will.

He was hardly missed during these hours, every second of which was by him fulfilled to its utmost extent by extremest effort that sinews and nerves could attain. Within the homestead the while, the easy moments went bright with words and looks of unwonted animation, for the kindly, hospitable instincts of the inmates were roused into cordial expression of welcome and interest by the grace and beauty of the returned stranger.

But Sweyn was eager and earnest, with more than a host's courteous warmth. The impression that at her first coming had charmed him, that had lived since through memory, deepened now in her actual presence. Sweyn, the matchless among men, acknowledged in this fair White Fell a spirit high and bold as his own, and a frame so firm and capable that only bulk was lacking for equal strength. Yet the white skin was moulded most smoothly, without such muscular swelling as made his might evident. Such love as his frank self-love could concede was called forth by an ardent admiration for this supreme stranger. More admiration than love was in his passion, and therefore he was free from a lover's hesitancy and delicate reserve and doubts. Frankly and boldly he courted her favour by looks and tones, and an address that came of natural ease, needless of skill by practice.

Nor was she a woman to be wooed otherwise. Tender whispers and sighs would never gain her ear; but her eyes would brighten and shine if she heard of a brave feat, and her prompt hand in sympathy fall swiftly on the axe-haft and clasp it hard. That movement ever fired Sweyn's admiration anew; he watched for it, strove to elicit it, and glowed when it came. Wonderful and beautiful was that wrist, slender and steel-strong; also the smooth shapely hand, that curved so fast and firm, ready to deal instant death.

Desiring to feel the pressure of these hands, this bold lover schemed with palpable directness, proposing that she should hear how their hunting songs were sung, with a chorus that signalled hands to be clasped. So his splendid voice gave the verses, and, as the chorus was taken up, he claimed her hands, and, even through the easy grip, felt, as he desired, the strength that was latent, and the vigour that quickened the very fingertips, as the song fired her, and her voice was caught out of her by the rhythmic swell, and rang clear on the top of the closing surge.

Afterwards she sang alone. For contrast, or in the pride of swaying moods by her voice, she chose a mournful song that drifted along in a minor chant, sad as a wind that dirges:

"Oh, let me go!
Around spin wreaths of snow;
The dark earth sleeps below.

"Far up the plain
Moans on a voice of pain:
'Where shall my babe be lain?'

"In my white breast
Lay the sweet life to rest!
Lay, where it can lie best!

"'Hush! hush its cries!
Dense night is on the skies:
Two stars are in thine eyes.'

"Come, babe, away!
But lie thou till dawn be grey,
Who must be dead by day.

"This cannot last;
But, ere the sickening blast,
All sorrow shall be past;

"And kings shall be
Low bending at thy knee,
Worshipping life from thee.

"For men long sore
To hope of what's before,—
To leave the things of yore.

"Mine, and not thine,
How deep their jewels shine!
Peace laps thy head, not mine."

Old Trella came tottering from her corner, shaken to additional palsy by an aroused memory. She strained her dim eyes towards the singer, and then bent her head, that the one ear yet sensible to sound might avail of every note. At the close, groping forward, she murmured with the high-pitched quaver of old age:

"So she sang, my Thora; my last and brightest. What is she like, she whose voice is like my dead Thora's? Are her eyes blue?"

"Blue as the sky."

"So were my Thora's! Is her hair fair, and in plaits to the waist?" "Even so," answered White Fell herself, and met the advancing hands with her own, and guided them to corroborate her words by touch.

"Like my dead Thora's," repeated the old woman; and then her trembling hands rested on the fur-clad shoulders, and she bent forward and kissed the smooth fair face that White Fell upturned, nothing loth, to receive and return the caress.

So Christian saw them as he entered.

He stood a moment. After the starless darkness and the icy night air, and the fierce silent two hours' race, his senses reeled on sudden entrance into warmth, and light, and the cheery hum of voices. A sudden unforeseen anguish assailed him, as now first he entertained the possibility of being overmatched by her wiles and her daring, if at the approach of pure death she should start up at bay transformed to a terrible beast, and achieve a savage glut at the last. He looked with horror and pity on the harmless, helpless folk, so unwitting of outrage to their comfort and security. The dreadful Thing in their midst, that was veiled from their knowledge by womanly beauty, was a centre of pleasant interest. There, before him, signally impressive, was poor old Trella, weakest and feeblest of all, in fond nearness. And a moment might bring about the revelation of a monstrous horror—a ghastly, deadly danger, set loose and at bay, in a circle of girls and women and careless defenceless men: so hideous and terrible a thing as might crack the brain, or curdle the heart stone dead.

And he alone of the throng prepared!

For one breathing space he faltered, no longer than that, while over him swept the agony of compunction that yet could not make him surrender his purpose.

He alone? Nay, but Tyr also; and he crossed to the dumb sole sharer of his knowledge.

So timeless is thought that a few seconds only lay between his lifting of the latch and his loosening of Tyr's collar; but in those few seconds succeeding his first glance, as lightning-swift had been the impulses of others, their motion as quick and sure. Sweyn's vigilant eye had darted upon him, and instantly his every fibre was alert with hostile instinct; and, half divining, half incredulous, of Christian's object in stooping to Tyr, he came hastily, wary, wrathful, resolute to oppose the malice of his wild-eyed brother.

But beyond Sweyn rose White Fell, blanching white as her furs, and with eyes grown fierce and wild. She leapt down the room to the door, whirling her long robe closely to her. "Hark!" she panted. "The signal horn! Hark, I must go!" as she snatched at the latch to be out and away.

For one precious moment Christian had hesitated on the half-loosened collar; for, except the womanly form were exchanged for the bestial, Tyr's jaws would gnash to rags his honour of manhood. Then he heard her voice, and turned—too late.

As she tugged at the door, he sprang across grasping his flask, but Sweyn dashed between, and caught him back irresistibly, so that a most frantic effort only availed to wrench one arm free. With that, on the impulse of sheer despair, he cast at her with all his force. The door swung behind her, and the flask flew into fragments against it. Then, as Sweyn's grasp slackened, and he met the questioning astonishment of surrounding faces, with a hoarse inarticulate cry: "God help us all!" he said. "She is a Were-Wolf."

Sweyn turned upon him, "Liar, coward!" and his hands gripped his brother's throat with deadly force, as though the spoken word could be killed so; and as Christian struggled, lifted him clear off his feet and flung him crashing backward. So furious was he, that, as his brother lay motionless, he stirred him roughly with his foot, till their mother came between, crying shame; and yet then he stood by, his teeth set, his brows knit, his hands clenched, ready to enforce silence again violently, as Christian rose staggering and bewildered.

But utter silence and submission were more than he expected, and turned his anger into contempt for one so easily cowed and held in subjection by mere force. "He is mad!" he said, turning on his heel as he spoke, so that he lost his mother's look of pained reproach at this sudden free utterance of what was a lurking dread within her.

Christian was too spent for the effort of speech. His hard-drawn breath laboured in great sobs; his limbs were powerless and unstrung in utter relax after hard service. Failure in his endeavour induced a stupor of misery and despair. In addition was the wretched humiliation of open violence and strife with his brother, and the distress of hearing misjudging contempt expressed without reserve; for he was aware that Sweyn had turned to allay the scared excitement half by imperious mastery, half by explanation and argument, that showed painful disregard of brotherly consideration. All this unkindness of his twin he charged upon the fell Thing who had wrought this their first dissension, and, ah! most terrible thought, interposed between them so effectually, that Sweyn was wilfully blind and deaf on her account, resentful of interference, arbitrary beyond reason.

Dread and perplexity unfathomable darkened upon him; unshared, the burden was overwhelming: a foreboding of unspeakable calamity, based upon his ghastly discovery, bore down upon him, crushing out hope of power to withstand impending fate.

Sweyn the while was observant of his brother, despite the continual check of finding, turn and glance when he would, Christian's eyes always upon him, with a strange look of helpless distress, discomposing enough to the angry aggressor. "Like a beaten dog!" he said to himself, rallying contempt to withstand compunction. Observation set him wondering on Christian's exhausted condition. The heavy labouring breath and the slack inert fall of the limbs told surely of unusual and prolonged exertion. And then why had close upon two hours' absence been followed by open hostility against White Fell?

Suddenly, the fragments of the flask giving a clue, he guessed all, and faced about to stare at his brother in amaze. He forgot that the motive scheme was against White Fell, demanding derision and resentment from him; that was swept out of remembrance by astonishment and admiration for the feat of speed and endurance. In eagerness to question he inclined to attempt a generous part and frankly offer to heal the breach; but Christian's depression and sad following gaze provoked him to self-justification by recalling the offence of that outrageous utterance against White Fell; and the impulse passed. Then other considerations counselled silence; and afterwards a humour possessed him to wait and see how Christian would find opportunity to proclaim his performance and establish the fact, without exciting ridicule on account of the absurdity of the errand.

This expectation remained unfulfilled. Christian never attempted the proud avowal that would have placed his feat on record to be told to the next generation.

That night Sweyn and his mother talked long and late together, shaping into certainty the suspicion that Christian's mind had lost its balance, and discussing the evident cause. For Sweyn, declaring his own love for White Fell, suggested that his unfortunate brother, with a like passion, they being twins in loves as in birth, had through jealousy and despair turned from love to hate, until reason failed at the strain, and a craze developed, which the malice and treachery of madness made a serious and dangerous force.

So Sweyn theorised, convincing himself as he spoke; convincing afterwards others who advanced doubts against White Fell; fettering his judgment by his advocacy, and by his staunch defence of her hurried flight silencing his own inner consciousness of the unaccountability of her action.

But a little time and Sweyn lost his vantage in the shock of a fresh horror at the homestead. Trella was no more, and her end a mystery. The poor old woman crawled out in a bright gleam to visit a bed-ridden gossip living beyond the fir-grove. Under the trees she was last seen, halting for her companion, sent back for a forgotten present. Quick alarm sprang, calling every man to the search. Her stick was found among the brushwood only a few paces from the path, but no track or stain, for a gusty wind was sifting the snow from the branches, and hid all sign of how she came by her death.

So panic-stricken were the farm folk that none dared go singly on the search. Known danger could be braced, but not this stealthy Death that walked by day invisible, that cut off alike the child in his play and the aged woman so near to her quiet grave.

"Rol she kissed; Trella she kissed!" So rang Christian's frantic cry again and again, till Sweyn dragged him away and strove to keep him apart, albeit in his agony of grief and remorse he accused himself wildly as answerable for the tragedy, and gave clear proof that the charge of madness was well founded, if strange looks and desperate, incoherent words were evidence enough.

But thenceforward all Sweyn's reasoning and mastery could not uphold White Fell above suspicion. He was not called upon to defend her from accusation when Christian had been brought to silence again; but he well knew the significance of this fact, that her name, formerly uttered freely and often, he never heard now: it was huddled away into whispers that he could not catch.

The passing of time did not sweep away the superstitious fears that Sweyn despised. He was angry and anxious; eager that White Fell should return, and, merely by her bright gracious presence, reinstate herself in favour; but doubtful if all his authority and example could keep from her notice an altered aspect of welcome; and he foresaw clearly that Christian would prove unmanageable, and might be capable of some dangerous outbreak.

For a time the twins' variance was marked, on Sweyn's part by an air of rigid indifference, on Christian's by heavy downcast silence, and a nervous apprehensive observation of his brother. Superadded to his remorse and foreboding, Sweyn's displeasure weighed upon him intolerably, and the remembrance of their violent rupture was a ceaseless misery. The elder brother, self-sufficient and insensitive, could little know how deeply his unkindness stabbed. A depth and force of affection such as Christian's was unknown to him. The loyal subservience that he could not appreciate had encouraged him to domineer; this strenuous opposition to his reason and will was accounted as furious malice, if not sheer insanity.

Christian's surveillance galled him incessantly, and embarrassment and danger he foresaw as the outcome. Therefore, that suspicion might be lulled, he judged it wise to make overtures for peace. Most easily done. A little kindliness, a few evidences of consideration, a slight return of the old brotherly imperiousness, and Christian replied by a gratefulness and relief that might have touched him had he understood all, but instead, increased his secret contempt.

So successful was this finesse, that when, late on a day, a message summoning Christian to a distance was transmitted by Sweyn, no doubt of its genuineness occurred. When, his errand proved useless, he set out to return, mistake or misapprehension was all that he surmised. Not till he sighted the homestead, lying low between the night-grey snow ridges, did vivid recollection of the time when he had tracked that horror to the door rouse an intense dread, and with it a hardly-defined suspicion.

His grasp tightened on the bear-spear that he carried as a staff; every sense was alert, every muscle strung; excitement urged him on, caution checked him, and the two governed his long stride, swiftly, noiselessly, to the climax he felt was at hand.

As he drew near to the outer gates, a light shadow stirred and went, as though the grey of the snow had taken detached motion. A darker shadow stayed and faced Christian, striking his life-blood chill with utmost despair.

Sweyn stood before him, and surely, the shadow that went was White Fell.

They had been together—close. Had she not been in his arms, near enough for lips to meet?

There was no moon, but the stars gave light enough to show that Sweyn's face was flushed and elate. The flush remained, though the expression changed quickly at sight of his brother. How, if Christian had seen all, should one of his frenzied outbursts be met and managed: by resolution? by indifference? He halted between the two, and as a result, he swaggered.

"White Fell?" questioned Christian, hoarse and breathless.

"Yes?"

Sweyn's answer was a query, with an intonation that implied he was clearing the ground for action.

From Christian came: "Have you kissed her?" like a bolt direct, staggering Sweyn by its sheer prompt temerity.

He flushed yet darker, and yet half-smiled over this earnest of success he had won. Had there been really between himself and Christian the rivalry that he imagined, his face had enough of the insolence of triumph to exasperate jealous rage.

"You dare ask this!"

"Sweyn, O Sweyn, I must know! You have!"

The ring of despair and anguish in his tone angered Sweyn, misconstruing it. Jealousy urging to such presumption was intolerable.

"Mad fool!" he said, constraining himself no longer. "Win for yourself a woman to kiss. Leave mine without question. Such an one as I should desire to kiss is such an one as shall never allow a kiss to you."

Then Christian fully understood his supposition.

"I—I!" he cried. "White Fell—that deadly Thing! Sweyn, are you blind, mad? I would save you from her: a Were-Wolf!"

Sweyn maddened again at the accusation—a dastardly way of revenge, as he conceived; and instantly, for the second time, the brothers were at strife violently.

But Christian was now too desperate to be scrupulous; for a dim glimpse had shot a possibility into his mind, and to be free to follow it the striking of his brother was a necessity. Thank God! he was armed, and so Sweyn's equal.

Facing his assailant with the bear-spear, he struck up his arms, and with the butt end hit hard so that he fell. The matchless runner leapt away on the instant, to follow a forlorn hope. Sweyn, on regaining his feet, was as amazed as angry at this unaccountable flight. He knew in his heart that his brother was no coward, and that it was unlike him to shrink from an encounter because defeat was certain, and cruel humiliation from a vindictive victor probable. Of the uselessness of pursuit he was well aware: he must abide his chagrin, content to know that his time for advantage would come. Since White Fell had parted to the right, Christian to the left, the event of a sequent* encounter did not occur to him. And now Christian, acting on the dim glimpse he had had, just as Sweyn turned upon him, of something that moved against the sky along the ridge behind the homestead, was staking his only hope on a chance, and his own superlative speed. If what he saw

* Following logically, as in a sequence.

was really White Fell, he guessed she was bending her steps towards the open wastes; and there was just a possibility that, by a straight dash, and a desperate perilous leap over a sheer bluff, he might yet meet her or head her. And then: he had no further thought.

It was past, the quick, fierce race, and the chance of death at the leap; and he halted in a hollow to fetch his breath and to look: did she come? had she gone?

She came.

She came with a smooth, gliding, noiseless speed, that was neither walking nor running; her arms were folded in her furs that were drawn tight about her body; the white lappets from her head were wrapped and knotted closely beneath her face; her eyes were set on a far distance. So she went till the even sway of her going was startled to a pause by Christian.

"Fell!"

She drew a quick, sharp breath at the sound of her name thus mutilated, and faced Sweyn's brother. Her eyes glittered; her upper lip was lifted, and shewed the teeth. The half of her name, impressed with an ominous sense as uttered by him, warned her of the aspect of a deadly foe. Yet she cast loose her robes till they trailed ample, and spoke as a mild woman.

"What would you?"

Then Christian answered with his solemn dreadful accusation:

"You kissed Rol—and Rol is dead! You kissed Trella: she is dead! You have kissed Sweyn, my brother; but he shall not die!"

He added: "You may live till midnight."

The edge of the teeth and the glitter of the eyes stayed a moment, and her right hand also slid down to the axe haft. Then, without a word, she swerved from him, and sprang out and away swiftly over the snow.

And Christian sprang out and away, and followed her swiftly over the snow, keeping behind, but half-a-stride's length from her side.

So they went running together, silent, towards the vast wastes of snow, where no living thing but they two moved under the stars of night.

Never before had Christian so rejoiced in his powers. The gift of speed, and the training of use and endurance were priceless to him now. Though midnight was hours away, he was confident that, go where that Fell Thing would, hasten as she would, she could not outstrip him nor escape from him. Then, when came the time for transformation, when the woman's form made no longer a shield against a man's hand, he could slay or be slain to save Sweyn. He had struck his dear brother in dire extremity, but he could not, though reason urged, strike a woman.

For one mile, for two miles they ran: White Fell ever foremost, Christian ever at equal distance from her side, so near that, now and again, her out-flying furs touched him. She spoke no word; nor he. She never turned her head to look at him, nor swerved to evade him; but, with set face looking forward, sped straight on, over rough, over smooth, aware of his nearness by the regular beat of his feet, and the sound of his breath behind.

In a while she quickened her pace. From the first, Christian had judged of her speed as admirable, yet with exulting security in his own excelling and enduring whatever her efforts. But, when the pace increased, he found himself put to the test as never had he been before in any race. Her feet, indeed, flew faster than his; it was only by his length of stride that he kept his place at her side. But his heart was high and resolute, and he did not fear failure yet.

So the desperate race flew on. Their feet struck up the powdery snow, their breath smoked into the sharp clear air, and they were gone before the air was cleared of snow and vapour. Now and then Christian glanced up to judge, by the rising of the stars, of the coming of midnight. So long—so long!

White Fell held on without slack. She, it was evident, with confidence in her speed proving matchless, as resolute to outrun her pursuer as he to endure till midnight and fulfil his purpose. And Christian held on, still self-assured. He could not fail; he would not fail. To avenge Rol and Trella was motive enough for him to do what man could do; but for Sweyn more. She had kissed Sweyn, but he should not die too: with Sweyn to save he could not fail.

Never before was such a race as this; no, not when in old Greece man and maid raced together with two fates at stake;* for the hard running was

* Probably a reference to the legend of Atalanta and Hippomenes. Atalanta was the swiftest maiden in the land, raised in the wild, and a great huntress. When her father insisted that she wed, she swore that she would only marry one who bested her in a race. Hippomenes asked the assistance of Aphrodite, who gave him three golden apples to place along the race course. When Atalanta stopped to pick up the apples, Hippomenes ran by her and won the race. Their marriage was less than harmonious, however, as Hippomenes failed to make regular offerings to Aphrodite, who was unforgiving.

sustained unabated, while star after star rose and went wheeling up towards midnight, for one hour, for two hours.

Then Christian saw and heard what shot him through with fear. Where a fringe of trees hung round a slope he saw something dark moving, and heard a yelp, followed by a full horrid cry, and the dark spread out upon the snow, a pack of wolves in pursuit.

Of the beasts alone he had little cause for fear; at the pace he held he could distance them, four-footed though they were. But of White Fell's wiles he had infinite apprehension, for how might she not avail herself of the savage jaws of these wolves, akin as they were to half her nature. She vouchsafed to them nor look nor sign; but Christian, on an impulse to assure himself that she should not escape him, caught and held the back-flung edge of her furs, running still.

She turned like a flash with a beastly snarl, teeth and eyes gleaming again. Her axe shone, on the upstroke, on the downstroke, as she hacked at his hand. She had lopped it off at the wrist, but that he parried with the bear-spear. Even then, she shore through the shaft and shattered the bones of the hand at the same blow, so that he loosed perforce.

Then again they raced on as before, Christian not losing a pace, though his left hand swung useless, bleeding and broken.

The snarl, indubitable, though modified from a woman's organs, the vicious fury revealed in teeth and eyes, the sharp arrogant pain of her maiming blow, caught away Christian's heed of the beasts behind, by striking into him close vivid realisation of the infinitely greater danger that ran before him in that deadly Thing.

When he bethought him to look behind, lo! the pack had but reached their tracks, and instantly slunk aside, cowed; the yell of pursuit changing to yelps and whines. So abhorrent was that fell creature to beast as to man.

She had drawn her furs more closely to her, disposing them so that, instead of flying loose to her heels, no drapery hung lower than her knees, and this without a check to her wonderful speed, nor embarrassment by the cumbering of the folds. She held her head as before; her lips were firmly set, only the tense nostrils gave her breath; not a sign of distress witnessed to the long sustaining of that terrible speed.

But on Christian by now the strain was telling palpably. His head weighed heavy, and his breath came labouring in great sobs; the bear spear would have been a burden now. His heart was beating like a hammer, but such a dulness oppressed his brain, that it was only by degrees he could realise his helpless state; wounded and weaponless, chasing that terrible Thing, that was a fierce, desperate, axe-armed woman, except she should assume the beast with fangs yet more formidable.

And still the far slow stars went lingering nearly an hour from midnight.

So far was his brain astray that an impression took him that she was fleeing from the midnight stars, whose gain was by such slow degrees that a time equalling days and days had gone in the race round the northern circle of the world, and days and days as long might last before the end—except she slackened, or except he failed.

But he would not fail yet.

How long had he been praying so? He had started with a self-confidence and reliance that had felt no need for that aid; and now it seemed the only means by which to restrain his heart from swelling beyond the compass of his body, by which to cherish his brain from dwindling and shrivelling quite away. Some sharp-toothed creature kept tearing and dragging on his maimed left hand; he never could see it, he could not shake it off; but he prayed it off at times.

The clear stars before him took to shuddering, and he knew why: they shuddered at sight of what was behind him. He had never divined before that strange things hid themselves from men under pretence of being snow-clad mounds or swaying trees; but now they came slipping out from their harmless covers to follow him, and mock at his impotence to make a kindred Thing resolve to truer form. He knew the air behind him was thronged; he heard the hum of innumerable murmurings together; but his eyes could never catch them, they were too swift and nimble. Yet he knew they were there, because, on a backward glance, he saw the snow mounds surge as they grovelled flatlings* out of sight; he saw the trees reel as they screwed themselves rigid past recognition among the boughs.

* This is an archaic way of saying "threw themselves flat on the ground."

And after such glance the stars for awhile returned to steadfastness, and an infinite stretch of silence froze upon the chill grey world, only deranged by the swift even beat of the flying feet, and his own—slower from the longer stride, and the sound of his breath. And for some clear moments he knew that his only concern was, to sustain his speed regardless of pain and distress, to deny with every nerve he had her power to outstrip him or to widen the space between them, till the stars crept up to midnight. Then out again would come that crowd invisible, humming and hustling behind, dense and dark enough, he knew, to blot out the stars at his back, yet ever skipping and jerking from his sight.

A hideous check came to the race. White Fell swirled about and leapt to the right, and Christian, unprepared for so prompt a lurch, found close at his feet a deep pit yawning, and his own impetus past control. But he snatched at her as he bore past, clasping her right arm with his one whole hand, and the two swung together upon the brink.

And her straining away in self preservation was vigorous enough to counter-balance his headlong impulse, and brought them reeling together to safety.

Then, before he was verily sure that they were not to perish so, crashing down, he saw her gnashing in wild pale fury as she wrenched to be free; and since her right hand was in his grasp, used her axe left-handed, striking back at him.

The blow was effectual enough even so; his right arm dropped powerless, gashed, and with the lesser bone broken, that jarred with horrid pain when he let it swing as he leaped out again, and ran to recover the few feet she had gained from his pause at the shock.

The near escape and this new quick pain made again every faculty alive and intense. He knew that what he followed was most surely Death animate: wounded and helpless, he was utterly at her mercy if so she should realise and take action. Hopeless to avenge, hopeless to save, his very despair for Sweyn swept him on to follow, and follow, and precede the kiss-doomed to death. Could he yet fail to hunt that Thing past midnight, out of the womanly form alluring and treacherous, into lasting restraint of the bestial, which was the last shred of hope left from the confident purpose of the outset?

"Sweyn, Sweyn, O Sweyn!" He thought he was praying, though his heart wrung out nothing but this: "Sweyn, Sweyn, O Sweyn!"

The last hour from midnight had lost half its quarters, and the stars went lifting up the great minutes; and again his greatening heart, and his shrinking brain, and the sickening agony that swung at either side, conspired to appal the will that had only seeming empire over his feet.

Now White Fell's body was so closely enveloped that not a lap nor an edge flew free. She stretched forward strangely aslant, leaning from the upright poise of a runner. She cleared the ground at times by long bounds, gaining an increase of speed that Christian agonised to equal.

Because the stars pointed that the end was nearing, the black brood came behind again, and followed, noising. Ah! if they could but be kept quiet and still, nor slip their usual harmless masks to encourage with their interest the last speed of their most deadly congener. What shape had they? Should he ever know? If it were not that he was bound to compel the fell Thing that ran before him into her truer form, he might face about and follow them. No—no—not so; if he might do anything but what he did—race, race, and racing bear this agony, he would just stand still and die, to be quit of the pain of breathing.

He grew bewildered, uncertain of his own identity, doubting of his own true form. He could not be really a man, no more than that running Thing was really a woman; his real form was only hidden under embodiment of a man, but what it was he did not know. And Sweyn's real form he did not know. Sweyn lay fallen at his feet, where he had struck him down—his own brother—he: he stumbled over him, and had to overleap him and race harder because she who had kissed Sweyn leapt so fast. "Sweyn, Sweyn, O Sweyn!"

Why did the stars stop to shudder? Midnight else had surely come!

The leaning, leaping Thing looked back at him with a wild, fierce look, and laughed in savage scorn and triumph. He saw in a flash why, for within a time measurable by seconds she would have escaped him utterly. As the land lay, a slope of ice sunk on the one hand; on the other hand a steep rose, shouldering forwards; between the two was space for a foot to be planted, but none for a body to stand; yet a juniper bough, thrusting out, gave a handhold secure enough for one with a resolute grasp to swing past the perilous place, and pass on safe.

Though the first seconds of the last moment were going, she dared to flash back a wicked look, and laugh at the pursuer who was impotent to grasp.

The crisis struck convulsive life into his last supreme effort; his will surged up indomitable, his speed proved matchless yet. He leapt with a rush, passed her before her laugh had time to go out, and turned short, barring the way, and braced to withstand her.

She came hurling desperate, with a feint to the right hand, and then launched herself upon him with a spring like a wild beast when it leaps to kill. And he, with one strong arm and a hand that could not hold, with one strong hand and an arm that could not guide and sustain, he caught and held her even so. And they fell together. And because he felt his whole arm slipping, and his whole hand loosing, to slack the dreadful agony of the wrenched bone above, he caught and held with his teeth the tunic at her knee, as she struggled up and wrung off his hands to overleap him victorious.

Like lightning she snatched her axe, and struck him on the neck, deep—once, twice—his life-blood gushed out, staining her feet.

The stars touched midnight.

The death scream he heard was not his, for his set teeth had hardly yet relaxed when it rang out; and the dreadful cry began with a woman's shriek, and changed and ended as the yell of a beast. And before the final blank overtook his dying eyes, he saw that She gave place to It; he saw more, that Life gave place to Death—causelessly, incomprehensibly.

For he did not presume that no holy water could be more holy, more potent to destroy an evil thing than the life-blood of a pure heart poured out for another in free willing devotion.

His own true hidden reality that he had desired to know grew palpable, recognisable. It seemed to him just this: a great glad abounding hope that he had saved his brother; too expansive to be contained by the limited form of a sole man, it yearned for a new embodiment infinite as the stars.

What did it matter to that true reality that the man's brain shrank, shrank, till it was nothing; that the man's body could not retain the huge pain of his heart, and heaved it out through the red exit riven at the neck; that the black noise came again hurtling from behind, reinforced by that dissolved shape, and blotted out for ever the man's sight, hearing, sense.

In the early grey of day Sweyn chanced upon the footprints of a man—of a runner, as he saw by the shifted snow; and the direction they had taken aroused curiosity, since a little farther their line must be crossed by the edge of a sheer height. He turned to trace them. And so doing, the length of the stride struck his attention—a stride long as his own if he ran. He knew he was following Christian.

In his anger he had hardened himself to be indifferent to the night-long absence of his brother; but now, seeing where the footsteps went, he was seized with compunction and dread. He had failed to give thought and care to his poor frantic twin, who might—was it possible?—have rushed to a frantic death.

His heart stood still when he came to the place where the leap had been taken. A piled edge of snow had fallen too, and nothing but snow lay below when he peered. Along the upper edge he ran for a furlong, till he came to a dip where he could slip and climb down, and then back again on the lower level to the pile of fallen snow. There he saw that the vigorous running had started afresh.

He stood pondering; vexed that any man should have taken that leap where he had not ventured to follow; vexed that he had been beguiled to such painful emotions; guessing vainly at Christian's object in this mad freak. He began sauntering along, half unconsciously following his brother's track; and so in a while he came to the place where the footprints were doubled.

Small prints were these others, small as a woman's, though the pace from one to another was longer than that which the skirts of women allow.

Did not White Fell tread so?

A dreadful guess appalled him, so dreadful that he recoiled from belief. Yet his face grew ashy white, and he gasped to fetch back motion to his checked heart. Unbelievable? Closer attention showed how the smaller footfall had altered for greater speed, striking into the snow with a deeper onset and a lighter pressure on the heels. Unbelievable? Could any woman but White Fell run so? Could any man but Christian run so? The guess became a certainty. He was following where alone in the dark night White Fell had fled from Christian pursuing.

Such villainy set heart and brain on fire with rage and indignation: such villainy in his own brother, till lately love-worthy, praiseworthy, though a fool for meekness. He would kill Christian; had he lives many as the footprints he had trodden, vengeance should demand them all. In a tempest of murderous hate he followed on in haste, for the track was plain enough, starting with such a burst of speed as could not be maintained, but brought him back soon to a plod for the spent, sobbing breath to be regulated. He cursed Christian aloud and called White Fell's name on high in a frenzied expense of passion. His grief itself was a rage, being such an intolerable anguish of pity and shame at the thought of his love, White Fell, who had parted from his kiss free and radiant, to be hounded straightway by his brother mad with jealousy, fleeing for more than life while her lover was housed at his ease. If he had but known, he raved, in impotent rebellion at the cruelty of events, if he had but known that his strength and love might have availed in her defence; now the only service to her that he could render was to kill Christian.

As a woman he knew she was matchless in speed, matchless in strength; but Christian was matchless in speed among men, nor easily to be matched in strength. Brave and swift and strong though she were, what chance had she against a man of his strength and inches, frantic, too, and intent on horrid revenge against his brother, his successful rival?

Mile after mile he followed with a bursting heart; more piteous, more tragic, seemed the case at this evidence of White Fell's splendid supremacy, holding her own so long against Christian's famous speed. So long, so long that his love and admiration grew more and more boundless, and his grief and indignation therewith also. Whenever the track lay clear he ran, with such reckless prodigality of strength, that it soon was spent, and he dragged on heavily, till, sometimes on the ice of a mere, sometimes on a wind-swept place, all signs were lost; but, so undeviating had been their line that a course straight on, and then short questing to either hand, recovered them again.

Hour after hour had gone by through more than half that winter day, before ever he came to the place where the trampled snow showed that a scurry of feet had come—and gone! Wolves' feet—and gone most amazingly! Only a little beyond he came to the lopped point of Christian's bear-spear; farther on he would see where the remnant of the useless shaft had been dropped. The snow here was dashed with blood, and the footsteps of the two had fallen closer together. Some hoarse sound of exultation came from him that might have been a laugh had breath sufficed. "O White Fell, my poor, brave love! Well struck!" he groaned, torn by his pity and great admiration, as he guessed surely how she had turned and dealt a blow.

The sight of the blood inflamed him as it might a beast that ravens. He grew mad with a desire to have Christian by the throat once again, not to loose this time till he had crushed out his life, or beat out his life, or stabbed out his life; or all these, and torn him piecemeal likewise: and ah! then, not till then, bleed his heart with weeping, like a child, like a girl, over the piteous fate of his poor lost love.

On—on—on—through the aching time, toiling and straining in the track of those two superb runners, aware of the marvel of their endurance, but unaware of the marvel of their speed, that, in the three hours before midnight had overpassed all that vast distance that he could only traverse from twilight to twilight. For clear daylight was passing when he came to the edge of an old marl-pit,* and saw how the two who had gone before had stamped and trampled together in desperate peril on the verge. And here fresh blood stains spoke to him of a valiant defence against his infamous brother; and he followed where the blood had dripped till the cold had staunched its flow, taking a savage gratification from this evidence that Christian had been gashed deeply, maddening afresh with desire to do likewise more excellently, and so slake his murderous hate. And he began to know that through all his despair he had entertained a germ of hope, that grew apace, rained upon by his brother's blood.

He strove on as best he might, wrung now by an access of hope, now of despair, in agony to reach the end, however terrible, sick with the aching of the toiled miles that deferred it.

And the light went lingering out of the sky, giving place to uncertain stars.

He came to the finish.

Two bodies lay in a narrow place. Christian's was one, but the other beyond not White Fell's. There where the footsteps ended lay a great white wolf.

---

* A pit from which "marl"—mud rich with calcium carbonate or lime—was dug to be used as fertilizer.

At the sight Sweyn's strength was blasted; body and soul he was struck down grovelling.

The stars had grown sure and intense before he stirred from where he had dropped prone. Very feebly he crawled to his dead brother, and laid his hands upon him, and crouched so, afraid to look or stir farther.

Cold, stiff, hours dead. Yet the dead body was his only shelter and stay in that most dreadful hour. His soul, stripped bare of all sceptic comfort, cowered, shivering, naked, abject; and the living clung to the dead out of piteous need for grace from the soul that had passed away.

He rose to his knees, lifting the body. Christian had fallen face forward in the snow, with his arms flung up and wide, and so had the frost made him rigid: strange, ghastly, unyielding to Sweyn's lifting, so that he laid him down again and crouched above, with his arms fast round him, and a low heart-wrung groan.

When at last he found force to raise his brother's body and gather it in his arms, tight clasped to his breast, he tried to face the Thing that lay beyond. The sight set his limbs in a palsy with horror and dread. His senses had failed and fainted in utter cowardice, but for the strength that came from holding dead Christian in his arms, enabling him to compel his eyes to endure the sight, and take into the brain the complete aspect of the Thing. No wound, only blood stains on the feet. The great grim jaws had a savage grin, though dead-stiff. And his kiss: he could bear it no longer, and turned away, nor ever looked again.

And the dead man in his arms, knowing the full horror, had followed and faced it for his sake; had suffered agony and death for his sake; in the neck was the deep death gash, one arm and both hands were dark with frozen blood, for his sake! Dead he knew him, as in life he had not known him, to give the right meed* of love and worship. Because the outward man lacked perfection and strength equal to his, he had taken the love and worship of that great pure heart as his due; he, so unworthy in the inner reality, so mean, so despicable, callous, and contemptuous towards the brother who had laid down his life to save him. He longed for utter annihilation, that so he might lose the agony of knowing himself so unworthy such perfect

* A deserved share or reward.

love. The frozen calm of death on the face appalled him. He dared not touch it with lips that had cursed so lately, with lips fouled by kiss of the horror that had been death.

He struggled to his feet, still clasping Christian. The dead man stood upright within his arm, frozen rigid. The eyes were not quite closed; the head had stiffened, bowed slightly to one side; the arms stayed straight and wide. It was the figure of one crucified, the blood-stained hands also conforming.*

So living and dead went back along the track that one had passed in the deepest passion of love, and one in the deepest passion of hate. All that night Sweyn toiled through the snow, bearing the weight of dead Christian, treading back along the steps he before had trodden, when he was wronging with vilest thoughts, and cursing with murderous hatred, the brother who all the while lay dead for his sake.

Cold, silence, darkness encompassed the strong man bowed with the dolorous burden; and yet he knew surely that that night he entered hell, and trod hell-fire along the homeward road, and endured through it only because Christian was with him. And he knew surely that to him Christian had been as Christ, and had suffered and died to save him from his sins.

* And let's not forget that his name was Christian!

Dora Sigerson Shorter (1866–1918) was born and raised in Ireland, the daughter of a noted Dublin surgeon and poet George Sigerson. She moved to London after she married Clement King Shorter, an English literary critic, in 1895. She is best known for her poetry and sculpture and is regarded today as one of the leading poets of the Irish Literary Revival. Her friendships extended beyond those circles, however, including author Katharine Tynan and political activist Alice Furlong. The following harrowing tale about the consequences of a transfer of souls first appeared in her 1900 collection *The Father Confessor,* subtitled *Stories of Death and Danger.*

Transmigration

by Dora Sigerson Shorter

I

Many men have tasted Hell some moments of their lives—a Hell of their own making, perhaps; but I, oh God! I have been in the Hell of the damned.

I cannot remember my father or my mother; oh, wretched that I am! Had I either to love one whom no man loves? No, I cannot remember. My memory goes back three months—no further. Every day I live those three months over and over again.

I had too much money when I came of age. I knew not how to use it. I threw it here and there, ever indulging in my own pleasure. Playing in the world till the dust of it rose up and clouded my eyes—till the hand of innocence I held in mine was changed for the hand of sin.

Playing in a world that I was sent to work in, I forgot I had a soul or that there was a God who had given it to me. I played until my selfish indulgences brought upon me the sickness of death. And then my three months of Hell commenced. Unloved, unfriended, I tossed upon my bed, blaspheming a God I did not believe in, swearing I would not die. Shrieking in my terror of that Hell, I felt myself approaching a Hell I had so often scoffed at. I heard my screams re-echo through the empty house, unreplied to, making my desolation complete. Then I lay still, gasping on my bed; so would my prayers soar up to Heaven, I thought, unanswered, unheard. But stay! a step on the stairs—nearer, nearer; the door has opened, and a man stands upon the threshold. Oh, eyes that beamed peace and love, you saved me from Heaven's vengeance for the moment—at what a cost! He came forward into the room when he saw me, and I thought for an instant it was an angel sent to comfort my misery.

"I heard you call," he said; "and, fearing you were ill, I entered. I am your neighbour, my latch-key fits your door. You must pardon my coming, but, thinking you were ill—and alone—"

"I am alone," I said—"alone, alone, deserted alike by God and man. Body and soul I am alone, and sick unto death."

"Despair not, my friend," said he. "I will attend you; you are sick, and morbid from being left alone. Rouse yourself, and I will try and help."

"Help me! no man can help me; I have helped no man. Unless you can give me another life to live with the knowledge I have of this."

"My dear friend, God alone can do that," his voice went on soothingly; "but you are truly sorry for your past?"

"Man," I cried, "there are no such things as death-bed repentances. Death is ever beside us a yawning precipice; as we walk along its edge we *know* that it is there. We look at the sky above it, at the flowers by its brink, but we never look at it; we turn our heads away, but we know that it is there. We feel the chill of it in the heat of the sun. We see its shadow on the petals of the flowers. We know that a false step, a stumble, and we are gone, plunged into Eternity in a moment. We say that sometime this path must come to an end, as we but follow it to our extermination, and when we see before us the black doors of death, *then* will we lay aside our flowers, and still our songs and laughter. And Heaven will pity our prayers and sighs. Talk not to me of such repentances; I believe them not, nor you, nor anyman."

"You are very ill," the stranger said, as I raved on.

"I will not die, I must live, though Heaven itself has shut its gates upon me. Hell—if such is my destination—must give me a year of life. I say, I will not die." A strange strength seemed to flow through my veins. I raised myself on my elbow. The stranger was standing at my bedside looking with divine pity at my convulsed face.

"You," I said. Oh, the horror of it! "You must die, you with your life of purity behind you; death should have no fears for you. The gates of Heaven are open for you; give me your body, your life, and let me live."

"Friend," he said, as though humouring me, "I cannot die; I have a mother who is old and requires my care, and a child, a darling little child."

"You must die!" I cried again. "I will care for your mother and child. You must die and let me live—I say, I will not die."

"You are very ill," was all he said, laying his hand upon my brow. And then, I know not how it came to pass, whether my cry to Heaven or Hell had been answered, or, whatever it was, by some great effort of my will, *but I stood by the bed looking down at my own sleeping body.* I dashed across the room to the glass. It was the stranger it reflected back—yes, the same high forehead, with fair, wavy hair, the same large, dreamy eyes; but his soul, ah! his soul lay sleeping in that motionless form upon the bed. I turned and left the haunted room, living, living, living!

II

Living, living—oh, the joy of it! I had died and was born again. How it came about, what cared I? "Who," I thought, as I bounded down the stairs, "so fortunate as I?" What man or woman thinking over the past has not said—"Oh, could I but live my life over again, I would not have done this thing or that"? And I, with my evil past laid out before me, could live it again, casting out the weeds and cultivating the trodden flowers; with nothing to hinder me, not even the sensual flesh that lay upstairs, a prison-house for the spirit of that good man whose body I was inhabiting and whose life I proposed to live.

I closed the door of my own house and went up the tiny garden to the next; as I did so, I heard the patter of little feet and a childish voice calling, "Here's papa! Here's papa!"

I opened the door and took the little darling into my arms. Never had I felt such happiness as when the innocent parted lips met mine and the soft baby-hands went round my neck. I stood still to take in the joy of it, but the child drew back in my arms and for a moment she sat quite quiet, and then she struggled until I had to let her down.

"It's not my papa!" she sobbed, running into the little sitting-room. "Oh, gran'ma, 'tis not my own papa!"

Mechanically I hung my hat upon the rack in the hall and followed the child. The room was small, but very bright and cosy; an old lady was seated in an arm-chair before the blazingfire; one withered hand was laid caressingly upon the golden head of the little girl, the other shaded her eyes as she anxiously watched the door. When I entered she smiled and turned to the weeping child.

"Why, what ailed you, darling? Look, Rosy, it is your own papa."

Rosy looked up through her tears, and, seeing me standing in the full glare of the lamp and fire, ran to me again. I sat down in a low chair opposite the old woman, and the little child climbed on to my knees.

"It's my dood papa," she said, laying her wet cheek against mine.

For an hour I sat thus tasting for the first time the joy of a home, and listening to the old woman as she told me tales of her son's youth—my youth now.

For some time she rambled on, in the fashion of the old, and at last for very joy I laughed aloud, waking the child, who had fallen asleep in my arms.

"Will you take her up to bed, Gilbert," said her grandmother; "she sat up for you that you might put her to sleep to-night."

I raised the child in my arms, the pretty little babe with her soft curls falling across her face, and she laid her drowsy head upon my shoulder. I pressed her with joy to my breast as I turned up the narrow, dark stairs; at my movement she sat up suddenly and pushed me from her with both her tiny hands. Oh, wonderful instinct of the child that in the light beheld her father, but in darkness knew me for a stranger!

"You're not my papa! Oh, I want papa!"

"Hush, hush!" I whispered; "I am your papa."

"You're not, you're not!" and she beat upon my breast with both her tiny fists. "Give me my own papa, you bad, bad man!"

Then a great fury seized me, and I held her over the banisters. "Call me your father, or I let you go."

"No, no; I want my own papa!"

"Call me your father, or I let you go."

"I want my dood papa!"

I did not mean it, Heaven knows I did not mean it, but my fingers loosed their hold. I shook the little hands from their terrified grasp upon my coat. The hall echoed the screams of a child and a sickening thud on the flags beneath. A terrible laugh followed, a laugh that might have come from the lowest pits of Hell. Was it I who uttered it? I looked into the hall beneath me. A trembling old woman knelt there, and, at her side, a servant with a lighted candle, but their white faces were not turned to the motionless body at their feet, but towards me, unspeaking, as though they were frozen by some terrible sight or sound. Had a devil entered into the body of Gilbert Graham during the time my spirit was passing from my own to it—a devil who, making me work its will, thus laughed in its hideous triumph? Surely devils were many round my bed when I lay dying. Its power had left me now, and I went, in bitter remorse, to the little child.

"She slipped from my arms," I whispered. "She slipped, mother."

She answered me nothing; but, as I raised the senseless babe, the servant sobbed, "Oh, Master Gilbert, we thought the shock had sent you mad!"

I laid the child upon the sofa, while the girl ran for a doctor. I stood as though stunned until he came, watching him then in a dream as he examined the soft limbs of the poor babe, and he shook his head as he arose.

"I am sorry to have to tell you that if she lives she will be a cripple all her life."

"Tell my mother," I whispered. I was not the one to tell her this.

"I am sorry," he said; "I am very sorry, Madam."

"Hush!" the old woman answered; "hush! You will waken her."

"She may never waken," he whispered. "Bear up, dear Madam."

"Hush!" the old woman said again, touching the golden curls that were stained with blood. "Hush! The fairies have come to her and laid red poppies in her hair."

And thus had I fulfilled my trust to care for his mother and child—one a cripple or dead, the other a muttering idiot.

I had launched my new life, and the waters that bore it were red human blood; but who or what was the dread pilot that guided it?

III

I stole out into the dimly lighted street. Of what use was I at home?

The little child still lingered. The old woman was still happy in her ignorance, babbling of fairies and red poppies. My hands were the fairies that had laid those terrible flowers on her babe's fair head, the sleep-giving poppies on her eyes.

The paper-boys were shouting in my ears as I passed, but I paid no attention to them. Their "terrible tragedies" could not equal mine; their cries of "Murder!" woke no horror in my heart; they only cried aloud the word that echoed there. I dare not think of the imprisoned soul that lay as dead in my room—the only one who sought me out in my hour of death's despair. My horrible cries, that had frightened the very servants from my house, but hastened his feet to my side; and now he slept, a thin wall between him and the reward I had given him—a ruined home.

Oh, how could I hear the city noises and a thousand cries within my breast—a thousand little hands beating upon my heart, "Give back! give back!"

And so I strode through the damp fog, caring not, thinking not where I was going. At last a bright light flashed in my eyes, and I started as though awaking. Before me was a lighted doorway, and above it, in the light of the lamp, hung a board, and upon it in red letters the word "Billiards." The place was a gambling-hell. I had known it but too well in the old days. I gazed about, half-hearing some one speaking, and saw a young man before me, his face flushed and his eyelids drooping.

"I could not help it, Graham; indeed I could not! I tried to keep away because of my promise to you and for my mother's sake."

His promise to me! I almost laughed aloud. Yes, I knew that boyish, effeminate face. It had been often opposite to me at the gambling-table inside. I had seen it grow white and tortured as the game went on. I had made its hairless lips grow sweet in a smile, or quiver pathetically like a girl's, by the turn of my hand; I had lured him on night after night with a hope I held between my fingers. His promise to me! I had forgotten. Something evil was rising in my heart. I felt it would claim my lips if I did not speak. I seized his arm.

"Go home," I said; "heed not what I may say to you after this, heed not what I may seem to you. The most beautiful statue is but hollow and moulded in common clay. The tiger's claws are soft as a lady's cheek, but they will tear you to pieces if you trust them. The moth sees the candle's flame, and, thinking it fair, he dies. I am not as you think—"

"I do not know what you mean, Graham. If you mean this den has any fairness for me, it is not so, unless it be the fascination of the bird to the serpent's eye."

"Leave me!" I cried despairingly, for devils' words were rising to my lips; and as he did not heed me, I turned and spoke them.

"Come in with me," I said, and laughed. "Come in with me, and I shall see fair play."

"With you!" He started. "With you, Graham! you who have preached of its dangers to me and its temptations and wickedness; you to whom I looked to save me from where it will lead me. Oh, Graham! I could laugh, 'tis so absurd!"

"I'll see fair play," I said again; "besides, you could not break yourself of the habit so easily and abruptly—I will wean you from it by degrees."

I took his arm, and we passed inside. No one took any notice of me when we entered, but they all gathered around my companion.

"Why, Varen, we thought you were going to leave us?"

"Did you hear of the discovery in Harrington Street last night? Poor Bulger! You remember Bulger, don't you? You lost a cool hundred to him one night here over the cards, eh? Got a cataleptic fit, they say; most interesting case. Went home in a most distressing state of mind the other night, commenced shouting like the devil, frightened the servant out of her wits and out of the house—says she hid in a doorway till dawn, afraid to go back; then she screwed up her courage and stole to the house; finding no answer to her knocks, and being unable to open the door, became alarmed, started for the police-station, and returned with some of the force. One got into the house by a low window and opened the door to the rest; they found poor Bulger lying on his bed—they thought—dead as a herring, but the doctors say 'tis a most interesting case of catalepsy."

I listened without speaking. "What a queer old world it is!" I thought; "we must have a name for everything, no matter how wonderful, or where would our doctors and men of science be? Nothing is left to the God who designed the whole. Our beliefs are superstitions, we laugh them away; we would explain the very law of life itself."

A hand was laid upon my arm.

"Play a game of cards, Graham? The fellows are asking me."

"No, no; this is no place for you—for me. Come out of it quickly." But the men surrounded us.

"You are not going yet? just one game, then?"

Fool that I was, I complied, and took my seat at the table. They thought I was a "green one," as was evident from their surprised looks when I swept up their little pile of silver at the end of the first game.

"You would think it was old Bulger himself," I heard one say; "he seems to have his accursed luck."

One game led to another; my companion's face grew pale; some demon arose within me, and I took a pleasure in its paleness.

Why is it innocence attracts the guilty so? Behind the bar connected with this card-room there was a young girl serving. I heard men make rude jests that brought the colour to her cheeks; she would hang her head if they called her endearing names, and the angry tears would spring to her eyes: she would shake off their hands with passion. For this girl they would leave their billiards and their cards to watch the red and white fly to her face; and now, when they speak to her, she answers their jests with similar ones; she answers their calls with a simper; she courts their caresses and their company; she is no longer attractive to them—she is one of themselves.

Why did I not pick out my prey among those evil, coarse faces—why did I seek to destroy the one exception? I know not; life preys upon that which is weaker than itself, not that which is its equal.

I swept pile after pile of silver into my pockets, Varen's white face growing whiter and whiter. At last he started to his feet—

"I'm cleared out—I have only a shilling left; I'm going home."

"Put it down," I said to him. "Why, man, you may win a pile on it yet. Finish this round, anyway."

Sullenly he sat down again and took up his cards.

I let him win game after game, and when he rose to depart he had won back a third of his losses.

"I'll come again to-morrow night and win the rest," he said, with a smile.

Why follow the downfall of that young life? Night after night we met in the same place, I hastening away from the ceaseless crying of a little, suffering child, calling for the father I had robbed her of; he from the complaints of a broken-hearted mother, powerless to draw her only son from the snare I had set for him. Night after night I robbed him of his earnings, leaving him to win back a third, to lure him with a hope, never to be fulfilled, that the next time he might win a fortune.

Paler each night grew the young face, shabbier the clothes, thinner the hands that grasped the cards so eagerly. Now he spoke no word of greeting to me; only his eyes revealed his thoughts: therein I could see the light of hope gleam faintly each night, fading, fading to give place to despair, returning again as the closing hours approached and the waiter's voice warned us it was time to stop.

One night Varen came hastily in, staggering as though he were drunk. Flinging himself down in a chair, he took his cards. There was no hope in his eyes; I saw only terrible anguish and despair. On one sleeve of his shabby coat I saw a broad band of crape.*

He played wildly—and won. I had slain my devil; he won again; I was glad. I saw his silver flow back to him; I was happy for the first time in many a weary hour. "I shall no longer be his curse," I thought; "through me he shall win back his fortune, his mother's blessing, his lost youth. I shall restore all."

* An armband worn in mourning after a death.

A cry recalled me. I had been dreaming. I gazed around bewildered; the candles were spluttering in their sockets, and on the side of one was a great roll of wax. It was turned towards Varen—I had heard old wives call it a winding-sheet. The dust of the day before lay white on the sideboard and table, disturbed only where the cards fell and by the track of our fingers. The dawn was creeping through the half-closed shutters of the window, making our faces grey and ghastly in the two lights.

Young Varen was staring at me with mad eyes, and on the table at my side lay a heap of silver. It was I who had been winning.

Varen leaned across the table and gazed into my face. "Are you a man," he said, "or are you a devil?"

I did not answer, but that terrible thing within me broke into a laugh. The men beside me started in horror as the sound came forth and echoed round the room as though a demon were in each corner to repeat it.

Varen's hand went to his breast.

"Devil in the shape of a man," he said, "your work is done! Cruelest of enemies in the guise of a friend! You won my trust and led me to this. What is pure, since you I believed so pure are as you are? What is the reward of love, since you I have loved reward me so? Through your aid I was fighting the old life from me, and rising to honour and esteem, to the knowledge of a mother's proud heart. And through your aid I fell to meanness and disgrace, to see a mother robbed of her necessaries, and worse—to lose her son's love and care and to die broken-hearted alone. Your hand had saved me from the precipice of Hell, and your hand it is that flings me into its hottest fire. Finish, then, your devil's work, for I dare not!"

He drew a pistol from his breast and handed it to me. I felt the cold steel in my hand, and saw the horrified looks of the men around us; they seemed powerless to cry out or interrupt us; before me the ghastly face of young Varen. A wild rage rose up in my heart; I panted like a mad dog, and foam fell from my mouth. I tried to pray, but could not.

A pistol-shot rang through the room, and the white face before me vanished. There was hot blood upon my hands; a terror seized me—what had I done? Hands were upon my shoulders. But I escaped them. I flew down the creaking stairs. People were shouting. Steps were coming after me. I flung wide the door and flew wildly, blindly, down the street. Feet were repeating the echo of mine. People were calling "Murder! murder!" Windows were flung open, men joined in the chase. People were calling "Murder!"—and my hands were red with blood. Ha! the well-known door—it was my own; *his* latch-key opened it. I let myself in and flew upstairs; there was a light in my old room; a nurse sat nodding over the fire. I saw my old form lying motionless upon the bed. I sprang to its side. Voices were calling at the hall-door—men were breaking it in. They had tracked me.

I seized the hand that lay upon the counterpane; a shudder ran through it. Steps were at the door, "Murder" ran through the house. There was a moment of nothingness and I woke.

It was all a terrible dream; I lay upon my own bed. The kind neighbour, hearing my cry, had called in to see if I needed anything; he was looking down with pity in his eyes, his hands cooling mine—he had dipped them in water. No! it was blood, BLOOD! and the room rang with the cries of "MURDERER!" I started up; they were putting manacles on his wrists. He was stunned, he knew not what to say; he answered not their insinuations, but passed his manacled hands now and again across his eyes, like a man who had been long sleeping.

A terrible laugh sounded round the room; it seemed to float through the doorway, and we heard it echo down the house, fading away into stillness. I tried to rise and speak, but fell back unconscious.

IV

I awoke to misery and despair. Lying still a moment, to gather my thoughts together, I heard some persons talking at the head of my bed. It was the nurse and a couple of men, doctors I soon knew them to be. They were talking excitedly, but in subdued voices; I heard every word distinctly: "Graham is to be hanged for the murder of young Varen." I started up, gazing at them in agony.

"He did not do it. I, and I alone, am guilty."

They had started back when I moved, in astonishment; but when I spoke they came beside me, trying to soothe me and make me lie down and rest again. To rest! O Heaven! there was no more rest for me in this world.

I told them I would explain, but they would not let me speak. I heard them whisper of my most extraordinary case. They thought I had gained consciousness while they were speaking of Graham, and, hearing their words at that critical moment, took the idea into my head that I had committed the crime.

"Let me go!" I moaned; "let me go!"

But they held me down in their cruel kindness till I had to do their bidding from very weakness.

But when the night came on, and when the old nurse was nodding in her chair, I arose in the darkness and went from the house. Up and down the streets I wandered till dawn grew grey, but no dawn arose in my heart, only black night for ever. Through the streets, never stopping, I walked till the sun grew hot and bright, and people crowded out into the pathways. I bought a paper from a newsvendor, and read the trial of Gilbert Graham. It was nearly over; all the evidence was against him. He had nothing to say for himself; once he spoke to ask if he might see his little child, and he was told she was dead. They said he seemed stunned, or as though in a dream. I read no more.

When the court was opened, and the trial came on again, I hid myself among the crowd that attended it. I saw the prisoner at the bar; he was not pale; a colour tinged his cheeks. He seemed as if he were asleep. I do not think he heard anything of what was going on. Witness after witness came to condemn him. I could not bear it. I put myself forward as a witness for the defence. They allowed me into the box. I tried to tell my story, but they would not listen to me; some laughed; some pitied me; but they would not let me speak.

"Will you not hear me?" I cried. "You cannot understand, but do not laugh; there are so many things men know nothing of, but do not scorn them because you do not understand them. Can you know what gives life to the smallest insect living on this earth? Can you explore a step beyond the grave? You cannot. I alone am guilty of this murder; by my own act, or by the act of Heaven or Hell, I know not."

A gentleman rose in the court; he sent a message to the Judge, whispered to a constable, and I was dragged out of the house. I heard a murmur of excited voices and a whisper.

"'Tis that poor fellow Bulger; they say his brain is turned since he had his cataleptic attack."

I was forced along by my doctor, his arm linked in mine. Calling a cab, he put me inside, and was about to follow, when a friend of his came up and spoke to him.

"Oh, yes," he answered, "I thought I'd find him there. He woke to consciousness just as Dr. Gill and myself were speaking of young Varen's death, and he seemed to get it into his head that he was the murderer. He escaped from the house last night, but from his ravings I thought it probable I should find him at court to-day."

I heard no more. Silently opening the door furthest from the speaker, I slipped out, and in the dusk of the evening made my escape.

How the night passed I know not, but, when the light came, I had but one thought: to seek out Graham and beg his forgiveness. Again I bought a morning paper, and read the finish of the trial. Graham was condemned to death.

After a day's wandering, or maybe more—I knew nothing of time in those blank hours—I found out the prison where he lay awaiting his doom, and craved admittance, saying I was a particular friend—a friend!

They let me see him for a moment, but he did not know me. He even smiled when I asked his forgiveness; even he would not believe me.

"I do not understand it at all," he said, laying his head on his hand wearily. "I cannot think, I cannot even feel these last few days," and then raised his head and gazed at me eagerly. "Do you know anything of my mother?"

I did not know of her, and turned away my face.

"I had a child!" he cried. "Oh, tell me of my little child!"

"Do you not remember?—she is dead," I told him, weeping.

He leaned his head upon his hand again. "I had forgotten."

He spoke no more to me, and I was taken out of the place. "He will forgive me tomorrow," I said.

But, hidden away in a low lodging-house, I was too ill to stir for many days; then early one morning I found myself at the prison door again; it opened for me readily, and when it closed I found myself confronted by my doctor and some of his friends.

"I thought our patient would turn up sooner or later," he said. "How fortunate you should choose the time we are here!"

"I will go anywhere you will if you but let me see him once again," I cried; "only once till he forgives me. Let me go! I must!" I cried, fighting them. "I cannot live unless I get his pardon."

"You cannot see him," they said.

"But I will—I must!"

"You cannot—he was hanged this morning at seven."

Mary E. Wilkins Freeman (1852–1930) was a prolific American writer of poems, novels, and short stories for children and adults. Born in Massachusetts to a strict religious family, she married at the age of 40 and moved to New Jersey. Primarily known for her depictions of New England life, she penned a dozen novels and as many short story collections, and much of her work explored the changing role of women, especially in rural settings. Wilkins Freeman also wrote of things supernatural. Her 1902 "Luella Miller" is a classic of vampire fiction, free of the influence of *Dracula* and its imitators and closer to the theme of Conan Doyle's 1894 novella *The Parasite.* In 1926, Wilkins Freeman became the first recipient of the William Dean Howells Medal for Distinction in Fiction from the American Academy of Arts and Letters. The following, which first appeared in *Everybody's Magazine* in February 1902 and in Wilkins Freeman's collection *The Wind in the Rose-Bush and Other Stories of the Supernatural* (published as Mary E. Wilkins in 1903), is a haunting tale of guilt and denial.

The Wind in the Rose-Bush

by Mary E. Wilkins Freeman

Ford Village has no railroad station, being on the other side of the river from Porter's Falls,* and accessible only by the ford which gives it its name, and a ferry line.

The ferry-boat was waiting when Rebecca Flint got off the train with her bag and lunch basket. When she and her small trunk were safely embarked she sat stiff and straight and calm in the ferry-boat as it shot

* There is a town called Porter's Falls in West Virginia, situated a few miles to the east of the Ohio River, but Wilkins Freeman is likely using fictitious locations throughout this story.

swiftly and smoothly across stream. There was a horse attached to a light country wagon on board, and he pawed the deck uneasily. His owner stood near, with a wary eye upon him, although he was chewing, with as dully reflective an expression as a cow. Beside Rebecca sat a woman of about her own age, who kept looking at her with furtive curiosity; her husband, short and stout and saturnine, stood near her. Rebecca paid no attention to either of them. She was tall and spare and pale, the type of a spinster, yet with rudimentary lines and expressions of matronhood. She all unconsciously held her shawl, rolled up in a canvas bag, on her left hip, as if it had been a child. She wore a settled frown of dissent at life, but it was the frown of a mother who regarded life as a forward child, rather than as an overwhelming fate.

The other woman continued staring at her; she was mildly stupid, except for an over-developed curiosity which made her at times sharp beyond belief. Her eyes glittered, red spots came on her flaccid cheeks; she kept opening her mouth to speak, making little abortive motions. Finally she could endure it no longer; she nudged Rebecca boldly.

"A pleasant day," said she.

Rebecca looked at her and nodded coldly. "Yes, very," she assented.

"Have you come far?"

"I have come from Michigan."

"Oh!" said the woman, with awe. "It's a long way," she remarked presently. "Yes, it is," replied Rebecca, conclusively.

Still the other woman was not daunted; there was something which she determined to know, possibly roused thereto by a vague sense of incongruity in the other's appearance. "It's a long ways to come and leave a family," she remarked with painful slyness.

"I ain't got any family to leave," returned Rebecca shortly.

"Then you ain't—"

"No, I ain't."

"Oh!" said the woman.

Rebecca looked straight ahead at the race of the river.

It was a long ferry. Finally Rebecca herself waxed unexpectedly loquacious. She turned to the other woman and inquired if she knew John Dent's widow who lived in Ford Village. "Her husband died about three years ago," said she, by way of detail.

The woman started violently. She turned pale, then she flushed; she cast a strange glance at her husband, who was regarding both women with a sort of stolid keenness.

"Yes, I guess I do," faltered the woman finally.

"Well, his first wife was my sister," said Rebecca with the air of one imparting important intelligence.

"Was she?" responded the other woman feebly. She glanced at her husband with an expression of doubt and terror, and he shook his head forbiddingly.

"I'm going to see her, and take my niece Agnes home with me," said Rebecca. Then the woman gave such a violent start that she noticed it.

"What is the matter?" she asked.

"Nothin', I guess," replied the woman, with eyes on her husband, who was slowly shaking his head, like a Chinese toy.

"Is my niece sick?" asked Rebecca with quick suspicion.

"No, she ain't sick," replied the woman with alacrity, then she caught her breath with a gasp.

"When did you see her?"

"Let me see; I ain't seen her for some little time," replied the woman. Then she caught her breath again.

"She ought to have grown up real pretty, if she takes after my sister. She was a real pretty woman," Rebecca said wistfully.

"Yes, I guess she did grow up pretty," replied the woman in a trembling voice.

"What kind of a woman is the second wife?"

The woman glanced at her husband's warning face. She continued to gaze at him while she replied in a choking voice to Rebecca:

"I—guess she's a nice woman," she replied. "I—don't know, I—guess so. I—don't see much of her."

"I felt kind of hurt that John married again so quick," said Rebecca; "but I suppose he wanted his house kept, and Agnes wanted care. I wasn't so situated that I could take her when her mother died. I had my own mother to care for, and I was school-teaching. Now mother has gone, and my uncle died six months ago and left me quite a little property, and I've given up my school, and I've come for Agnes. I guess she'll be glad to go with me, though I suppose her stepmother is a good woman, and has always done for her."

The man's warning shake at his wife was fairly portentous. "I guess so," said she.

"John always wrote that she was a beautiful woman," said Rebecca. Then the ferry-boat grated on the shore.

John Dent's widow had sent a horse and wagon to meet her sister-in-law. When the woman and her husband went down the road, on which Rebecca in the wagon with her trunk soon passed them, she said reproachfully:

"Seems as if I'd ought to have told her, Thomas."

"Let her find it out herself," replied the man. "Don't you go to burnin' your fingers in other folks' puddin', Maria."

"Do you s'pose she'll see anything?" asked the woman with a spasmodic shudder and a terrified roll of her eyes.

"See!" returned her husband with stolid scorn. "Better be sure there's anything to see."

"Oh, Thomas, they say—"

"Lord, ain't you found out that what they say is mostly lies?"

"But if it should be true, and she's a nervous woman, she might be scared enough to lose her wits," said his wife, staring uneasily after Rebecca's erect figure in the wagon disappearing over the crest of the hilly road.

"Wits that so easy upset ain't worth much," declared the man. "You keep out of it, Maria."

Rebecca in the meantime rode on in the wagon, beside a flaxen-headed boy, who looked, to her understanding, not very bright. She asked him a question, and he paid no attention. She repeated it, and he responded with a bewildered and incoherent grunt. Then she let him alone, after making sure that he knew how to drive straight.

They had traveled about half a mile, passed the village square, and gone a short distance beyond, when the boy drew up with a sudden Whoa! before a very prosperous-looking house. It had been one of the aboriginal cottages of the vicinity, small and white, with a roof extending on one side over a piazza, and a tiny "L" jutting out in the rear, on the right hand. Now the cottage was transformed by dormer windows, a bay window on the piazzaless side, a carved railing down the front steps, and a modern hard-wood door.

"Is this John Dent's house?" asked Rebecca.

The boy was as sparing of speech as a philosopher. His only response was in flinging the reins over the horse's back, stretching out one foot to the shaft, and leaping out of the wagon, then going around to the rear for the trunk. Rebecca got out and went toward the house. Its white paint had a new gloss; its blinds were an immaculate apple green; the lawn was trimmed as smooth as velvet, and it was dotted with scrupulous groups of hydrangeas and cannas.

"I always understood that John Dent was well-to-do," Rebecca reflected comfortably. "I guess Agnes will have considerable. I've got enough, but it will come in handy for her schooling. She can have advantages."

The boy dragged the trunk up the fine gravel-walk, but before he reached the steps leading up to the piazza, for the house stood on a terrace, the front door opened and a fair, frizzled head of a very large and handsome woman appeared. She held up her black silk skirt, disclosing voluminous ruffles of starched embroidery, and waited for Rebecca. She smiled placidly, her pink, double-chinned face widened and dimpled, but her blue eyes were wary and calculating. She extended her hand as Rebecca climbed the steps.

"This is Miss Flint, I suppose," said she.

"Yes, ma'am," replied Rebecca, noticing with bewilderment a curious expression compounded of fear and defiance on the other's face.

"Your letter only arrived this morning," said Mrs. Dent, in a steady voice. Her great face was a uniform pink, and her china-blue eyes were at once aggressive and veiled with secrecy.

"Yes, I hardly thought you'd get my letter," replied Rebecca. "I felt as if I could not wait to hear from you before I came. I supposed you would be so situated that you could have me a little while without putting you out too much, from what John used to write me about his circumstances, and when I had that money so unexpected I felt as if I must come for Agnes. I suppose you will be willing to give her up. You know she's my own blood, and of course she's no relation to you, though you must have got attached to her. I know from her picture what a sweet girl she must be, and John always said she looked like her own mother, and Grace was a beautiful woman, if she was my sister."

Rebecca stopped and stared at the other woman in amazement and alarm. The great handsome blonde creature stood speechless, livid, gasping, with her hand to her heart, her lips parted in a horrible caricature of a smile.

"Are you sick!" cried Rebecca, drawing near. "Don't you want me to get you some water!"

Then Mrs. Dent recovered herself with a great effort. "It is nothing," she said. "I am subject to—spells. I am over it now. Won't you come in, Miss Flint?"

As she spoke, the beautiful deep-rose colour suffused her face, her blue eyes met her visitor's with the opaqueness of turquoise—with a revelation of blue, but a concealment of all behind.

Rebecca followed her hostess in, and the boy, who had waited quiescently, climbed the steps with the trunk. But before they entered the door a strange thing happened. On the upper terrace close to the piazza-post, grew a great rose-bush, and on it, late in the season though it was, one small red, perfect rose.

Rebecca looked at it, and the other woman extended her hand with a quick gesture. "Don't you pick that rose!" she brusquely cried.

Rebecca drew herself up with stiff dignity.

"I ain't in the habit of picking other folks' roses without leave," said she.

As Rebecca spoke she started violently, and lost sight of her resentment, for something singular happened. Suddenly the rose-bush was agitated violently as if by a gust of wind, yet it was a remarkably still day. Not a leaf of the hydrangea standing on the terrace close to the rose trembled.

"What on earth—" began Rebecca, then she stopped with a gasp at the sight of the other woman's face. Although a face, it gave somehow the impression of a desperately clutched hand of secrecy.

"Come in!" said she in a harsh voice, which seemed to come forth from her chest with no intervention of the organs of speech. "Come into the house. I'm getting cold out here."

"What makes that rose-bush blow so when there isn't any wind?" asked Rebecca, trembling with vague horror, yet resolute.

"I don't see as it is blowing," returned the woman calmly. And as she spoke, indeed, the bush was quiet.

"It was blowing," declared Rebecca.

"It isn't now," said Mrs. Dent. "I can't try to account for everything that blows out-of-doors. I have too much to do."

She spoke scornfully and confidently, with defiant, unflinching eyes, first on the bush, then on Rebecca, and led the way into the house.

"It looked queer," persisted Rebecca, but she followed, and also the boy with the trunk.

Rebecca entered an interior, prosperous, even elegant, according to her simple ideas. There were Brussels carpets, lace curtains, and plenty of brilliant upholstery and polished wood.

"You're real nicely situated," remarked Rebecca, after she had become a little accustomed to her new surroundings and the two women were seated at the tea-table.

Mrs. Dent stared with a hard complacency from behind her silver-plated service. "Yes, I be," said she.

"You got all the things new?" said Rebecca hesitatingly, with a jealous memory of her dead sister's bridal furnishings.

"Yes," said Mrs. Dent; "I was never one to want dead folks' things, and I had money enough of my own, so I wasn't beholden to John. I had the old duds put up at auction. They didn't bring much."

"I suppose you saved some for Agnes. She'll want some of her poor mother's things when she is grown up," said Rebecca with some indignation.

The defiant stare of Mrs. Dent's blue eyes waxed more intense. "There's a few things up garret," said she.

"She'll be likely to value them," remarked Rebecca. As she spoke she glanced at the window. "Isn't it most time for her to be coming home?" she asked.

"Most time," answered Mrs. Dent carelessly; "but when she gets over to Addie Slocum's she never knows when to come home."

"Is Addie Slocum her intimate friend?"

"Intimate as any."

"Maybe we can have her come out to see Agnes when she's living with me," said Rebecca wistfully. "I suppose she'll be likely to be homesick at first."

"Most likely," answered Mrs. Dent.

"Does she call you mother?" Rebecca asked.

"No, she calls me Aunt Emeline," replied the other woman shortly. "When did you say you were going home?"

"In about a week, I thought, if she can be ready to go so soon," answered Rebecca with a surprised look.

She reflected that she would not remain a day longer than she could help after such an inhospitable look and question.

"Oh, as far as that goes," said Mrs. Dent, "it wouldn't make any difference about her being ready. You could go home whenever you felt that you must, and she could come afterward."

"Alone?"

"Why not? She's a big girl now, and you don't have to change cars."

"My niece will go home when I do, and not travel alone; and if I can't wait here for her, in the house that used to be her mother's and my sister's home, I'll go and board somewhere," returned Rebecca with warmth.

"Oh, you can stay here as long as you want to. You're welcome," said Mrs. Dent.

Then Rebecca started. "There she is!" she declared in a trembling, exultant voice. Nobody knew how she longed to see the girl.

"She isn't as late as I thought she'd be," said Mrs. Dent, and again that curious, subtle change passed over her face, and again it settled into that stony impassiveness.

Rebecca stared at the door, waiting for it to open. "Where is she?" she asked presently. "I guess she's stopped to take off her hat in the entry," suggested Mrs. Dent.

Rebecca waited. "Why don't she come? It can't take her all this time to take off her hat." For answer Mrs. Dent rose with a stiff jerk and threw open the door.

"Agnes!" she called. "Agnes!" Then she turned and eyed Rebecca. "She ain't there."

"I saw her pass the window," said Rebecca in bewilderment.

"You must have been mistaken."

"I know I did," persisted Rebecca.

"You couldn't have."

"I did. I saw first a shadow go over the ceiling, then I saw her in the glass there"—she pointed to a mirror over the sideboard opposite—" and then the shadow passed the window."

"How did she look in the glass?"

"Little and light-haired, with the light hair kind of tossing over her forehead."

"You couldn't have seen her."

"Was that like Agnes?"

"Like enough; but of course you didn't see her. You've been thinking so much about her that you thought you did."

"You thought YOU did."

"I thought I saw a shadow pass the window, but I must have been mistaken. She didn't come in, or we would have seen her before now. I knew it was too early for her to get home from Addie Slocum's, anyhow."

When Rebecca went to bed Agnes had not returned. Rebecca had resolved that she would not retire until the girl came, but she was very tired, and she reasoned with herself that she was foolish. Besides, Mrs. Dent suggested that Agnes might go to the church social with Addie Slocum. When Rebecca suggested that she be sent for and told that her aunt had come, Mrs. Dent laughed meaningly.

"I guess you'll find out that a young girl ain't so ready to leave a sociable, where there's boys, to see her aunt," said she.

"She's too young," said Rebecca incredulously and indignantly.

"She's sixteen," replied Mrs. Dent; "and she's always been great for the boys."

"She's going to school four years after I get her before she thinks of boys," declared Rebecca.

"We'll see," laughed the other woman.

After Rebecca went to bed, she lay awake a long time listening for the sound of girlish laughter and a boy's voice under her window; then she fell asleep.

The next morning she was down early. Mrs. Dent, who kept no servants, was busily preparing breakfast.

"Don't Agnes help you about breakfast?" asked Rebecca.

"No, I let her lay," replied Mrs. Dent shortly.

"What time did she get home last night?"

"She didn't get home."

"What?"

"She didn't get home. She stayed with Addie. She often does."

"Without sending you word?"

"Oh, she knew I wouldn't worry."

"When will she be home?"

"Oh, I guess she'll be along pretty soon."

Rebecca was uneasy, but she tried to conceal it, for she knew of no good reason for uneasiness. What was there to occasion alarm in the fact of one young girl staying overnight with another? She could not eat much breakfast. Afterward she went out on the little piazza, although her hostess strove furtively to stop her.

"Why don't you go out back of the house? It's real pretty—a view over the river," she said.

"I guess I'll go out here," replied Rebecca. She had a purpose: to watch for the absent girl.

Presently Rebecca came hustling into the house through the sitting-room, into the kitchen where Mrs. Dent was cooking.

"That rose-bush!" she gasped.

Mrs. Dent turned and faced her. "What of it?"

"It's a-blowing."

"What of it?"

"There isn't a mite of wind this morning."

Mrs. Dent turned with an inimitable toss of her fair head. "If you think I can spend my time puzzling over such nonsense as—" she began, but Rebecca interrupted her with a cry and a rush to the door.

"There she is now!" she cried. She flung the door wide open, and curiously enough a breeze came in and her own gray hair tossed, and a paper blew off the table to the floor with a loud rustle, but there was nobody in sight.

"There's nobody here," Rebecca said. She looked blankly at the other woman, who brought her rolling-pin down on a slab of pie-crust with a thud.

"I didn't hear anybody," she said calmly.

"I SAW SOMEBODY PASS THAT WINDOW!"

"You were mistaken again."

"I KNOW I saw somebody."

"You couldn't have. Please shut that door."

Rebecca shut the door. She sat down beside the window and looked out on the autumnal yard, with its little curve of footpath to the kitchen door.

"What smells so strong of roses in this room?" she said presently. She sniffed hard.

"I don't smell anything but these nutmegs."

"It is not nutmeg."

"I don't smell anything else."

"Where do you suppose Agnes is?"

"Oh, perhaps she has gone over the ferry to Porter's Falls with Addie. She often does. Addie's got an aunt over there, and Addie's got a cousin, a real pretty boy."

"You suppose she's gone over there?"

"Mebbe. I shouldn't wonder."

"When should she be home?"

"Oh, not before afternoon."

Rebecca waited with all the patience she could muster. She kept reassuring herself, telling herself that it was all natural, that the other woman could not help it, but she made up her mind that if Agnes did not return that afternoon she should be sent for.

When it was four o'clock she started up with resolution. She had been furtively watching the onyx clock on the sitting-room mantel; she had timed herself. She had said that if Agnes was not home by that time she should demand that she be sent for. She rose and stood before Mrs. Dent, who looked up coolly from her embroidery.

"I've waited just as long as I'm going to," she said. "I've come 'way from Michigan to see my own sister's daughter and take her home with me. I've been here ever since yesterday—twenty-four hours—and I haven't seen her. Now I'm going to. I want her sent for."

Mrs. Dent folded her embroidery and rose.

"Well, I don't blame you," she said. "It is high time she came home. I'll go right over and get her myself."

Rebecca heaved a sigh of relief. She hardly knew what she had suspected or feared, but she knew that her position had been one of antagonism if not accusation, and she was sensible of relief.

"I wish you would," she said gratefully, and went back to her chair, while Mrs. Dent got her shawl and her little white head-tie. "I wouldn't trouble you, but I do feel as if I couldn't wait any longer to see her," she remarked apologetically.

"Oh, it ain't any trouble at all," said Mrs. Dent as she went out. "I don't blame you; you have waited long enough."

Rebecca sat at the window watching breathlessly until Mrs. Dent came stepping through the yard alone. She ran to the door and saw, hardly noticing it this time, that the rose-bush was again violently agitated, yet with no wind evident elsewhere.

"Where is she?" she cried.

Mrs. Dent laughed with stiff lips as she came up the steps over the terrace. "Girls will be girls," said she. "She's gone with Addie to Lincoln. Addie's got an uncle who's conductor on the train, and lives there, and he got 'em passes, and they're goin' to stay to Addie's Aunt Margaret's a few days. Mrs. Slocum said Agnes didn't have time to come over and ask me before the train went, but she took it on herself to say it would be all right, and—"

"Why hadn't she been over to tell you?" Rebecca was angry, though not suspicious. She even saw no reason for her anger.

"Oh, she was putting up grapes. She was coming over just as soon as she got the black off her hands. She heard I had company, and her hands were a sight. She was holding them over sulphur matches."

"You say she's going to stay a few days?" repeated Rebecca dazedly.

"Yes; till Thursday, Mrs. Slocum said."

"How far is Lincoln from here?"

"About fifty miles. It'll be a real treat to her. Mrs. Slocum's sister is a real nice woman."

"It is goin' to make it pretty late about my goin' home."

"If you don't feel as if you could wait, I'll get her ready and send her on just as soon as I can," Mrs. Dent said sweetly.

"I'm going to wait," said Rebecca grimly.

The two women sat down again, and Mrs. Dent took up her embroidery.

"Is there any sewing I can do for her?" Rebecca asked finally in a desperate way. "If I can get her sewing along some—"

Mrs. Dent arose with alacrity and fetched a mass of white from the closet. "Here," she said, "if you want to sew the lace on this nightgown. I was going to put her to it, but she'll be glad enough to get rid of it. She ought to have this and one more before she goes. I don't like to send her away without some good underclothing."

Rebecca snatched at the little white garment and sewed feverishly.

That night she wakened from a deep sleep a little after midnight and lay a minute trying to collect her faculties and explain to herself what she was listening to. At last she discovered that it was the then popular strains of "The Maiden's Prayer"* floating up through the floor from the piano in the sitting-room below. She jumped up, threw a shawl over her nightgown, and hurried downstairs trembling. There was nobody in the sitting-room; the piano was silent. She ran to Mrs. Dent's bedroom and called hysterically:

"Emeline! Emeline!"

"What is it?" asked Mrs. Dent's voice from the bed. The voice was stern, but had a note of consciousness in it.

"Who—who was that playing 'The Maiden's Prayer' in the sitting-room, on the piano?"

"I didn't hear anybody."

"There was some one."

"I didn't hear anything."

"I tell you there was some one. But—THERE AIN'T ANYBODY THERE."

"I didn't hear anything."

"I did—somebody playing 'The Maiden's Prayer' on the piano. Has Agnes got home? I WANT TO KNOW."

"Of course Agnes hasn't got home," answered Mrs. Dent with rising inflection. "Be you gone crazy over that girl? The last boat from Porter's Falls was in before we went to bed. Of course she ain't come."

"I heard—"

"You were dreaming."

---

* "A Maiden's Prayer" is by Polish composer Tekla Bądarzewska-Baranowska; first published in 1856, it became a popular piece in American country music.

"I wasn't; I was broad awake."

Rebecca went back to her chamber and kept her lamp burning all night.

The next morning her eyes upon Mrs. Dent were wary and blazing with suppressed excitement. She kept opening her mouth as if to speak, then frowning, and setting her lips hard. After breakfast she went upstairs, and came down presently with her coat and bonnet.

"Now, Emeline," she said, "I want to know where the Slocums live."

Mrs. Dent gave a strange, long, half-lidded glance at her. She was finishing her coffee. "Why?" she asked.

"I'm going over there and find out if they have heard anything from her daughter and Agnes since they went away. I don't like what I heard last night."

"You must have been dreaming."

"It don't make any odds whether I was or not. Does she play 'The Maiden's Prayer' on the piano? I want to know."

"What if she does? She plays it a little, I believe. I don't know. She don't half play it, anyhow; she ain't got an ear."

"That wasn't half played last night. I don't like such things happening. I ain't superstitious, but I don't like it. I'm going. Where do the Slocums live?"

"You go down the road over the bridge past the old grist mill, then you turn to the left; it's the only house for half a mile. You can't miss it. It has a barn with a ship in full sail on the cupola."

"Well, I'm going. I don't feel easy."

About two hours later Rebecca returned. There were red spots on her cheeks. She looked wild. "I've been there," she said, and there isn't a soul at home. Something HAS happened."

"What has happened?"

"I don't know. Something. I had a warning last night. There wasn't a soul there. They've been sent for to Lincoln."

"Did you see anybody to ask?" asked Mrs. Dent with thinly concealed anxiety.

"I asked the woman that lives on the turn of the road. She's stone deaf. I suppose you know. She listened while I screamed at her to know where the Slocums were, and then she said, 'Mrs. Smith don't live here.' I didn't see anybody on the road, and that's the only house. What do you suppose it means?"

"I don't suppose it means much of anything," replied Mrs. Dent coolly. "Mr. Slocum is conductor on the railroad, and he'd be away anyway, and Mrs. Slocum often goes early when he does, to spend the day with her sister in Porter's Falls. She'd be more likely to go away than Addie."

"And you don't think anything has happened?" Rebecca asked with diminishing distrust before the reasonableness of it.

"Land, no!"

Rebecca went upstairs to lay aside her coat and bonnet. But she came hurrying back with them still on.

"Who's been in my room?" she gasped. Her face was pale as ashes. Mrs. Dent also paled as she regarded her.

"What do you mean?" she asked slowly.

"I found when I went upstairs that—little nightgown of—Agnes's on—the bed, laid out. It was—LAID OUT. The sleeves were folded across the bosom, and there was that little red rose between them. Emeline, what is it? Emeline, what's the matter? Oh!"

Mrs. Dent was struggling for breath in great, choking gasps. She clung to the back of a chair. Rebecca, trembling herself so she could scarcely keep on her feet, got her some water.

As soon as she recovered herself Mrs. Dent regarded her with eyes full of the strangest mixture of fear and horror and hostility.

"What do you mean talking so?" she said in a hard voice.

"It IS THERE."

"Nonsense. You threw it down and it fell that way."

"It was folded in my bureau drawer."

"It couldn't have been."

"Who picked that red rose?"

"Look on the bush," Mrs. Dent replied shortly.

Rebecca looked at her; her mouth gaped. She hurried out of the room. When she came back her eyes seemed to protrude. (She had in the meantime hastened upstairs, and come down with tottering steps, clinging to the banisters.)

"Now I want to know what all this means?" she demanded.

"What what means?"

"The rose is on the bush, and it's gone from the bed in my room! Is this house haunted, or what?"

"I don't know anything about a house being haunted. I don't believe in such things. Be you crazy?" Mrs. Dent spoke with gathering force. The colour flashed back to her cheeks.

"No," said Rebecca shortly. "I ain't crazy yet, but I shall be if this keeps on much longer. I'm going to find out where that girl is before night."

Mrs. Dent eyed her.

"What be you going to do?"

"I'm going to Lincoln."

A faint triumphant smile overspread Mrs. Dent's large face. "You can't," said she; "there ain't any train."

"No train?"

"No; there ain't any afternoon train from the Falls to Lincoln."

"Then I'm going over to the Slocums' again to-night."

However, Rebecca did not go; such a rain came up as deterred even her resolution, and she had only her best dresses with her. Then in the evening came the letter from the Michigan village which she had left nearly a week ago. It was from her cousin, a single woman, who had come to keep her house while she was away. It was a pleasant unexciting letter enough, all the first of it, and related mostly how she missed Rebecca; how she hoped she was having pleasant weather and kept her health; and how her friend, Mrs. Greenaway, had come to stay with her since she had felt lonesome the first night in the house; how she hoped Rebecca would have no objections to this, although nothing had been said about it, since she had not realized that she might be nervous alone. The cousin was painfully conscientious, hence the letter. Rebecca smiled in spite of her disturbed mind as she read it, then her eye caught the postscript. That was in a different hand, purporting to be written by the friend, Mrs. Hannah Greenaway, informing her that the cousin had fallen down the cellar stairs and broken her hip, and was in a dangerous condition, and begging Rebecca to return at once, as she herself was rheumatic and unable to nurse her properly, and no one else could be obtained.

Rebecca looked at Mrs. Dent, who had come to her room with the letter quite late; it was half-past nine, and she had gone upstairs for the night.

"Where did this come from?" she asked.

"Mr. Amblecrom brought it," she replied.

"Who's he?"

"The postmaster. He often brings the letters that come on the late mail. He knows I ain't anybody to send. He brought yours about your coming. He said he and his wife came over on the ferry-boat with you."

"I remember him," Rebecca replied shortly. "There's bad news in this letter." Mrs. Dent's face took on an expression of serious inquiry.

"Yes, my Cousin Harriet has fallen down the cellar stairs—they were always dangerous—and she's broken her hip, and I've got to take the first train home to-morrow."

"You don't say so. I'm dreadfully sorry."

"No, you ain't sorry!" said Rebecca, with a look as if she leaped. "You're glad. I don't know why, but you're glad. You've wanted to get rid of me for some reason ever since I came. I don't know why. You're a strange woman. Now you've got your way, and I hope you're satisfied."

"How you talk."

Mrs. Dent spoke in a faintly injured voice, but there was a light in her eyes.

"I talk the way it is. Well, I'm going to-morrow morning, and I want you, just as soon as Agnes Dent comes home, to send her out to me. Don't you wait for anything. You pack what clothes she's got, and don't wait even to mend them, and you buy her ticket. I'll leave the money, and you send her along. She don't have to change cars. You start her off, when she gets home, on the next train!"

"Very well," replied the other woman. She had an expression of covert amusement.

"Mind you do it."

"Very well, Rebecca."

Rebecca started on her journey the next morning. When she arrived, two days later, she found her cousin in perfect health. She found, moreover, that the friend had not written the postscript in the cousin's letter. Rebecca would have returned to Ford Village the next morning, but the fatigue and nervous strain had been too much for her. She was not able to move from her bed. She had a species of low fever induced by anxiety and fatigue. But she could write, and she did, to the Slocums, and she received no answer. She also wrote to Mrs. Dent; she even sent numerous telegrams, with no response. Finally she wrote to the postmaster, and an answer arrived by the first possible mail. The letter was short, curt, and to the purpose. Mr. Amblecrom, the postmaster, was a man of few words, and especially wary as to his expressions in a letter.

"Dear madam," he wrote, "your favour rec'ed. No Slocums in Ford's Village. All dead. Addie ten years ago, her mother two years later, her father five. House vacant. Mrs. John Dent said to have neglected stepdaughter. Girl was sick. Medicine not given. Talk of taking action. Not enough evidence. House said to be haunted. Strange sights and sounds. Your niece, Agnes Dent, died a year ago, about this time.

"Yours truly,

"THOMAS AMBLECROM."

Herminie Templeton Kavanagh (1861–1933), born Herminie McGibney to an Irish major, is best remembered as an English writer of short stories about Darby O'Gill, collected in two volumes, *Darby O'Gill and the Good People* (1903), published under the name Herminie Templeton (the name of her first husband) and *Ashes of Old Wishes and Other Darby O'Gill Tales* (1926), published as Herminie Templeton Kavanagh (Kavanagh being her second husband). She also wrote two plays in 1903. The O'Gill stories proved very popular, and Walt Disney Productions produced a live-action feature film combining the following story and others into *Darby O'Gill and the Little People*. In the following story, first published in May 1903 in *McClure's Magazine*, Darby is a "lad"—in the Disney version, he is an aging caretaker, originally intended to be played by Barry Fitzgerald but ultimately portrayed by Albert Sharpe (who was age 74 at the time of the film's release).

The Banshee's Halloween

by Herminie Templeton Kavanagh

I

Halloween night, to all unhappy ghosts, is about the same as St. Patrick's Day is to you or to me—'tis a great holiday in every churchyard.* An' no one knew this betther or felt it keener than did Darby O'Gill,† that same Halloween night, as he stood on his own doorstep with

* In ancient Scottish and Irish folklore, Halloween was believed to be a night when the borders between worlds were at their thinnest, and malicious fairies—or *sidh*—could cross into our world (along with spirits of the dead) and cause mischief and mayhem.

† Yes, that Darby O'Gill: *Darby O'Gill and the Little People* is a 1959 film starring Albert Sharpe, Janet Munro, Sean Connery and Jimmy O'Dea, based on Kavanagh's books of tales about the Irishman and produced by Walt Disney Productions.

the paper of black tay* for Eileen McCarthy safely stowed away in the crown of his top-hat.

No one in that barony was quicker than he at an act of neighbourly kindness, but now, as he huddled himself together in the shelter of his own eaves, and thought of the dangers before, an' of the cheerful fire an' comfortable bed he was leaving behint, black raybellion rushed shouting across his heart.

"Oh, my, oh, my, what a perishin' night to turn a man out into!" he says. "It'd be half a comfort to know I was goin' to be kilt before I got back, just as a warnin' to Bridget," says he.

The misthrayted lad turned a sour eye on the chumultuous weather, an' groaned deep as he pulled closer about his chowldhers the cape of his greatcoat an' plunged into the daysarted an' flooded roadway.

Howsumever, 'twas not the pelting rain, nor the lashing wind, nor yet the pitchy darkness that bothered the heart out of him as he wint splashin' an' stumbling along the road. A thought of something more raylentless than the storm, more mystarious than the night's blackness put pounds of lead into the lad's unwilling brogues; for somewhere in the shrouding darkness that covered McCarthy's house the banshee† was waiting this minute, purhaps, ready to jump out at him as soon as he came near her.

And, oh, if the banshee nabbed him there, what in the worruld would the poor lad do to save himself?

At the raylisation of this sitiwation, the goose-flesh crept up his back an' settled on his neck an' chowldhers. He began to cast about in his mind for a bit of cheer or a scrap of comfort, as a man in such sarcumstances will do. So, grumblin' an' sore-hearted, he turned over Bridget's parting words. "If one goes on an errant of marcy," Bridget had said, "a score of God's white angels with swoords in their hands march before an' beside an' afther him, keeping his path free from danger."

---

* Tea

† The literal translation of "banshee" is "female fairy." Banshees appear frequently in Irish folklore, where their wailing announces the death of someone nearby; in some versions of the legend, they visit over three consecutive nights, with their wailing increasing in volume and intensity with each appearance.

He felt anxious in his hat for the bit of charitable tay he was bringin', and was glad to find it there safe an' dhry enough, though the rest of him was drenched through an' through.

"Isn't this an act of charity I'm doin', to be bringin' a cooling drink to a dyin' woman?" he axed himself aloud. "To be sure it is. Well, then, what rayson have I to be afeared?" says he, pokin' his two hands into his pockets. "Arrah, it's aisy enough to bolsther up one's heart with wise sayin' an' hayroic praycepts when sitting comodious by one's own fire; but talkin' wise words to one's self is mighty poor comfort when you're on the lonely high-road of a Halloween night, with a churchyard waitin' for ye on the top of the hill not two hundred yards away. If there was only one star to break through the thick sky an' shine for him, if there was but one friendly cow to low or a distant cock to break the teeming silence, 'twould put some heart into the man. But not a sound was there only the swish and wailing of the wind through the inwisible hedges.

"What's the matther with the whole worruld? Where is it wanished to?" says Darby. "If a ghost were to jump at me from the churchyard wall, where would I look for help? To run is no use," he says, "an' to face it is—"

Just then the current of his misdoubtings ran whack up against a sayin' of ould Peggy O'Callaghan. Mrs. O'Callaghan's repitation for truth and voracity, whin it come to fairy tales or ghost stories, be it known, was ayquil if not shuparior to the best in Tipperary. Now, Peggy had towld Ned Mullin, an' Ned Mullin had towld Bill Donahue, the tinker, an' the tinker had adwised Darby that no one need ever be afeared of ghosts if he only had the courage to face them.

Peggy said, "The poor crachures ain't roamin' about shakin' chains an' moanin' an' groanin', just for the sport of scarin' people, nor yet out of maneness. 'Tis always a throuble that's on their minds—a message they want sint, a saycret they're endayvouring to unload. So instead of flyin' from the onhappy things, as most people generally do," she said, "one should walk up bowld to the apparraytion, be it gentle or common, male or faymale, an' say, 'What throubles ye, sir?' or 'What's amiss with ye, ma'am?' An' take my worrud for it," says she, "ye'll find yourself a boneyfactor to them when you laste expect it," she says.

'Twas a quare idee, but not so onraysonable afther all whin one comes to think of it; an' the knowledgeable man fell to dayliberatin' whether he'd have the hardness to folly it out if the chanst came. Sometimes he thought he would, then agin he was sure he wouldn't. For Darby O'Gill was one who bint quick undher trouble like a young three before a hurrycane, but he only bint—the throuble never broke him. So, at times his courage wint down to a spark like the light of a candle in a gust of wind, but before you could turn on your heel 'twas blazing up sthrong and fiercer than before.

Whilst thus contimplatin' an' meditaytin', his foot sthruck the bridge in the hollow just below the berrin'-ground, an' there as the boy paused a minute, churning up bravery enough to carry him up the hill an' past the mystarious gravestones, there came a short quiver of lightning, an' in its sudden flare he was sure he saw not tin yards away, an' comin' down the hill toward him, a dim shape that took the breath out of his body.

"Oh, be the powers!" he gasped, his courage emptying out like wather from a spilt pail.

It moved, a slow, grey, formless thing without a head, an' so far as he was able to judge it might be about the size of an ulephant. The parsecuted lad swung himself sideways in the road, one arrum over his eyes an' the other stretched out at full length, as if to ward off the terrible wisitor.

The first thing that began to take any shape in his bewildhered brain was Peggy O'Callaghan's adwice. He thried to folly it out, but a chatterin' of teeth was the only sound he made. An' all this time a thraymendous splashin', like the floppin' of whales, was coming nearer an' nearer.

The splashin' stopped not three feet away, an' the ha'nted man felt in the spine of his back an' in the calves of his legs that a powerful, unhowly monsther towered over him.

Why he didn't swoonge in his tracks is the wondher. He says he would have dhropped at last if it weren't for the distant bark of his own good dog, Sayser, that put a throb of courage intil his bones. At that friendly sound he opened his two dhry lips an' stutthered this sayin':

"Whoever you are, an' whatever shape ye come in, take heed that I'm not afeared," he says. "I command ye to tell me your throubles an' I'll be your boneyfactor. Then go back dacint an' rayspectable where you're buried. Spake an' I'll listen," says he.

He waited for a reply, an' getting none, a hot splinther of shame at bein' so badly frightened turned his sowl into wexation. "Spake up," he says, "but come no furder, for if you do, be the hokey I'll take one thry at ye, ghost or no ghost!" he says. Once more he waited, an' as he was lowering the arrum from his eyes for a peek, the ghost spoke up, an' its answer came in two pitiful, disthressed roars. A damp breath puffed acrost his face, an' openin' his eyes, what should the lad see but the two dhroopin' ears of Solomon, Mrs. Kilcannon's grey donkey. Foive different kinds of disgust biled up into Darby's throat an' almost sthrangled him. "Ye murdherin', big-headed imposture!" he gasped.

Half a minute afther a brown hoot-owl, which was shelthered in a near-by black-thorn three, called out to his brother's fambly which inhabited the belfry of the chapel above on the hill that some black-minded spalpeen* had hoult of Solomon Kilcannon be the two ears an' was kickin' the ribs out of him, an' that the langwidge the man was usin' to the poor baste was worse than scan'lous.

Although Darby couldn't undherstand what the owl was sayin', he was startled be the blood-curdlin' hoot, an' that same hoot saved Solomon from any further exthrayornery throuncin', bekase as the angry man sthopped to hearken there flashed on him the rayilisation that he was bating an' crool maulthraytin' a blessing in dishguise. For this same Solomon had the repitation of being the knowingest, sensiblist thing which walked on four legs in that parish. He was a fayvourite with young an' old, especially with childher, an' Mrs. Kilcannon said she could talk to him as if he were a human, an' she was sure he under-sthood. In the face of thim facts the knowledgeable man changed his chune, an' puttin' his arrum friendly around the disthressed animal's neck, he said:

"Aren't ye ashamed of yerself, Solomon, to be payradin' an' mayandherin' around the churchyard Halloween night, dishguisin' yerself this away as an outlandish ghost, an' you havin' the foine repitation for daciency an' good manners?" he says, excusin' himself. "I'm ashamed of you, so I am, Solomon," says he, hauling the baste about in the road, an' turning him till

* A rascal.

his head faced once more the hillside. "Come back with me now to Cormac McCarthy's, avourneen.* We've aich been in worse company, I'm thinkin'; at laste you have, Solomon," says he.

At that, kind an' friendly enough, the forgivin' baste turned with him, an' the two keeping aich other slitherin' company, went stumblin' an' scramblin' up the hill toward the chapel. On the way Darby kept up a one-sided conwersation about all manner of things, just so that the ring of a human woice, even if 'twas only his own, would take a bit of the crool lonesomeness out of the dark hedges.

"Did you notice McDonald's sthrame as you came along the night, Solomon? It must be a roarin' torrent be this, with the pourin' rains, an' we'll have to cross it," says he. "We could go over McDonald's stone bridge that stands ferninst McCarthy's house, with only Nolan's meadow betwixt the two, but," says Darby, laying a hand, confaydential on the ass's wet back, "'tis only a fortnit since long Faylix, the blind beggarman, fell from the same bridge and broke his neck, an' what more natural," he axed, "than that the ghost of Faylix would be celebraytin' its first Halloween, *as* a ghost, at the spot where he was kilt?"

You may believe me or believe me not, but at thim worruds Solomon sthopped dead still in his thracks an' rayfused to go another step till Darby coaxed him on be sayin':

"Oh, thin, we won't cross it if you're afeared, little man," says he, "but we'll take the path through the fields on this side of it, and we'll cross the sthrame by McCarthy's own wooden foot-bridge. 'Tis within tunty feet of the house. Oh, ye needn't be afeared," he says agin; "I've seen the cows cross it, so it'll surely hould the both of us."

A sudden raymembrance whipped into his mind of how tall the stile was, ladin' into Nolan's meadow, an' the boy was puzzling deep in his mind to know how was Solomon to climb acrost that stile, whin all at once the gloomy western gate of the graveyard rose quick be their side.

The two shied to the opposite hedge, an' no wondher they did.

Fufty ghosts, all in their shrouds, sat cheek be jowl along the churchyard wall, never caring a ha'porth for the wind or the rain.

---

* Darling, sweetheart—a term of endearment.

There was little Ted Rogers, the humpback, who was dhrownded in Mullin's well four years come Michaelmas; there was black Mulligan, the game-keeper, who shot Ryan, the poacher, sittin' with a gun on his lap, an' he glowerin'; beside the game-keeper sat the poacher, with a jagged black hole in his forehead; there was Thady Finnegan, the scholar, who was disappointed in love an' died of a daycline; furder on sat Mrs. Houlihan, who dayparted this life from ating of pizen musherooms; next to *her* sat—oh, a hundhred others!

Not that Darby *saw* thim, do ye mind. He had too good sinse to look that way at all. He walked with his head turned out to the open fields, an' his eyes squeeged shut. But something in his mind toult him they were there, an' he felt in the marrow of his bones that if he gave them the encouragement of one glance two or three'd slip off the wall an' come moanin' over to tell him their throubles.

What Solomon saw an' what Solomon heard, as the two wint shrinkin' along'll never be known to living man, but once he gave a jump, an' twice Darby felt him thrimblin', an' whin they raiched at last the chapel wall the baste broke into a swift throt. Purty soon he galloped, an' Darby wint gallopin' with him, till two yallow blurs of light across in a field to the left marked the windys of the stone-cutter's cottage.

'Twas a few steps only, thin, to the stile over into Nolan's meadow, an' there the two stopped, lookin' helpless at aich other. Solomon had to be lifted, and there was the throuble. Three times Darby thried be main strength to hist his compagnen up the steps, but in vain, an' Solomon was clane dishgusted.

Only for the tendher corn on our hayro's left little toe, I think maybe that at length an' at last the pair would have got safe over. The kind-hearted lad had the donkey's two little hoofs planted on the top step, an' whilst he himself was liftin' the rest of the baste in his arrums, Solomon got onaisy that he was goin' to be trun, an' so began to twisht an' squirm; of course, as he did, Darby slipped an' wint thump on his back agin the stile, with Solomon sittin' comfortable on top of the lad's chist. But that wasn't the worst of it, for as the baste scrambled up he planted one hard little hoof on Darby's left foot, an' the knowledgeable man let a yowl out of him that must have frightened all the ghosts within miles.

Seein' he'd done wrong, Solomon boulted for the middle of the road an' stood there wiry an' attentive, listening to the names flung at him from where his late comerade sat on the lowest step of the stile nursin' the hurted foot.

'Twas an excited owl in the belfry that this time spoke up an' shouted to his brother down in the blackthorn:

"Come up, come up quick!" it says. "Darby O'Gill is just afther calling Solomon Kilcannon a malayfactor."

Darby rose at last, an' as he climbed over the stile he turned to shake his fist toward the middle of the road.

"Bad luck to ye for a thick-headed, on-grateful informer!" he says; "you go your way an' I'll go mine—we're sundhers,"* says he. So sayin', the crippled man wint limpin' an' grumplin' down the boreen,† through the meadow, whilst his desarted friend sint rayproachful brays afther him that would go to your heart.

The throbbin' of our hayro's toe banished all pity for the baste, an' even all thoughts of the banshee, till a long, gurgling, swooping sound in front toult him that his fears about the rise in McDonald's sthrame were undher rather than over the actwil conditions.

Fearin' that the wooden foot-bridge might be swept away, as it had been the year purvious, he hurried on.

Most times this sthrame was only a quiet little brook that ran betwixt purty green banks, with hardly enough wather in it to turn the broken wheel in Chartres' runed mill; but to-night it swept along an angry, snarlin', growlin' river that overlept its banks an' dhragged wildly at the swaying willows.

Be a narrow throw of light from McCarthy's side windy our thraveller could see the maddened wathers thrivin' an' tearing to pull with it the props of the little foot-bridge; an' the boards shook an' the centre swayed undher his feet as he passed over. "Bedad, I'll not cross this way goin' home, at any rate," he says, looking back at it.

The worruds were no sooner out of his mouth than there was a crack, an' the middle of the foot-bridge lifted in the air, twishted round for a second,

* "Sunders"—separated.

† A narrow country lane.

an then hurled itself into the sthrame, laving the two inds still standing in their place on the banks.

"Tunder an' turf!" he cried, "I mustn't forget to tell the people within of this, for if ever there was a thrap set by evil spirits to drownd a poor, unwary mortial, there it stands. Oh, ain't the ghosts terrible wicious on Halloween!"

He stood dhrippin' a minute on the threshold, listening; thin, without knockin', lifted the latch an' stepped softly into the house.

II

Two candles burned above the blue and white chiney dishes on the table, a bright fire blazed on the hearth, an' over in the corner where the low bed was set the stone-cutter was on his knees beside it.

Eileen lay on her side, her shining hair sthrealed out on the pillow. Her purty, flushed face was turned to Cormac, who knelt with his forehead hid on the bed-covers. The colleen's two little hands were clasped about the great fist of her husband, an' she was talking low, but so airnest that her whole life was in every worrud.

"God save all here!" said Darby, takin' off his hat, but there was no answer. So deep were Cormac an' Eileen in some conwersation they were having together that they didn't hear his coming. The knowledgeable man didn't know what to do. He raylised that a husband and wife about to part for ever were lookin' into aich other's hearts, for maybe the last time. So he just sthood shifting from one foot to the other, watching thim, unable to daypart, an' not wishin' to obtrude.

"Oh, it isn't death at all that I fear," Eileen was saying. "No, no, Cormac asthore, 'tis not that I'm misdoubtful of; but, ochone mavrone,* 'tis you I fear!"

The kneelin' man gave one swift upward glance, and dhrew his face nearer to the sick wife. She wint on, thin, spakin' tindher an' half smiling an' sthrokin' his hand:

* An expression of sorrow—each word is occasionally used alone—like "alas and alack."

"I know, darlint, I know well, so you needn't tell me, that if I were to live with you a thousand years you'd never sthray in mind or thought to any other woman, but it's when I'm gone—when the lonesome avenings folly aich other through days an' months, an' maybe years, an' you sitting here at this fireside without one to speak to, an' you so handsome an' gran', an' with the penny or two we've put away—"

"Oh, asthore machree,* why can't ye banish thim black thoughts!" says the stone-cutter. "Maybe," he says, "the banshee will not come again. Ain't all the counthry-side prayin' for ye this night, an' didn't Father Cassidy himself bid you to hope? The saints in Heaven couldn't be so crool!" says he.

But the colleen wint on as though she hadn't heard him, or as if he hadn't intherrupted her:

"An' listen," says she; "they'll come urging ye, the neighbours, an' raysonin' with you. Your own flesh an' blood'll come, an', no doubt, me own with them, an' they all sthriving to push me out of your heart, an' to put another woman there in my place. I'll know it all, but I won't be able to call to you, Cormac machree, for I'll be lying silent undher the grass, or undher the snow up behind the church."

While she was sayin' thim last worruds, although Darby's heart was meltin' for Eileen, his mind began running over the colleens of that townland to pick out the one who'd be most likely to marry Cormac in the ind. You know how far-seeing an' quick-minded was the knowledgeable man. He settled sudden on the Hanlon girl, an' daycided at once that she'd have Cormac before the year was out. The ondaycency of such a thing made him furious at her.

He says to himself, half crying, "Why, then, bad cess† to you for a shameless, red-haired, forward baggage, Bridget Hanlon, to be runnin' afther the man, an' throwing yourself in his way, an' Eileen not yet cowld in her grave!" he says.

While he was saying them things to himself, McCarthy had been whuspering fierce to his wife, but what it was the stone-cutter said the friend of

* Terms of endearment.

† "Bad cess" is an Irish version of "bad luck."

the fairies* couldn't hear. Eileen herself spoke clean enough in answer, for the faver gave her onnatural strength.

"Don't think," she says, "that it's the first time this thought has come to me. Two months ago, whin I was sthrong an' well an' sittin' happy as a meadow-lark at your side, the same black shadow dhrifted over me heart. The worst of it an' the hardest to bear of all is that they'll be in the right, for what good can I do for you when I'm undher the clay," says she.

"It's different with a woman. If you were taken an' I left I'd wear your face in my heart through all me life, an' ax for no sweeter company."

"Eileen," says Cormac, liftin' his hand, an' his woice was hoarse as the roar of the say, "I swear to you on me bendid knees ——"

With her hand on his lips, she sthopped him. "There'll come on ye by daygrees a great cravin' for sympathy, a hunger an' a longing for affection, an' you'll have only the shadow of my poor, wanished face to comfort you, an' a recollection of a woice that is gone for ever. A new, warm face'll keep pushin' itself betwixt us ——"

"Bad luck to that red-headed hussy!" mutthered Darby, looking around disthressed. "I'll warn father Cassidy of her an' of her intintions the day afther the funeral."

There was silence for a minute; Cormac, the poor lad, was sobbing like a child. By-and-by Eileen wint on again, but her woice was failing an' Darby could see that her cheeks were wet.

"The day'll come when you'll give over," she says. "Ah, I see how it'll all ind. Afther that you'll visit the churchyard be stealth, so as not to make the other woman sore-hearted."

"My, oh, my, isn't she the far-seein' woman?" thought Darby.

"Little childher'll come," she says, "an' their soft, warm arrums will hould you away. By-and-by you'll not go where I'm laid at all, an' all thoughts of these few happy months we've spent together—Oh! Mother in Heaven, how happy they were——"

* In the first of the Darby O'Gill stories, "Darby O'Gill and the Good People," Darby goes after the fairies when they steal his favorite cow, but after he tricks them, they concede and the fairy King becomes Darby's friend.

The girl started to her elbow, for, sharp an' sudden, a wild, wailing cry just outside the windy startled the shuddering darkness. 'Twas a long cry of terror and of grief, not shrill, but piercing as a knife-thrust. Every hair on Darby's head stood up an' pricked him like a needle. 'Twas the banshee!

"Whist, listen!" says Eileen. "Oh, Cormac asthore, it's come for me again!" With that, stiff with terror, she buried herself undher the pillows.

A second cry follyed the first, only this time it was longer, and rose an' swelled into a kind of a song that broke at last into the heart-breakingest moan that ever fell on mortial ears. "Ochone!" it sobbed.

The knowledgeable man, his blood turned to ice, his legs thremblin' like a hare's, stood looking in spite of himself at the black windy-panes, expecting some frightful wision.

Afther that second cry the woice balanced itself up an' down into the awful death keen. One word made the whole song, and that was the turruble worrud, "Forever!"

"Forever an' forever, oh, forever!" swung the wild keen, until all the deep meaning of the worrud burned itself into Darby's sowl, thin the heart-breakin' sob, "Ochone!" inded always the varse.

Darby was just wondherin' whether he himself wouldn't go mad with fright, whin he gave a sudden jump at a hard, sthrained woice which spoke up at his very elbow.

"Darby O'Gill," it said, and it was the stone-cutter who spoke, "do you hear the death keen? It came last night; it'll come to-morrow night at this same hour, and thin—oh, my God!"

Darby tried to answer, but he could only stare at the white, set face an' the sunken eyes of the man before him.

There was, too, a kind of fierce quiet in the way McCarthy spoke that made Darby shiver.

The stone-cutter wint on talkin' the same as though he was goin' to dhrive a bargain. "They say you're a knowledgeable man, Darby O'Gill," he says, "an' that on a time you spint six months with the fairies. Now I make you this fair, square offer," he says, laying a forefinger in the palm of the other hand. "I have fifty-three pounds that Father Cassidy's keeping for me. Fifty-three pounds," he says agin. "An' I have this good bit of a farm that me father was born on, an' his father was born on, too, and the grandfather of him. An' I have the grass of seven cows. You know that. Well, I'll give it all to you, all, every stiver* of it, if you'll only go outside an' dhrive away that cursed singer." He trew his head to one side an' looked anxious up at Darby.

The knowledgeable man racked his brains for something to speak, but all he could say was, "I've brought you a bit of tay from the wife, Cormac."

McCarthy took the tay with unfeeling hands, an' wint on talking in the same dull way. Only this time there came a hard lump in his throat now and then that he stopped to swally.

"The three cows I have go, of course, with the farm," says he. "So does the pony an' the five pigs. I have a good plough an' a foine harrow; but you must lave my stone-cutting tools, so little Eileen an' I can earn our way wherever we go, an' it's little the crachure ates the best of times."

The man's eyes were dhry an' blazin'; no doubt his mind was cracked with grief. There was a lump in Darby's throat, too, but for all that he spoke up scolding-like.

"Arrah, talk rayson, man," he says, putting two hands on Cormac's chowlders; "if I had the wit or the art to banish the banshee, wouldn't I be happy to do it an' not a fardin' to pay?"

"Well, then," says Cormac, scowling, an' pushin' Darby to one side, "I'll face her myself—I'll face her an' choke that song in her throat if Sattin himself stood at her side."

With those words, an' before Darby could sthop him, the stone-cutter flung open the door an' plunged out into the night. As he did so the song outside sthopped. Suddenly a quick splashing of feet, hoarse cries, and shouts gave tidings of a chase. The half-crazed gossoon† had stharted the banshee—of that there could be no manner of doubt. A raymembrance of the awful things that she might do to his friend paythrefied the heart of Darby.

Even afther these cries died away he stood listenling a full minute, the sowls of his two brogues glued to the floor. The only sounds he heard now were the deep ticking of a clock and a cricket that chirped slow an' solemn

* A "stiver" is the smallest amount of money.

† A boy.

on the hearth, an' from somewhere outside came the sorrowful cry of a whipperwill. All at once a thought of the broken bridge an' of the black, treacherous waters caught him like the blow of a whip, an' for a second drove from his mind even the fear of the banshee.

In that one second, an' before he rayalised it, the lad was out undher the dhripping trees, and running for his life toward the broken foot-bridge. The night was whirling an' beating above him like the flapping of thraymendous wings, but as he ran Darby thought he heard above the rush of the water and through, the swish of the wind Cormac's woice calling him.

The friend of the fairies stopped at the edge of the foot-bridge to listen. Although the storm had almost passed, a spiteful flare of lightning lept up now an' agin out of the western hills, an' afther it came the dull rumble of distant thunder; the water splashed spiteful against the bank, and Darby saw that seven good feet of the bridge had been torn out of its centre, laving uncovered that much of the black, deep flood.

He stood sthraining his eyes an' ears in wondheration, for now the woice of Cormac sounded from the other side of the sthrame, and seemed to be floating toward him through the field over the path Darby himself had just thravelled. At first he was mightily bewildhered at what might bring Cormac on the other side of the brook, till all at once the murdhering scheme of the banshee burst in his mind like a gunpowdher explosion.

Her plan was as plain as day—she meant to dhrown the stone-cutter. She had led the poor, daysthracted man straight from his own door down to and over the new stone bridge, an' was now dayludherin' him on the other side of the sthrame, back agin up the path that led to the broken foot-bridge.

In the glare of a sudden blinding flash from the middle of the sky Darby saw a sight he'll never forget till the day he dies. Cormac, the stone-cutter, was running toward the death-trap, his bare head trun back, an' his two arrums stretched out in front of him. A little above an' just out of raich of them, plain an' clear as Darby ever saw his wife Bridget, was the misty white figure of a woman. Her long, waving hair sthrealed back from her face, an' her face was the face of the dead.

At the sight of her Darby thried to call out a warning, but the words fell back into his throat. Thin again came the stifling darkness. He thried to run away, but his knees failed him, so he turned around to face the danger.

As he did so he could hear the splash of the man's feet in the soft mud. In less than a minute Cormac would be sthruggling in the wather. At the thought Darby, bracing himself body and sowl, let a warning howl out of him.

"Hould where you are!" he shouted; "she wants to drownd ye—the bridge is broke in the middle!" but he could tell, from the rushing footsteps an' from the hoarse swelling curses which came nearer an' nearer every second, that the dayludhered man, crazed with grief, was deaf an' blind to everything but the figure that floated before his eyes.

At that hopeless instant Bridget's parting words popped into Darby's head.

"When one goes on an errant of marcy a score of God's white angels, with swoords in their hands, march before an' beside an' afther him, keeping his path free from danger."

How it all come to pass he could never rightly tell, for he was like a man in a dhrame, but he recollects well standing on the broken ind of the bridge, Bridget's words ringing in his ears, the glistening black gulf benathe his feet, an' he swinging his arrums for a jump. Just one thought of herself and the childher, as he gathered himself for a spring, an' then he cleared the gap like a bird.

As his two feet touched the other side of the gap a turrific screech—not a screech, ayther, but an angry, frightened shriek—almost split his ears. He felt a rush of cowld, dead air agin his face, and caught a whiff of newly turned clay in his nosthrils; something white stopped quick before him, an' then, with a second shriek, it shot high in the darkness an' disappeared. Darby had frightened the wits out of the banshee.

The instant afther the two men were clinched an' rowling over an' over aich other down the muddy bank, their legs splashing as far as the knees in the dangerous wather, an' McCarthy raining wake blows on the knowledgeable man's head an' breast.

Darby felt himself goin' into the river. Bits of the bank caved undher him, splashing into the current, an' the lad's heart began clunking up an' down like a churn-dash.

"Lave off, lave off!" he cried, as soon as he could ketch his breath. "Do you take me for the banshee?" says he, giving a dusperate lurch an' rowling himself on top of the other.

"Who are you, then? If you're not a ghost you're the divil, at any rate," gasped the stone-cutter.

"Bad luck to ye!" cried Darby, clasping both arrums of the haunted man. "I'm no ghost, let lone the divil—I'm only your friend, Darby O'Gill."

Lying there, breathing hard, they stared into the faces of aich other a little space till the poor stone-cutter began to cry.

"Oh, is that you, Darby O'Gill? Where is the banshee? Oh, haven't I the bad fortune," he says, sthriving to raise himself.

"Rise up," says Darby, lifting the man to his feet an' steadying him there. The stone-cutter stared about like one stunned be a blow.

"I don't know where the banshee flew, but do you go back to Eileen as soon as you can," says the friend of the fairies. "Not that way, man alive," he says, as Cormac started to climb the foot-bridge, "it's broke in the middle; go down an' cross the stone bridge. I'll be afther you in a minute," he says.

Without a word, meek now and biddable as a child, Cormac turned, an' Darby saw him hurry away into the blackness.

The raysons Darby raymained behind were two: first an' foremost, he was a bit vexed at the way his clothes were muddied an' dhraggled, an' himself had been pounded an' hammered; an' second, he wanted to think. He had a quare cowld feeling in his mind that something was wrong—a kind of a foreboding, as one might say.

As he stood thinking a rayalisation of the caylamity sthruck him all at once like a rap on the jaw—he had lost his fine brier pipe. The lad groaned as he began the anxious sarch. He slapped furiously at his chist an' side pockets, he dived into his throwsers and greatcoat, and at last, sprawlin' on his hands an' feet like a monkey, he groped savagely through the wet, sticky clay.

"This comes," says the poor lad, grumblin' an' gropin', "of pokin' your nose into other people's business. Hallo, what's this?" says he, straightening himself. "'Tis a comb. Be the powers of pewther, 'tis the banshee's comb."

An' so indade it was. He had picked up a goold comb the length of your hand an' almost the width of your two fingers. About an inch of one ind was broken off, an' dhropped into Darby's palm. Without thinkin', he put the broken bit into his weskit pocket, an' raised the biggest half close to his eyes, the betther to view it.

"May I never see sorrow," he says, "if the banshee mustn't have dhropped her comb. Look at that, now. Folks do be sayin' that 'tis this gives her the foine singing voice, bekase the comb is enchanted," he says. "If that sayin' be thrue, it's the faymous lad I am from this night. I'll thravel from fair to fair, an' maybe at the ind they'll send me to parliament."

With these worruds he lifted his caubeen* an' stuck the comb in the top tuft of his hair.

Begor, he'd no sooner guv it a pull than a sour, singing feelin' begun at the bottom of his stomick, an' it rose higher an' higher. When it raiched his chist he was just going to let a bawl out of himself only that he caught sight of a thing ferninst him that froze the marrow in his bones.

He gasped short an' jerked the comb out of his hair, for there, not tin feet away, stood a dark, shadowy woman, tall, thin, an' motionless, laning on a crutch.

During a breath or two the persecuted hayro lost his head completely, for he never doubted that the banshee had changed her shuit of clothes to chase back afther him.

The first clear aymotion that rayturned to him was to fling the comb on the ground an' make a boult of it. On second thought he knew that 'twould be aisier to bate the wind in a race than to run away from the banshee.

"Well, there's a good Tipperary man done for this time," groaned the knowledgeable man, "unless in some way I can beguile her." He was fishing in his mind for its civilest worrud when the woman spoke up, an' Darby's heart jumped with gladness as he raycognised the cracked voice of Sheelah Maguire,† the spy for the fairies.

"The top of the avenin' to you, Darby O'Gill," says Sheelah, peering at him from undher her hood, the two eyes of her glowing like tallow candles; "amn't I kilt with a-stonishment to see you here alone this time of the night," says the ould witch.

Now, the clever man knew as well as though he had been tould, when Sheelah said thim worruds, that the banshee had sent her to look for the comb, an' his heart grew bould; but he answered her polite enough, "Why,

* An Irish beret.

† Darby first met Sheelah in "Darby O'Gill and the Good People."

thin, luck to ye, Misthress Maguire, ma'am," he says, bowing grand, "sure, if you're kilt with a-stonishment, amn't I sphlit with inkerdoolity to find yourself mayandherin' in this lonesome place on Halloween night."

Sheelah hobbled a step or two nearer, an' whispered confaydential.

"I was wandherin' hereabouts only this morning," she says, "an' I lost from me hair a goold comb—one that I've had this forty years. Did ye see such a thing as that, agra?"* An' her two eyes blazed.

"Faix, I dunno," says Darby, putting his two arrums behind him. "Was it about the length of ye're hand an' the width of ye're two fingers?" he axed.

"It was," says she, thrusting out a withered paw.

"Thin I didn't find it," says the tantalising man. "But maybe I did find something summillar, only 'twasn't yours at all, but the banshee's," he says, chuckling.

Whether the hag was intentioned to welt Darby with her staff, or whether she was only liftin' it for to make a sign of enchantment in the air, will never be known, but whatsomever she meant the hayro doubled his fists an' squared off; at that she lowered the stick, an' broke into a shrill, cackling laugh.

"Ho, ho!" she laughed, houldin' her sides, "but aren't ye the bould, distinguishable man. Becourse 'tis the banshee's comb; how well ye knew it! Be the same token I'm sint to bring it away; so make haste to give it up, for she's hiding an' waiting for me down at Chartres' mill. Aren't you the courageous blaggard, to grabble at her, an' thry to ketch her. Sure, such a thing never happened before, since the worruld began," says Sheelah.

The idee that the banshee was hiding an' afeared to face him was great news to the hayro. But he only tossed his head an' smiled shuparior as he made answer.

"'Tis yourself that knows well, Sheelah Maguire, ma'am," answers back the proud man, slow an' dayliberate, "that whin one does a favour for an unearthly spirit he may daymand for pay the favours of three such wishes as the spirit has power to give. The worruld knows that. Now I'll take three good wishes, such as the banshee can bestow, or else I'll carry the goolden

* Agra has the same meaning as the English slang expression "luv," used in referring to a person.

comb straight to Father Cassidy. The banshee hasn't goold nor wor'ly goods, as the sayin' is, but she has what suits me betther."

This cleverness angered the fairy-woman so she set in to abuse and to frighten Darby. She ballyragged, she browbate, she trajooced, she threatened, but 'twas no use. The bould man hildt firm, till at last she promised him the favours of the three wishes.

"First an' foremost," says he, "I'll want her never to put her spell on me or any of my kith an' kin."

"That wish she gives you, that wish she grants you, though it'll go sore agin the grain," snarled Sheelah.

"Then," says Darby, "my second wish is that the black spell be taken from Eileen McCarthy."

Sheelah flusthered about like an angry hin. "Wouldn't something else do as well?" she says.

"I'm not here to argify," says Darby, swingin' back an' forrud on his toes.

"Bad scran to you,"* says Sheelah. "I'll have to go an' ask the banshee herself about that. Don't stir from that spot till I come back."

You may believe it or not, but with that sayin' she bent the head of her crutch well forward, an' before Darby's very face she trew—savin' your presence—one leg over the stick as though it had been a horse, an' while one might say Jack Robinson the crutch riz into the air an' lifted her, an' she went sailing out of sight.

Darby was still gaping an' gawpin' at the darkness where she disappeared whin—whisk! she was back agin an' dismountin' at his side.

"The luck is with you," says she, spiteful. "That wish I give, that wish I grant you. You'll find seven crossed rushes undher McCarthy's door-step; uncross them, put them in fire or in wather, an' the spell is lifted. Be quick with the third wish—out with it!"

"I'm in a more particular hurry about that than you are," says Darby. "You must find me my brier pipe," says he.

"You omadhaun,"† sneered the fairy-woman, "'tis sthuck in the band of your hat, where you put it when you left your own house the night. No,

---

* "Bad food [or fare] to you!"—a curse.

† A fool or simpleton.

no, not in front," she says, as Darby put up his hand to feel. "It's stuck in the back. Your caubeen's twishted," she says.

Whilst Darby was standing with the comb in one hand an' the pipe in the other, smiling daylighted, the comb was snatched from his fingers and he got a welt in the side of the head from the crutch. Looking up, he saw Sheelah tunty feet in the air, headed for Chartres' mill, an' she cacklin' an' screechin' with laughter. Rubbing his sore head an' mutthering unpious words to himself, Darby started for the new bridge.

In less than no time afther, he had found the seven crossed rushes undher McCarthy's door-step, an' had flung them into the stream. Thin, without knocking, he pushed open McCarthy's door an' tiptoed quietly in.

Cormac was kneelin' beside the bed with his face buried in the pillows, as he was when Darby first saw him that night. But Eileen was sleeping as sound as a child, with a sweet smile on her lips. Heavy pursperation beaded her forehead, showing that the faver was broke.

Without disturbing aither of them our hayro picked up the package of tay from the floor, put it on the dhresser, an' with a glad heart sthole out of the house an' closed the door softly behind him.

Turning toward Chartres' mill he lifted his hat an' bowed low. "Thank you kindly, Misthress Banshee," he says. "'Tis well for us all I found your comb this night. Public or private, I'll always say this for you—you're a woman of your worrud," he says.

Frances Hodgson Burnett (1849–1924) was born in Manchester, England, but moved with her family to Tennessee in 1865. Frances's father died suddenly of a stroke when she was three, and she began writing at 16 to bring in extra money. In 1868 she started selling stories to popular ladies' magazines, followed by the publication of her first novel, *That Lass o'Lowrie's*, in 1877. However, after meeting Louisa May Alcott in 1879, she turned her hand to children's literature, and produced three classics: *Little Lord Fauntleroy* (1886), *A Little Princess* (1905), and *The Secret Garden* (1911). In her personal life, Burnett was a spiritualist and Christian Scientist whose 1898 divorce from her first husband, Swan Burnett, caused a minor scandal. Her second marriage (to Stephen Townsend) was unhappy and ended after two years. Burnett, who had divided her time between Great Britain and America, spent the last 17 years of her life on Long Island, New York. "In the Closed Room" was originally published in 1904 by itself in a lovely edition illustrated by the renowned Jessie Willcox Smith; it was well-reviewed, although one British newspaper noted that "most emphatically should it be said that the book is not a suitable one for a child to read."

In the Closed Room

by Frances Hodgson Burnett

PART ONE

In the fierce airless heat of the small square room the child Judith panted as she lay on her bed. Her father and mother slept near her, drowned in the heavy slumber of workers after their day's labour. Some people in the next flat were quarrelling, irritated probably by the appalling heat and their miserable helplessness against it. All the hot emanations of the sun-baked city streets seemed to combine with their clamour and unrest, and rise to the flat in which the child lay gazing at the darkness. It was situated but a few feet from the track of the Elevated Railroad and existence seemed to pulsate to the rush and roar of the demon which swept past the windows every few minutes. No one knew that Judith held the thing in horror, but it was a truth that she did. She was only seven years old, and at that age it is not easy to explain one's self so that older people can understand.

She could only have said, "I hate it. It comes so fast. It is always coming. It makes a sound as if thunder was quite close. I can never get away from it." The children in the other flats rather liked it. They hung out of the window perilously to watch it thunder past and to see the people who crowded it pressed close together in the seats, standing in the aisles, hanging on to the straps. Sometimes in the evening there were people in it who were going to the theatre, and the women and girls were dressed in light colours and wore hats covered with white feathers and flowers. At such times the children were delighted, and Judith used to hear the three in the next flat calling out to each other, "That's MY lady! That's MY lady! That one's mine!"

Judith was not like the children in the other flats. She was a frail, curious creature, with silent ways and a soft voice and eyes. She liked to play by herself in a corner of the room and to talk to herself as she played. No one knew what she talked about, and in fact no one inquired. Her mother was always too busy. When she was not making men's coats by the score at the whizzing sewing machine, she was hurriedly preparing a meal which was always in danger of being late. There was the breakfast, which might not be ready in time for her husband to reach his "shop" when the whistle blew; there was the supper, which might not be in time to be in waiting for him when he returned in the evening. The midday meal was a trifling matter, needing no special preparation. One ate anything one could find left from supper or breakfast.

Judith's relation to her father and mother was not a very intimate one. They were too hard worked to have time for domestic intimacies, and a feature of their acquaintance was that though neither of them was sufficiently articulate to have found expression for the fact—the young man and woman felt the child vaguely remote. Their affection for her was tinged with something indefinitely like reverence. She had been a lovely baby with a peculiar magnolia whiteness of skin and very large, sweetly smiling eyes of dark blue, fringed with quite black lashes. She had exquisite pointed fingers and slender feet, and though Mr. and Mrs. Foster were—perhaps fortunately—unaware of it, she had been not at all the baby one would have expected to come to life in a corner of the hive of a workman's flat a few feet from the Elevated Railroad.

"Seems sometimes as if somehow she couldn't be mine," Mrs. Foster said at times. "She ain't like me, an' she ain't like Jem Foster, Lord knows. She ain't like none of either of our families I've ever heard of—'ceptin' it might be her Aunt Hester—but SHE died long before I was born. I've only heard mother tell about her. She was a awful pretty girl. Mother said she had that kind of lily-white complexion and long slender fingers that was so supple she could curl 'em back like they was double-jointed. Her eyes was big and had eyelashes that stood out round 'em, but they was brown. Mother said she wasn't like any other kind of girl, and she thinks Judith may turn out like her. She wasn't but fifteen when she died. She never was ill in her life—but one morning she didn't come down to breakfast, and when they went up to call her, there she was sittin' at her window restin' her chin on her hand, with her face turned up smilin' as if she was talkin' to some one. The doctor said it had happened hours before, when she had come to the window to look at the stars. Easy way to go, wasn't it?"

Judith had heard of her Aunt Hester, but she only knew that she herself had hands like her and that her life had ended when she was quite young. Mrs. Foster was too much occupied by the strenuousness of life to dwell upon the passing of souls. To her the girl Hester seemed too remote to appear quite real. The legends of her beauty and unlikeness to other girls seemed rather like a sort of romance.

As she was not aware that Judith hated the Elevated Railroad, so she was not aware that she was fond of the far away Aunt Hester with the long-pointed fingers which could curl backwards. She did not know that when she was playing in her corner of the room, where it was her way to sit on her little chair with her face turned towards the wall, she often sat curving her small long fingers backward and talking to herself about Aunt Hester. But this—as well as many other things—was true. It was not secretiveness which caused the child to refrain from speaking of certain things. She herself could not have explained the reasons for her silence; also it had never occurred to her that explanation and reasons were necessary. Her mental attitude was that of a child who, knowing a certain language, does not speak it to those who have never heard and are wholly ignorant of it. She knew her Aunt Hester as her mother did not. She had seen her often in her dreams and had a secret fancy that she could dream of her when she wished to do so. She was very fond of dreaming of her. The places where she came upon Aunt Hester were strange and lovely places where the air one breathed smelled like flowers and everything was lovely in a new way, and when one moved one felt so light that movement was delightful, and when one wakened one had not quite got over the lightness and for a few moments felt as if one would float out of bed.

The healthy, vigourous young couple who were the child's parents were in a healthy, earthly way very fond of each other. They had made a genuine love match and had found it satisfactory. The young mechanic Jem Foster had met the young shop-girl Jane Hardy, at Coney Island one summer night and had become at once enamoured of her shop-girl good looks and high spirits. They had married as soon as Jem had had the "raise" he was anticipating and had from that time lived with much harmony in the flat building by which the Elevated train rushed and roared every few minutes through the day and a greater part of the night. They themselves did not object to the "Elevated"; Jem was habituated to uproar in the machine shop, in which he spent his days, and Jane was too much absorbed in the making of men's coats by the dozens to observe anything else. The pair had healthy appetites and slept well after their day's work, hearty supper, long cheerful talk, and loud laughter over simple common joking.

"She's a queer little fish, Judy," Jane said to her husband as they sat by the open window one night, Jem's arm curved comfortably around the young woman's waist as he smoked his pipe. "What do you think she says to me to-night after I put her to bed?"

"Search ME!" said Jem oracularly.

Jane laughed.

"'Why,' she says, 'I wish the Elevated train would stop.'

"'Why?' says I.

"'I want to go to sleep,' says she. 'I'm going to dream of Aunt Hester.'"

"What does she know about her Aunt Hester," said Jem. "Who's been talkin' to her?"

"Not me," Jane said. "She don't know nothing but what she's picked up by chance. I don't believe in talkin' to young ones about dead folks. 'Tain't healthy."

"That's right," said Jem. "Children that's got to hustle about among live folks for a livin' best keep their minds out of cemeteries. But, Hully Gee, what a queer thing for a young one to say."

"And that ain't all," Jane went on, her giggle half amused, half nervous. "'But I don't fall asleep when I see Aunt Hester,' says she. 'I fall awake. It's more awake there than here.'

"'Where?' says I, laughing a bit, though it did make me feel queer.

"'I don't know' she says in that soft little quiet way of hers. 'There.' And not another thing could I get out of her."

On the hot night through whose first hours Judith lay panting in her corner of the room, tormented and kept awake by the constant roar and rush and flash of lights, she was trying to go to sleep in the hope of leaving all the heat and noise and discomfort behind, and reaching Aunt Hester. If she could fall awake she would feel and hear none of it. It would all be unreal and she would know that only the lightness and the air like flowers and the lovely brightness were true. Once, as she tossed on her cot-bed, she broke into a low little laugh to think how untrue things really were and how strange it was that people did not understand—that even she felt as she lay in the darkness that she could not get away. And she could not get away unless the train would stop just long enough to let her fall asleep. If she could fall asleep between the trains, she would not awaken. But they came so quickly one after the other. Her hair was damp as she pushed it from her forehead, the bed felt hot against her skin, the people in the next flat quarreled more angrily, Judith heard a loud slap, and then the woman began to cry. She was a young married woman, scarcely more than a girl. Her marriage had not been as successful as that of Judith's parents. Both husband and wife had irritable tempers. Through the thin wall Judith could hear the girl sobbing angrily as the man flung himself out of bed, put on his clothes and went out, banging the door after him.

"She doesn't know," the child whispered eerily, "that it isn't real at all."

There was in her strange little soul a secret no one knew the existence of. It was a vague belief that she herself was not quite real—or that she did not belong to the life she had been born into. Her mother and father loved her and she loved them, but sometimes she was on the brink of telling them that she could not stay long—that some mistake had been made. What mistake—or where was she to go to if she went, she did not know. She used to catch her breath and stop herself and feel frightened when she had been near speaking of this fantastic thing. But the building full of workmen's flats, the hot room, the Elevated Railroad, the quarrelling people, were all a mistake. Just once or twice in her life she had seen places and things which did not seem so foreign. Once, when she had been taken to the Park in the spring, she had wandered away from her mother to a sequestered place among shrubs and trees, all waving tender, new pale green, with the leaves a few early hot days had caused to rush out and tremble unfurled. There had been a stillness there and scents and colours she knew. A bird had come and swung upon a twig quite near her and, looking at her with bright soft full eyes, had sung gently to her, as if he were speaking. A squirrel had crept up onto her lap and had not moved when she stroked it. Its eyes had been full and soft also, and she knew it understood that she could not hurt it. There was no mistake in her being among the new fair greenness, and the woodland things who spoke to her. They did not use words, but no words were needed. She knew what they were saying. When she had pushed her way through the greenness of the shrubbery to the driveway she had found herself quite near to an open carriage, which had stopped because the lady who sat in it was speaking to a friend on the path. She was a young woman, dressed in delicate spring colours, and the little girl at her side was dressed in white cloth, and it was at the little girl Judith found herself gazing. Under her large white hat and feathers her little face seemed like a white flower. She had a deep dimple near her mouth. Her hair was a rich coppery red and hung heavy and long about her cheeks and shoulders. She lifted her head a little when the child in the common hat and frock pressed through the greenness of the bushes and she looked at Judith just as the bird and the squirrel had looked at her. They gazed as if they had known each other for ages of years and were separated by nothing.

Each of them was quite happy at being near the other, and there was not in the mind of either any question of their not being near each other again. The question did not rise in Judith's mind even when in a very few minutes the carriage moved away and was lost in the crowd of equipages rolling by.

At the hottest hours of the hot night Judith recalled to herself the cool of that day. She brought back the fresh pale greenness of the nook among the bushes into which she had forced her way, the scent of the leaves and grass which she had drawn in as she breathed, the nearness in the eyes of the bird, the squirrel, and the child. She smiled as she thought of these things, and as she continued to remember yet other things, bit by bit, she felt less hot—she gradually forgot to listen for the roar of the train—she smiled still more—she lay quite still—she was cool—a tiny fresh breeze fluttered through the window and played about her forehead. She was smiling in soft delight as her eyelids drooped and closed.

"I am falling awake," she was murmuring as her lashes touched her cheek.

Perhaps when her eyes closed the sultriness of the night had changed to the momentary freshness of the turning dawn, and the next hour or so was really cooler. She knew no more heat but slept softly, deeply, long—or it seemed to her afterwards that she had slept long—as if she had drifted far away in dreamless peace.

She remembered no dream, saw nothing, felt nothing until, as it seemed to her, in the early morning, she opened her eyes. All was quite still and clear—the air of the room was pure and sweet. There was no sound anywhere and, curiously enough, she was not surprised by this, nor did she expect to hear anything disturbing.

She did not look round the room. Her eyes remained resting upon what she first saw—and she was not surprised by this either. A little girl about her own age was standing smiling at her. She had large eyes, a deep dimple near her mouth, and coppery red hair which fell about her cheeks and shoulders. Judith knew her and smiled back at her.

She lifted her hand—and it was a pure white little hand with long tapering fingers.

"Come and play with me," she said—though Judith heard no voice while she knew what she was saying. "Come and play with me."

Then she was gone, and in a few seconds Judith was awake, the air of the room had changed, the noise and clatter of the streets came in at the window, and the Elevated train went thundering by. Judith did not ask herself how the child had gone or how she had come. She lay still, feeling undisturbed by everything and smiling as she had smiled in her sleep.

While she sat at the breakfast table she saw her mother looking at her curiously.

"You look as if you'd slept cool instead of hot last night," she said. "You look better than you did yesterday. You're pretty well, ain't you, Judy?"

Judith's smile meant that she was quite well, but she said nothing about her sleeping.

The heat did not disturb her through the day, though the hours grew hotter and hotter as they passed. Jane Foster, sweltering at her machine, was obliged to stop every few minutes to wipe the beads from her face and neck. Sometimes she could not remain seated, but got up panting to drink water and fan herself with a newspaper.

"I can't stand much more of this," she kept saying. "If there don't come a thunderstorm to cool things off I don't know what I'll do. This room's about five hundred."

But the heat grew greater and the Elevated trains went thundering by.

When Jem came home from his work his supper was not ready. Jane was sitting helplessly by the window, almost livid in her pallor. The table was but half spread.

"Hullo," said Jem; "it's done you up, ain't it?"

"Well, I guess it has," good-naturedly, certain of his sympathy. "But I'll get over it presently, and then I can get you a cold bite. I can't stand over the stove and cook."

"Hully Gee, a cold bite's all a man wants on a night like this. Hot chops'd give him the jim-jams. But I've got good news for you—it's cheered me up myself."

Jane lifted her head from the chair back.

"What is it?"

"Well, it came through my boss. He's always been friendly to me. He asks a question or so every now and then and seems to take an interest. To-day he was asking me if it wasn't pretty hot and noisy down here, and after I told him how we stood it, he said he believed he could get us a better place to stay in through the summer. Some one he knows has had illness and trouble in his family and he's obliged to close his house and take his wife away into the mountains. They've got a beautiful big house in one of them far up streets by the Park and he wants to get caretakers in that can come well recommended. The boss said he could recommend us fast enough. And there's a big light basement that'll be as cool as the woods. And we can move in to-morrow. And all we've got to do is to see that things are safe and live happy."

"Oh, Jem!" Jane ejaculated. "It sounds too good to be true! Up by the Park! A big cool place to live!"

"We've none of us ever been in a house the size of it. You know what they look like outside, and they say they're bigger than they look. It's your business to go over the rooms every day or so to see nothing's going wrong in them—moths or dirt, I suppose. It's all left open but just one room they've left locked and don't want interfered with. I told the boss I thought the basement would seem like the Waldorf-Astoria to us. I tell you I was so glad I scarcely knew what to say."

Jane drew a long breath.

"A big house up there," she said. "And only one closed room in it. It's too good to be true!"

"Well, whether it's true or not we'll move out there to-morrow," Jem answered cheerfully. "To-morrow morning bright and early. The boss said the sooner the better."

A large house left deserted by those who have filled its rooms with emotions and life, expresses a silence, a quality all its own. A house unfurnished and empty seems less impressively silent. The fact of its devoidness of sound is upon the whole more natural. But carpets accustomed to the pressure of constantly passing feet, chairs and sofas which have held human warmth, draperies used to the touch of hands drawing them aside to let in daylight, pictures which have smiled back at thinking eyes, mirrors which have reflected faces passing hourly in changing moods, elate or dark or longing, walls which have echoed back voices—all these things when left alone seem to be held in strange arrest, as if by some spell intensifying the effect of the pause in their existence.

The child Judith felt this deeply throughout the entirety of her young being.

"How STILL it is," she said to her mother the first time they went over the place together.

"Well, it seems still up here—and kind of dead," Jane Foster replied with her habitual sociable half-laugh. "But seems to me it always feels that way in a house people's left. It's cheerful enough down in that big basement with all the windows open. We can sit in that room they've had fixed to play billiards in. We shan't hurt nothing. We can keep the table and things covered up. Tell you, Judy, this'll be different from last summer. The Park ain't but a few steps away an' we can go and sit there too when we feel like it. Talk about the country—I don't want no more country than this is. You'll be made over the months we stay here."

Judith felt as if this must veritably be a truth. The houses on either side of the street were closed for the summer. Their occupants had gone to the seaside or the mountains and the windows and doors were boarded up. The street was a quiet one at any time, and wore now the aspect of a street in a city of the dead. The green trees of the Park were to be seen either gently stirring or motionless in the sun at the side of the avenue crossing the end of it. The only token of the existence of the Elevated Railroad was a remote occasional hum suggestive of the flying past of a giant bee. The thing seemed no longer a roaring demon, and Judith scarcely recognized that it was still the centre of the city's rushing, heated life.

The owners of the house had evidently deserted it suddenly. The windows had not been boarded up and the rooms had been left in their ordinary condition. The furniture was not covered or the hangings swathed. Jem Foster had been told that his wife must put things in order.

The house was beautiful and spacious, its decorations and appointments were not mere testimonies to freedom of expenditure, but expressions of a dignified and cultivated thought. Judith followed her mother from room to room in one of her singular moods. The loftiness of the walls, the breadth and space about her made her, at intervals, draw in her breath with pleasure. The pictures, the colours, the rich and beautiful textures she saw brought to her the free—and at the same time soothed—feeling she remembered as the chief feature of the dreams in which she "fell awake." But beyond all other things she rejoiced in the height and space, the sweep of view through one large room into another. She continually paused and stood with her face lifted looking up at the pictured things floating on a ceiling above her. Once, when she had stood doing this long enough to forget herself, she was startled by her mother's laugh, which broke in upon the silence about them with a curiously earthly sound which was almost a shock.

"Wake up, Judy; have you gone off in a dream? You look all the time as if you was walking in your sleep."

"It's so high," said Judy. "Those clouds make it look like the sky."

"I've got to set these chairs straight," said Jane. "Looks like they'd been havin' a concert here. All these chairs together an' that part of the room clear."

She began to move the chairs and rearrange them, bustling about cheerfully and talking the while. Presently she stooped to pick something up.

"What's this," she said, and then uttered a startled exclamation. "Mercy! they felt so kind of clammy they made me jump. They HAVE had a party. Here's some of the flowers left fallen on the carpet."

She held up a cluster of wax-white hyacinths and large heavy rosebuds, faded to discoloration.

"This has dropped out of some set piece. It felt like cold flesh when I first touched it. I don't like a lot of white things together. They look too kind of mournful. Just go and get the wastepaper basket in the library, Judy. We'll carry it around to drop things into. Take that with you."

Judith carried the flowers into the library and bent to pick up the basket as she dropped them into it.

As she raised her head she found her eyes looking directly into other eyes which gazed at her from the wall. They were smiling from the face of a child in a picture. As soon as she saw them Judith drew in her breath and stood still, smiling, too, in response. The picture was that of a little girl in a floating white frock. She had a deep dimple at one corner of her mouth, her hanging hair was like burnished copper, she held up a slender hand with pointed fingers and Judith knew her. Oh! she knew her quite well. She had never felt so near any one else throughout her life.

"Judy, Judy!" Jane Foster called out. "Come here with your basket; what you staying for?"

Judith returned to her.

"We've got to get a move on," said Jane, "or we shan't get nothin' done before supper time. What was you lookin' at?"

"There's a picture in there of a little girl I know," Judith said. "I don't know her name, but I saw her in the Park once and—and I dreamed about her."

"Dreamed about her? If that ain't queer. Well, we've got to hurry up. Here's some more of them dropped flowers. Give me the basket."

They went through the whole house together, from room to room, up the many stairs, from floor to floor, and everywhere Judith felt the curious stillness and silence. It can not be doubted that Jane Foster felt it also.

"It is the stillest house I was ever in," she said. "I'm glad I've got you with me, Judy. If I was sole alone I believe it 'ud give me the creeps. These big places ought to have big families in them."

It was on the fourth floor that they came upon the Closed Room. Jane had found some of the doors shut and some open, but a turn of the handle gave entrance through all the unopened ones until they reached this one at the back on the fourth floor.

"This one won't open," Jane said, when she tried the handle. Then she shook it once or twice. "No, it's locked," she decided after an effort or two. "There, I've just remembered. There's one kept locked. Folks always has things they want locked up. I'll make sure, though."

She shook it, turned the handle, shook again, pressed her knee against the panel. The lock resisted all effort.

"Yes, this is the closed one," she made up her mind. "It's locked hard and fast. It's the closed one."

It was logically proved to be the closed one by the fact that she found no other one locked as she finished her round of the chambers.

Judith was a little tired before they had done their work. But her wandering pilgrimage through the large, silent, deserted house had been a revelation of new emotions to her. She was always a silent child. Her mind was so full of strange thoughts that it seemed unnecessary to say many words. The things she thought as she followed her from room to room, from floor to floor, until they reached the locked door, would have amazed and puzzled Jane Foster if she had known of their existence. Most of all, perhaps, she would have been puzzled by the effect the closed door had upon the child. It puzzled and bewildered Judith herself and made her feel a little weary.

She wanted so much to go into the room. Without in the least understanding the feeling, she was quite shaken by it. It seemed as if the closing of all the other rooms would have been a small matter in comparison with the closing of this one. There was something inside which she wanted to see—there was something—somehow there was something which wanted to see her. What a pity that the door was locked! Why had it been done? She sighed unconsciously several times during the evening, and Jane Foster thought she was tired.

"But you'll sleep cool enough to-night, Judy," she said. "And get a good rest. Them little breezes that comes rustling through the trees in the Park comes right along the street to us."

She and Jem Foster slept well. They spent the evening in the highest spirits and—as it seemed to them—the most luxurious comfort. The space afforded them by the big basement, with its kitchen and laundry and pantry, and, above all, the specially large room which had been used for billiard playing, supplied actual vistas. For the sake of convenience and coolness they used the billiard room as a dormitory, sleeping on light cots, and they slept with all their windows open, the little breezes wandering from among the trees of the Park to fan them. How they laughed and enjoyed themselves over their supper, and how they stretched themselves out with sighs of joy in the darkness as they sank into the cool, untroubled waters of deep sleep.

"This is about the top notch," Jem murmured as he lost his hold on the world of waking life and work.

But though she was cool, though she was undisturbed, though her body rested in absolute repose, Judith did not sleep for a long time. She lay and listened to the quietness. There was mystery in it. The footstep of a belated passer-by in the street woke strange echoes; a voice heard in the distance in a riotous shout suggested weird things. And as she lay and listened, it was as if she were not only listening but waiting for something. She did not know at all what she was waiting for, but waiting she was.

She lay upon her cot with her arms flung out and her eyes wide open. What was it that she wanted—that which was in the closed room? Why had they locked the door? If they had locked the doors of the big parlours it would not have mattered. If they had locked the door of the library—her mind paused—as if for a moment, something held it still. Then she remembered that to have locked the doors of the library would have been to lock in the picture of the child with the greeting look in her eyes and the fine little uplifted hand. She was glad the room had been left open. But the room up-stairs—the one on the fourth floor—that was the one that mattered most of all. She knew that to-morrow she must go and stand at the door and press her cheek against the wood and wait—and listen. Thinking this and knowing that it must be so, she fell—at last—asleep.

PART TWO

Judith climbed the basement stairs rather slowly. Her mother was busy rearranging the disorder the hastily departing servants had left. Their departure had indeed been made in sufficient haste to have left behind the air of its having been flight. There was a great deal to be done, and Jane Foster, moving about with broom and pail and scrubbing brushes, did not dislike the excitement of the work before her. Judith's certainty that she would not be missed made all clear before her. If her absence was observed her mother would realize that the whole house lay open to her and that she was an undisturbing element wheresoever she was led either by her fancy or by circumstance. If she went into the parlours she would probably sit and talk to herself or play quietly with her shabby doll. In any case she would be finding pleasure of her own and would touch nothing which could be harmed.

When the child found herself in the entrance hall she stopped a few moments to look about her. The stillness seemed to hold her and she paused to hear and feel it. In leaving the basement behind, she had left the movement of living behind also. No one was alive upon this floor—nor upon the next—nor the next. It was as if one had entered a new world—a world in which something existed which did not express itself in sound or in things which one could see. Chairs held out their arms to emptiness—cushions were not pressed by living things—only the people in the pictures were looking at something, but one could not tell what they were looking at.

But on the fourth floor was the Closed Room, which she must go to—because she must go to it—that was all she knew.

She began to mount the stairs which led to the upper floors. Her shabby doll was held against her hip by one arm, her right hand touched the wall as she went, she felt the height of the wall as she looked upward. It was such a large house and so empty. Where had the people gone and why had they left it all at once as if they were afraid? Her father had only heard vaguely that they had gone because they had had trouble.

She passed the second floor, the third, and climbed towards the fourth. She could see the door of the Closed Room as she went up step by step, and she found herself moving more quickly. Yes, she must get to it—she must put her hand on it—her chest began to rise and fall with a quickening of her breath, and her breath quickened because her heart fluttered—as if with her haste. She began to be glad, and if any one could have seen her they would have been struck by a curious expectant smile in her eyes.

She reached the landing and crossed it, running the last few steps lightly. She did not wait or stand still a moment. With the strange expectant smile on her lips as well as in her eyes, she put her hand upon the door—not upon the handle, but upon the panel. Without any sound it swung quietly open. And without any sound she stepped quietly inside.

The room was rather large and the light in it was dim. There were no shutters, but the blinds were drawn down. Judith went to one of the windows and drew its blind up so that the look of the place might be clear to her. There were two windows and they opened upon the flat roof of an extension, which suggested somehow that it had been used as a place to walk about in. This, at least, was what Judith thought of at once—that some one who had used the room had been in the habit of going out upon the roof and staying there as if it had been a sort of garden. There were rows of flower pots with dead flowers in them—there were green tubs containing large shrubs, which were dead also—against the low parapet certain of them held climbing plants which had been trained upon it. Two had been climbing roses, two were clematis, but Judith did not know them by name. The ledge of the window was so low that a mere step took her outside. So taking it, she stood among the dried, withered things and looked in tender regret at them.

"I wish they were not dead," she said softly to the silence. "It would be like a garden if they were not dead."

The sun was hot, but a cool, little breeze seemed straying up from among the trees of the Park. It even made the dried leaves of the flowers tremble and rustle a little. Involuntarily she lifted her face to the blue sky and floating white clouds. They seemed so near that she felt almost as if she could touch them with her hand. The street seemed so far—so far below—the whole world seemed far below. If one stepped off the parapet it would surely take one a long time to reach the earth. She knew now why she had come up here. It was so that she might feel like this—as if she was upheld far away from things—as if she had left everything behind—almost as if she had fallen awake again. There was no perfume in the air, but all was still and sweet and clear.

Suddenly she turned and went into the room again, realizing that she had scarcely seen it at all and that she must see and know it. It was not like any other room she had seen. It looked more simple, though it was a pretty place. The walls were covered with roses, there were bright pictures, and shelves full of books. There was also a little writing desk and there were two or three low chairs, and a low table. A closet in a corner had its door ajar and Judith could see that inside toys were piled together. In another corner a large doll's house stood, looking as if some one had just stopped playing with it. Some toy furniture had been taken out and left near it upon the carpet.

"It was a little girl's room," Judith said. "Why did they close it?"

Her eye was caught by something lying on a sofa—something covered with a cloth. It looked almost like a child lying there asleep—so fast asleep that it did not stir at all. Judith moved across to the sofa and drew the cloth aside. With its head upon a cushion was lying there a very large doll, beautifully dressed in white lace, its eyes closed, and a little wreath of dead flowers in its hair.

"It looks almost as if it had died too," said Judith.

She did not ask herself why she said "as if it had died too"—perhaps it was because the place was so still—and everything so far away—that the flowers had died in the strange, little deserted garden on the roof.

She did not hear any footsteps—in fact, no ghost of a sound stirred the silence as she stood looking at the doll's sleep—but quite quickly she ceased to bend forward, and turned round to look at something which she knew was near her. There she was—and it was quite natural she should be there—the little girl with the face like a white flower, with the quantity of burnished coppery hair and the smile which deepened the already deep dimple near her mouth.

"You have come to play with me," she said.

"Yes," answered Judith. "I wanted to come all night. I could not stay down-stairs."

"No," said the child; "you can't stay down-stairs. Lift up the doll."

They began to play as if they had spent their lives together. Neither asked the other any questions. Judith had not played with other children, but with this one she played in absolute and lovely delight. The little girl knew where all the toys were, and there were a great many beautiful ones. She told Judith where to find them and how to arrange them for their games. She invented wonderful things to do—things which were so unlike anything Judith had ever seen or heard or thought of that it was not strange that she realized afterwards that all her past life and its belongings had been so forgotten as to be wholly blotted out while she was in the Closed Room. She did not know her playmate's name, she did not remember that there were such things as names. Every moment was happiness. Every moment the little girl seemed to grow more beautiful in the flower whiteness of her face and hands and the strange lightness and freedom of her movements. There was an ecstasy in looking at her—in feeling her near.

Not long before Judith went down-stairs she found herself standing with her outside the window in among the withered flowers.

"It was my garden," the little girl said. "It has been so hot and no one has been near to water them, so they could not live."

She went lightly to one of the brown rose-bushes and put her pointed-fingered little hand quite near it. She did not touch it, but held her hand near—and the leaves began to stir and uncurl and become fresh and tender again, and roses were nodding, blooming on the stems. And she went in the same manner to each flower and plant in turn until all the before dreary little garden was bright and full of leaves and flowers.

"It's Life," she said to Judith. Judith nodded and smiled back at her, understanding quite well just as she had understood the eyes of the bird who had swung on the twig so near her cheek the day she had hidden among the bushes in the Park.

"Now, you must go," the little girl said at last. And Judith went out of the room at once—without waiting or looking back, though she knew the white figure did not stir till she was out of sight.

It was not until she had reached the second floor that the change came upon her. It was a great change and a curious one. The Closed Room became as far away as all other places and things had seemed when she had stood upon the roof feeling the nearness of the blueness and the white clouds—as when she had looked round and found herself face to face with the child in the Closed Room. She suddenly realized things she had not known before. She knew that she had heard no voice when the little girl spoke to her—she knew that it had happened, that it was she only who had lifted the doll—who had taken out the toys—who had arranged the low table for their feast, putting all the small service upon it—and though they had played with such rapturous enjoyment and had laughed and feasted—what had they feasted on? That she could not recall—and not once had she touched or been touched by the light hand or white dress—and though they seemed to express their thoughts and intentions freely she had heard no voice at all. She was suddenly bewildered and stood rubbing her hand over her forehead and her eyes—but she was happy—as happy as when she had fallen awake in her sleep—and was no more troubled or really curious than she would have been if she had had the same experience every day of her life.

"Well, you must have been having a good time playing up-stairs," Jane Foster said when she entered the big kitchen. "This is going to do you good, Judy. Looks like she'd had a day in the country, don't she, Jem?"

Through the weeks that followed her habit of "playing up-stairs" was accepted as a perfectly natural thing. No questions were asked and she knew it was not necessary to enter into any explanations.

Every day she went to the door of the Closed Room and, finding it closed, at a touch of her hand upon the panel it swung softly open. There she waited—sometimes for a longer, sometimes for a shorter time—and the child with the coppery hair came to her. The world below was gone as soon as she entered the room, and through the hours they played together joyously as happy children play. But in their playing it was always Judith who touched the toys—who held the doll—who set the little table for their feast. Once as she went down-stairs she remembered that when she had that day made a wreath of roses from the roof and had gone to put it on her playmate's head, she had drawn back with deepened dimple and, holding up her hand, had said, laughing: "No. Do not touch me."

But there was no mystery in it after all. Judith knew she should presently understand.

She was so happy that her happiness lived in her face in a sort of delicate brilliance. Jane Foster observed the change in her with exceeding comfort, her view being that spacious quarters, fresh air, and sounder sleep had done great things for her.

"Them big eyes of hers ain't like no other child's eyes I've ever seen," she said to her husband with cheerful self-gratulation. "An' her skin's that fine an' thin an' fair you can jest see through it. She always looks to me as if she was made out of different stuff from me an' you, Jem. I've always said it."

"She's going to make a corking handsome girl," responded Jem with a chuckle.

They had been in the house two months, when one afternoon, as she was slicing potatoes for supper, Jane looked round to see the child standing at the kitchen doorway, looking with a puzzled expression at some wilted flowers she held in her hand. Jane's impression was that she had been coming into the room and had stopped suddenly to look at what she held.

"What've you got there, Judy?" she asked.

"They're flowers," said Judith, her eyes still more puzzled.

"Where'd you get 'em from? I didn't know you'd been out. I thought you was up-stairs."

"I was," said Judith quite simply. "In the Closed Room."

Jane Foster's knife dropped into her pan with a splash.

"Well," she gasped.

Judith looked at her with quiet eyes.

"The Closed Room!" Jane cried out. "What are you saying? You couldn't get in?"

"Yes, I can."

Jane was conscious of experiencing a shock. She said afterwards that suddenly something gave her the creeps.

"You couldn't open the door," she persisted. "I tried it again yesterday as I passed by—turned the handle and gave it a regular shove and it wouldn't give an inch."

"Yes," the child answered; "I heard you. We were inside then."

A few days later, when Jane weepingly related the incident to awe-stricken and sympathizing friends, she described as graphically as her limited vocabulary would allow her to do so, the look in Judith's face as she came nearer to her.

"Don't tell me there was nothing happening then," she said. "She just came up to me with them dead flowers in her hand an' a kind of look in her eyes as if she was half sorry for me an' didn't know quite why.

"'The door opens for me,' she says. 'That's where I play every day. There's a little girl comes and plays with me. She comes in at the window, I think. She is like the picture in the room where the books are. Her hair hangs down and she has a dimple near her mouth.'

"I couldn't never tell any one what I felt like. It was as if I'd got a queer fright that I didn't understand.

"'She must have come over the roof from the next house,' I says. 'They've got an extension too—but I thought the people were gone away.'

"'There are flowers on our roof,' she said. 'I got these there.' And that puzzled look came into her eyes again. 'They were beautiful when I got them—but as I came down-stairs they died.'

"'Well, of all the queer things,' I said. She put out her hand and touched my arm sort of lovin' an' timid.

"'I wanted to tell you to-day, mother,' she said. 'I had to tell you to-day. You don't mind if I go play with her, do you? You don't mind?'

"Perhaps it was because she touched me that queer little loving way—or was it the way she looked—it seemed like something came over me an' I just grabbed her an' hugged her up.

"'No,' I says. 'So as you come back. So as you come back.'

"And to think!" And Jane rocked herself sobbing.

A point she dwelt on with many tears was that the child seemed in a wistful mood and remained near her side—bringing her little chair and sitting by her as she worked, and rising to follow her from place to place as she moved from one room to the other.

"She wasn't never one as kissed you much or hung about like some children do—I always used to say she was the least bother of any child I ever knew. Seemed as if she had company of her own when she sat in her little chair in the corner whispering to herself or just setting quiet." This was a thing Jane always added during all the years in which she told the story. "That was what made me notice. She kept by me and she kept looking at me different from any way I'd seen her look before—not pitiful exactly—but something like it. And once she came up and kissed me and once or twice she just kind of touched my dress or my hand—as I stood by her. SHE knew. No one need tell me she didn't."

But this was an error. The child was conscious only of a tender, wistful feeling, which caused her to look at the affectionate healthy young woman who had always been good to her and whom she belonged to, though she remotely wondered why—the same tenderness impelled her to touch her arm, hand and simple dress, and folding her arms round her neck to kiss her softly. It was an expression of gratitude for all the rough casual affection of the past. All her life had been spent at her side—all her life on earth had sprung from her.

When she went up-stairs to the Closed Room the next day she told her mother she was going before she left the kitchen.

"I'm going up to play with the little girl, mother," she said.

"You don't mind, do you?"

Jane had had an evening of comfortable domestic gossip and joking with Jem, had slept, slept soundly and eaten a hearty breakfast. Life had reassumed its wholly normal aspect. The sun was shining hot and bright and she was preparing to scrub the kitchen floor. She believed that the child was mistaken as to the room she had been in.

"That's all right," she said, turning the hot water spigot over the sink so that the boiling water poured forth at full flow into her pail, with clouds of steam. "But when I've done my scrubbing I'm comin' up to see if it IS the Closed Room you play in. If it is, I guess you'd better play somewhere else—and I want to find out how you get that door open. Run along if you like."

Judith came back to her from the door. "Yes," she said, "come and see. But if she is there," putting her hand on Jane's hip gently, "you mustn't touch her."

Jane turned off the hot water and stared.

"Her!"

"The little girl who plays. *I* never touch her. She says I must not."

Jane lifted her pail from the sink, laughing outright.

"Well, that sounds as if she was a pretty airy young one," she said. "I guess you're a queer little pair. Run on. I must get at this floor."

Judith ran up the three flights of stairs lightly. She was glad she had told her mother, though she wondered vaguely why it had never seemed right to tell her until last night, and last night it had seemed not so much necessary as imperative. Something had obliged her to tell her. The time had come when she must know. The Closed Room door had always shut itself gently after Judith had passed through it, and yesterday, when her mother passing by chance, had tried the handle so vigorously, the two children inside the room had stood still gazing at each other, but neither had spoken and Judith had not thought of speaking. She was out of the realm of speech, and without any sense of amazement was aware that she was out of it. People with voices and words were in that faraway world below.

The playing to-day was even a lovelier, happier thing than it had ever been before. It seemed to become each minute a thing farther and farther away from the world in the streets where the Elevated Railroad went humming past like a monster bee. And with the sense of greater distance came a sense of greater lightness and freedom. Judith found that she was moving about the room and the little roof garden almost exactly as she had moved in the waking dreams where she saw Aunt Hester—almost as if she was floating and every movement was ecstasy. Once as she thought this she looked at her playmate, and the child smiled and answered her as she always did before she spoke.

"Yes," she said; "I know her. She will come. She sent me."

She had this day a special plan with regard to the arranging of the Closed Room. She wanted all the things in it—the doll—the chairs—the toys—the little table and its service to be placed in certain positions. She told Judith what to do. Various toys were put here or there—the little table was set with certain dishes in a particular part of the room. A book was left lying upon the sofa cushion, the large doll was put into a chair near the sofa, with a smaller doll in its arms, on the small writing desk a letter, which Judith found in a drawer—a half-written letter—was laid, the pen was left in the ink. It was a strange game to play, but somehow Judith felt it was very pretty. When it was all done—and there were many curious things to do—the Closed Room looked quite different from the cold, dim, orderly place the door had first opened upon. Then it had looked as if everything had been swept up and set away and covered and done with forever—as if the life in it had ended and would never begin again. Now it looked as if some child who had lived in it and loved and played with each of its belongings, had just stepped out from her play—to some other room quite near—quite near. The big doll in its chair seemed waiting—even listening to her voice as it came from the room she had run into.

The child with the burnished hair stood and looked at it with her delicious smile.

"That is how it looked," she said. "They came and hid and covered everything—as if I had gone—as if I was Nowhere. I want her to know I come here. I couldn't do it myself. You could do it for me. Go and bring some roses."

The little garden was a wonder of strange beauty with its masses of flowers. Judith brought some roses from the bush her playmate pointed out. She put them into a light bowl which was like a bubble of thin, clear glass and stood on the desk near the letter.

"If they would look like that," the little girl said, "she would see. But no one sees them like that—when the Life goes away with me."

After that the game was finished and they went out on the roof garden and stood and looked up into the blue above their heads. How blue—how blue—how clear—how near and real! And how far and unreal the streets and sounds below. The two children stood and looked up and laughed at the sweetness of it.

Then Judith felt a little tired.

"I will go and lie down on the sofa," she said.

"Yes," the little girl answered. "It's time for you to go to sleep."

They went into the Closed Room and Judith lay down. As she did so, she saw that the door was standing open and remembered that her mother was coming up to see her and her playmate.

The little girl sat down by her. She put out her pretty fine hand and touched Judith for the first time. She laid her little pointed fingers on her forehead and Judith fell asleep.

It seemed only a few minutes before she wakened again. The little girl was standing by her.

"Come," she said.

They went out together onto the roof among the flowers, but a strange—a beautiful thing had happened. The garden did not end at the parapet and the streets and houses were not below. The little garden ended in a broad green pathway—green with thick, soft grass and moss covered with trembling white and blue bell-like flowers. Trees—fresh leaved as if spring had just awakened them—shaded it and made it look smiling fair. Great white blossoms tossed on their branches and Judith felt that the scent in the air came from them. She forgot the city was below, because it was millions and millions of miles away, and this was where it was right to be. There was no mistake. This was real. All the rest was unreal—and millions and millions of miles away.

They held each other's slim-pointed hands and stepped out upon the broad, fresh green pathway. There was no boundary or end to its beauty, and it was only another real thing that coming towards them from under the white, flowering trees was Aunt Hester.

In the basement Jane Foster was absorbed in her labours, which were things whose accustomedness provided her with pleasure. She was fond of her scrubbing, she enjoyed the washing of her dishes, she definitely entertained herself with the splash and soapy foam of her washtubs and the hearty smack and swing of her ironing. In the days when she had served at the ribbon counter in a department store, she had not found life as agreeable as she had found it since the hours which were not spent at her own private sewing machine were given to hearty domestic duties providing cleanliness, savoury meals, and comfort for Jem.

She was so busy this particular afternoon that it was inevitable that she should forget all else but the work which kept her on her knees scrubbing floors or on a chair polishing windows, and afterwards hanging before them bits of clean, spotted muslin.

She was doing this last when her attention being attracted by wheels in the street stopping before the door, she looked out to see a carriage door open and a young woman, dressed in exceptionally deep mourning garb, step onto the pavement, cross it, and ascend the front steps.

"Who's she?" Jane exclaimed disturbedly. "Does she think the house is to let because it's shut?" A ring at the front door bell called her down from her chair. Among the duties of a caretaker is naturally included that of answering the questions of visitors. She turned down her sleeves, put on a fresh apron, and ran up-stairs to the entrance hall.

When she opened the door, the tall, young woman in black stepped inside as if there were no reason for her remaining even for a moment on the threshold.

"I am Mrs. Haldon," she said. "I suppose you are the caretaker?"

Haldon was the name of the people to whom the house belonged. Jem Foster had heard only the vaguest things of them, but Jane remembered that the name was Haldon, and remembering that they had gone away because they had had trouble, she recognized at a glance what sort of trouble it had been. Mrs. Haldon was tall and young, and to Jane Foster's mind, expressed from head to foot the perfection of all that spoke for wealth and fashion. Her garments were heavy and rich with crape, the long black veil, which she had thrown back, swept over her shoulder and hung behind her, serving to set forth, as it were, more pitifully the white wornness of her pretty face, and a sort of haunting eagerness in her haggard eyes. She had been a smart, lovely, laughing and lovable thing, full of pleasure in the world, and now she was so stricken and devastated that she seemed set apart in an awful lonely world of her own.

She had no sooner crossed the threshold than she looked about her with a quick, smitten glance and began to tremble. Jane saw her look shudder away from the open door of the front room, where the chairs had seemed left as if set for some gathering, and the wax-white flowers had been scattered on the floor.

She fell into one of the carved hall seats and dropped her face into her hands, her elbows resting on her knees.

"Oh! No! No!" she cried. "I can't believe it. I can't believe it!"

Jane Foster's eyes filled with good-natured ready tears of sympathy.

"Won't you come up-stairs, ma'am?" she said. "Wouldn't you like to set in your own room perhaps?"

"No! No!" was the answer. "She was always there! She used to come into my bed in the morning. She used to watch me dress to go out. No! No!"

"I'll open the shutters in the library," said Jane.

"Oh! No! No! No! She would be sitting on the big sofa with her fairy story-book. She's everywhere—everywhere! How could I come! Why did I! But I couldn't keep away! I tried to stay in the mountains. But I couldn't. Something dragged me day and night. Nobody knows I am here!" She got up and looked about her again. "I have never been in here since I went out with HER," she said. "They would not let me come back. They said it would kill me. And now I have come—and everything is here—all the things we lived with—and SHE is millions and millions—and millions of miles away!"

"Who—who—was it?" Jane asked timidly in a low voice.

"It was my little girl," the poor young beauty said. "It was my little Andrea. Her portrait is in the library."

Jane began to tremble somewhat herself. "That—?" she began—and ended: "She is DEAD?"

Mrs. Haldon had dragged herself almost as if unconsciously to the stairs. She leaned against the newel post and her face dropped upon her hand.

"Oh! I don't KNOW!" she cried. "I cannot believe it. How COULD it be? She was playing in her nursery—laughing and playing—and she ran into the next room to show me a flower—and as she looked up at me—laughing, I tell you—laughing—she sank slowly down on her knees—and the flower fell out of her hand quietly—and everything went out of her face—everything was gone away from her, and there was never anything more—never!"

Jane Foster's hand had crept up to her throat. She did not know what made her cold.

"My little girl—" she began, "her name is Judith—"

"Where is she?" said Mrs. Haldon in a breathless way.

"She is up-stairs," Jane answered slowly. "She goes—into that back room—on the fourth floor—"

Mrs. Haldon turned upon her with wide eyes.

"It is locked!" she said. "They put everything away. I have the key."

"The door opens for her," said Jane. "She goes to play with a little girl—who comes to her. I think she comes over the roof from the next house."

"There is no child there!" Mrs. Haldon shuddered. But it was not with horror. There was actually a wild dawning bliss in her face. "What is she like?"

"She is like the picture." Jane scarcely knew her own monotonous voice. The world of real things was being withdrawn from her and she was standing without its pale—alone with this woman and her wild eyes. She began to shiver because her warm blood was growing cold. "She is a child with red hair—and there is a deep dimple near her mouth. Judith told me. You must not touch her."

She heard a wild gasp—a flash of something at once anguish and rapture blazed across the haggard, young face—and with a swerving as if her slight body had been swept round by a sudden great wind, Mrs. Haldon turned and fled up the stairs.

Jane Foster followed. The great wind swept her upward too. She remembered no single intake or outlet of breath until she was upon the fourth floor.

The door of the Closed Room stood wide open and Mrs. Haldon was swept within.

Jane Foster saw her stand in the middle of the room a second, a tall, swaying figure. She whirled to look about her and flung up her arms with an unearthly rapturous, whispered cry:

"It is all as she left it when she ran to me and fell. She has been here—to show me it is not so far!"

She sank slowly upon her knees, wild happiness in her face—wild tears pouring down it.

"She has seen her!" And she stretched forth yearning arms towards the little figure of Judith, who lay quiet upon the sofa in the corner. "Your little girl has seen her—and I dare not waken her. She is asleep."

Jane stood by the sofa—looking down. When she bent and touched the child the stillness of the room seemed to have got into her blood.

"No," she said, quivering, but with a strange simplicity. "No! not asleep! It was this way with her Aunt Hester."

Olivia Howard Dunbar (1873–1953) was born and lived her life in the eastern United States. She started as a reporter but turned to short stories after joining a literary circle that included Edwin Arlington Robinson and Ridgely Torrence. She married the latter in 1914. Although she wrote biographies, essays, and articles as well, she's now chiefly remembered for her handful of beautifully-crafted and disturbing short stories. "The Dream-Baby" first appeared in *Harper's Bazar* in 1904.

The Dream-baby

by Olivia Howard Dunbar

"It will seem a little like dying, won't it?" grimly commented Miss Agatha Holt, pausing to contemplate, as though for the first time, her immediate future.

Miss Emily, in the opposite corner of the fragrant little sitting-room, that was unacquainted with other disorder than the present quite legitimate one of packing, was wrapping with delicately conscientious fingers certain precious bits of china. The windows were open, and there surged gently in a relaxed June atmosphere. The draperies at doors and windows stirred sleepily.

"Rather more like heaven, Agatha," amended Miss Emily, in a thin, girlish voice that was not so incongruous, after all, with the unmistakable gray bands in her brown hair. It was not unlikely that this lovable lady would remain an *ingénue* to the brink of senility. Then something in Miss Agatha's expression made her add: "Now, if you're going to regret it, dear, we won't 'retire' at all. It's not too late. Perhaps we might not get together as large a school next year, but—"

"Nonsense!" brusquely interrupted the other, accelerating the executive precision of her packing. "I want nothing of the sort. There's no sweeter sorrow than parting with text-books and kindergarten cubes. Then I haven't the anguish of a schoolroom full of shorn friendships, as you know, dear. Oh no, I've never been 'dear teacher'! It isn't that. But to me, because I am well and strong, there is, perversely enough, something like humiliation in confessing, at fifty-three, that one has hung up one's tools for good. Why, one almost despises oneself!"

"I don't, Agatha," protested Miss Emily, putting on her glasses for a closer study of Miss Agatha's mood.

"I know; it's because you're fortunate enough to be consistently feminine. You appreciate that we are about to enter upon a dignified and harmonious spinsterly existence, whose pleasures we have amply earned. Well, so do I, and I naturally want to live up to my opportunities. Only, I have rough corners, you know, Emily, and I don't doubt you'll feel them sharper than ever, now."

"But that's something to be proud of, my dear," Emily gently chirped. "Most people's corners are worn smooth in the schoolroom."

"Poor darling!" Where her idol was concerned, Miss Agatha's pity overflowed at a word. "They did sandpaper you, the little wretches! You always were absurdly soft, Emily, and the schoolroom is no place for softness. I shall never become reconciled to your having missed your proper background, which, as I've told you often enough, would have been fireside domesticity. Don't talk to me of destiny!"

But indeed Miss Emily appeared to have no wish to. Her lack of zest in a discussion of this order was always indicated by some sweet irrelevance. "Agatha, have we any more tissue-paper?" served the purpose at this point.

For a week past, the atmosphere in the little flat had been singularly vibrant; the week, that is, since school had closed—with a definite, final snap, this time—and preparations for the summer flitting had begun. These latter were based, it is true, on an exaggerated estimate of the ravages that may be wrought in a summer by the moth and rust that do corrupt domestic treasures; but any less stalwart battery of defence would have failed to accommodate the ladies' delicately balanced consciences to the enjoyment of their approaching summer in Gloucester, with its delights, familiar now these many years, of wandering over wind-swept moors, intelligently admiring sunsets and storms, reading up neglected volumes of history and experiencing contact with the sublimated cultivation of Massachusetts. The "retiring" from their profession, the flurry of an unaccustomed concern with matters of finance, the ritualistic elaboration of their packing—these had, in combination, imparted to the two ladies an extraordinary state of tension, an unnatural aliveness to what was going on about them. Twelfth Street, upon which they had looked daily for years, had, as Miss Agatha said, a "final" look, though they were certainly returning in the autumn. And their friends bade them farewell for the summer—though this, again, was but their distorted perception of it—as though the two ladies were already remote from the familiar currents. What more natural, under these stimulating circumstances, than that Miss Agatha should have been driven, from mere "nerves," to frequent caustic comments?—or that Miss Emily should have timidly confessed that only twice before within her memory had she been so emotionally torn up by the roots:—once, when she had secured her first position as teacher, and again, when she and Agatha hadmade their first trip to Europe, bent on a decorous tour of the English cathedral towns.

For twenty-five years, it should be understood, this delightful pair had worked side by side. For fifteen years a certain door had borne the legend: "Miss Holt and Miss Vanderkoep: Classes for Young Children." As "Miss-Holt-and-Miss-Vanderkoep" they were, indeed, invariably known. Socially or professionally, the concept of them was single rather than dual. When, at half past eight in the morning, two persons of authority would approach the schoolroom, one slight, smiling, tranquil, one taller, breezier, and, to the infant mind, infinitely more terrible and "sarcastic"—appalling characteristic in a teacher!—those members of the "classes for young children" who were lingering reticently in the background, would exchange the unnecessary observation, "Here come Miss-Holt-and-Misa-Vanderkoep!" When the mothers of these very young persons wished to confer, as it were, a social nod upon the accomplished instructors, phrases of affectionate condescension would invite "My-dear-Miss-Holt-and-Miss-Vanderkoep." To their friends, to their butcher, to their clergyman, to their janitor, they were, always, "Miss-Holt-and-Miss-Vanderkoep." So, quite naturally, the devoted pair, though by no means lacking in individuality, had long ceased to think of themselves as divisible, and it seemed probable they would continue indefinitely, "Miss-Holt-and-Miss-Vanderkoep."

Once in serene possession of the recuperative joys upon which they had so properly counted, the monumental fact of their "retirement" acquired a certain agreeable dimness. There were moments when Miss Agatha and Miss Emily almost forgot that they had attained the parting of the ways,—that chill, academic routine lay behind, and graceful and improving leisure lay before. It was incredible that it should have been so disconcerting, after years of longing, to be brought face to face, at last, with the opportunity for graceful and improving leisure!

Invariably, heretofore, the two ladies had returned to town on the fifteenth of September, a date that is widely conceded to be appropriate and dignified. This year, when the eighth of September came, Miss Agatha asked, a little nervously, "Have you begun to pack yet, dear?"

Miss Emily tried to pretend she did not understand.

"My dear, we've always gone back on the fifteenth. I—wrote Hotchkiss we were coming then. He asked, you know, about the floors."

"I've always fancied it must be wonderful here in October," said Miss Emily, sentimentally. "You know we've so often wished—"

"I know." Miss Agatha appeared to be reflecting. "To me, I confess, it seems a little absurd to stay over an extra six weeks simply for the idle consideration of landscape. Still, Emily, if you really wish to—And what in the world did we 'retire' for if not to do exactly as we please?"

Miss Emily paused in her turn. "Well, then," she said, with the air of one making an original observation, "let us go on the fifteenth. Will you see about the stateroom, Agatha?"

The economical decision of the previous June to do without a maid was a thousand times mentally applauded by Miss Agatha, who was quite ready to confess to herself that she would otherwise have found the autumn days uncomfortably long; and who, as it was, quite immoderately indulged herself in the riotous pastime of sweeping the rooms. All the drudgery, indeed, of the new regimen was firmly appropriated by Miss Agatha, and for two reasons. It helped, she thought, to justify an existence that now seemed sadly purposeless; and it secured her the happiness of seeing Emily's slender, ladylike hands engaged in the lighter and showier of the domestic tasks. Emily in conjunction with the breakfast china or the linen-closet was a spectacle peculiarly appropriate and charming; while at a glimpse of Emily preparing a cake, fond-hearted Miss Agatha could have indulged, with all the zest in the world, in just some such affectionate panegyric as pretty Ruth Pinch* evoked, stirring together her immortal pudding.

In proportion as Miss Agatha felt the dreariness of exclusion from blackboards and chalk, primers and basket-weaving, and the sound of sweet, unreasonable little voices, she characteristically strove to keep a knowledge of her feeling from Miss Emily. It came about that certain topics were never mentioned between them. Agatha, who had always taken the lead, had the air of protecting the younger woman from—neither of them could have told what. Certainly not from this charming, unfettered life they had so long yearned for! Meanwhile, Agatha so tenderly feared that her friend suffered from conditions she herself had brought about that she did not even dare ask the questions that might have ended her suspense.

One day poor Agatha's clouded conscience lightened. "Emily darling," she exclaimed, "shouldn't you like to be at home to some of the children on Wednesday afternoons? It would please them, you know, they're so fond of you."

"Why, Agatha!"

"Should you like it?"

"I think it would be perfectly lovely," gushed Miss Emily, in all sincerity.

The success of the first of these cheerful if a trifle tumultuous occasions was complete. Agatha, who, after a brief welcome of the guests, had retired to the kitchen, ostensibly in the interests of domestic affairs, smiled and frowned alternately. "Poor Emily!" she anxiously commented. "She's happier with those children than she has been in six months. Poor dear!"

At breakfast, a few mornings later, Miss Agatha was unusually silent. "I've something very odd to tell you, Emily," she remarked at last, "I dreamed of you last night."

* Ruth Pinch is a character in Charles Dickens's 1844 *Martin Chuzzlewit*; sweet-natured and domestic, she works as a governess and a housewife.

"Oh dear!" Miss Emily, hidden away in her bureau drawers, kept a "dream-book," and she well knew, from trustful consultation, just how direfully portentous it is to dream of—

"Oh, but this was a delightful dream," Miss Agatha hastened to assure her. "It was a dream of you and a baby. You've always had a Madonna look, you know, Emily, but there you were all Madonna. I can see the little thing now with its sensitive wee face—it wasn't more than six months old—and a patrician dot of a nose and mysterious blue eyes. And what was most curious was that you seemed to exercise some uncanny maternal spell over it; for when it fretted you said"—Miss Agatha paused and smiled to herself at the tender absurdity of the recollection—"you said, 'Hush, Vanderkoep!'—and he hushed."

"Vanderkoep!" echoed Miss Emily. "And I always thought it would be such a good name for a boy. But, Agatha, what was the rest of it?"

"There was nothing else. Or if there was, I failed to realize it. Just you and Vanderkoep projected against space. There may, of course, have been—some other members of the family, but I didn't see them."

"How curious," gently commented Miss Emily, who, held in the thrall of this unusual narrative, had quite forgotten to drink her coffee. "And he was pretty?"

"Altogether charming. Not the plump Cupid type. One could fancy him developing into something really distinguished. Oh, I should know him anywhere, it was all so startlingly vivid. It seemed almost," she went on, with an effort to be quite explicit, "like a supernatural realization of what might have been, of what should have been. With such a very slightly different turn of the wheel, Emily,—Ah, how we all like to ponder on the 'ifs'!"

Miss Emily reflected a little. "How soft and sweet they are, aren't they?" she said, tenderly. "Babies, I mean."

"Very," agreed Miss Agatha.

Again and again through the day Agatha found her friend regarding her with a kind of silent eagerness. And, though affecting not to notice this, she too discovered, a little to her discomfort, that the impression of her singular dream was strangely slow to fade.

It was with a greatly disquieted air that she came to breakfast the next morning.

"Did you sleep well, dear?" inquired Miss Emily, with a new timidity.

"Not in the least well. A succession of nightmares. And when I've been dieting, too. It's preposterous!"

"Why didn't you call me?"

"It's precisely what I did, and frantically, in my sleep. I have passed my night, Emily, in a mad chase after that baby of yours, that Vanderkoep. If you will believe me, he fell down-stairs before my very eyes!"

"Oh, Agatha!"

"But I picked him up, and when I found he wasn't killed I put him in a hot bath as a restorative. However, he almost drowned himself, for he was so smooth and slippery I couldn't hold him. Emily, I must ask you to give me another cup of coffee and to make it strong. I feel a literal fatigue."

"And there was no one with him?"

"You reappeared at last, and when you took him in your arms you both looked so pretty I couldn't scold either of you!"

"Was he good when I took him?" asked Miss Emily, as if she were sure of the answer.

"Perfectly. Did I tell you, Emily, that the child has beautiful eyes? And one of his dimples corresponds with that one of yours that you ought to have outgrown long ago!"

"What kind of sounds does he make?"

"Why, something like this,"—Miss Agatha obligingly made a desperate endeavor to imitate the formless gurgles of the dream-baby.

"Of course," beamed Miss Emily, in complete approval. "How dear he will be when he talks," she added, unconsciously.

Agatha looked up in wonder. Nor did her later reflections on this conversation prove reassuring.

Meanwhile, the dream-baby maintained in the family interests a prominence altogether unaccountable. Peculiarly susceptible to his shadowy fascination, Miss Emily expressed her affectionate absorption by the most significant of omissions. For the first time in her life, she neglected her embroidery, and it became her inexplicable habit to sit idle, almost motionless, through several hours. Or, adroitly succeeding in the introduction of Vanderkoep as a subject of conversation, she would devote herself to a strained effort to transfer from Miss Agatha's mental vision to her own every detail of the tantalizing image.

At close intervals Miss Agatha—oh, quite in spite of herself! for she had vowed that she would never dream of Vanderkoep again, and had forsworn her nightly glass of milk, lest that modest nutriment be responsible—had further visions of the engaging phantom who, in his peculiar and insubstantial fashion, had made himself so integral a part of the little family. And with each dream her perception of him became more consistently rational; there were no lurid escapes from sudden deaths in these later visions. And while, actually, Miss Agatha had never conspicuously succeeded in expressing her sympathy with children, having been, indeed, through all her pedagogical experience, rather hopelessly at odds with them, with Vanderkoep she got on a singularly satisfactory footing. He would, she lamented, never sit in her lap with the same look of rapturous content that he wore while held in Emily's tenderly maternal embrace. But his amiable, if picturesquely incomplete remarks showed that there were no reservations in his affection; and the most harmonious understanding pervaded those intangible domestic scenes where Emily and the baby, an altogether radiant picture, would suffer Agatha to sit by, their happy and admiring complement.

Secretly, however, the fact that the dreams became increasingly unlike dreams was a matter of serious concern to Miss Agatha, that most sensible and clear-headed of women, that substantial compound of keen humor and broad common sense! Dreams with the magnificent incoherence of ordinary, familiar dreamland, she could have tolerated; but visions that dared again and again to shape themselves into so audacious—and, yes, so bewitching!—a semblance of reality, beset her with vague terrors. She had become far too expert in the uncanny business for her sadly disturbed peace of mind.

It might have been expected that Vanderkoep's progress in life would be by unnatural fits and starts, something after the manner of the immortal Alice.* Quite on the contrary, his development kept pace with the calendar;

---

* A reference to the scene in Lewis Carroll's 1865 *Alice's Adventures in Wonderland* in which she grows and shrinks from drinking from a mysterious bottle and eating a small cake.

and his accomplishments, as the months went by, corresponded precisely with the measure of his existence. He crept, sat erect, and otherwise asserted himself at, in each case, the normal period. It is true that neither of the two ladies could have divined this gratifying fact; but having formed the habit of jotting down Vanderkoep's exploits in an ornate book designed for that purpose, and blushingly bought by Miss Emily at a department store, they discovered, on comparing these notes with the information given each month in *Baby and his Ways,* the magazine for which Miss Emily had promptly subscribed, that there was absolutely nothing to criticise in the dream-baby's development. "Though what we should do about it, if there was. Heaven only knows!" Miss Agatha had remarked in a candid outburst that quite wounded sensitive Miss Emily.

One day Agatha came in from a meeting of the "Municipal Government Club" which she had joined on the assurance of its president that it would "enrich her life," and found Emily sedulously erasing the evidence of tears. Suspicion flew like an arrow and hit the mark.

"I suppose it's that baby again," groaned Agatha.

"He hasn't done anything," sobbed Emily, in superfluous defence of the dream-baby. "I suppose it's his not really belonging to me that I mind so much. And then, I might as well tell you, Agatha, that the worst of it is—that nobody ever had a baby before without being able to make clothes for it!" Here the poor lady's grief quite overcame her.

"Hush, hush, dear!"

"I want to sew him a little dress more than I want anything, Agatha! And you know how beautifully I could make it. I have thought how I should have it out square, so as to show the exquisite back of his neck. You were telling me yesterday how I loved to kiss him there. . . . Agatha!"—Emily was very timid—"what should you think if I bought,—well, perhaps not a dress, but some flannel and made him a little jacket, just to please myself?"

"Emily, I beg of you never to talk in this way again. I blame myself beyond all telling. Please, dear, let us try to forget it all!"

The sobbing figure seemed not to hear. "Agatha," she said, "I want you to promise me something,—that you will never keep from me anything in regard to Vanderkoep. It is my right to know everything and at once. So you must not only tell me, but it must be immediately, the next morning—whatever, whatever, it may be."

Agatha, whose affection for her friend was ever her line of least resistance, succumbed.

"Why, yes, dear, I promise," she agreed, nervously. "Let me make you some tea."

Within the few months of Vanderkoep's spectral existence there had at times threatened to appear—though the admission could not have been wrung from either of the two friends—a narrow rift within the exquisitely close tissue of their intimacy. The lack was perhaps not so much of understanding as of sincerity, of outspokenness, between them; and Miss Agatha, who suffered excruciatingly from the knowledge of this, was also painfully aware of the cause. Quite unconsciously, Emily was jealous of her more intimate knowledge of Vanderkoep. And why, thought the unhappy Agatha, should she not be? How grotesquely cruel it was that Emily should always be obliged to learn at second hand of Vanderkoep's countless physical perfections and delicious infant waywardnesses! that she should be denied the mirrored joy of once holding her own dream-baby in her arms! It was so simple a thing to dream—why might not poor dear Emily yield herself to at least one radiant delusion?

Early in May, according to the arithmetic of Miss Agatha's visions, Vanderkoep attained the dignity of his first anniversary. Truthful and conscientious to a fault, she communicated the report of this festival, though with an evident unwillingness.

"We will let the china wait a little," said Miss Emily, with determination. "Sit down and tell me all about it. What did he say?"

"He said 'mamma,'" replied Miss Agatha, with the tender patience of one teaching the blind, "and hugged you with that happy little scream of his."

Miss Emily nodded.

"And then he laughed mischievously, showing all his cunning little teeth."

"Five of them," interjected Miss Emily, accurately.

"And when I tried to find out what pleased him so much, I saw that he was holding tightly under his arm a toy elephant—"

"Where had he gotten it?"

"Why, it was one of his birthday presents from you. I think you must have given him a dozen. One was a fine bay horse, harnessed into a cart, with real harness and all that. It seemed to delight him particularly."

"Boys always love horses so," said Miss Emily, wisely.

"And though I tried to make him come to me, he wouldn't. He stayed with you and cuddled."

Thus was the narrative continued and pieced out and refitted and every least detail adjusted to its place. At the close of which Miss Emily put on her glasses and sat down at her desk to enter faithfully into the book devoted to Vanderkoep the full and unabridged history of his first birthday.

A few days later the first prolonged heat wave swept blightingly over the city.

"I think we cannot get away too soon. Emily," observed Miss Agatha. "How fortunate it is we haven't to wait till June!"

Miss Emily said nothing.

"What do you think, my dear?" pursued Miss Agatha.

"I suppose I might as well say, now," said Miss Emily, "that I think we cannot go out of town this summer."

"But why?"

"Because of Vanderkoep," Miss Emily came out flatly.

"Well?"

"His very existence is exclusively associated with our rooms here. Do you feel confident, Agatha, that if we went away and interrupted our psychic connection with these surroundings—I hardly know how to put it—"

"I know I should dream of Vanderkoep anywhere," declared Miss Agatha, wearily.

"But how do you know? Have you ever been able to control—"

"No," confessed Miss Agatha.

"And yet you would venture—"

"It would make you unhappy, would it not, Emily, to go away?" interrupted Miss Agatha, to whom these discussions were painful, she could not tell why. "Very well, then, we will stay. I suppose we would better have a maid in for the summer."

So, through the listless warmth of May, the determined heat of June, and the relentless blaze of July, the two ladies lingered on in the little flat in Twelfth Street. There was little enough to interest or stimulate. Existence itself seemed a perfunctory and in no way desirable affair. The two ladies availed themselves to the fullest of their library subscription, corresponded with friends spending the summer in Europe—and talked of Vanderkoep. Miss Agatha proved herself of heroic stuff by suppressing her almost intolerable longing for cool air and the smell of the sea; Miss Emily suffered the heat and discomfort in significant silence.

During the first week of August came the crisis of the summer's feverish violence. The ominous stillness associated with extreme heat pervaded places where hitherto one had been conscious of nothing but noise. The torrid, throbbing nights were less to be borne than the burning days; sleep, except in snatches, was impossible. From the whole stricken city seemed to rise continuous, unlovely exhalations of sickness, suffering, death.*

Miss Emily's never too robust strength yielded to the cruel heat, and for days Miss Agatha nursed her faithfully. During one feverish evening, in particular, when no night coolness came to bring relief, Miss Agatha spent all her strength in the effort to gain a little comfort for her friend. At midnight, exhausted, she lay down without undressing in her own room and slept till dawn. When she awoke, it was with a cry. Miss Emily, lightly dozing in the next room, heard it.

"What is it, Agatha dear?" she asked. Receiving no answer, she called again, then went into Agatha's room. Her friend was sitting upright with a curious expression on her tired face.

An almost supernatural intuition directed Miss Emily's challenge, "You have been dreaming of Vanderkoep!"

"I am not myself, Emily." Miss Agatha began to talk very fast. "It's the heat. It muddles one's head so. I'm really not responsible. I'm not, indeed. Don't talk of it, Emily. Let us wait till another time."

"I know," said Miss Emily. "You need not tell me. He's dead. My baby's dead."

She went and stood by the window and looked vaguely out. "What killed him?" She turned sharply to Miss Agatha.

---

* Prior to the introduction of electric fans and air conditioning, hundreds would die in heat waves; one such period in 1911 killed 211 people in New York alone.

"Emily, I feel like a murderer!" she broke out. "Don't, don't!"

"What killed him?" persisted Miss Emily, in a hard voice.

"Darling—he died from a fever. I think it must have been the heat. We did everything for him. He did not seem to suffer, Emily!"

Miss Emily said nothing, but continued to stand by the window. Her back was rigid. She wrung her hands incessantly.

"Emily," begged Miss Agatha, clasping her about the shoulders, "you must not suffer so. It is not too late. Listen, dear,—you must wait until I can get a strong sleeping-powder from the drug-store. Then I shall take it and let it put me to sleep, and I shall dream—of course I shall. I shall dream him back again. I know, Emily, that this was not a true dream. You see, dear, the heat and all!"

"And could that comfort me—that you should dream a lying dream? What are you doing to me, Agatha? Why should you want to lie to me, now, when my baby's dead?"

Outside, in the street, there was the first stir of day. Miss Emily, ignoring her friend's entreaties, hurriedly dressed herself, tied a veil neatly over her hat and buttoned her cotton gloves. Then, still in silence, she went to the outer door and turned the knob.

"Emily!" cried the agonized Miss Agatha, "where are you going?"

Miss Emily paused a moment. "Why, I am going," she said, steadily, "to get some flowers for my baby."

Edith Nesbit (1858–1924) was a highly popular British writer of more than 60 children's books written under the name "E. Nesbit," including *The Railway Children* (1906). She was also a socialist and political activist, and co-founder of the Fabian Society, later affiliated with the Labour Party. Nesbit wrote dozens of short stories, including many for adult audiences. Her collections of horror stories entitled *Grim Tales* and *Something Wrong* were both first published in 1903, and another collection including supernatural fiction appeared in 1906. The following, a chilling cautionary tale with overtones of *Frankenstein* and *The Strange Case of Dr. Jekyll and Mr. Hyde*, first appeared in the *Strand Magazine* of February 1908 under her married name **E. Bland**.

The Third Drug

by E. Bland (Edith Nesbit)

I

Roger Wroxham looked round his studio before he blew out the candle, and wondered whether, perhaps, he looked for the last time. It was large and empty, yet his trouble had filled it and, pressing against him in the prison of those four walls, forced him out into the world, where lights and voices and the presence of other men should give him room to draw back, to set a space between it and him, to decide whether he would ever face it again—he and it alone together. The nature of his trouble is not germane to this story. There was a woman in it, of course, and money, and a friend, and regrets and embarrassments—and all of these reached out tendrils that wove and interwove till they made a puzzle problem of which heart and brain were now weary.

He blew out the candle and went quietly downstairs. It was nine at night, a soft night of May in Paris. Where should he go? He thought of the Seine, and took—an omnibus. When at last it stopped he got off, and so strange was the place to him that it almost seemed as though the trouble itself had been left behind. He did not feel it in the length of three or four streets that he traversed slowly. But in the open space, very light and lively, where he recognised the Taverne de Paris and knew himself in Montmartre, the trouble set its teeth in his heart again, and he broke away from the lamps and the talk to struggle with it in the dark, quiet streets beyond.

A man braced for such a fight has little thought to spare for the details of his surroundings. The next thing that Wroxham knew of the outside world was the fact which he had known for some time that he was not alone in the street. There was someone on the other side of the road keeping pace with him—yes, certainly keeping pace, for, as he slackened his own, the feet on the other pavement also went more slowly. And now they were four feet, not two. Where had the other man sprung from? He had not been there a moment ago. And now, from an archway a little ahead of him, a third man came.

Wroxham stopped. Then three men converged upon him, and, like a sudden magic-lantern picture on a sheet prepared, there came to him all that he had heard and read of Montmartre—dark archways, knives, Apaches,* and men who went away from homes where they were beloved and never again returned. He, too—well, if he never returned again, it would be quicker than the Seine, and, in the event of ultramundane possibilities, safer.

He stood still and laughed in the face of the man who first reached him.

"Well, my friend?" said he; and at that the other two drew close.

"Monsieur walks late," said the first, a little confused, as it seemed, by that laugh.

"And will walk still later if it pleases him," said Roger. "Good night, my friends."

---

* Members of the criminal underworld of Paris, first named such in 1904 in an article in a French newspaper that likened the criminals to the well-known Native American tribe.

"Ah!" said the second, "friends do not say adieu so quickly. Monsieur will tell us the hour."

"I have not a watch," said Roger, quite truthfully.

"I will assist you to search for it," said the third man, and laid a hand on his arm.

Roger threw it off. The man with the hand staggered back.

"The knife searches more surely," said the second.

"No, no," said the third, quickly; "he is too heavy. I for one will not carry him afterwards."

They closed round him, hustling him between them. Their pale, degenerate faces spun and swung round him in the struggle. For there was a struggle. He had not meant that there should be a struggle. Someone would hear—someone would come.

But if any heard none came. The street retained its empty silence; the houses, masked in close shutters, kept their reserve. The four were wrestling, all pressed close together in a writhing bunch, drawing breath hardly through set teeth, their feet slipping and not slipping on the rounded cobblestones.

It was then that Roger felt the knife. Its point glanced off the cigarette-case in his breast pocket and bit sharply at his inner arm. And at the sting of it Roger knew, suddenly and quite surely, that he did not desire to die. He feigned a reeling weakness, relaxed his grip, swayed sideways, and then suddenly caught the other two in a new grip, crushed their faces together, flung them off, and ran. It was but for an instant that his feet were the only ones that echoed in the street. Then he knew that the others too were running.

He ran more swiftly—he was running now for his life—the life that he had held so cheap three minutes before. And all the streets were empty—empty like dream-streets, with all their windows dark and unhelpful, their doors fast closed against his need. Only now and again he glanced to right or left, if perchance some window might show light to justify a cry for help, some door advance the welcome of an open inch.

There was at last such a door. He did not see it till it was almost behind him. Then there was the drag of the sudden stop—the eternal instant of indecision. Was there time? There must be. He dashed his fingers through the inch-crack, grazing the backs of them, leapt within, drew the door after him, felt madly for a lock or bolt, found a key, and, hanging his whole weight on it, managed to get the door home and turned the key. Then someone cursed breathlessly outside; there was the sound of feet that went away.

He found himself listening, listening, and there was nothing to hear but the silence, and once, before he thought to twist his handkerchief round it, the drip of blood from his hand.

By and by he knew that he was not alone in this house, for from far away there came the faint sound of a footstep, and, quite near, the faint answering echo of it. And at a window high up on the other side of the courtyard a light showed. Light and sound and echo intensified, the light passing window after window, till at last it moved across the courtyard and the little trees threw black shifting shadows as it came towards him—a lamp in the hand of a man.

It was a short, bald man, with pointed beard and bright, friendly eyes. He held the lamp high as he came, and when he saw Roger he drew his breath in an inspiration that spoke of surprise, sympathy, pity.

"Hold! hold!" he said, in a singularly pleasant voice; "there has been a misfortune? You are wounded, monsieur?'"

"Apaches," said Roger, and was surprised at the weakness of his own voice.

"Fortunately," said the other, "I am a surgeon. Allow me."

He set the lamp on the step of a closed door, took off Roger's coat, and quickly tied his own handkerchief round the wounded arm.

"Now," he said, "courage! I am alone in the house. No one comes here but me. If you can walk up to my rooms you will save us both much trouble. If you cannot, sit here and I will fetch you a cordial. But I advise you to try to walk. That *portecochère* is, unfortunately, not very strong, and the lock is a common spring lock, and your friends may return with *their* friends; whereas the door across the courtyard is heavy, and the bolts are new."

Roger moved towards the heavy door whose bolts were new. The stairs seemed to go on for ever. The doctor lent his arm, but the carved banisters and their lively shadows whirled before Roger's eyes. Also he seemed to be shod with lead, and to have in his legs bones that were red hot. Then the stairs ceased, and there was light, and a cessation of the dragging of those leaden feet. He was on a couch, and his eyes might close.

When next he saw and heard he was lying at ease, the close intimacy of a bandage clasping his arm, and in his mouth the vivid taste of some cordial.

The doctor was sitting in an arm chair near a table, looking benevolent through gold-rimmed pince-nez.

"Better?" he said. "No; lie still, you'll be a new man soon."

"I am desolated," said Roger, "to have occasioned you all this trouble."

"In a big house like this," said the doctor, as it seemed a little sadly, "there are many empty rooms, and some rooms which are not empty. There is a bed altogether at your service, monsieur, and I counsel you not to delay in seeking it. You can walk?"

Wroxham stood up. "Why, yes," he said, stretching himself. "I feel, as you say, a new man."

A narrow bed and rush-bottomed chair showed like doll's-house furniture in the large, high, gaunt room to which the doctor led him.

"You are too tired to undress yourself," said the doctor; "rest—only rest," and covered him with a rug, snugly tucked him up, and left him.

"I leave the door open," he said, "in case you should have any fever. Good night. Do not torment yourself. All goes well."

Then he took away the lamp, and Wroxham lay on his back and saw the shadows of the window-frames cast by the street lamps on the high ceiling. His eyes, growing accustomed to the darkness, perceived the carving of the white panelled walls and mantelpiece. There was a door in the room, another door than the one which the doctor had left open. Roger did not like open doors. The other door, however, was closed. He wondered where it led, and whether it were locked. Presently he got up to see. It was locked. He lay down again.

His arm gave him no pain, and the night's adventure did not seem to have overset his nerves. He felt, on the contrary, calm, confident, extraordinarily at ease, and master of himself. The trouble—how could that ever have seemed important? This calmness—it felt like the calmness that precedes sleep. Yet sleep was far from him. What was it that kept sleep away? The bed was comfortable—the pillows soft. What was it? It came to him presently that it was the scent which distracted him, worrying him with a memory that he could not define. A faint scent of—what was it? Perfumery? Yes—and camphor—and something else—something vaguely disquieting. He had not noticed it before he had risen and tried the handle of that other door. But now he covered his face with the sheet, but through the sheet he smelt it still. He rose and threw back one of the long French windows. It opened with a click and a jar, and he looked across the dark well of the courtyard. He leaned out, breathing the chill pure air of the May night, but when he withdrew his head the scent was there again. Camphor—perfume—and something else. What was it that it reminded him of?

He stood up and went, with carefully-controlled swiftness, towards the open door. He wanted light and a human voice. The doctor was in the room upstairs; he—

The doctor was face to face with him on the landing, not a yard away, moving towards him quietly in shoeless feet.

"I can't sleep," said Wroxham, a little wildly; "it's too dark and—"

"Come upstairs," said the doctor, and Wroxham went.

There was comfort in the large, lighted room. A green shaded lamp stood on the table.

"What's behind that door," said Wroxham, abruptly—"that door downstairs?"

"Specimens," the doctor answered; "preserved specimens. My line is physiological research. You understand?"

So that was it.

"I feel quite well, you know," said Wroxham, laboriously explaining—"fit as any man—only I can't sleep."

"I see," said the doctor.

"It's the scent from your specimens, I think," Wroxham went on; "there's something about that scent—"

"Yes," said the doctor.

"It's very odd." Wroxham was leaning his elbow on his knee and his chin on his hand. "I feel so frightfully well—and yet—There's a strange feeling—"

"Yes," said the doctor. "Yes, tell me exactly how you feel."

"I feel," said Wroxham, slowly, "like a man on the crest of a wave."

The doctor stood up.

"You feel well, happy, full of life and energy—as though you could walk to the world's end, and yet—"

"And yet," said Roger, "as though my next step might be my last—as though I might step into a grave."

He shuddered.

"Do you," asked the doctor, anxiously—"do you feel thrills of pleasure—something like the first waves of chloroform—thrills running from your hair to your feet?"

"I felt all that," said Roger, slowly, "downstairs before I opened the window."

The doctor looked at his watch, frowned, and got up quickly. "There is very little time," he said.

Suddenly Roger felt an unexplained thrill of pain.

The doctor went to a long laboratory bench with bottle-filled shelves above it, and on it crucibles and retorts, test tubes, beakers—all a chemist's apparatus—reached a bottle from a shelf, and measured out certain drops into a graduated glass, added water, and stirred it with a glass rod.

"Drink that," he said.

"You may be giving me poison," Roger gasped, his hands at his heart.

"I may," said the doctor. "What do you suppose poison makes you feel like? What do you feel like now?"

"I feel," said Roger, "like death."

Every nerve, every muscle thrilled to a pain not too intense to be underlined by a shuddering nausea.

"Like death," he said again.

"Then drink," cried the doctor, in tones of such cordial entreaty, such evident anxiety, that Wroxham half held his hand out for the glass.

"Drink! Believe me, it is your only chance."

Again the pain swept through him like an electric current. The beads of sweat sprang out on his forehead.

"That wound," the doctor pleaded, standing over him with the glass held. "For Heaven's sake, drink! Don't you understand, man? You *are* poisoned. Your wound—"

"The knife?" Wroxham murmured, and as he spoke his eyes seemed to swell in his head, and his head itself to grow enormous. "Do you know the poison—and its antidote?"

"I know all." The doctor soothed him. "Drink, then, my friend."

As the pain caught him again in a clasp more close than any lover's he clutched at the glass and drank. The drug met the pain and mastered it. Roger, in the ecstasy of pain's cessation, saw the world fade and go out in a haze of vivid violet.

II

Faint films of lassitude shot with contentment wrapped him round. He lay passive as a man lies in the convalescence that follows a long fight with Death.

"I'm better now," he said, in a voice that was a whisper—tried to raise his hand from where it lay helpless in his sight, failed, and lay looking at it in confident repose—"much better."

"Yes," said the doctor, and his pleasant, soft voice had grown softer, pleasanter. "You are now in the second stage. An interval is necessary before you can pass to the third. I will enliven the interval by conversation. Is there anything you would like to know?"

"Nothing," said Roger; "I am quite happy—quite contented."

"This is very interesting," said the doctor. "Tell me exactly how you feel."

Roger faintly and slowly told him.

"Ah!" the doctor said, "I have not before heard this. You are the only one of them all who ever passed the first stage. The others—"

"The others?" said Roger, but he did not care much about the others.

"The others," said the doctor, frowning, "were unsound. Decadent students, degenerate Apaches. You are highly trained—in fine physical condition. And your brain! The Lord be good to the Apaches who so delicately excited it to just the degree of activity needed for my purpose."

"The others?" Wrexham insisted.

"The others? They are in the room whose door was locked. Look—you should be able to see them. The second drug should lay your consciousness before me like a sheet of white paper on which I can write what I choose. If I choose that you should see my specimens—*Allons donc.*[*] I have no secrets from you now. Look—look—strain your eyes. In theory I know all that you can do and feel and see in this second stage. But practically—Enlighten me—look—shut your eyes and look!"

Roger closed his eyes and looked. He saw the gaunt, uncarpeted staircase, the open doors of the big rooms, passed to the locked door, and it opened at his touch. The room inside was, like the other, spacious and panelled. A lighted lamp with a blue shade hung from the ceiling, and below it an effect of spread whiteness. Roger looked. There *were* things to be seen.

With a shudder he opened his eyes on the doctor's delightful room, the doctor's intent face.

"What did you see?" the doctor asked. "Tell me!"

"Did you kill them all?" Roger asked back.

"They died—of their own inherent weakness," the doctor said. "And you saw them?"

"I saw," said Roger, "the quiet people lying all along the floor in their death clothes—the people who have come in at that door of yours that is a trap—for robbery, or curiosity, or shelter—and never gone out any more."

"Right," said the doctor. "Right. My theory is proved at every point. You can see what I choose you to see. Yes; decadents all. It was in embalming that I was a specialist before I began these other investigations."

"What," Roger whispered—"what is it all for?"

"To make the superman," said the doctor. "I will tell you."

He told. It was a long story—the story of a man's life, a man's work, a man's dreams, hopes, ambitions.

"The secret of life," the doctor ended. "That is what all the alchemists sought. They sought it where Fate pleased. I sought it where I have found it—in death."

"And the secret is?" asked Roger.

---

* "So, let's go."

"I have told you," said the doctor, impatiently; "it is in the third drug that life—splendid, superhuman life—is found. I have tried it on animals. Always they became perfect, all that an animal should be. And more, too—much more. They were too perfect, too near humanity. They looked at me with human eyes. I could not let them live. Such animals it is not necessary to embalm. I had a laboratory in those days—and assistants. They called me the Prince of Vivisectors."

The man on the sofa shuddered.

"What is the third drug?" Roger asked, lying limp and flat on his couch.

"It is the Elixir of Life," said the doctor. "I am not its discoverer; the old alchemists knew it well, but they failed because they sought to apply the elixir to a normal—that is, a diseased and faulty—body. I knew better. One must have first a body abnormally healthy, abnormally strong. Then, not the elixir, but the two drugs that prepare. The first excites prematurely the natural conflict between the principles of life and death, and then, just at the point where Death is about to win his victory, the second drug intensifies life so that it conquers—intensifies, and yet chastens. Then the whole life of the subject, risen to an ecstasy, falls prone in an almost voluntary submission to the coming super-life. Submission—submission! The garrison must surrender before the splendid conqueror can enter and make the citadel his own. Do you understand? Do you submit?"

"I submit," said Roger, for, indeed, he did. "But—soon—quite soon—I will not submit."

He was too weak to be wise, or those words had remained unspoken.

The doctor sprang to his feet.

"It works too quickly!" he cried. "Everything works too quickly with you. Your condition is too perfect. So now I bind you."

From a drawer beneath the bench where the bottles gleamed the doctor drew rolls of bandages—violet, like the haze that had drowned, at the urgence of the second drug, the consciousness of Roger. He moved, faintly resistant, on his couch. The doctor's hands, most gently, most irresistibly, controlled his movement.

"Lie still," said the gentle, charming voice. "Lie still; all is well." The clever, soft hands were unrolling the bandages—passing them round arms and throat—under and over the soft narrow couch. "I cannot risk your life, my poor boy. The least movement of yours might ruin everything. The third drug, like the first, must be offered directly to the blood which absorbs it. I bound the first drug as an unguent upon your knife-wound."

The swift hands passed the soft bandages back and forth, over and under—flashes of violet passed to and fro in the air like the shuttle of a weaver through his warp. As the bandage clasped his knees Roger moved.

"For Heaven's sake, no!" the doctor cried; "the time is so near. If you cease to submit it is death."

With an incredible accelerated swiftness he swept the bandages round and round knees and ankles, drew a deep breath—stood upright.

"I must make an incision," he said—"in the head this time. It will not hurt. See! I spray it with the Constantia Nepenthe;* that also I discovered. My boy, in a moment you know all things—you are as a god. Be patient. Preserve your submission."

Roger did not feel the knife that made the cross cut on his temple, but he felt the hot spurt of blood that followed the cut, he felt the cool flap of a plaster spread with some sweet, clean-smelling unguent that met the blood and stanched it. There was a moment—or was it hours?—of nothingness. Then from that cut on his forehead there seemed to radiate threads of infinite length, and of a strength that one could trust to—threads that linked one to all knowledge past and present. He felt that he controlled all wisdom, as a driver controls his four-in-hand. Knowledge, he perceived, belonged to him, as the air belongs to the eagle. He swam in it, as a great fish in a limitless ocean.

He opened his eyes and met those of the doctor, who sighed as one to whom breath has grown difficult.

"Ah, all goes well. Oh, my boy, was it not worth it? What do you feel?"

"I. Know. Everything," said Roger, with full stops between the words.

"Everything? The future?"

"No. I know all that man has ever known."

---

* Nepenthe is described in Homer's *Odyssey* as a drug banishing grief or troubles; "constantia Nepenthe" is apparently the mad doctor's name for a topical anaesthetic.

"Look back—into the past. See someone. See Pharaoh. You see him—on his throne?"

"Not on his throne. He is whispering in a corner of his great gardens to a girl who is the daughter of a water-carrier."

"Bah! Any poet of my dozen decadents who lie so still could have told me that. Tell me secrets—the *Masque de Fer*."*

The other told a tale, wild and incredible, but it satisfied the listener.

"That too—it might be imagination. Tell me the name of the woman I loved and—"

The echo of the name of the anaesthetic came to Roger, and "Constantia," said he, in an even voice.

"Ah!" the doctor cried, "now I see you know all things. It was not murder. I hoped to dower her with all the splendours of the super-life."

"Her bones lie under the lilacs, where you used to kiss her in the spring," said Roger, quite without knowing what it was that he was going to say.

"It is enough," the doctor cried. He sprang up, ranged certain bottles and glasses on a table convenient to his chair. "You know all things. It was not a dream, this, the dream of my life. It is true. It is a fact accomplished. Now I, too, will know all things. I will be as the gods."

He sought among leather cases on a far table and came back swiftly into the circle of light that lay below the green-shaded lamp.

Roger, floating contentedly on the new sea of knowledge that seemed to support him, turned eyes on the trouble that had driven him out of that large, empty studio so long ago, so far away. His newfound wisdom laughed at that problem, laughed and solved it. "To end that trouble I must do so-and-so, say such-and-such," Roger told himself again and again.

And now the doctor, standing by the table, laid on it his pale, plump hand outspread. He drew a knife from a case—a long, shiny knife—and scored his hand across and across its back, as a cook scores pork for cooking. The slow blood followed the cuts in beads and lines.

---

* "The Iron Mask." The doctor refers to the near-legendary French prisoner whose identity was never known. In Dumas's 1830 *Man in the Iron Mask*, he is revealed to be the twin of Louis XIV.

Into the cuts he dropped a green liquid from a little bottle, replaced its stopper, bound up his hand, and sat down.

"The beginning of the first stage," he said; "almost at once I shall begin to be a new man. It will work quickly. My body, like yours, is sane and healthy."

There was a long silence.

"Oh, but this is good," the doctor broke it to say. "I feel the hand of Life sweeping my nerves like harp-strings."

Roger had been thinking, the old common sense that guides an ordinary man breaking through this consciousness of illimitable wisdom. "You had better," he said, "unbind me; when the hand of Death sweeps your nerves you may need help."

"No," the doctor said, and no, and no, and no many times. "I am afraid of you. You know all things, and even in your body you are stronger than I."

And then suddenly and irresistibly the pain caught him. Roger saw his face contorted with agony, his hands clench on the arm of his chair; and it seemed that either this man was less able to bear pain than he, or that the pain was much more violent than had been his own. And the plump, pale hand, writhing and distorted by anguish, again and again drew near to take the glass that stood ready on the table, and with convulsive self-restraint again and again drew back without it.

The short May night was waning—the shiver of dawn rustled the leaves of the plant whose leaves were like red misshaped hearts.

"Now!" The doctor screamed the word, grasped the glass, drained it, and sank back in his chair. His hand struck the table beside him. Looking at his limp body and head thrown back one could almost see the cessation of pain, the coming of kind oblivion.

III

The dawn had grown to daylight, a poor, grey, rain-stained daylight, not strong enough to pierce the curtains and persiennes,* and yet not so weak but that it could mock the lamp, now burnt low and smelling vilely.

* Window shutters.

Roger lay very still on his couch, a man wounded, anxious, and extravagantly tired. In those hours of long, slow dawning, face to face with the unconscious figure in the chair, he had felt, slowly and little by little, the recession of that sea of knowledge on which he had felt himself float in such large content. The sea had withdrawn itself, leaving him high and dry on the shore of the normal. The only relic that he had clung to and that he still grasped was the answer to the problem of the trouble—the only wisdom that he had put into words. These words remained to him, and he knew that they held wisdom—very simple wisdom, too.

"To end the trouble I must do so-and-so and say such-and-such."

Slowly a dampness spread itself over Wroxham's forehead and tingled among the roots of his hair. He writhed in his bonds. They held fast. He could not move hand or foot. Only his head could turn a little, so that he could at will see the doctor or not see him. A shaft of desolate light pierced the persienne at its hinge and rested on the table, where an overturned glass lay.

Wroxham thrilled from head to foot. The body in the chair stirred—hardly stirred—shivered, rather—and a very faint, far-away voice said:—

"Now the third—give me the third."

"What?" said Roger, stupidly; and he had to clear his throat twice before he could say even that.

"The moment is now," said the doctor. "I remember all. I made you a god. Give me the third drug."

"Where is it?" Roger asked.

"It is at my elbow," the doctor murmured. "I submit—I submit. Give me the third drug, and let me be as you are."

"As *I* am?" said Roger. "You forget. *I* am bound."

"Break your bonds," the doctor urged, in a quick, small voice. "I trust you now. You are stronger than all men, as you are wiser. Stretch your muscles, and the bandages will fall asunder like snow-wreaths."

"It is too late," Wroxham said, and laughed; "all that is over. I am not wise any more, and I have only the strength of a man. I am tired and wounded. I cannot break my bonds—I cannot help you!"

"But if you cannot help me—it is death," said the doctor.

"It is death," said Roger. "Do you feel it coming on you?"

"I feel life returning," said the doctor, "it is now the moment—the one possible moment. And I cannot reach it. Oh, give it me—give it me!"

Then Roger cried out suddenly, in a loud voice: "Now, by all that's sacred, you infernal decadent, I am *glad* that I cannot give it. Yes, if it costs me my life, it's worth it, you madman, so that your life ends too. Now be silent, and die like a man if you have it in you."

Roger lay and watched him, and presently he writhed from the chair to the floor, tearing feebly at it with his fingers, moaned, shuddered, and lay very still.

Of all that befell Roger in that house the worst was now. For now he knew that he was alone with the dead, and between him and death stretched certain hours and days. For the *porte-cochere* was locked; the doors of the house itself were locked—heavy doors and the locks new.

"I am alone in the house," the doctor had said. "No one comes here but me."

No one would come. He would die there—he, Roger Wroxham—"poor old Roger Wroxham, who was no one's enemy but his own." Tears pricked his eyes. He shook his head impatiently and they fell from his lashes.

"You fool," he said, "can't *you* die like a man either?"

Then he set his teeth and made himself lie still. It seemed to him that now Despair laid her hand on his heart. But, to speak truth, it was Hope whose hand lay there. This was so much more than a man should be called on to bear—it could not be true. It was an evil dream. He would awake presently. Or if it were, indeed, real—then someone would come, someone must come. God could not let nobody come to save him.

And late at night, when heart and brain had been stretched almost to the point where both break and let in the sea of madness, someone came.

The interminable day had worn itself out. Roger had screamed, yelled, shouted till his throat was dried up, his lips baked and cracked. No one heard. How should they? The twilight had thickened and thickened till at last it made a shroud for the dead man on the floor by the chair. And there were other dead men in that house; and as Roger ceased to see the one he saw the others—the quiet, awful faces, the lean hands, the straight, stiff limbs laid out one beyond another in the room of death. They at least were not bound. If they should rise in their white wrappings and, crossing that empty sleeping-chamber very softly, come slowly up the stairs—

A stair creaked.

His ears, strained with hours of listening, thought themselves befooled. But his cowering heart knew better.

Again a stair creaked. There was a hand on the door.

"Then it is all over," said Roger in the darkness, "and I *am* mad."

The door opened very slowly, very cautiously. There was no light. Only the sound of soft feet and draperies that rustled.

Then suddenly a match spurted—light struck at his eyes; a flicker of lit candle-wick steadying to flame. And the things that had come were not those quiet people creeping up to match their death with his death in life, but human creatures, alive, breathing, with eyes that moved and glittered, lips that breathed and spoke.

"He must be here," one said. "Lisette watched all day; he never came out. He must be here—there is nowhere else."

Then they set up the candle-end on the table, and he saw their faces. They were the Apaches who had set on him in that lonely street, and who had sought him here—to set on him again.

He sucked his dry tongue, licked his dry lips, and cried aloud:—

"Here I am! Oh, kill me! For the love of Heaven, brothers, kill me *now*!"

And even before he spoke they had seen him, and seen what lay on floor.

"He died this morning. I am bound. Kill me, brothers; I cannot die slowly here alone. Oh, kill me, for pity's sake!"

But already the three were pressing on each other at a doorway suddenly grown too narrow. They could kill a living man, but they could not face death, quiet, enthroned. "For the love of Heaven," Roger screamed, "have pity! Kill me outright! Come back—come back!"

And then, since even Apaches are human, they did come back. One of them caught up the candle and bent over Roger, knife in hand. "Make sure," said Roger, through set teeth.

"*Nom d'un nom*," said the Apache, with worse words, and cut the bandages here, and here, and here again, and there, and lower, to the very feet.

Then between them the three men carried the other out and slammed the outer door, and presently set him against a gate-post in another street, and went their wicked ways.

And after a time a girl with furtive eyes brought brandy and hoarse muttered kindnesses, and slid away in the shadows.

Against that gate-post the police came upon him. They took him to the address they found on him. When they came to question him he said, "Apaches," and his variations on that theme were deemed sufficient, though not one of them touched truth or spoke of the third drug.

There has never been anything in the papers about that house. I think it is still closed, and inside it still lie in the locked room the very quiet people; and above, there is the room with the narrow couch and the scattered, cut, violet bandages, and the Thing on the floor by the chair, under the lamp that burned itself out in that May dawning.

Mary Austin was born in Carlinville, Illinois in 1868, but she's now thought of primarily as a southwestern writer, thanks largely to her classic *The Land of Little Rain* (1903). At the age of 19, Austin moved with her family to California, where they'd been offered public land to homestead, but they arrived in a drought. Times were tough, so at 22 she married a novice farmer named Stanford Wallace Austin. The marriage was not happy, and the arrival of their severely handicapped daughter Ruth added further strain to the family. Mary found most of her comfort hiking the desert with Ruth strapped to her back and writing about it. Divorcing her husband in 1907, she moved to Carmel, California where her friends included Jack London and Willa Cather. This story comes from her 1909 collection *Lost Borders,* although "The Pocket-Hunter" was first introduced in *The Land of Little Rain,* where she says she liked him "for his clean, companionable talk." Austin died in 1934.

The Pocket-Hunter's Story

by Mary Austin

The crux of this story for the PocketHunter* was that he had known the two men, Mac and Creelman, before they came into it; known them, in fact, in the beginning of that mutual distrust which grew out of an earlier friendliness into one of those expansive enmities which in the spined and warted humanity of the camps have as ready an acceptance as the devoted partnerships of which Wells Bassit

* In her book *The Land of Little Rain*, Mary Austin describes the Pocket-Hunter as a kind of prospector in search of pockets: "A pocket, you must know, is a small body of rich ore occurring by itself, in a vein of poorer stuff. Nearly every mineral ledge contains such, if only one has the luck to hit upon them without too much labor."

furnished the pre-eminent example. It was, he believed, in some such relationship their acquaintance had begun, and from which they now drew the sustenance of those separate devils of hate that, nesting in corrosive hollows of their hosts, rose to froth and rage, each at the mere intimation of a merit in the other.

No one knew what the turn of the screw had been that set them gnashing, but it was supposed, on no better evidence, perhaps, than that such trouble is at the bottom of most quarrels in the camps, to have been about a mine. The final crisis, the very memory of which seemed to hold for him a moment of recurrent, hairlifting horror, was known by the Pocket-Hunter, and by some of the others, to have been brought on by an Indian woman down Parrimint-way.

She was Mac's woman; though, except as being his, he was not thought to set particular store by her. He used to leave her in his cabin while he was off in the Hills for a three weeks' *pasear;** but the tacit admission of an Indian woman as no fit subject for whitemen to fight over forbade his being put to the ordinary provocation on account of her. Therefore, when Creelman projected his offence, which was to excite in his enemy the desire for killing without providing him with a sufficient excuse, there was a vague notion moving in the heavy fibre of his mind that there was a species of humor in what he was about to do. But he would probably not have gone on to Tres Piños† and told of it, if he had known how soon it was to come to Mac's ears.

This, you understand, was long after their grudge had climbed by inconsiderable occasions to the point where Mac had several times offered to kill Creelman on no motion but the pleasure of being rid of his company.

Mac was a sickly man, and by that, and his having had the worst of it in their earlier encounters, his rage so much the more possessed him that, when he had come back to his cabin and the Indian woman had told him her story, he was able by that mere spur of a possession trifled with to take the short leap from intent to performance at a bound. There was no such bodily leap possible, of course; he had to trudge the whole

* Spanish for "walk"

† A few place names in Austin's fiction are real, but for the most part her colorful place names are fictitious.

of one day on foot to Tres Piños, an old weakness battling with his rage. He was one of those illy-furnished souls whom the wilderness despoils most completely—hair, beard, and skin of him burned to one sandy sallowness, the eyelashes of no color, the voice of no timbre, more or less stiffened at the joints by the poison of leaded ores, his very name shorn of its distinguishing syllable; no more of him left, in fact, than would serve as a vehicle for hating Creelman. When he came to Tres Piños and learned that the other had gone on from there, nobody would tell him where, the rage of bafflement threw him into some kind of a fit, and blood gushed from his nose and mouth.

All this the Pocket-Hunter was possessed of when he set out shortly after with his pack and burros, prospecting toward the Dry Creek district, where in due time he crossed the trail of Shorty Wells and Long Tom Bassit. There was no particular reason why Wells should have been called Shorty, except that Long Tom was of a stature to give to any average man in his vicinity a title to that adjective. Further than that he gave no other warrant to the virtues, aptitudes, propensities with which Shorty credited him, than the negative one of not denying them. In camps where they were known the opinion gained ground that there was very little to Long Tom but his size and his amiability, which was remarked upon, but, that Shorty, having discovered this creditable baggage in his own pack, had laid it to Bassit, not being able to say else how he came by it; but there they were, as inveterate a pair of partners as the camps ever bred, owning to no greater satisfaction than just to be abroad in the hills together following the Golden Hope; and there on a day between Dry Creek and Denman's the Pocket-Hunter found them.

The way he came to tell me about it was this. I had laid by for a nooning under the quaking asp* by Peterscreek on the trail from Tunawai, and found him before me with his head under one of those woven shelters of living boughs which the sheep-herders leave in that country, and he moved out to make room for me in its hand's-breadth of shade.

Understand, there *was* no more shade to be got there. Straight before us went the meagre sands; to every yard or so of space its foothigh, sapless shrub. Somewhere at the back of us lifted, out of a bank of pinkish-violet

* A quaking-aspen tree.

mist, sierras white and airy. Eastward where the earth sagged on its axis, in some dreary, beggared sleep, pale, wispish clouds went up. Now and then to no wind the quaking-asps clattered their dry bones of leaves.

We had been talking, the Pocket-Hunter and I, of that curious obsession of travel by which the mind, pressing on in the long, open trail ahead of the dragging desert pace, seems often to develop a capacity for going on alone in it, so that it becomes involved in one sliding picture, as it were, of what is ahead and what at hand, until, when the body stops for necessary rest and food, it is impossible to say if it is here where it halted, or there where the mind possessed. I had said that this accounted to me not only for the extraordinary feats of endurance in desert travel, but for the great difficulty prospectors have in relocating places they have marked, so mazed they are by that mixed aspect of strangeness and familiarity that every district wears, which, long before it has been entered by the body, has been appraised by the eye of the mind.

"But suppose," said the Pocket-Hunter, "it really does go on by itself?"

"And where," I wished to know, "would be the witness to that, unless it brought back a credible report of what it had seen?"

"Or done," suggested the Pocket-Hunter, "what it set out to do. That would clinch it, I fancy."

"But the mind can only take notice," I protested. "It can't *do* anything without its body."

"Or another one," suggested the PocketHunter.

"Ah," said I, "tell me the story."

It was, went on the Pocket-Hunter, after he had told me all that I have set down about the four men who made the story, about nine of the morning when he came to Dry Creek on the way to Jawbone Cañon, and the day was beginning to curl up and smoke along the edges with the heat, rocking with the motion of it, and water of mirage rolling like quicksilver in the hollows. What the Pocket-Hunter said exactly was that it was a morning in May, but it comes to the same thing. He had just come out of the wash by Cactus Flat when he was aware of a man chasing about in the heat fog, and making out to want something more than common. Even as early as that in the incident the Pocket-Hunter thought he had encountered some faint, floating films from that coil of inexplicable dreadfulness in which he was so soon to find himself involved, and yet he was not sure that it might not have been chiefly in the extraordinary manner of the man's approach, seeing him caught up in the mirage, drawn out and dwarfed again, "like some kind of human accordion," said the Pocket-Hunter, and now rolled toward him with limbs grotesquely multiplied in a river of mist.

Presently, however, he got the man between him and the sun, in such a way that he was able to make out it was himself who was wanted, and when he had slewed the burros round to come up to him, he could see plainly who it was, and it was Wells. It was altogether so unusual a circumstance to find Shorty Wells anywhere out of eyeshot of Tom Bassit that it was not reassuring, and Shorty himself was so sensible of it that almost before any greeting passed, he had let out with certain swallowing of the throat that Tom was dead.

It appeared the two of them had come over Tinpah* two days before, and Bassit, who had a weakness of the heart that made high places a menace to him, had accomplished the Pass apparently in good order. But when they had taken the immense drop that carries one from the crest of Tinpah to Dry Creek like a bucket in a shaft, something had gone suddenly, irretrievably wrong. There had been a half collapse at the foot of the trail, and a complete one a few miles back on the trail to Denman's, toward which they had turned in extremity. Tom had suffered agonizingly, so that if there had been any place nearer from which help might conceivably have come, Shorty could not have left him to go and fetch it; and along about the hour which the Indians call, all in one word, the bluish-light-of-dawn, Tom had died.

All the way back to camp, after he had met the Pocket-Hunter, Shorty kept arguing with himself as to whether, if he had done the one thing or had not done the other, it would have been better for poor Tom, and the Pocket-Hunter assuring him for his comfort that it would not, keeping back, by some native stroke of sympathy, what he had lately heard at Tres Piños that Creelman had a cabin in the Jawbone, and was living in it what time Mac was camping on his trail. It was no farther from the foot of Tinpah than they had come toward Denman's, but in the opposite direction, and from

* "Tinpah" is probably a play on "Tonopah," a silver-rich Nevada mining town.

their not turning there it seemed likely they had not heard of it—kinder if Shorty might never come to know, seeing he had not known it in time to be of use to Tom. And this was a point the Pocket-Hunter was presently to make sure of, that neither Shorty nor Long Tom was acquainted with the location of the cabin, nor with Mac nor Creelman by sight.

As it was, he made the most of comforting Shorty for having stayed by his partner to the last.

"I never left him till he croaked," Shorty told him. "It was along toward morning he went quiet, and just as I was goin' for to cover him with the blanket, he croaked—and I come away."

There was that touch of dread in him which ever the figure of death excites in simple minds, which, perhaps as much as the wish to bring help to the burial, had turned him from the body of the friend who was, and now kept his eyes fixed persistently upon the ground as they came back to it across the flat, which here, made smooth in shining, leprous patches of alkali, presented no screen to the disordered camp higher than the sickly pickle-weed about its borders. The Pocket-Hunter, therefore, as they came on toward the place where from two crossed sticks of Shorty's fire a thin point of flame wavered upward, had time for wondering greatly at what he saw, which was so little what he had been led to expect there that he had not found yet any warrant for mentioning it, when Shorty, gathering himself toward what he had to face, lifting up his eyes, let out a kind of howl and ran.

The Pocket-Hunter said he did not know how soon Shorty grasped the fact, which he himself perceived with his eyes some time before his intelligence took hold of it, that the body lying doubled on the sand some yards from the empty bed was not the same that Shorty had left stiffening under the blanket. He thought they must have both taken account of it at the same time, and been stricken dumb by the sheer horror of it, for he could not remember a word spoken by either of them, between Shorty's sharp yell of astonishment and the time when they took it by the shoulders and turned it to the sun.

The limbs were still lax enough with recent life to settle slowly as they stirred the body; there were no wounds upon it, but blood had gushed freely from the nose and mouth. It was a smallish man of no particular color or complexion, with that slight distortion of the joints common in a country of leaded ores. By these marks, as they discovered themselves in the sharp light, the Pocket-Hunter was able to identify him as a man Shorty had never seen, last heard of at Tres Piños, where he had fallen by rage into some such seizure as had apparently overtaken him upon the trail. That he should be here at all, and in such a case as this, was sufficiently horrifying, but it was nothing to the appalling wonder as to what had become of Tom.

There was the impress of his body upon the bed, and the blanket, shed in loose folds across the foot, now lifted a little and buoyed by the wind, and in all the wide day nothing to hide a man, except where, miles behind, the sheer bulk of Tinpah was split by shadowy gulfs of cañons. Shorty was, for the time, fairly tottering in his mind. He would pry foolishly about the camp, getting back by quick turns and pounces to the stretched body on the sand, as though in the interim it might have recovered from its extraordinary illusion and become the body of his friend again. By degrees the Pocket-Hunter constrained him to piece out the probable circumstance.

They had to begin, of course, with Tom's not being dead, and to go on from that to the previous fact of Mac working his poor body over the long stretches between Tres Piños and the Jawbone, where he must have learned that Creelman was hiding. Well, he *had* a poor body, and it must have given out under him just as he arrived in camp, very shortly after Shorty had left it, and, over-ridden by his errand, had persuaded Long Tom, then recovering from his trance or swoon, to rise and go on with it.

"To kill Creelman! Tom?"

Shorty's imagination flagged visibly in the eye of Tom's huge amiability, but the PocketHunter came around triumphantly.

"Well, he went!"

"But he couldn't have," Shorty put forward, hopefully, as if any bar to his partner's leaving the camp might somehow result in proving him still there. "He hadn't stood on his feet for twenty-four hours, and suffered something awful. Besides, he didn't know there was a cabin; if he had, I'd have gone there yesterday."

"Mac would have told him, of course."

Shorty drooped dejectedly before a supposition that, however large the hope it entailed of finding his partner still in the flesh, afforded no relief to the incontrovertible persistence of evidence in his own mind. "But he croaked, I tell you—they're dead when they croak, ain't they?"

Whatever was said to that was said by the zt-z-z-t of desert flies punctuating the heavy heat. At the sound of it little beads of sweat broke out on Shorty's face.

"Look a-here," he brought out, finally, "if this other fellow, Mac here, was as bad off as you say, why didn't Tom go to him; kind of ease him off like? What for did he go off and leave him crumpled up like that?"

"He wouldn't have died until after Tom left, Mac wouldn't," the Pocket-Hunter reminded him. "What makes you so sure?"

"Tom never walked none after we struck camp." Shorty was secure of his ground here. "And there's no tracks of him except where he came in alongside of me—and goin' out—*there!*" The print of Tom's large feet had turned toward the Jawbone. "Besides," he returned to it with anxiety, "what would he go to Creelman's for?"

This was a point, and the Pocket-Hunter took as much time as was necessary to shroud the dead man in Tom's blanket to consider it. He found this at last:

"Tom," he said, "was a peaceable man?"

"None peaceabler," admitted Tom's partner.

"Well, then, when he found this little—" (the adjective checked out of respect to the object of it being as he was) "Mac here so set on killing, he thought it no more than right to get on ahead and give Creelman a hint of what was coming to him."

This being so much what might have been expected of Tom, it appeared insensibly to give greater plausibility to the whole occasion. It left them for the moment free to set out on Tom's trail with almost a movement of naturalness. It lasted, however, only long enough to see them into the steady, flowing stride of desert travel; the recurrence of that motion, perhaps, set up again in Shorty's mind the consciousness of loss in which it had some two hours earlier begun, and the consideration of mere practical details, such as the distance from the camp to Creelman's, swept back to the full conviction of unreality.

Looking ahead at the long trudge between them and the mouth of the cañon, where in that clear light, on that level mesa, no man could have moved unespied by them, where, in fact, no man at that moment was moving, he broke out in a kind of exasperated wail:

"But he couldn't have, I tell you; he couldn't have walked it. . . . He was dead, I tell you. . . . He croaked and I covered him up. . . ."

It became momentarily clearer to the PocketHunter that unless they came soon, behind some screening weed, in some unguessed hollow, upon Long Tom's huddled body, collapsed in the recurrent weakness of his disorder, so to restore the event to reasonableness, he must find himself swamped again in the horror of the inexplicable, out of which they had been speciously pulled by the Pocket-Hunter's argument.

It was not until they came to the loose shale and sand at the mouth of the cañon that Shorty reverted again to the form of his amazement.

"Did you notice," said he, "anything queer about Tom's tracks?"

"Queer, how?"

"Well—different?"

"Like he thought he had a game leg?" suggested the Pocket-Hunter.

"Well, he hadn't . . . but the other man . . . back yonder . . . *he* had a game leg."

"Shorty! Shorty!" the Pocket-Hunter fairly begged. "You ain't . . . you mustn't . . . let your mind run on them things!"

"Well, he had," persisted Wells. His voice clicked with dryness, trailed off whispering. It seemed to the Pocket-Hunter, suddenly, that the twenty steps or so between the man so certainly dead in his tracks on one side the fire back there, and the supposedly dead arising in his on the other, had swelled to immeasurable space. It was then there came into his mind the remainder of that singular obsession of the trail in the notice of which our conversation had begun. He saw on the instant Mac inching out from Tres Piños on his unmatched poor legs, his hate riding far before him, blown forward by some devil's blast, tugging at him like a kite at its ballast, lifting him past incredible stretches of hot sand and cutting stone, until it dropped him there. He wrenched his mind away from that by an effort, and fixed it on the pale pine-colored square of Creelman's cabin, where it began to show in the shadowy gulf of the cañon.

The door was open and the curtains of the two small windows on either side half drawn against a glare which would have been gone from that side of the canon more than an hour ago.

Here, as they halted to take notice of it, some expiring gasps of bluish smoke from Creelman's breakfast fire went up from the tin chimney against the basalt wall. As they came near they observed a large flaccid hand hanging out over the sill. What they made out further was Creelman's body, extended face downward, barring the door. A small lizard tic-tacked on the unpainted boards across the hand that did not start at it, and disappeared into the shadow of the room, where, as if this intrusion gave them leave to look, they perceived among the broken plates and disordered furniture a broken pack-stick, Creelman's knife, open and blooded—the figure of Long Tom, half propped against the footboard of the bunk, dropping weakly from a wound. It *was* Tom, though over his face as it leered up at them was spread a strange new expressiveness, such a superficial and furtive change as frivolous passers-by will add sometimes to the face of a poster with pencil touches, provoking to half-startled laughter; plain enough to have shocked them back, even as against the witness of clothes and hair and features, from the instant's recognition, to produce in them an amazement, momentary, yet long enough for the dying man to take note of them unfriendlily, and to have addressed himself to the Pocket-Hunter.

"Came to see the fight, did you? It's damned well over . . . but I did for him . . . the—, —, — !" His body sank visibly with the stream of curses.

But the faith of Shorty was proof even against this. He had cleared the body of Creelman at a stride, and was on his knees beside his partner, crying very simply.

"Oh, Tom, Tom," he begged, "you never done it? Say you never done it, pardner, say you never!"

"Aw, who the hell are you?" The lewd eyes rolled up at him, he gave two or three long gasps which ended in a short choking gurgle, the body started slightly, and dropped.

"Come away, Shorty, he's croaked," said the Pocket-Hunter not unkindly; but Shorty knelt on there, crying quietly as he watched the dead man's features settle and stiffen to the likeness of his friend.

Marjorie Bowen (1885–1952) was a prolific British writer of over 150 books, mainly in the genres of historical fiction, horror tales, popular history, and biographies (including *This Shining Woman*, about Mary Wollstonecraft Godwin, Mary Shelley's mother). She wrote her first novel, *The Viper of Milan*, at 16; when it was published, it became a bestseller. Bowen would go on to be cited as an influence by Graham Greene, and her entry in *The Penguin Encyclopedia of Horror and the Supernatural* (1986) calls her "one of the great supernatural writers of this century." "Twilight" first appeared in her collection *God's Playthings* (1912), in which each story is about a different historical figure, their name announced just below the title.

Twilight

by Marjorie Bowen

*Lucrezia Borgia, Duchess d'Este**

Three women stood before a marble-margined pool in the grounds of the Ducal palace at Ferrara;† behind them three cypresses waved against a purple sky from which the sun was beginning to fade; at the base

* Lucrezia Borgia (1480–1519) was the daughter of Pope Alexander VI (born Rodrigo de Borja in Spain); she was an educated woman, skilled at administration, who would become (in) famous for her rumored involvement in a number of murders (using poison that she supposedly kept in a ring) and for her numerous affairs. She died at the age of 39, ten days after giving birth to her seventh child (although some biographers argue it was actually her tenth), so Bowen is taking literary license in this story by suggesting she was elderly.

† Lucrezia's third and final marriage, in 1502, was to Alfonso d'Este, Duke of Ferrara, a province and city in Northern Italy.

of these trees grew laurel, ilex, and rose bushes. Round the pool was a sweep of smooth green across which the light wind lifted and chased the red, white and pink rose leaves.

Beyond the pool the gardens descended, terrace on terrace of opulent trees and flowers; behind the pool the square strength of the palace rose, with winding steps leading to balustraded balconies. Further still, beyond palace and garden, hung vineyard and cornfield in the last warm maze of heat.

All was spacious, noble, silent; ambrosial scents rose from the heated earth–the scent of pine, lily, rose and grape.

The centre woman of the three who stood by the pool was the Spanish Duchess, Lucrezia, daughter of the Borgia Pope. The other two held her up under the arms, for her limbs were weak beneath her.

The pool was spread with the thick-veined leaves of water-lilies and upright plants with succulent stalks broke the surface of the water. In between the sky was reflected placidly, and the Duchess looked down at the counterfeit of her face as clearly given as if in a hand-mirror.

It was no longer a young face; beauty was painted on it skilfully; false red, false white, bleached hair cunningly dyed, faded eyes darkened on brow and lash, lips glistening with red ointment, the lost loveliness of throat and shoulders concealed under a lace of gold and pearls, made her look like a portrait of a fair woman, painted crudely.

And, also like one composed for her picture, her face was expressionless save for a certain air of gentleness, which seemed as false as everything else about her—false and exquisite, inscrutable and alluring—alluring still with a certain sickly and tainted charm, slightly revolting as were the perfumes of her unguents when compared to the pure scents of trees and flowers. Her women had painted faces, too, but they were plainly gowned, one in violet, one in crimson, while the Duchess blazed in every device of splendour.

Her dress, of citron-coloured velvet, trailed about her in huge folds, her bodice and her enormous sleeves sparkled with tight-sewn jewels; her hair was twisted into plaits and curls and ringlets; in her ears were pearls so large that they touched her shoulders.

She trembled in her splendour and her knees bent; the two women stood silent, holding her up–they were little more than slaves.

She continued to gaze at the reflection of herself; in the water she was fair enough. Presently she moistened her painted lips with a quick movement of her tongue.

"Will you go in, Madonna?" asked one of the women.

The Duchess shook her head; the pearls tinkled among the dyed curls.

"Leave me here," she said.

She drew herself from their support and sank heavily and wearily on the marble rim of the pool.

"Bring me my cloak."

They fetched it from a seat among the laurels; it was white velvet, unwieldy with silver and crimson embroidery.

Lucrezia drew it round her shoulders with a little shudder.

"Leave me here," she repeated.

They moved obediently across the soft grass and disappeared up the laurel-shaded steps that led to the terraces before the high-built palace.

The Duchess lifted her stiff fingers, that were rendered almost useless by the load of gems on them, to her breast.

Trails of pink vapour, mere wraiths of clouds began to float about the west; the long Italian twilight had fallen.

A young man parted the bushes and stepped on to the grass; he carried a lute slung by a red ribbon across his violet jacket; he moved delicately, as if reverent of the great beauty of the hour.

Lucrezia turned her head and watched him with weary eyes.

He came lightly nearer, not seeing her. A flock of homing doves passed over his head; he swung on his heel to look at them and the reluctantly departing sunshine was golden on his upturned face.

Lucrezia still watched him, intently, narrowly; he came nearer again, saw her, and paused in confusion, pulling off his black velvet cap.

"Come here," she said in a chill, hoarse voice.

He obeyed with an exquisite swiftness and fell on one knee before her; his dropped hand touched the ground a pace beyond the furthest-flung edge of her gown.

"Who are you?" she asked.

"Ormfredo Orsini,* one of the Duke's gentlemen, Madonna," he answered.

He looked at her frankly surprised to see her alone in the garden at the turn of the day. He was used to see her surrounded by her poets, her courtiers, her women; she was the goddess of a cultured court and persistently worshipped.

"One of the Orsini," she said. "Get up from your knees."

He thought she was thinking of her degraded lineage, of the bad, bad blood in her veins. As he rose he considered these things for the first time. She had lived decorously at Ferrara for twenty-one years,† nearly the whole of his lifetime; but he had heard tales, though he had never dwelt on them.

"You look as if you were afraid of me—"

"Afraid of you—I, Madonna?"

"Sit down," she said.

He seated himself on the marble rim and stared at her; his fresh face wore a puzzled expression.

"What do you want of me, Madonna?" he asked.

"Ahè!" she cried. "How very young you are, Orsini!"

Her eyes flickered over him impatiently, greedily; the twilight was beginning to fall over her, a merciful veil; but he saw her for the first time as an old woman. Slightly he drew back, and his lute touched the marble rim as he moved, and the strings jangled.

"When I was your age," she said, "I had been betrothed to one man and married to another, and soon I was wedded to a third. I have forgotten all of them."

"You have been so long our lady here," he answered. "You may well have forgotten the world, Madonna, beyond Ferrara."

"You are a Roman?"

"Yes, Madonna."

She put out her right hand and clasped his arm.

"Oh, for an hour of Rome!—in the old days!"

---

* From the 12th century on, the Orsinis were a renowned Italian family. In 1502, several members of the family participated in a failed plot against Cesare Borgia, Lucrezia's brother.

† Lucrezia actually lived in Ferrara for 17 years.

Her whole face, with its artificial beauty and undisguisable look of age, was close to his; he felt the sense of her as the sense of something evil.

She was no longer the honoured Duchess of Ferrara, but Lucrezia, the Borgia's lure, Cesare's sister, Alessandro's daughter, the heroine of a thousand orgies, the inspiration of a hundred crimes.

The force with which this feeling came over him made him shiver; he shrank beneath her hand.

"Have you heard things of me?" she asked in a piercing voice.

"There is no one in Italy who has not heard of you, Madonna."

"That is no answer, Orsini. And I do not want your barren flatteries."

"You are the Duke's wife," he said, "and I am the servant of the Duke."

"Does that mean that you must lie to me?"

She leant even nearer to him; her whitened chin, circled by the stiff goldwork of her collar, touched his shoulder.

"Tell me I am beautiful," she said. "I must hear that once more—from young lips."

"You are beautiful, Madonna."

She moved back and her eyes flared.

"Did I not say I would not have your flatteries?"

"What, then, was your meaning?"

"Ten years ago you would not have asked; no man would have asked. I am old. Lucrezia old!–ah, Gods above!"

"You are beautiful," he repeated. "But how should I dare to touch you with my mouth?"

"You would have dared, if you had thought me desirable," she answered hoarsely. "You cannot guess how beautiful I was—before you were born, Orsini."

He felt a sudden pity for her; the glamour of her fame clung round her and gilded her. Was not this a woman who had been the fairest in Italy seated beside him?

He raised her hand and kissed the palm, the only part that was not hidden with jewels.

"You are sorry for me," she said.

Orsini started at her quick reading of his thoughts.

"I am the last of my family," she added. "And sick. Did you know that I was sick, Orsini?"

"Nay, Madonna."

"For weeks I have been sick. And wearying for Rome."

"Rome," he ventured, "is different now, Madonna."

"Ahè!" she wailed. "And I am different also."

Her hand lay on his knee; he looked at it and wondered if the things he had heard of her were true. She had been the beloved child of her father, the old Pope, rotten with bitter wickedness; she had been the friend of her brother, the dreadful Cesare—her other brother, Francesco, and her second husband—was it not supposed that she knew how both had died?*

But for twenty-one years she had lived in Ferrara, patroness of poet and painter, companion of such as the courteous gentle Venetian, Pietro Bembo.†

And Alfonso d'Este, her husband, had found no fault with her; as far as the world could see, there had been no fault to find.

Ormfredo Orsini stared at the hand sparkling on his knee and wondered.

"Suppose that I was to make you my father confessor?" she said. The white mantle had fallen apart and the bosom of her gown glittered, even in the twilight.

"What sins have you to confess, Madonna?" he questioned.

She peered at him sideways.

"A Pope's daughter should not be afraid of the Judgment of God," she answered. "And I am not. I shall relate my sins at the bar of Heaven and say I have repented—Ahè—if I was young again!"

"Your Highness has enjoyed the world," said Orsini.

"Yea, the sun," she replied, "but not the twilight."

---

* Francesco II Gonzaga was Lucrezia's brother-in-law, with whom she had a long affair that was discontinued after he contracted syphilis. However, Bowen may be thinking of Lucrezia's brother Giovanni, who was murdered in 1497, possibly by her brother Gioffre. Her second husband, Alfonso d'Aragon, was murdered in 1500, and the killer was rumored to be her brother Cesare.

† Bembo was known for reintroducing the works of Petrarch and the development of the madrigal, but he also had an affair with Lucrezia Borgia beginning in 1502.

"The twilight?"

"It has been twilight now for many years," she said, "ever since I came to Ferrara."

The moon was rising behind the cypress trees, a slip of glowing light. Lucrezia took her chin in her hand and stared before her; a soft breeze stirred the tall reeds in the pool behind her and gently ruffled the surface of the water.

The breath of the night-smelling flowers pierced the slumbrous air; the palace showed a faint shape, a marvellous tint; remote it looked and uncertain in outline.

Lucrezia was motionless; her garments were dim, yet glittering, her face a blur; she seemed the ruin of beauty and graciousness, a fair thing dropped suddenly into decay.

Orsini rose and stepped away from her; the perfume of her unguents offended him. He found something horrible in the memory of former allurement that clung to her; ghosts seemed to crowd round her and pluck at her, like fierce birds at carrion.

He caught the glitter of her eyes through the dusk; she was surely evil, bad to the inmost core of her heart; her stale beauty reeked of dead abomination. . . . Why had he never noticed it before?

The ready wit of his rank and blood failed him; he turned away towards the cypress trees.

The Duchess made no attempt to detain him; she did not move from her crouching, watchful attitude.

When he reached the belt of laurels he looked back and saw her dark shape still against the waters of the pool that were beginning to be touched with the argent glimmer of the rising moon. He hurried on, continually catching the strings of his lute against the boughs of the flowering shrubs; he tried to laugh at himself for being afraid of an old, sick woman; he tried to ridicule himself for believing that the admired Duchess, for so long a decorous great lady, could in truth be a creature of evil.

But the conviction flashed into his heart was too deep to be uprooted.

She had not spoken to him like a Duchess of Ferrara, but rather as the wanton Spaniard whose excesses had bewildered and sickened Rome.

A notable misgiving was upon him; he had heard great men praise her, Ludovico Ariosto,* Cardinal Ippolito's secretary and the noble Venetian Bembo; he had himself admired her remote and refined splendour. Yet, because of these few moments of close talk with her, because of a near gaze into her face, he felt that she was something horrible, the poisoned offshoot of a bad race.

He thought that there was death on her glistening painted lips, and that if he had kissed them he would have died, as so many of her lovers were reputed to have died.

He parted the cool leaves and blossoms and came on to the borders of a lake that lay placid under the darkling sky.

It was very lonely; bats twinkled past with a black flap of wings; the moon had burnt the heavens clear of stars; her pure light began to fill the dusk. Orsini moved softly, with no comfort in his heart.

The stillness was intense; he could hear his own footfall, the soft leather on the soft grass. He looked up and down the silence of the lake.

Then suddenly he glanced over his shoulder. Lucrezia Borgia was standing close behind him; when he turned her face looked straight into his.

He moaned with terror and stood rigid; awful it seemed to him that she should track him so stealthily and be so near to him in this silence and he never know of her presence.

"Eh, Madonna!" he said.

"Eh, Orsini," she answered in a thin voice, and at the sound of it he stepped away, till his foot was almost in the lake.

His unwarrantable horror of her increased, as he found that the glowing twilight had confused him; for, whereas at first he had thought she was the same as when he had left her seated by the pool, royal in dress and bearing, he saw now that she was leaning on a stick, that her figure had fallen together, that her face was yellow as a church candle, and that her head was bound with plasters, from the under edge of which her eyes twinkled, small and lurid.

---

* The author of the 1516 Italian masterpiece *Orlando Furioso* and the creator of the term "humanism," he also served as secretary to Cardinal Ippolito, who was Lucrezia's brother-in-law.

She wore a loose gown of scarlet brocade that hung open on her arms that showed lean and dry; the round bones at her wrist gleamed white under the tight skin, and she wore no rings.

"Madonna, you are ill," muttered Ormfredo Orsini. He wondered how long he had been wandering in the garden.

"Very ill," she said. "But talk to me of Rome. You are the only Roman at the Court, Orsini."

"Madonna, I know nothing of Rome," he answered, "save our palace there and sundry streets—"

She raised one hand from the stick and clutched his arm.

"Will you hear me confess?" she asked. "All my beautiful sins that I cannot tell the priest? All we did in those days of youth before this dimness at Ferrara?"

"Confess to God," he answered, trembling violently.

Lucrezia drew nearer.

"All the secrets Cesare taught me," she whispered. "Shall I make you heir to them?"

"Christ save me," he said, "from the Duke of Valentinois'* secrets!"

"Who taught you to fear my family?" she questioned with a cunning accent. "Will you hear how the Pope feasted with his Hebes and Ganymedes?† Will you hear how we lived in the Vatican?"

Orsini tried to shake her arm off; anger rose to equal his fear.

"Weed without root or flower, fruitless uselessness!" he said hoarsely. "Let me free of your spells!"

She loosed his arm and seemed to recede from him without movement; the plasters round her head showed ghastly white, and he saw all the wrinkles round her drooped lips and the bleached ugliness of her bare throat.

---

* Louis XII of France appointed Cesare Borgia Duke of Valentinois in 1498, one of the reasons behind Cesare's nickname "Il Valentino."

† Hebe was the Greek goddess of youth, who also served the gods nectar and ambrosia; the Church of England later created a story that she had fallen during her service and exposed her body. Ganymede was a beautiful youth who was taken by Zeus to Mount Olympus to serve as cup-bearer to the gods. His legend is associated with pederasty and homosexuality.

"Will you not hear of Rome?" she insisted in a wailing whisper. He fled from her, crashing through the bushes.

Swiftly and desperately he ran across the lawns and groves, up the winding steps to the terraces before the palace, beating the twilight with his outstretched hands as if it was an obstacle in his way.

Stumbling and breathless, he gained the painted corridors that were lit with a hasty blaze of wax light. Women were running to and fro, and he saw a priest carrying the Holy Eucharist cross a distant door.

One of these women he stopped.

"The Duchess—" he began, panting.

She laid her finger on her lip.

"They carried her in from the garden an hour ago; they bled and plastered her, but she died—before she could swallow the wafer—(hush! she was not thinking of holy things, Orsini!)—ten minutes ago—"

Regina Miriam Bloch (1889–1938) is surely one of the most enigmatic female authors from the turn of the last century. She was born in Germany, but at some point moved to London, where she initially found success as a poet. She released two collections, *The Swine-Gods and Other Visions* (1917) and *The Book of Strange Loves* (1918). Although both books were well-received, she never published another work of fiction and fell into obscurity for unknown reasons. To add to the mystery, it was sometimes claimed that she was also the famed author Rebecca West, although West—after first seeming to confirm the fact in a 1921 magazine interview—denied it in 1922. Bloch, who never married, was also interested in eastern philosophy and spiritualism. In fact, most of what she wrote during the last twenty years of her life were book reviews for occult and spiritualist journals. The story chosen for this book—"The Swine-Gods"—marks the first time Bloch's fiction has seen print in over a century.

The Swine-Gods

by Regina Miriam Bloch

In my dream I wandered along an endless lane, gray as the smoke of twilight ere night hath kindled the fires of her stars upon God's hearth-place. It wound ceaselessly on and on as a grey serpent uncoiling; the trees were lean and dismal, and gloomed like clouds through the besetting mists.

I grew weary wandering its arid space; my feet saddened and my heart sank within me.

And there came by a little child whose face was peaked with sobbing, and whose hair was wild, and that had a broken wing upon its shoulder.

I said: "Where am I?"

It said: "This is the Long Lane of the Lost, and I am a Lost Love."

And it passed on.

And there came another child, with an elfin face that held a ruined laughter, and whose rose-red robe was tattered.

I said: "Who art thou?"

She said: "I am a lost Hour of Delight and there is mud upon my feet."

And she went on.

She was followed by a third child in a gown that had once been skyey-blue, but was faded to drabness by wind and weather. She bare withered lilies in her arm and at her kirtle* hung a broken lute.

I said: "Who art thou?"

And she looked at me with eyes wherein the violets had paled and said: "I am a Lost Illusion, for all things lost wander along this Lane."

I said: "Is there no house within it? For I am weary of my bitter wayfaring, and it hath no end."

She made answer: "There is no rest-house but one."

I said: "Where?"

Then she pointed, saying: "Yonder," and passed by also.

I looked where she had shewn to me and saw, beyond the mist, a palace with mighty walls frowning on high and pinnaces and towers that were fashioned curiously.

I went on towards it and lo! the bridge fell clashing from invisible hands above a river that ran murk and drear about it. The gates and doorways of bronze stood wide and nowhere was there a keeper and straightway I entered in.

As I passed I heard from afar, a moaning as of one in pain and the baying of a distant pack. I wondered who it was that hunted a-down the Long Lane of the Lost.

And I went marveling into the silent palace.

I found myself within a hall greater than any dreamed of by men, and built entirely with pillars and walls of black porphyry and basalt.

The heavy columns frowned stupendously; a sable dome seemed to soar above me in its giddy heights, where beasts and bats with harpy

* A type of woman's gown from the Middle Ages.

faces and dusk wings, circled without cess,* flapping and screaming. The floors were of black jade that shimmered like a haunted mere.† And from the pillars hung pendants of black crystal shining frostily, while in the crevices of the flags, the pediments and colonnades, raven flowers like creatures of death moved and spread their petals until they seemed as greedy, voracious mouths. At either end of the hall there was a furnace of red fire, in the midst whereof, beyond steps of black marble, loomed a terrific Baal‡ of iron to which many acolytes were sacrificing.

I went towards the Baal at the right end of the hall.

The glow of the fires in all that surrounding opaqueness dazzled me. For a time I stood deafened by the crackle and roar of the flames from the core of the furnace. Then as my sight cleared, I saw a huge Moloch,§ with wide-open jaws and molten flaring hands and a head fashioned in the image of a Swine, whose snout belched fire.

Before him were priests with shaven heads and leering faces, attired also in black. And each one bare a little silent flame of blue or white or red or green towards a High-Priest, who stood in the centre of the uppermost step before the Baal.

The High-Priest towered above the others and his robes shone with black jade. I could not see his face, but upon his head there were eagle-feathers and his foot was cloven.¶

---

* Bloch likely meant either "cease" or "cessation" here, since "cess" refers to either "luck" or a type of tax (both Irish meanings).

† A body of water.

‡ Baal was originally the name of various gods in the Mesopotamian and Semitic religions, but after the Protestant Reformation it was more commonly applied to icons and false gods.

§ Moloch was originally a Canaanite god that demanded child sacrifice, but it has come to refer to anything demanding a heavy sacrifice. Moloch also appears in Milton's 1667 *Paradise Lost*, in Fritz Lang's 1927 silent classic *Metropolis*, and even in episode 8 of the first season of *Buffy the Vampire Slayer.*

¶ Cloven-hoofed feet are often listed as a characteristic of the Devil.

And the High-Priest chanted, saying: "Master Mammon,[*] O God Mammon, always we find thy fuel and thy eternal fires never die, although thy hands are burnt unto white embers. O God above the other Gods of whom the world craves grace, since the dawning hath thy house been set upon sure foundations. Thy lures are deeper than the sockets of the sea; thy pride is ever fed, thy tents spread out their mighty camps in mockery of the Lord.

"Behold! begetter of men, we do thine ancient service."

And one of the priests came forward and the little flame that burnt upon the platter in his hands was white.

And he gave it to him of the cloven foot, droning: "Arch-Flamen,[†] this is the soul of a very young maid. Her limbs and body are as folded flowers, but her parents have sold her to an old man who hath much gold in his coffers. His lips are frore[‡] and blue, his breath is as the odour of death and his heart is as a satyr's."

Then the Arch-Priest lifted the white flame high, so that it lay close beneath the searing fire of the Swine-Baal's snout.

And crying: "O Mammon, the sweet savour of thy Virgin-bride!" he cast it down into the molten hands.

The fire hissed up once and crackled and burnt on.

Now there came a second priest, with a little blue flame, saying: "This is the soul of a poet who dreamt exquisite dreams and went hungerful and there were very few to hearken.

"Yet desire came to him, so he cast away his dreams and sang of vileness and abominable things. But the people flocked to hear and cried: 'More! More!'

"He said: 'Verily, I will give ye more of my obscenities, if ye will give me your gold.'

"Then they laughed, and stripped the coins from their hair and the bracelets from their arms.

"And he sang on."

---

* Mammon is a Hebrew word meaning "money," but is sometimes personified as a demonic deity. He also appears in Milton's *Paradise Lost*.

† A flamen was a priest of the ancient Roman religion.

‡ Frozen or frosty.

And the High-Priest cast the blue flame in, saying: "All the dreams and songs, the ideals and quests of the world are thine, O Master Mammon."

Next there came one bearing a red flame, who said: "This is the heart of a man who loved a maiden dearly.

"She had only one gown and no jewels for her anklets, but her soul was pure as the dews of the dawn.

"And he came unto a house wherein there dwelt a harlot, who had been the dancing-woman of the Caliphs. Her bed was hung with silk, her tables were of chalcedony, her ewers of silver and she had pearls upon her kirtle-zone.

"And she said: 'I lust for thy youth and strength. Thou art as an oak and I as a palm that is broken. Abide with me!'

"Then he looked upon her pearls and the chalcedony and barred the doors of her house against his love in the robe of white linen.

"And her heart brake, but he drank of the wine in the ewers and forgat."

The red flame fell into the crimson fire and the Arch-Priest said: "O Master Mammon, O Breaker and Maker of hearts, O shaper of ways and wielder of destinies!"

Thereon came a priest bearing a yellow flame and he said:

"This is the soul of a man who was the favourite Vizier of the King, who had raised him up from the poor of his city and set him within his gates.

"The King gave him of his lands and much power besides, wherefore his house was almost as rich as the palace of his master.

"But this Vizier had a wife who had also been of the poor of the King's city and could not rise to fit her place. And the Vizier left her and she grew old as a crone.

"Then he cast his eyes upon the King's wife, who was fair and wore a tiara of emeralds on her head. And the King's wife looked upon him and he won her favours, for she was vain and his tongue was subtle.

"And one night as he was secretly in the Queen's closet, he gazed about him at the rare traceries of gems and gold, and said:

"'My house is not so great nor my wife so young and lovely. There is priceless treasure within the treasure-chambers. Why should not I wear the royal cloak and crown and make this woman my Queen?'

"Then he rose up from her arms and stole privily into the bed-chamber of the King and stabbed him to death in his sleep."

And the Arch-Priest cast the yellow flame into the scarlet pit, chanting: "All the flowers of the world's envy and the fruits of the world's passion are woven into thy garland, Master Mammon!"

But I was sickened, and turned away and went over to the Baal that stood in the fiery furnace at the left end of the hall.

And lo! here too were priests bearing the soul-flames. Only their vessels were not of gold and silver, but of iron and steel. And the head of the Moloch was different, for it was that of a boar. From his jaws protruded two great tusks like spikes and from them burst alternate flame and smoke, amid an angry roaring that clattered through all his tremendous iron bulk.

But the High-Priest before him was as the one before the image of Mammon and had a cloven foot also.

And he chanted: "O Master Mars,* O Master Mars, all nature is thy pawn. Thou battenest upon the weak in the numberless degrees of thy strength. Thou art the lord of the sharp fang, the ravenous maw, the piercing beak, the leaping beast. The Christs, Messiahs and prophets, the priests and angels fail before thee. The rot of thy carrion and the stench of thy carcasses ascend unto the portals of Heaven and their hellish incense defies the rose-haunted closes of Paradise . . .

"Thou art the lord of the Valley of the Shadow, the moving scythe of death; thy arms grapple with youth immortally. Thou art the despoiler of the divine in Man; thou demandest unending sacrifice and lo! it is given. For every son of woman, every creature of earth and sea and air are thine, thou Ravisher of the Eternities!"

And there came a priest bearing a flame, who said, "Lord, this is the soul of a young man who was the only son of his mother and she a widow.

"They dwelt happily together, for he tilled her field and gat her oil and cracknels† with the labour of his hands; while she gloried in the strength of him and the hair which was a gold fleece on his head and as the hair of the lover of her youth.

* The Roman god of war.

† Small cakes or crackers.

"But the great Kings quarrelled in high places. They carried division into the land and laid it waste and despoiled its maidens.

"Then the young husbandman said: 'My mother, I must lay by the plough-share and the pruning-hook and seize a lance and buckler in their stead. Farewell!'

"She clung to him, tearless and numb for the greatness of her sorrow, and said: 'Haste home to me again. For thou art my all in the world and there is no other footfall that comes to me over the hills.'

"He said: 'I will return.'

"But he never came, for the sling-stone of a foeman struck his temple and he was trampled out of human semblance and into blood and mire by the stampeding chargers of the King's horsemen.

"And his mother died alone of her broken heart."

Then the Arch-Priest seized the flame and hurled it in, saying:

"May this fair fume arise to thee, my Sire! Thine is the sweet first-fruit of all manhood. Thine the eye-apple of maternity, thine the throne-jewels of a Sultan's vassalry."

Next there came a second priest, with a blood-red flame.

He said: "This is the soul of one who was the maker of machines of torment and torture.

"He pored by night and by day to evolve strange gases that slay and metal monsters that devour.

"He joyed when the fields ran foul with gore and entrails, where myriads of men had stood an hour a-gone, because of his devices.

"He was crowned with glory and given great rewards by the ruler of his land."

And the Arch-Priest cast it in, saying: "O Mars, thou unknitter of bones, thou destroyer of flesh, thou glutton of limbs, thou wine-bibber of blood: accept thy sacrament!"

Yet there came another priest, bearing a flame that was almost black upon a platter of iron.

He spake: "This is the soul of a mighty King.

"His palaces were gemmed with the riches of the world, his ships traversed the seven seas, his merchants sate in conclave, his armies were strong as the hosts of heaven, his throne was firm as the plinth of the sun.

"He dreamed long beneath his canopies of his exceeding wealth, all things were at his service and decree. One day as he sat thus upon the dais of his pleasure-palace, idly toying with his scepter, he said unto his minister: 'Hast thou ever seen a greater ruby or one of more brilliance than that upon my head-band?'

"The counsellor replied: 'Yea, my Liege, for there is a larger one of more surpassing luster in the fillet of the King of the Yonder-Land.'

"The King said: 'Have it brought unto me!'

"But the minister replied: 'I cannot, for it belongeth to this King and is the heirloom of his heritage.'

"The King asked: 'Hath he other jewels?'

"The counsellor answered: 'His is the only realm which rivalleth thine. His caskets overflow, his daughters are fair, his kingdom is peaceful, his people happy and toil pleasantly in the fertile fields.'

"But the King's face grew dark with envy and his nostrils distended.

"He said: 'Call out my guards and mariners, for I will wrest his kingdom from him. There shall be no other King but me, no other Empire but mine own; I will rule unto the four ends of the earth.'

"And he sent his rushing armies upon the Yonder-Land. Its rich fields were turned to seas of mud, its houses and temples to ruins, its castles looted, its Kings and young men slain, its Virgins defiled, its children and old women murdered.

"But the ruby of the Yonder-Land glowed beside the other ruby in the head-band of the baleful King.

"And he cried to his overseers and chamberlains: 'My Empire hath grown greater and there are now no other Kings on land or sea.

"Whip up my slaves with your scourges, O overseers; tax my people, O satraps, and let them rebuild the Yonder-Land and found new palaces unto my paramours and temples to my gods.'"

And the Arch-Priest cast the flame into the fire, saying: "Thou art the King of the blood-stained places, of the desolate and razed cities; thine are the women killed with child, the ravished, the brutally slaughtered. Thine are tyranny and persecution, the anguish of wounded beasts, the offerings of the oppressed and tithed. Thine are the groans of slaves, the whistle of whips, the sweats of exceeding labour, O Master Mars, O God of War!"

Then sorrow seized upon me and I ran forth as one possessed from that sable House of Mammon and Mars, with its dirging priests, its jeering litanies, its ceaseless sacrifices of human souls, its molten Swine-Gods amid its howling, insatiable fires.

As I sped out through the brazen gates and over the drawbridge, I heard again the baying of dogs and monotonous moaning.

And as I reached the Long Lane of the Lost, there swept past me a pack of hounds in full cry.

Some were yellow as flame, some red as fire and others black as night. And they belled* and raced like the wind.

As I gazed at them aghast, there came a clattering of hooves and behold! upon a great white horse, which had a crystal jewel set between its eyes and whose mane flew out in the storm, rode an Angel clad in black, who blew that wailing music upon a silver horn.

He had neither saddle nor stirrup nor rein, and yet rode fleetly after the manner of God's legionaries.

I caught at his robe, crying: "Huntsman! Huntsman!"

He paused a moment, saying: "What wouldst thou?"

And I saw that his face was white and sad as that of one whom chill winds have beaten. His hair was dewy and his great wings draggled with rain.

I said: "What pack be this?"

He said: "The sleuth-hounds of God are passing down the Long Lane of the Lost. The black hounds are the moments of Pain, the red of Passion and the yellow of Remorse. We are hard upon the heels of a human soul that is seeking for the House of Mammon and Mars."

I said: "O Huntsman, who art thou?"

Then he smiled upon me with the sadness of his eyes, and answered: "The Eternal Conscience."

And blowing a mournful "Halloo! Hallo!" upon his silver horn, he shook me loose and was gone after the yelping pack.

And I cried out in terror and awoke.

* Bellowed or roared.

Ellen Glasgow (1873–1945) was a lifelong Virginian, a suffragist, a prolific author, and a Pulitzer Prize winner for her 1942 novel *In This Our Life*, which was considered groundbreaking for its realistic portrayals of African Americans and the injustice they suffered. Most of her work was set in the post-Reconstruction South, and this story—which first appeared in her 1923 collection *The Shadowy Third and Other Stories*—is a fine example of early Southern Gothic and has been compared to Edgar Allan Poe's 1839 "The Fall of the House of Usher."

Jordan's End

by Ellen Glasgow

At the fork of the road there was the dead tree where buzzards were roosting, and through its boughs I saw the last flare of the sunset. On either side the November woods were flung in broken masses against the sky. When I stopped they appeared to move closer and surround me with vague, glimmering shapes. It seemed to me that I had been driving for hours; yet the ancient negro who brought the message had told me to follow the Old Stage Road till I came to Buzzard's Tree at the fork. "F'om dar on hit's moughty nigh ter Marse Jur'dn's place," the old man had assured me, adding tremulously, "en young Miss she sez you mus' come jes' ez quick ez you kin." I was young then (that was more than thirty years ago), and I was just beginning the practice of medicine in one of the more remote counties of Virginia.

My mare stopped, and leaning out, I gazed down each winding road, where it branched off, under half bared boughs, into the autumnal haze of the distance. In a little while the red would fade from the sky, and the chill night would find me still hesitating between those dubious ways which seemed to stretch into an immense solitude. While I waited uncertainly there was a stir in the boughs overhead, and a buzzard's feather floated down and settled slowly on the robe over my knees. In the effort to drive off depression, I laughed aloud and addressed my mare in a jocular tone:

"We'll choose the most God-forsaken of the two, and see where it leads us."

To my surprise the words brought an answer from the trees at my back. "If you're goin' to Isham's store, keep on the Old Stage Road," piped a voice from the underbrush.

Turning quickly, I saw the dwarfed figure of a very old man, with a hunched back, who was dragging a load of pine knots out of the woods. Though he was so stooped that his head reached scarcely higher than my wheel, he appeared to possess unusual vigour for one of his age and infirmities. He was dressed in a rough overcoat of some wood brown shade, beneath which I could see his overalls of blue jeans. Under a thatch of grizzled hair his shrewd little eyes twinkled cunningly, and his bristly chin jutted so far forward that it barely escaped the descending curve of his nose. I remember thinking that he could not be far from a hundred; his skin was so wrinkled and weather-beaten that, at a distance, I had mistaken him for a negro.

I bowed politely. "Thank you, but I am going to Jordan's End," I replied.

He cackled softly. "Then you take the bad road. Thar's Jur'dn's turnout." He pointed to the sunken trail, deep in mud, on the right. "An' if you ain't objectin' to a little comp'ny, I'd be obleeged if you'd give me a lift. I'm bound thar on my own o' count, an' it's a long ways to tote these here lightwood knots."

While I drew back my robe and made room for him, I watched him heave the load of resinous pine into the buggy, and then scramble with agility to his place at my side.

"My name is Peterkin," he remarked by way of introduction. "They call me Father Peterkin along o' the gran'child'en." He was a garrulous soul, I suspected, and would not be averse to imparting the information I wanted.

"There's not much travel this way," I began, as we turned out of the cleared space into the deep tunnel of the trees. Immediately the twilight enveloped us, though now and then the dusky glow in the sky was still visible. The air was sharp with the tang of autumn; with the effluvium of rotting leaves, the drift of wood smoke, the ripe flavour of crushed apples.

"Thar's nary a stranger, thoughten he was a doctor, been to Jur'dn's End as fur back as I kin recollect. Ain't you the new doctor?"

"Yes, I am the doctor." I glanced down at the gnomelike shape in the wood brown overcoat. "Is it much farther?"

"Naw, suh, we're all but thar jest as soon as we come out of Whitten woods."*

"If the road is so little travelled, how do you happen to be going there?"

Without turning his head, the old man wagged his crescent shaped profile. "Oh, I live on the place. My son Tony works a slice of the farm on shares, and I manage to lend a hand at the harvest or corn shuckin', and, now-and-agen, with the cider. The old gentleman used to run the place that away afore he went deranged, an' now that the young one is laid up, thar ain't nobody to look arter the farm but Miss Judith. Them old ladies don't count. Thar's three of 'em, but they're all addle-brained an' look as if the buzzards had picked 'em. I reckon that comes from bein' shut up with crazy folks in that thar old tumbledown house. The roof ain't been patched fur so long that the shingles have most rotted away, an' thar's times, Tony says, when you kin skearcely hear yo' years fur the rumpus the wrens an' rats are makin' overhead."

"What is the trouble with them—the Jordans, I mean?"

"Jest run to seed, suh, I reckon."

"Is there no man of the family left?"

For a minute Father Peterkin made no reply. Then he shifted the bundle of pine knots, and responded warily. "Young Alan, he's still livin' on the old place, but I hear he's been took now, an' is goin' the way of all the rest of 'em. 'Tis a hard trial for Miss Judith, po' young thing, an' with a boy nine year old that's the very spit an' image of his pa. Wall, wall, I kin recollect away back yonder when old Mr. Timothy Jur'dn was the proudest man any whar aroun' in these parts; but arter the War things sorter begun to go down hill with him, and he was obleeged to draw in his horns . . ."†

* An area located near Roanoke, Virginia.

† A slang expression meaning to become less assertive or visible.

"Is he still living?"

The old man shook his head. "Mebbe he is, an' mebbe he ain't. Nobody knows but the Jur'dn's, an' they ain't tellin' fur the axin'."

"I suppose it was this Miss Judith who sent for me?"

"'T would most likely be she, suh. She was one of the Yardlys that lived over yonder at Yardly's Field; an' when young Mr. Alan begun to take notice of her, 'twas the first time sence way back that one of the Jur'dn's had gone courtin' outside the family. That's the reason the blood went bad like it did, I reckon. Thar's a sayin' down aroun' here that Jur'dn an' Jur'dn won't mix." The name was invariably called Jurdin by all classes; but I had already discovered that names are rarely pronounced as they are spelled in Virginia.

"Have they been married long?"

"Ten year or so, suh. I remember as well as if 'twas yestiddy the day young Alan brought her home as a bride, an' thar warn't a soul besides the three daft old ladies to welcome her. They drove over in my son Tony's old buggy, though 'twas spick an' span then. I was goin' to the house on an arrant, an' I was standin' right down thar at the ice pond when they come by. She hadn't been much in these parts, an' none of us had ever seed her afore. When she looked up at young Alan her face was pink all over and her eyes war shinin' bright as the moon. Then the front do' opened an' them old ladies, as black as crows, flocked out on the po'ch. Thar never was anybody as peart-lookin' as Miss Judith was when she come here; but soon arterwards she begun to peak an' pine, though she never lost her sperits an' went mopin' roun' like all the other women folks at Jur'dn's End. They married sudden, an' folks do say she didn't know nothin' about the family, an' young Alan didn't know much mo' than she did. The old ladies had kep' the secret away from him, sorter believin' that what you don't know cyarn' hurt you. Anyways they never let it leak out tell arter his chile was born. Thar ain't never been but that one, an' old Aunt Jerusly declars he was born with a caul over his face,* so mebbe things will be all right fur him in the long run."

"But who are the old ladies? Are their husbands living?"

* A caul is a thin piece of the amniotic tissue that forms over a baby's head. It is rare, and was once considered a good omen for the child.

When Father Peterkin answered the question he had dropped his voice to a hoarse murmur. "Deranged. All gone deranged," he replied.

I shivered, for a chill depression seemed to emanate from the November woods. As we drove on, I remembered grim tales of enchanted forests filled with evil faces and whispering voices. The scents of wood earth and rotting leaves invaded my brain like a magic spell. On either side the forest was as still as death. Not a leaf quivered, not a bird moved, not a small wild creature stirred in the underbrush. Only the glossy leaves and the scarlet berries of the holly appeared alive amid the bare interlacing branches of the trees. I began to long for an autumn clearing and the red light of the afterglow.

"Are they living or dead?" I asked presently.

"I've hearn strange tattle," answered the old man nervously, "but nobody kin tell. Folks do say as young Alan's pa is shut up in a padded place, and that his gran'pa died thar arter thirty years. His uncles went crazy too, an' the daftness is beginnin' to crop out in the women. Up tell now it has been mostly the men. One time I remember old Mr. Peter Jur'dn tryin' to burn down the place in the dead of the night. Thar's the end of the wood, suh. If you'll jest let me down here. I'll be gittin' along home across the old-field, an' thanky too."

At last the woods ended abruptly on the edge of an abandoned field which was thickly sown with scrub pine and broomsedge. The glow in the sky had faded now to a thin yellow-green, and a melancholy twilight pervaded the landscape. In this twilight I looked over the few sheep huddled together on the ragged lawn, and saw the old brick house crumbling beneath its rank growth of ivy. As I drew nearer I had the feeling that the surrounding desolation brooded there like some sinister influence.

Forlorn as it appeared at this first approach, I surmised that Jordan's End must have possessed once charm as well as distinction. The proportions of the Georgian front were impressive, and there was beauty of design in the quaint doorway, and in the steps of rounded stone which were brocaded now with a pattern of emerald moss. But the whole place was badly in need of repair. Looking up, as I stopped, I saw that the eaves were falling away, that crumbled shutters were sagging from loosened hinges, that odd scraps of hemp sacking or oil cloth were stuffed into windows where panes were missing. When I stepped on the floor of the porch, I felt the rotting boards give way under my feet.

After thundering vainly on the door, I descended the steps, and followed the beaten path that led round the west wing of the house. When I had passed an old boxwood tree at the corner, I saw a woman and a boy of nine years or so come out of a shed, which I took to be the smokehouse, and begin to gather chips from the woodpile. The woman carried a basket made of splits* on her arm, and while she stooped to fill this, she talked to the child in a soft musical voice. Then, at a sound that I made, she put the basket aside, and rising to her feet, faced me in the pallid light from the sky. Her head was thrown back, and over her dress of some dark calico, a tattered gray shawl clung to her figure. That was thirty years ago; I am not young any longer; I have been in many countries since then, and looked on many women; but her face, with that wan light on it, is the last one I shall forget in my life. Beauty! Why, that woman will be beautiful when she is a skeleton, was the thought that flashed into my mind.

She was very tall, and so thin that her flesh seemed faintly luminous, as if an inward light pierced the transparent substance. It was the beauty, not of earth, but of triumphant spirit. Perfection, I suppose, is the rarest thing we achieve in this world of incessant compromise with inferior forms; yet the woman who stood there in that ruined place appeared to me to have stepped straight out of legend or allegory. The contour of her face was Italian in its pure oval; her hair swept in wings of dusk above her clear forehead; and, from the faintly shadowed hollows beneath her brows, the eyes that looked at me were purple-black, like dark pansies.

"I had given you up," she began in a low voice, as if she were afraid of being overheard. "You are the doctor?"

"Yes, I am the doctor. I took the wrong road and lost my way. Are you Mrs. Jordan?"

She bowed her head. "Mrs. Alan Jordan. There are three Mrs. Jordans besides myself. My husband's grandmother and the wives of his two uncles."

"And it is your husband who is ill?"

* A basket made from thin strips of white oak.

"My husband, yes. I wrote a few days ago to Doctor Carstairs." (Thirty years ago Carstairs, of Baltimore, was the leading alienist* in the country.) "He is coming to-morrow morning; but last night my husband was so restless that I sent for you to-day." Her rich voice, vibrating with suppressed feeling, made me think of stained glass windows and low organ music.

"Before we go in," I asked, "will you tell me as much as you can?"

Instead of replying to my request, she turned and laid her hand on the boy's shoulder. "Take the chips to Aunt Agatha, Benjamin," she said, "and tell her that the doctor has come."

While the child picked up the basket and ran up the sunken steps to the door, she watched him with breathless anxiety. Not until he had disappeared into the hall did she lift her eyes to my face again. Then, without answering my question, she murmured, with a sigh which was like the voice of that autumn evening, "We were once happy here." She was trying, I realized, to steel her heart against the despair that threatened it.

My gaze swept the obscure horizon, and returned to the mouldering woodpile where we were standing. The yellow-green had faded from the sky, and the only light came from the house where a few scattered lamps were burning. Through the open door I could see the hall, as bare as if the house were empty, and the spiral staircase which crawled to the upper story. A fine old place once, but repulsive now in its abject decay, like some young blood of former days who has grown senile.

"Have you managed to wring a living out of the land?" I asked, because I could think of no words that were less compassionate.

"At first a poor one," she answered slowly. "We worked hard, harder than any negro in the fields, to keep things together, but we were happy. Then three years ago this illness came, and after that everything went against us. In the beginning it was simply brooding, a kind of melancholy, and we tried to ward it off by pretending that it was not real, that we imagined it. Only of late, when it became so much worse, have we admitted the truth, have we faced the reality—"

This passionate murmur, which had almost the effect of a chant rising out of the loneliness, was addressed, not to me, but to some abstract and

* A psychiatrist.

implacable power. While she uttered it her composure was like the tranquility of the dead. She did not lift her hand to hold her shawl, which was slipping unnoticed from her shoulders, and her eyes, so like dark flowers in their softness, did not leave my face.

"If you will tell me all, perhaps I may be able to help you," I said.

"But you know our story," she responded. "You must have heard it."

"Then it is true? Heredity, intermarriage, insanity?"

She did not wince at the bluntness of my speech. "My husband's grandfather is in an asylum, still living after almost thirty years. His father—my husband's, I mean—died there a few years ago. Two of his uncles are there. When it began I don't know, or how far back it reaches. We have never talked of it. We have tried always to forget it—Even now I cannot put the thing into words—My husband's mother died of a broken heart, but the grandmother and the two others are still living. You will see them when you go into the house. They are old women now, and they feel nothing."

"And there have been other cases?"

"I do not know. Are not four enough?"

"Do you know if it has assumed always the same form?" I was trying to be as brief as I could.

She flinched, and I saw that her unnatural calm was shaken at last. "The same, I believe. In the beginning there is melancholy, moping, Grandmother calls it, and then—" She flung out her arms with a despairing gesture, and I was reminded again of some tragic figure of legend.

"I know, I know," I was young, and in spite of my pride, my voice trembled. "Has there been in any case partial recovery, recurring at intervals?"

"In his grandfather's case, yes. In the others none. With them it has been hopeless from the beginning."

"And Carstairs is coming?"

"In the morning. I should have waited, but last night—" Her voice broke, and she drew the tattered shawl about her with a shiver. "Last night something happened. Something happened," she repeated, and could not go on. Then, collecting her strength with an effort which made her tremble like a blade of grass in the wind, she continued more quietly, "To-day he has been better. For the first time he has slept, and I have been able to leave him. Two of the hands from the fields are in the room." Her tone changed suddenly, and a note of energy passed into it. Some obscure resolution brought a tinge of colour to her pale cheek. "I must know," she added, "if this is as hopeless as all the others."

I took a step toward the house. "Carstairs's opinion is worth as much as that of any man living," I answered.

"But will he tell me the truth?"

I shook my head. "He will tell you what he thinks. No man's judgment is infallible."

Turning away from me, she moved with an energetic step to the house. As I followed her into the hall the threshold creaked under my tread, and I was visited by an apprehension, or, if you prefer, by a superstitious dread of the floor above. Oh, I got over that kind of thing before I was many years older; though in the end I gave up medicine, you know, and turned to literature as a safer outlet for a suppressed imagination.

But the dread was there at that moment, and it was not lessened by the glimpse I caught, at the foot of the spiral staircase, of a scantily furnished room, where three lean black-robed figures, as impassive as the Fates, were grouped in front of a wood fire. They were doing something with their hands. Knitting, crocheting, or plaiting straw?

At the head of the stairs the woman stopped and looked back at me. The light from the kerosene lamp on the wall fell over her, and I was struck afresh not only by the alien splendour of her beauty, but even more by the look of consecration, of impassioned fidelity that illumined her face.

"He is very strong," she said in a whisper. "Until this trouble came on him he had never had a day's illness in his life. We hoped that hard work, not having time to brood, might save us; but it has only brought the thing we feared sooner."

There was a question in her eyes, and I responded in the same subdued tone. "His health, you say, is good?" What else was there for me to ask when I understood everything?

A shudder ran through her frame. "We used to think that a blessing, but now—" She broke off and then added in a lifeless voice, "We keep two field hands in the room day and night, lest one should forget to watch the fire, or fall asleep."

A sound came from a room at the end of the hall, and, without finishing her sentence, she moved swiftly toward the closed door. The apprehension, the dread, or whatever you choose to call it, was so strong upon me, that I was seized by an impulse to turn and retreat down the spiral staircase. Yes, I know why some men turn cowards in battle.

"I have come back, Alan," she said in a voice that wrung my heartstrings.

The room was dimly lighted; and for a minute after I entered, I could see nothing clearly except the ruddy glow of the wood fire in front of which two negroes were seated on low wooden stools. They had kindly faces, these men; there was a primitive humanity in their features, which might have been modelled out of the dark earth of the fields.

Looking round the next minute, I saw that a young man was sitting away from the fire, huddled over in a cretonne*-covered chair with a high back and deep wings. At our entrance the negroes glanced up with surprise; but the man in the winged chair neither lifted his head nor turned his eyes in our direction. He sat there, lost within the impenetrable wilderness of the insane, as remote from us and from the sound of our voices as if he were the inhabitant of an invisible world. His head was sunk forward; his eyes were staring fixedly at some image we could not see; his fingers, moving restlessly, were plaiting and unplaiting the fringe of a plaid shawl. Distraught as he was, he still possessed the dignity of mere physical perfection. At his full height he must have measured not under six feet three; his hair was the colour of ripe wheat, and his eyes, in spite of their fixed gaze, were as blue as the sky after rain. And this was only the beginning, I realized. With that constitution, that physical frame, he might live to be ninety.

"Alan!" breathed his wife again in her pleading murmur.

If he heard her voice, he gave no sign of it. Only when she crossed the room and bent over his chair, he put out his hand, with a gesture of irritation, and pushed her away, as if she were a veil of smoke which came between him and the object at which he was looking. Then his hand fell back to its old place, and he resumed his mechanical plaiting of the fringe.

---

* A heavy cotton fabric with a floral print.

The woman lifted her eyes to mine. "His father did that for twenty years," she said in a whisper that was scarcely more than a sigh of anguish.

When I had made my brief examination, we left the room as we had come, and descended the stairs together. The three old women were still sitting in front of the wood fire. I do not think they had moved since we went upstairs; but, as we reached the hall below, one of them, the youngest, I imagine, rose from her chair, and came out to join us. She was crocheting something soft and small, an infant's sacque, I perceived as she approached, of pink wool. The ball had rolled from her lap as she stood up, and it trailed after her now, like a woollen rose, on the bare floor. When the skein pulled at her, she turned back and stooped to pick up the ball, which she rewound with caressing fingers. Good God, an infant's sacque in that house!

"Is it the same thing?" she asked.

"Hush!" responded the younger woman kindly. Turning to me she added, "We cannot talk here," and opening the door, passed out on the porch. Not until we had reached the lawn, and walked in silence to where my buggy stood beneath an old locust tree, did she speak again.

Then she said only, "You know now?"

"Yes, I know," I replied, averting my eyes from her face while I gave my directions as briefly as I could. "I will leave an opiate," I said. "To-morrow, if Carstairs should not come, send for me again. If he does come," I added, "I will talk to him and see you afterward."

"Thank you," she answered gently; and taking the bottle from my hand, she turned away and walked quickly back to the house.

I watched her as long as I could; and then getting into my buggy, I turned my mare's head toward the woods, and drove by moonlight, past Buzzard's Tree and over the Old Stage Road, to my home. "I will see Carstairs to-morrow," was my last thought that night before I slept.

But, after all, I saw Carstairs only for a minute as he was taking the train. Life at its beginning and its end had filled my morning; and when at last I reached the little station, Carstairs had paid his visit, and was waiting on the platform for the approaching express. At first he showed a disposition to question me about the shooting, but as soon as I was able to make my errand clear, his jovial face clouded.

"So you've been there?" he said. "They didn't tell me. An interesting case, if it were not for that poor woman. Incurable, I'm afraid, when you consider the predisposing causes. The race is pretty well deteriorated, I suppose. God! what isolation! I've advised her to send him away. There are three others, they tell me, at Staunton."*

The train came; he jumped on it, and was whisked away while I gazed after him. After all, I was none the wiser because of the great reputation of Carstairs.

All that day I heard nothing more from Jordan's End; and then, early next morning, the same decrepit negro brought me a message.

"Young Miss, she tole me ter ax you ter come along wid me jes' ez soon ez you kin git ready."

"I'll start at once, Uncle, and I'll take you with me."

My mare and buggy stood at the door. All I needed to do was to put on my overcoat, pick up my hat, and leave word, for a possible patient, that I should return before noon. I knew the road now, and I told myself, as I set out, that I would make as quick a trip as I could. For two nights I had been haunted by the memory of that man in the armchair, plaiting and unplaiting the fringe of the plaid shawl. And his father had done that, the woman had told me, for twenty years!

It was a brown autumn morning, raw, windless, with an overcast sky and a peculiar illusion of nearness about the distance. A high wind had blown all night, but at dawn it had dropped suddenly, and now there was not so much as a ripple in the broomsedge. Over the fields, when we came out of the woods, the thin trails of blue smoke were as motionless as cobwebs. The lawn surrounding the house looked smaller than it had appeared to me in the twilight, as if the barren fields had drawn closer since my last visit. Under the trees, where the few sheep were browsing, the piles of leaves lay in windrifts along the sunken walk and against the wings of the house.

When I knocked the door was opened immediately by one of the old women, who held a streamer of black cloth or rusty crape in her hands.

---

* The Western State Hospital (later the Staunton Correctional Center) at Staunton operated from 1828 to 2003.

"You may go straight upstairs," she croaked; and, without waiting for an explanation, I entered the hall quickly, and ran up the stairs.

The door of the room was closed, and I opened it noiselessly, and stepped over the threshold. My first sensation, as I entered, was one of cold. Then I saw that the windows were wide open, and that the room seemed to be full of people, though, as I made out presently, there was no one there except Alan Jordan's wife, her little son, the two old aunts, and an aged crone of a negress. On the bed there was something under a yellowed sheet of fine linen (what the negroes call "a burial sheet," I suppose), which had been handed down from some more affluent generation.

When I went over, after a minute, and turned down one corner of the covering, I saw that my patient of the other evening was dead. Not a line of pain marred his features, not a thread of gray dimmed the wheaten gold of his hair. So he must have looked, I thought, when she first loved him. He had gone from life, not old, enfeebled and repulsive, but enveloped still in the romantic illusion of their passion.

As I entered, the two old women, who had been fussing about the bed, drew back to make way for me, but the witch of a negress did not pause in the weird chant, an incantation of some sort, which she was mumbling. From the rag carpet in front of the empty fireplace, the boy, with his father's hair and his mother's eyes, gazed at me silently, broodingly, as if I were trespassing; and by the open window, with her eyes on the ashen November day, the young wife stood as motionless as a statue. While I looked at her a redbird flew out of the boughs of a cedar, and she followed it with her eyes.

"You sent for me?" I said to her.

She did not turn. She was beyond the reach of my voice, of any voice, I imagine; but one of the palsied old women answered my question.

"He was like this when we found him this morning," she said. "He had a bad night, and Judith and the two hands were up with him until daybreak. Then he seemed to fall asleep, and Judith sent the hands, turn about, to get their breakfast."

While she spoke my eyes were on the bottle I had left there. Two nights ago it had been full, and now it stood empty, without a cork, on the mantelpiece. They had not even thrown it away. It was typical of the pervading inertia of the place that the bottle should still be standing there awaiting my visit.

For an instant the shock held me speechless; when at last I found my voice it was to ask mechanically.

"When did it happen?"

The old woman who had spoken took up the story. "Nobody knows. We have not touched him. No one but Judith has gone near him." Her words trailed off into unintelligible muttering. If she had ever had her wits about her, I dare-say fifty years at Jordan's End had unsettled them completely.

I turned to the woman at the window. Against the gray sky and the black intersecting branches of the cedar, her head, with its austere perfection, was surrounded by that visionary air of legend. So Antigone might have looked on the day of her sacrifice, I reflected. I had never seen a creature who appeared so withdrawn, so detached, from all human associations. It was as if some spiritual isolation divided her from her kind.

"I can do nothing," I said.

For the first time she looked at me, and her eyes were unfathomable. "No, you can do nothing," she answered. "He is safely dead."

The negress was still crooning on; the other old women were fussing helplessly. It was impossible in their presence, I felt, to put in words the thing I had to say.

"Will you come downstairs with me?" I asked. "Outside of this house?"

Turning quietly, she spoke to the boy. "Run out and play, dear. He would have wished it." Then, without a glance toward the bed, or the old women gathered about it, she followed me over the threshold, down the stairs, and out on the deserted lawn. The ashen day could not touch her, I saw then. She was either so remote from it, or so completely a part of it, that she was impervious to its sadness. Her white face did not become more pallid as the light struck it; her tragic eyes did not grow deeper; her frail figure under the thin shawl did not shiver in the raw air. She felt nothing, I realized suddenly.

Wrapped in that silence as in a cloak, she walked across the windrifts of leaves to where my mare was waiting. Her step was so slow, so unhurried, that I remember thinking she moved like one who had all eternity before her. Oh, one has strange impressions, you know, at such moments!

In the middle of the lawn, where the trees had been stripped bare in the night, and the leaves were piled in long mounds like double graves, she stopped and looked in my face. The air was so still that the whole place might have been in a trance or asleep. Not a branch moved, not a leaf rustled on the ground, not a sparrow twittered in the ivy; and even the few sheep stood motionless, as if they were under a spell. Farther away, beyond the sea of broomsedge, where no wind stirred, I saw the flat desolation of the landscape. Nothing moved on the earth, but high above, under the leaden clouds, a buzzard was sailing.

I moistened my lips before I spoke. "God knows I want to help you!" At the back of my brain a hideous question was drumming. How had it happened? Could she have killed him? Had that delicate creature nerved her will to the unspeakable act? It was incredible. It was inconceivable. And yet . . .

"The worst is over," she answered quietly, with that tearless agony which is so much more terrible than any outburst of grief. "Whatever happens, I can never go through the worst again. Once in the beginning he wanted to die. His great fear was that he might live too long, until it was too late to save himself. I made him wait then. I held him back by a promise."

So she had killed him, I thought. Then she went on steadily, after a minute, and I doubted again.

"Thank God, it was easier for him than he feared it would be," she murmured.

No, it was not conceivable. He must have bribed one of the negroes. But who had stood by and watched without intercepting? Who had been in the room? Well, either way! "I will do all I can to help you," I said.

Her gaze did not waver. "There is so little that any one can do now," she responded, as if she had not understood what I meant. Suddenly, without the warning of a sob, a cry of despair went out of her, as if it were torn from her breast. "He was my life," she cried, "and I must go on!"

So full of agony was the sound that it seemed to pass like a gust of wind over the broomsedge. I waited until the emptiness had opened and closed over it. Then I asked as quietly as I could: "What will you do now?"